Circle of Deceit

by
Thomas Hill

Fusion Press

Published by Fusion Press
A publishing service of Authorlink
(http://www.authorlink.com)
3720 Millswood Dr.
Irving, Texas 75062, USA

First published by Fusion Press
A publishing service of Authorlink
First Printing, July, 2000

Copyright © Thomas Hill, 2000
All rights reserved

Without limiting the rights under copyright reserved above, no part of this book may be reproduced, or introduced into a retrieval system, or transmitted, in any form, or by any means (electronic, mechanical, photocopying, recording, or otherwise) without written permission of the publisher and copyright holder.

Printed in the United States of America

ISBN 192870479 4

For those friends there with encouragement…
And for Fred, my dog
who came from out of nowhere
and made things easier.

With Special Thanks
To my editor
Kate Kitchen
Publicist/Writer
Laguna Nigel, California

This is a work of fiction. All the names, characters, organizations, and events portrayed in this book are either the product of the author's imagination or are used fictitiously for verisimilitude. Any other resemblance to any organization, event, or actual person, living or dead, is unintended and entirely coincidental.

Chapter One

She spent her last precious seconds of life knowing she was going to die. Her cherry-red manicured nails clutched frantically to the side of the rain-soaked cliff, mud oozing through her slender fingers as she desperately grasped, again and again, to find something solid to cling to. Clawing at rocks, brush and clumps of soil, she lost her footing as the saturated ground gave way beneath her struggling body. Slipping down over the rocks and mud, she lost sight of the blue sky, edged with cumulous clouds not quite finished with their days of pouting.

As her screams of terror pierced the solitude of the peaceful, green-rolling hills overlooking Bodega Bay, she fell tumbling to the jagged rocks and pounding surf two hundred feet below, her body broken and shattered, her voice forever silenced. As she lay at the bottom, crumpled over the rocks as if she were a broken mannequin, her long, black hair floated about her face with the rhythm of the waves as they teased their way onto the rocks. Her unseeing eyes focused forever at the top of the cliff and the figure that stood, unmoving, at the very spot from which she had fallen. It was minutes before the lone figure turned and walked away.

The story of the socialite's death hit the small California town like a fifty-foot wave. The incident dwarfed all other news. Unrelenting rains and storms of past weeks no longer competed for the daily topic of interest at the local café. A shock wave of grief permeated the entire community. Joanne Hall, tall, slender, the attractive wife of a prominent scientist, was dead at forty-three, fallen—or pushed, off a muddy cliff just outside of town. The tranquility of Bodega Bay was shattered. People talked of little else.

Marshall Hall, the victim's husband, still ruggedly handsome at forty-seven, had told authorities over and over what had happened. That he had wanted to talk with her about something important and had suggested a walk along the grassy hillside just two miles from their home. They had planned a walk, then cocktails at home and an early dinner. The Halls lived in a small but elegant estate in the private, gated Sea Cliff community. They had driven from their home to the parking area near the cliffs. It was a blustery afternoon between storms. He had recalled her words before they left the house, "Take something warm, Marshall. The winds are still kicking up from this morning's storm."

As he helped her on with her favorite lamb's wool jacket, he felt a momentary pang of anguish. He remembered wondering if this were really what he wanted to do. He had grabbed his bulky blue sweater before leaving the house. It was always windy on the cliffs.

His recorded statement to the police was nearly verbatim, both times, much too perfect.

"Joanne was walking about ten feet ahead. I'd warned her that the ground was soft and she was getting too close to the edge, when it suddenly gave way, it just—gave way! I grabbed at her. I really grabbed! But I was too late. My God, I keep hearing her scream! I didn't know what to do! I ran back for my car phone and called the sheriff." His words now were barely audible on the tape, full of anxiety and fear.

The detectives played and replayed his frantic call. It had come in at 3:35 p.m.

"911 Emergency."

"Please, I need—I need help! It's my wife. She slipped! She— the ground—" the caller's voice was uneven, as if he were trying to catch his breath, his message nearly indistinguishable.

"Sir, what is the nature of your emergency?"

"My wife fell—she's in the water, on the rocks. She's on the rocks! Hurry!"

"Sir, what is your location?"

"Where you park, near the trails—Bodega Bay." There were other muffled sounds, and then the phone went dead, but not before the operator had been able to determine the location. The area was called "Lover's Bluff" and the sheriff's office made routine patrols there every weekend, discouraging under-aged beer drinkers and over-exuberant teenage Romeos.

After his call, county rescue and police were on the scene in less than twenty minutes. Joanne's body was recovered in time for the news of her tragic death to make the five o'clock broadcasts in

San Francisco.

Emergency Medical Technician Paul Shore shook his head as he zipped shut the red body bag. "What a beautiful woman. Looks like she never had a chance. Must have been a mudslide. It looks like part of the cliff gave way."

The medical examiner would perform tests on the body the following day, to check for alcohol, drugs or any sign of foul play.

Marshall Hall stood in the lobby at the sheriff's office, unable to move appearing dazed and emotionally drained. He had left his car at the scene and driven in with a deputy. Jack and Bonnie Bradford, his next-door neighbors, had heard the news and had come to take him to their home. Another friend had picked up the car and driven it back to Sea Cliff.

Joanne had many friends in this small, beach community, which lay just north of San Francisco. Her philanthropy with the arts and the youth community plus her outgoing personality had endeared her to every one she met. She became an instant friend to all. It only took one meeting. A lovely woman with free-flowing hair, she complemented her academic husband in looks and charm.

The Halls were well known for their work with local environmental groups. In fact, on Saturday, at a quaint, local café, they had attended a brunch with friends to discuss solutions to the beach's increasing erosion. That day, Kappy Anderson, the owner of the café was teasing her, saying good-naturedly, "You've got it all, Joanne—great looking husband, beautiful daughter, more money than you can count and a house at Sea Cliff!"

Kappy was referring to Renee, Joanne's daughter from an earlier marriage. Renee was a senior at College of the Pacific in Stockton. Extremely close to her mother, she was the only one who had noticed the couple growing apart in recent years. Renee's visits had become less frequent as a result of the increasing animosity she had witnessed between her mother and stepfather.

The police questioned members of the group who had attended the meeting, but there had been no apparent stress between the handsome couple.

Kappy, the café owner, recounted her comments along with Joanne's brisk response to her husband. Marshall had said, "See? You are stunning. The other women are jealous." To which Joanne had replied, "She knows, doesn't she, Marshall? All of this is just too humiliating!" she said, and turning abruptly, walked out to their car.

Mike Staples had come to Bodega Bay three years ago, after fifteen years as a vice cop with the San Francisco Police Department. After losing his wife in a drive-by shooting as she waited for him outside the precinct, then watching the perpetrator get off on a technicality because of a slick lawyer, Staples had experienced enough big city life and big city crime. Now a detective with the local sheriff's office, as Bodega Bay wasn't large enough for a municipal police force, he was assigned by the county attorney to make the required investigation of the Hall case.

There was an outpouring of sympathy for the husband—none of their country club friends considered foul play. It seemed purely routine—an investigation of a tragic accident. The mayor had remarked to the detective, "Marshall's a friend, Mike, and straight as an arrow. He and Joanne have done a lot for this town, let alone the scientific community with his drug research at Maxco-Litton. Take it easy on him, okay?"

Mike Staples needed questions answered regarding the scene of the fall. It appeared to him as if there had been a scuffle close to the edge of the cliff. He wasn't a soil expert, but it didn't appear as though the cliff had just arbitrarily given way.

Due to Joanne's prominence in the community, Marshall had scheduled a public memorial service for Wednesday and a private funeral to be held Friday, for family and close friends. That would give Mike a few days to gather information.

Renee, Joanne's daughter was leaving the dorm for dinner when her roommate shouted after her, "Renee, It's for you!" She mouthed the words, 'stepfather,' and Renee shook her head, then came back to pick up the phone.

"Renee, I have terrible news." The voice on the other end sounded strangely quiet, not authoritarian and crisp as usual.

The two had never been close and Marshall had spent nearly every waking hour at his lab and the rest of the time at home in his 'unapproachable' study, preparing grant review documents and seeking funding for his research projects.

The conversation was short lived. Marshall offered to have a car pick up Renee and drive her home. She assured him she would manage but thought she should wait until morning. She was too upset to travel. Marshall agreed.

Turning away from the phone, Renee fell into the rattan chair, stunned. As if it were an automatic response, she picked up the phone and dialed Jill's number in Scottsdale.

Jill Rushly had been close to Renee and her mother for as long as the girl could remember. It was Joanne Hall who had comforted Jill when a drunk driver killed Jill's parents years past. And it was Joanne who encouraged Jill during those trying days to pursue her dream, a career in law enforcement. Jill had joined the Scottsdale Police Department and had worked her way through the ranks to become a respected and levelheaded detective with natural instincts for crime solving.

Overcome with grief, Renee reached out to the one woman she knew would give her comfort. Jill Rushly had often commented to Joanne how much she would have loved to have Renee for a daughter. It was a good friendship and would offer Renee a support system at this difficult time.

Jill and her husband were just finishing dinner. "Oh, no," Jill groaned when the phone rang. "I forgot I'm on call tonight. I hope it isn't the station."

"Jill Rushly," she answered, crossing her fingers and holding her breath. The sound of the familiar voice startled her.

"Jill, it' it's Renee. It's my mom. I—she fell! There's an investigation!"

"What! Renee, what is it? Are you okay? What's going on? Okay, slow down and take a couple of deep breaths. You need to tell me what happened." Jill suddenly felt sick to her stomach. She sat down and waited, afraid to hear what might be coming. It took several minutes for her to gather the complete story.

"Mom had an accident this afternoon. She was walking along Lover's Bluff with Marshall, you know the place. There was a mudslide or something. Jesus, Jill, I just can't believe it. She fell—" her voice overcome by sobs, she tried to catch her breath. "Mom fell to the rocks. She's dead. My mom's dead!" The young woman stopped speaking, stunned by the impact of what she had said. "Jill, I just talked to her yesterday, and now she's dead!"

The immediate silence was deafening. Shaken, Jill tried to gather her thoughts. As a police officer, she had been trained to handle tragedy. But she wasn't prepared for this. A feeling of incredible loss enveloped her. The woman who had for years been her best friend was gone. In a soft, barely audible voice, Jill responded, "Renee, I'm so sorry. I wish I could be there to comfort you. This is terrible news."

"Jill, I need you so badly. Can you come? I don't think I can do this without you. I can't—there is so much to do."

"I'll be there, Renee," Jill replied, gently. "We'll get through this together. I know this is horrible for you. I'll catch the first flight in the morning."

"Okay, Jill, thanks," Renee responded, quieter now. "I can't talk anymore. I need to go home." Renee had decided to drive the three hours to her mother's home in Bodega Bay that night, after all. She just wanted to be closer to her mother, wherever she was.

"I'll call as soon as I get to San Francisco," Jill promised.

Quieter now, Renee thanked Jill gratefully.

Slowly and carefully, Jill replaced the receiver back in its cradle, afraid, somehow, to lose the connection for fear the reality of it all would be too much to bear. She began to cry softly, but wasn't quite sure who she was crying for, Joanne, Renee or herself.

John Rushly had become concerned about his wife's obvious anguish. He knew something tragic had happened, but had been careful not to interrupt.

"Jill, what is it?" he asked, touching her on the back of the neck. That's all she needed. Spinning around into his arms, she began to sob against his chest. He held her tightly, his strong hands stroking her sweet smelling, strawberry-blonde hair.

"It's Joanne," Jill cried, still in shock. "There's been an accident. She's *dead*, John. I just can't believe it." She nestled into his arms, grateful for his calm.

"What kind of accident? What the hell happened? What can I do, honey? Was that Renee?" Receiving a muffled response and a nod, he continued to soothe her, his touch having a quieting effect. "She must be devastated."

Jill gathered her strength, stepped away from John and tried to regain her composure.

"I'll have to leave, John. Renee needs me. I'll be gone at least a week." She looked up at him, her clear, blue eyes filled with tears.

"You go ahead, sweetheart." It broke his heart to see her looking up at him, obviously in such grief, and yet there was nothing he could do to take away her pain. "If I could get away, I'd go with you, you know that." But John Rushly was needed at home. Special Agent of the FBI, he was in charge of the Phoenix Field Office. Both in law enforcement, they had met on a previous case and married within a year.

His tall, handsome athletic build contrasted sharply against Jill's five-foot, four-inch frame and pixie quality. He was fond of teasing her for her girlish look, and would often say, "Watch out for that lady if she's got a .38 Special in her hand!" Then he would affectionately tousle her hair, which she hated, and laugh at her pretended discomfort.

Fiery, feisty and freckle-faced, that was Jill Rushly, and she could handle her "big, strong FBI agent, make no mistake about it!" she'd exclaim threateningly, when he challenged her. She would stand facing him directly, looking up at his strong, chiseled features, her hands on her hips and fire in her big, blue eyes.

"John, hold me—I love you so much." Now she wasn't feeling so feisty. The young woman was distraught and his job at this moment was to love her. Jill stood leaning against her husband, remembering her terrible loss of two years past. Just at the climax of a very long complicated case, Dick, her partner had sacrificed his life to save hers. *Now,* she thought, *more tragedy—Joanne is dead. Poor Renee,* she thought, remembering she had to call the Department to get her leave approved. She hugged John before she turned away to make the necessary phone calls. She would spend the evening packing.

It rained hard on the day of the memorial service. The damp and dreary procession walked into the small church just outside of town, filling the sanctuary. The weight of their sadness could be felt as well as seen.

Just outside the church, before the service, Jill was introduced to the local detective in charge of the case. Mike Staples, a broad-shouldered, ruddy-complexioned guy with a clean but rumpled appearance, agreed to give Jill details of his preliminary investigation. Although initially reluctant to share information with a civilian, once he knew she was a fellow officer, and was reminded of a famous case she had helped to solve in Phoenix, she no longer seemed like an outsider. He sensed the deep loss felt by this lovely lady. Surprised at her diminutive stature, as he stood near, he noticed a tremendous strength in her eyes and her manner. The story of her exploits had become well known in law enforcement circles. The two detectives had the makings of becoming good friends.

The mood was somber. The woman who had done so much for this community lay still and quiet in a white casket. Dressed in a soft jersey, long-sleeved white gown, she held one single white rose delicately in her hand. Her hair, now fresh and clean with no traces of mud, flowed gently over her shoulders.

Jill and Renee sat together, comforting each other. The grief-stricken widower had found this occasion rather awkward, as if he felt guilty for letting Jill's friend die. Polite but distant, Marshall sat quietly, not listening to the service, trying to figure out what could have gone so wrong in a marriage that had lasted seventeen years.

Jill was asked to say a few words. She stepped up to the podium, hands trembling, and took a deep breath. She had composed a short poem on her brief flight from Phoenix to San Francisco. Jill and her friend had exchanged poetry throughout their friendship and she had thought this a fitting tribute.

"Joanne Hall was more than a friend to me," she started, hoping to ease the pain of those sitting before her. "She helped me by offering herself so generously during a tragic period of my life. I'll never forget her. I know she did a lot for this community and that you loved her, too." Jill turned toward Renee. "Renee, words cannot describe how much your mother meant to me. I hope this helps a little." Jill began to read.

"You were our angel here on earth,
You gave to us, you believed in us,
You shared with us, as angels do

Now gracing the halls of Heaven,

The other angels are the lucky ones.
For you are there with them,
And we are here, alone.
We will miss you, dear friend."

By Thursday, the town had settled into some semblance of normality. The private funeral would take place the following day. The townspeople didn't believe there was any need for an investigation. They assumed that Detective Staples would conclude his queries with the medical examiner's report, and the matter would be closed. In reality, Mike Staples had asked for more time to gather additional information. As he put it to his superior, "I need to tie up some loose ends."

"What's the problem?" Lieutenant Ramsey responded. He was more than curious. Mike decided to level with his boss.

"This whole thing bothers me. Did you know there was a seven hundred fifty thousand dollar life insurance policy on Marshall's wife?" Mike continued. "The M.E. found strands of a blue sweater embedded under the fingernails of the victim. I went back over the police report. The husband stated that his wife was walking ahead and he couldn't reach her in time. I know the sweater thing doesn't prove much. They could have embraced or something. But the scene just does not look right. I have some soil guys out there. They're getting back to me later today. I want permission to dig into the husband's personal business."

"Okay, Mike, but try to keep this quiet. This investigation could backfire. It's a small town. Incidentally, I don't think it's a good idea to be so cozy with the Scottsdale lady. Besides her being a cop, her husband is a FBI agent. We don't need any unnecessary interference."

"Lieutenant, I like her. She's a sharp lady. But I know what you mean," he replied. "Hey, I'll keep my inquiry low key. Don't worry."

Following the memorial service, Marshall Hall made a half-hearted attempt to comfort his stepdaughter before retreating to his office in Novato, a short, half-hour drive from his home. The scientists working under his direction, while sympathetic to

Marshall's loss, had remained hard at work all week, dealing with a critical research deadline. Their project was expected to be approved by the FDA within six months, but Marshall had recently uncovered serious questions as to the validity of the data. The tragedy at home could not have struck at a worse time.

Kimberly Weitzel arrived at the Novato office late on Wednesday. She hadn't attended the memorial service, realizing it might seem inappropriate. At thirty-six, the stunning executive secretary and mistress to Marshall Hall had kept a low profile for several days, wanting desperately to contact him, but afraid his stepdaughter would answer the home phone. She had fallen deeply in love with this charismatic, golden boy of the pharmaceutical world.

Daughter of Dr. Julian Weitzel, Marshall's mentor and senior associate at the research facility, Kimberly felt steeped in her own measure of guilt. She hadn't expected Marshall to be in and was startled to see him at his desk.

"Marshall," her throaty voice was even more sensuous than usual, with the emotion of the moment. "I am so sorry." It was a typical comment under the circumstances and Marshall looked up, grateful to see her.

"I've been wanting to call you, Kimberly, he smiled gently. "I've been going through hell." In the half-light coming from the lamps on the table behind her, she looked even more voluptuous and desirable than he had remembered. Her soft, full lips seemed almost pouty and her cherubic face was framed perfectly by shoulder-length, soft blonde hair. Painfully forcing his mind back to reality, he tried to appear detached. He shook his head, repeating himself. "I've been going through hell."

"I can imagine," came the soft reply in that low voice he loved so much. "What can I do?" It was awkward for them both. His attempts at trying to be natural agitated him further.

"I feel so guilty! How did it come to this? My God, Kimberly, she's dead!" Had a staff member walked by just then, the looks on their faces would have betrayed them both. He continued, "I don't think we should see each other for awhile. I have a lot of doubts about what has happened. Right now, I don't feel right and I'm confused. I'm having a really hard time with this." He paused, changing direction, "I also need to talk to you about your father, but not now." His voice sounded strained. Usually every bit the cool, calm and collected scientist, he sounded disoriented.

"Marshall, it was an accident," she whispered, trying to calm him. There is nothing you could have done." She felt him slipping away from her, shutting her out.

"We shouldn't have been arguing," Marshall replied, shaking his head. "I was determined to tell her about us. If Joanne hadn't been so upset, she might still be here."

"You can't blame yourself, darling."

"Look, Kimberly, I can't even breathe right now. I need some space, some time. My wife is dead. I didn't mean for that to happen. She was a good woman. What was I thinking? A lot has happened." He paused, looking away, "I'll be taking some time off. Maybe you should, too."

Under the circumstances, Kimberly knew he was right. She touched his hand briefly before returning to her desk. She knew little of the pressures brought down on her boss by the intense, corporate head of Maxco-Litton. Roger Maxco was Marshall's employer as well as her father's. She knew there was something extremely stressful going on and he had earlier confided in her that his wife had raised some serious objections to his work situation. Feeling shut out and afraid, she was petrified of losing Marshall. Things had been going so well for them.

For Detective Staples, a circumstantial case was building. Meetings with the county Medical Examiner and talks with the soil engineers had brought several things to light. Mike outlined his findings in a memo to his lieutenant.

✓ Fibers from husband's sweater under victim's fingernail
✓ $750,000 life insurance police
✓ Affair between Marshall Hall and Kimberly Weitzel
✓ Victim's daughter and stepfather estranged
✓ Recent transfer of large sum of money into KW's account
✓ Accident site shows possible scuffle

The site inspectors had found a cigarette butt about twenty feet below the top of the cliff. The police had overlooked it. Someone had apparently flicked the Kool butt over the cliff. The brand was distinctive. *Not many people smoke KOOLS anymore*, Mike thought. They had also taken casts of footprints, footprints of a man and a woman.

Mike wrestled with the facts as he finished the memo. *Someone other than Hall could have flicked the butt—maybe a worker at the scene*, he thought. But still, it looked suspicious. "If that's his brand," Mike told his lieutenant, "I can't imagine anyone pausing for a cigarette, then flicking the butt off the cliff after his wife fell two hundred feet to her death!"

"Damn!" the Lieutenant exploded, pulling his feet off the desk. He slammed his fist against the filing cabinet. "An arrest warrant of a man as prominent as Marshall Hall will turn this town upside down. I don't want a fucking media circus here!" Settling back into his chair, he thought for a moment, then looked up at his deputy. "We need hard facts, Mike. You probably have enough, preliminarily, for the County Prosecutor, but I'm worried about the fallout. Take more time. Let's tie this down tight."

Mike was getting through to the lieutenant. His case, although weak, raised disturbing questions. Mike responded, "You got it. I believe the money angle is worth pursuing. I'll need some help."

Ramsey had the last word. "Let's get a court order for his records. I'll assign a lawyer to go through documents. I'll give the sheriff your impressions. The prosecutor will sit tight for a few days. Unless we get hard evidence, this guy could walk. But remember, Mike, this is all circumstantial and he could be innocent. No mistakes!"

Mike Staples had returned to his office. The phone rang. The call was from Jill.

"Mike, I can't stop worrying about what you told me at the memorial service. Please tell me Marshall isn't a suspect." She wanted to believe it was truly an accident.

"I'll tell you what I just told Ramsey." Mike related what he had outlined to his lieutenant an hour before. The story of the cigarette butt was particularly disturbing to Jill. *If it belonged to Marshall*, Jill thought, *the callousness of the act redefines the word despicable. And worse,* she shuddered, *Renee could be in danger!*

It was Friday. The simple but dignified funeral went smoothly. Marshall had left the arrangements to Jill and Renee who had worked out all the details for the service, from selecting the pallbearers to the place of interment. The memorial service had given the townspeople a chance to say goodbye to Joanne. Now the family could share their grief privately.

Jill was scheduled to fly back to Phoenix at seven o'clock that evening. She tried to talk with Marshall before she left, but he still seemed distant and preoccupied. Renee had wanted her to stay longer—the two were closer than ever, now. Renee had casually mentioned to her friend that her mother and stepfather had been having problems. She didn't elaborate.

Before leaving the cemetery, Jill watched the flower-draped casket as it was lowered into the wet ground. A short distance away, Marshall had paused to acknowledge some friends leaving the gravesite. As he turned away, he opened a pack of cigarettes. Lighting up, he slipped the pack of KOOLS back into his pocket. Jill noticed the brand and catching her breath, turned angrily away, got into her rental car, and headed for the airport.

As the America West 707 lifted into the evening sky, Jill whispered a final farewell. "I'll find the truth, my dear friend. I promise."

Chapter Two

Marshall Hall had been dealt the trump cards of an idyllic life. He was brought up in Iowa in a home of affluence, his parents being successful corporate farmers. From his early childhood, Marshall had a thirst for knowledge and a gift for mathematics and the sciences. Biology was his favorite subject and he was forever talking to classmates about wanting to discover the cure for cancer. He was well respected by his peers for his brilliance as well as integrity.

After graduating from high school at sixteen, the young genius registered at Drake University in Des Moines. By twenty-four, he had earned a dual-doctorate in biochemistry and chemical engineering from the University of Chicago. A professor once remarked, in a reference for his doctoral candidacy, "This student is absolutely focused. His integrity is beyond reproach. Neither a social scientist, nor a humanist, Mr. Hall prefers to leave discussions of those disciplines to the teachers and philosophers."

He arbitrarily adopted scientific truth as his only personal philosophy. In 1982, immediately upon receiving his doctorate, he was recruited to a research position in the Microbiology and Immunology Department at Scripps Research Institute in La Jolla. It was on a walk above those cliffs that the young man met and fell in love with his future wife, Joanne Burton. The daughter of the prominent Jonathan H. Burton, professor at the University of Southern California, was a stockbroker and had, in eight short years, amassed a sizable portfolio. Joanne had made the mistake of marrying young, and had divorced her alcoholic college man shortly after the birth of their daughter Renee.

Marshall and Joanne made a striking couple. He was totally oblivious to his own dashing good looks, which were in stark contrast to his academic demeanor. Until he met Joanne, science and the pursuit of greatness were his whole life. He was thought by many to be cold and distant. Joanne, however, was flattered by his intentions. His qualities suited her perfectly—handsome, intelligent, confident and ambitious. Her warmth toward everyone she met contrasted starkly with his aloofness, but it didn't matter.

After dating for six months, they left Renee with friends and flew to Puerto Vallarta to get married. When they returned from their brief honeymoon, three days later, a letter was waiting for Marshall at his office. He had been invited to join the prestigious, international pharmaceutical firm of Maxco-Litton. It was the dream job for any respected research scientist and more than double his salary at Scripps. After a year, there would be stock options and the gift of a membership to the private club as well as a substantial down payment on a home at the exclusive Sea Cliff Estates.

After three meetings with the executives, and a tour of the sophisticated research lab that would be his, he was offered all the autonomy and funds he needed to utilize his extraordinary talents. Being allowed to handpick his research staff clinched the deal. The company was preparing for something huge, he was told, and the project required the finest minds in the world. In his initial eight years as a research scientist, Marshall had acquired a tremendous reputation, a reputation that was about to pay off.

A month after his marriage, Marshall took his bride and his soon-to-be-adopted daughter up the coast to their new apartment in Bodega Bay.

The board of Directors at Maxco-Litton was so pleased with Marshall's progress in the first six months, they authorized his membership in the Sea Cliff subdivision, and a one hundred thousand-dollar bonus to move the couple into their new home, high above the surf at Bodega Bay. Joanne, having left her financial career in Southern California, now had something to do. She had an entire house to furnish. This, along with her chairing the local arts council and working on other civic groups, immeasurably enhanced their standing in the community. What Marshall supported with an occasional donation, Joanne supported with effort. They settled into their new life quickly, separately but together.

They had both fallen in love with the seaside town, a quaint village with spectacular ocean views and crashing surfs. Marshall drove thirty miles each day into the town of Novato, just forty miles north of San Francisco. That's when Marshall's day would start, as he drove through the heavy, wrought iron security gates into his exclusive domain, his very own private laboratory ensconced safely on the top floor of the West Coast Research Facility of Maxco-Litton. And he enjoyed, as well, the late-night return.

After a challenging twelve-hour day, he would head back up the coast, the moon trailing close behind. Playing Pachelbel's Canon, he was soothed by the sight and sound of the surf crashing into the shoreline as he made his way home. By the time his Lincoln coasted into his private driveway, his expensive but comfortably furnished executive home stood before him, bathed in soft moonlight, overlooking the edge of the world. If Joanne had waited up, they would have a cocktail and light dinner. That was the pattern for seventeen years

And for seventeen years, the brilliant researcher had been of inestimable value to the conglomerate. Maxco-Litton was the largest and most sophisticated research laboratory and pharmaceutical manufacturer in the world.

For five years, Marshall and his senior advisor and colleague, Dr. Julian Weitzel had been working at a feverish pace. They had developed and painstakingly tested a new vaccine that would prevent breast cancer. With nearly two hundred thousand new cases of breast cancer in the United States each year, the clamor for the new vaccine would be overwhelming. Statistics were solid. There were nearly forty-five thousand deaths each year with one out of every eight women contracting the disease during her lifetime. And *they* had discovered the vaccine!

Accurate, verifiable data was essential to present this monumentally vital drug to the FDA and ultimately the world! But Marshall had uncovered damaging evidence, faulty data from Dr. Julian Weitzel that had disproved the scientists' original hypothesis. That discovery now threatened the project, and the company. In addition, the result of prematurely manufacturing and distributing the vaccine without all the contraindications communicated to the medical community, could summarily cause the deaths of tens of thousands of women. The human toll would eventually be staggering, worldwide.

Maxco-Litton would serve to make-or lose billions of dollars with the initial distribution of this drug. The profit potential was so astronomical, accurate projections were nearly impossible to make. Marshall Hall was the single person who held this ethical dilemma in his hands. *Do I dare stop this project?* He wondered. There was only one question that ate away at every fiber of his being. *I must speak with Julian,* he thought as he drove home. *I have to know if he presented faulty data to me, his own partner, or did he just overlook it.* Either answer was unacceptable. Weitzel was too ethical for the former, too professional and experienced for the latter. *The stakes are indeed enormous,* he thought, remembering Roger's threat. *Roger Maxco knows it and I know it.* A shiver ran up his spine.

Roger Maxco, CEO of Maxco-Litton, had generously bestowed upon Dr. Hall an advance against future bonuses to be realized by the success of this project—nearly three hundred thousand dollars. Extended as a professional courtesy on the surface, in actuality, it was offered to keep the brilliant scientist quiet. In fact, Maxco had pleaded with Marshall to forget about the money. Roger perceived Marshall, with his newly acquired discovery of the flawed data, to be a serious threat to the project's completion. The CEO was determined to buy the scientist's silence, whatever the cost.

Marshall's idyllic life was now history. His entire world had turned upside down. Leaving his office late Monday evening, he noticed it was still raining, as it had been for weeks. Speeding north to his turnoff at Petaluma, the widower's thoughts began to accelerate as he drove faster and faster. He felt as though the weight of the universe were on his shoulders. The memory of Joanne's shrill screams of terror continued to haunt him.

The phone call two weeks ago from his boss had somehow worked its way into Marshall's thoughts. He could still hear those words, the nearly ominous mutterings of Roger Maxco, calling from his New York conference room. They kept replaying in his head.

He recalled the conversation, nearly word for word.

"Marshall, do you understand our position? This vaccine you and Julian have been working on—it's vital that it gets FDA approval without delay! Granted, there are questions, but it's nothing as serious as you suggest. Every new drug has a couple of side effects. Goddamn it, Marshall! There is no compromise on this. Take some time off. Forget about the money; it's a gift! Hasn't Julian proved himself to be your best friend, your mentor, your most trusted colleague? You both have done brilliant work on this project! Don't fuck it up!" Roger was yelling now.

"This is a once-in-a-lifetime medical discovery! Remember, Marshall, if you blow this, your entire life's work and Julian's reputation is on your head. Just think of what you'll do to his family! Not to mention your own precious career!"

He was suddenly shaken back to his senses by nearly running over what was left of a huge tire on the road, evidently from an eighteen-wheeler. Adrenaline pumping, the near-accident only served to clear his head. He steadied his hands on the wheel and reached into his glove compartment for a cigarette. He hated himself for starting to smoke again, but after Roger's phone call, stress had gotten the better of him and he had succumbed to his earlier vice. Closing the car window and lighting up, he settled in and thought about that phone call.

Marshall knew better. It had been their joint project. But Marshall was the one who had discovered and challenged the questionable data submitted by his colleague. Dr. Julian Weitzel had submitted, in his forty-year career, more than a hundred brilliant papers regarding cancer research. With a degree in medicine, a specialty in clinical oncology and a Ph.D. in genetic engineering, he was well known in medical and academic circles. Weitzel had been published in the New England Journal of Medicine, JAMA, the Journal of the American Medical Association and was on the editorial board of the prestigious Journal of Clinical Oncology. How could Marshall question this brilliant man, his mentor, the man he had worked with, side by side for years?

Initially, Julian had convinced Marshall the data was solid and that he would be given exactly what he needed to prove his original hypothesis. This data was being carefully constructed to pave the way for FDA approval. The agency had made mistakes in the past but if Marshall Hall were correct in his assessment of the data submitted by Julian, this error wouldn't be attributed to the FDA. It would be due to miscalculations by Dr. Julian Weitzel, acceptance of it by Dr. Marshall Hall, and would reflect directly on Maxco-Litton. It would bring the pharmaceutical giant to its knees.

Upon discovering the errors and reviewing the calculations, Marshall had found himself thinking, *Julian is the best researcher there is! Could he possibly have done this on purpose just to get the drug approved? The firm would stand to make billions. We will all become instant millionaires. I wonder.*

From the beginning, the testing process had been painstakingly slow and frustrating. In addition to the omission of the contraindications of the vaccine for women with high cholesterol or high blood pressure among other pathologies, Marshall's look at the flawed data suggested that one known chemical initiator and promoter had not been neutralized. Viral oncogenes inserted in connection with a cellular oncogene could induce malignant tumors. That could not be allowed to happen.

Julian's data had given the 'all clear' to this last stumbling block. Marshall had at first accepted the data without question. It was a case of desperately wanting to believe. After further investigation, he felt compelled to request a private meeting with Roger Maxco. That had taken place several weeks ago, before Joanne's death.

A life's work destroyed and a sensitive and brilliant man discredited, he thought, unable to get Roger's threats out of his head. *Along with all this,* he thought painfully, *there was Kimberly. She would never forgive him.*

The narrow two-lane road between State Highway 101 and Bodega Bay was dark. There was no traffic and the road up ahead was flooded. Marshall saw the flooded road just in time. He hit the brakes and the heavy Lincoln responded quickly, sliding to a stop. A gray Suburban rolled up next to him. There was a brief discussion about the depth of the water. The passenger in the Suburban stepped out, presumably to survey the road. Marshall did not see the second man.

The blow came swift and hard, leaving a mark on Marshall's head. The heavy car was pushed off the road into the wash and rapidly rising water. Satisfied that their quarry was dead, two men got back into the Suburban, turned around and quickly headed back to Highway 101, then south into San Francisco.

A California Highway Patrol officer discovered the scene of the accident at seven o'clock the next morning. Rescue efforts began downstream since there was no body found in the car. Mike Staples arrived on the scene an hour after the car had been spotted. Monty Newton from County Rescue greeted him, laughing as usual at the deputy's appearance.

Colleagues frequently razzed Mike for his appearance, calling him Colombo. He almost always wore a raincoat that had probably seen its last pressing more than five years ago. His ruddy complexion and healthy shock of thick, sandy-colored hair, always in need of a cut, matched his rumpled coat and complementing his casual appearance. But he was a good detective and had been trained well. Newton had thought to call the deputy because they had identified the Lincoln as Marshall Hall's and Newton had heard of his buddy's investigation into the wife's death.

"Staples," he said, "I understand you're interested in the owner of this vehicle. The problem is, we can't find him. He may have been washed downstream. It's possible he could end up in the ocean." Newton did not sound optimistic.

"Yeah," Mike responded. "I have a great deal of interest. I'm still wondering if his wife's death was accidental. Circumstances seem mysterious. Does this look like an accident to your people? Or could he have just tried to bail and left the scene?"

Newton responded, "It has all the earmarks. With the water rushing as fast as it was during the night, anything could have happened out here. My guess is that he skidded off the road after slamming on his brakes. The driver's door was opened. He probably tried to get out and was swept away."

Mike Staples was not convinced. Marshall Hall had known the road well and would have been alert to serious flooding. Further, his vehicle had every safety option, including ABS brakes. Once again, things just didn't add up. Mike turned toward Newton, handing him his card. "Let me know if you find anything, anything at all. Thanks for the call."

"Sure thing, Mike. Hey, buy an iron, why don't you?"

The deputy shot him a graphic gesture, smiled good-naturedly and walked away. Doubling back toward Highway 101, he decided to stop at several small stores along the way before reaching the main highway. He asked several people if they had noticed anything unusual the night before. There was one interesting observation made just six miles from the turnoff.

"Earlier, I noticed a large GMC or Chevy Suburban heading toward Bodega Bay," the coffee shop owner said. "About an hour later, it came racing back." He concluded the road must have been washed out and the truck was looking for another route.

Well, Mike thought to himself, *this may be the end of my case against Marshall Hall.* He hoped the body would turn up and bring closure to the incident at Bodega Bay.

Her grief had taken its toll on Jill Rushly. She asked her chief for a few days of vacation leave. She also wanted time to follow up with Mike regarding what, if anything, he may have learned about Joanne's death.

Jill's husband had returned from a meeting at FBI headquarters in Washington, D.C. Called away from his home office, John had just helped to complete an extremely complicated case that had taken a year to solve.

That evening at dinner, Jill broached the subject, asking her husband for advice in pursuing the Bodega Bay incident.

Leaning over her to refill her coffee cup, he thought for a moment. "There may be a circumstantial case against Marshall Hall, Jill, but you know as well as I do that you can never be sure of anything without solid physical evidence." They were about to have dessert when the phone rang. It was Mike Staples calling from his office four hundred miles away. Jill answered the phone.

"Hey, Jill. It's Mike. Sorry to interrupt your evening, but something important has come up. Do you have a minute?" he sounded excited.

"Yes, of course Mike. Go ahead," she caught her breath, waiting.

"It appears that Marshall Hall has had a serious accident along the road just off the main highway. He hit a flooded area and his car skidded into the water. Rescue thinks he may have been washed out to sea. There's no trace."

This is crazy, Jill thought. "What do you think happened, Mike? It seems awfully coincidental, doesn't it?" Jill, like her husband, was not keen on unusual and fortuitous circumstances. The news, insofar as Jill was concerned, posed more questions than answers.

"Jill, the case is building against Marshall. Though I have to admit it is still largely circumstantial. This just doesn't add up. An analytical brain like Marshall's is not going to take a chance and try to make it across raging water. Something else happened. It may or may not be related to the death of his wife. To tell you the truth, I'm stumped."

"Mike, I want answers, too. Please keep me informed. Thank you so much for bringing me into this. I want to think about it, okay?"

"I understand," came the swift reply. "I have no idea where this case is going, Jill, but I thought I'd better let you know."

"I really appreciate your call, Mike. Oh, my God, has anyone thought to notify Renee?"

Her question was met with an awkward silence.

"Never mind, Mike, I'll do it." She dreaded having to make that call. Stepfather or not, he was the only parent Renee had left.

"John, did you hear?"

But he had already concluded that his lovely detective-wife was going to be intimately involved in a case, albeit off-duty, a long way from home. He understood Jill's commitment to her friend and was determined to support her. "It sounds like this case is becoming complicated," he said. "Talk to me."

As Jill filled her husband in on the details, she couldn't help wondering, *where is this all going?*

Chapter Three

The prestigious, executive offices of Maxco-Litton occupied the top three floors in one of the twin towers of the famous World Trade Center in New York City. The top floor was reserved for the chosen few. A board of Directors, made up of twelve individuals, kept the giant firm on course. Prestige and performance earned offices with impressive views of the spectacular Manhattan skyline. Two men wielded absolute power and discretion—Roger Maxco and Arthur Litton. Elizabeth Martin, the only woman in the hierarchy, ran a close third. Few questioned her authority.

Recruited straight out of Princeton, by Litton, Elizabeth was the third largest shareholder in the conglomerate. Her prestige as Chief Financial Officer had gained her a phenomenal reputation as an administrator, giving her the ability to affect company policy. Smart, sophisticated and dressed impeccably in Armani suits, her dark auburn hair always gathered pristinely in a French twist or a bun at the nape of her neck, Elizabeth made heads turn every time she walked through the reception area and down the west wing toward the executive suites. At five feet ten and a half in heels, she towered over the other Directors. She didn't hesitate to use her height as a psychological advantage as she chaired board meetings, urging her colleagues to support her proposals.

Throughout her fifteen years at the firm, Elizabeth, with her tailored elegance, was never spotted socializing, inside or outside of her work environment. She attended the annual, black-tie affair at the country club that acknowledged the major donors only because it was required of her. On a rare occasion, she would have a late-night cocktail with the board members after a particularly long Director meeting. It was safe to say that men were not comfortable around Elizabeth, although she was striking and feminine in appearance, and her ethics were impeccable.

A department head had explained her mystique once, saying, "She's sharp, smart and savvy, a straight shooter. But she can lie back, then without warning, strike like a rattler if she's cornered. I

pity the poor man who would get involved with her." No one did, she wouldn't permit it. Elizabeth had married her career and it didn't seem as if a divorce was imminent any day soon.
   Her instincts had served her well. She had invested her own money, tucking away a full third of her salary since day one with the firm, and could retire at any time. The company realized that and did everything to keep her happy. Elizabeth was responsible, perhaps more than anyone else, for creating the financial solvency Maxco-Litton enjoyed. The challenge of being so near the top of one of the most solvent pharmaceutical firms in the world, however, had kept her happily ensconced in the executive wing. The other nine Directors, much less inspired to work for a living, looked to this powerful triumvirate to guide them through the day-to-day decision-making process of running this four billion-dollar empire. It was an awesome task.

   Roger Maxco was beginning a private meeting with his personal attorney, Michael Lowe. The subject at hand was not something to be shared with fellow Directors. They spoke in hushed voices.
   "I guess we'll never know about Hall's wife," Roger remarked. "Do you think he killed her? It would have been so against his nature."
   "I have no idea," Michael replied, adding, "he was cozy with Weitzel's daughter, everyone knew that and pretended not to. But still, It doesn't make a lot of sense."
   "Frankly, I don't give a damn. It's just as well," Roger said. "She did approach me once at a benefit and asked me what was going on with her husband and Julian at the lab. He evidently was worried about the data and confiding in her. Son of a bitch!"
   "They're both gone, Roger—hopefully that's the end of it."
   The CEO nodded and the two men concluded their meeting.
   Driven by power, greed, and little else, Roger Maxco at fifty-seven was looked upon by the pharmaceutical community as someone not to trifle with. He had built a pharmaceutical firm prior to coming to the company, his firm being Maxco-Litton's only serious competitor. There had been suggestions, although unconfirmed, that his previous firm's holdings had resulted from

highly questionable dealings.

Supposedly, he had supplied black market drugs to a third world country for a great deal of money. They were drugs that had not passed quality assurance and according to him, had been destroyed. The error had not been caught in time to save production costs and the entire batch had been contaminated. The sale would have netted the firm millions, but certainly not as garbage. However, once discovered, no one had witnessed any destruction of the drugs, as was required and customary. As a matter of fact, an unidentified, large shipment had left the warehouse surreptitiously one night, and was never traced. Nothing was ever proved. There was no evidence, no indictment, and only a private query from the president of the board. Maxco had suddenly left the firm and was recruited immediately by Arthur Litton, who at his advancing age had decided to offer a full partnership to this man with a proven financial track record. There was money to be made and Litton had never been one to hold back on taking risks for profit.

Maxco's education, wit and knowledge of corporate law could not be denied. No one knew anything about his personal life, however. Although he was supposedly married, no one had ever met his wife. Rarely socializing with business acquaintances, his life outside of these sacred halls appeared to be a mystery. He could turn on the charm in an instant and raise a million dollars for a research grant at a party before the night was halfway over. But he had a side that was rarely seen, a malevolent streak that appeared whenever he felt threatened. He was careful never to show that side to Elizabeth. With her ability to manage the company's complex portfolios, he needed to stay on her good side. And charisma was all he showed her.

At the other side of the helm stood Arthur Litton. At sixty-three, the gentle-speaking, slender, mustached elder was less intimidating to the others than Maxco. He was much more accessible and his open door policy was well respected, although rarely used. Litton was either on the golf course, at the racetrack or at his estate on Long Island. His gambling debts were enormous. With three children at Harvard, twin sons in medical school and a daughter in law school, his financial responsibilities were astronomical. No one knew how he managed, but neither did they question him. The staff, from Elizabeth on down to the switchboard operator in reception, adored him. He knew everyone's first and last name, whether they were married or not, and always remembered to ask about their children. Everyone trusted him implicitly and respected him enough to steer clear of speculation as to his gambling debts. There was never a hint of scandal surrounding Arthur Litton, and he was careful to keep it that way.

He had climbed the corporate ladder the hard way. Married to a woman from New York's prominent social registry, Litton had a lovely mansion on Long Island. A shrewd man, he had an uncanny sense of timing. Always in the right place at the right time, his colleagues marveled at this bright and competent Philadelphia lawyer. He had been responsible for recruiting Elizabeth, quite a feather in his cap. He had mentored her from day one and she had caught on fast, quickly proving herself deserving of his friendship and trust.

It had been a full week since Marshall's unfortunate automobile accident. Management adjustments within the research arm of Maxco-Litton had already taken place.

Julian, even in the throes of grieving for his associate, was given total autonomy over the vaccine and its preparation for the FDA process. Approval had been expected within a six-month period. Due to the tragedy and the FDA administrator's respect for both Marshall and Julian Weitzel, the approval time was expected to accelerate. The two had, for years, made notable contributions to the industry, their reputations flawless and credentials impeccable.

The man in Room 212 lay on the soft, almond-colored blanket at the Best Western Motel in Walnut Creek. A wealthy suburb fifty miles northwest of San Francisco, this had been his refuge for eight days. He had kept to himself, afraid to further endanger his life. Fortunately, he had several hundred dollars in cash with him when he was attacked. Dr. Marshall Hall had not been swept out to sea. He was alive and well in Walnut Creek, California.

The blow to his head had been discomforting, but not serious. When his Lincoln was pushed into the wash, Marshall had pretended to be dead. In fact, he had swallowed such a significant amount of water, he was trying to keep from choking. He was afraid he would be discovered. From the roadway, the two assailants were convinced they had completed their job—a job ordered by someone with a New York connection. For security reasons, the two would-be assassins had never met the person who had ordered the hit. They were to be paid by a third party and were not interested in any other details.

That night had been a long one for Marshall. Fortunately, before the arrival of the California Highway Patrol, he had found a ride into Petaluma where he was able to rent a car. He had said he'd slipped in the mud trying to change a flat, and had to walk from the outskirts of town in the pouring rain. The rental agent hardly took notice of his story, afraid he would miss part of a rerun of M*A*S*H on his six-inch TV screen. The drive to Walnut Creek was short and he began to regain his composure after just one day. Wisely, he kept a low profile and took the time to formulate a plan.

One of the calls he decided to make was to Kimberly. He knew she could be trusted. The ethical question of exposing her father gnawed at his conscience. There was no doubt that whoever participated in the attempt on his life should pay. How they would pay and who else would suffer as a result was the question he needed to sort out. Kimberly could help. He looked at his watch. It was the middle of the evening. *She's thought of me dead for eight days*, he thought, reminding himself to be careful.

Her sultry voice shot through him like a knife as she answered on the first ring. "Hello?"

Marshall could barely bring himself to speak. "—Kimberly? Honey, it's Marshall."

"What? Marshall? Oh, no! Is it really you?" She could hardly control her voice.

"Yes, are you alone? I need to know, are you alone?" Becoming dizzy, she grabbed for the table beside her, then sat down quickly. *Please let this be him*, she thought, trying to cling to hope when everything in the real world told her he was dead.

"Everyone thinks—" She couldn't bring herself to say the

words. Holding the phone tightly, she whispered, "Marshall, what happened? How did you survive? *Where are you?*" She was trying unsuccessfully to collect her composure. *I need to get to him!* she thought.

"Listen carefully. Someone tried to kill me. I need your help. It's about the project your dad and I worked on. You must come alone and make sure *no one* knows where you are going, not even Julian. My life depends on it. Please understand, Kimberly. I really need you!"

"Of course, Marshall. Dear God! I can't believe this! Where are you?"

"I'm in Walnut Creek." He gave her directions and they arranged to meet a noon on Monday. "I can't wait to see you. Honey," he said more softly, "I love you." The agenda had changed. With her help, he could now move forward with his plan to deal with Maxco-Litton. But there was one more call he had to make that evening, a call to the Rushly home in Scottsdale.

John and Jill had continued their conversation relating to the incidents at Bodega Bay. An hour after receiving the call from Mike, the phone rang again. This time, John picked up the receiver.

"Agent Rushly, this is Marshall Hall. I called to speak to your wife but I really need to talk to you too. Do you have a few moments?" John motioned for Jill to pick up the extension.

"Yes, of course, Mr. Hall. It appears that the stories regarding your death have been greatly exaggerated," he quipped. "This call is quite unexpected." John Rushly had, in a second, established a semblance of rapport with the caller, and Marshall Hall felt safe for the first time in over a week.

"Mr. Rushly, my near drowning was no accident. Two men attacked me. It was planned. The reason I was targeted is complicated and far-reaching. I know I may be a suspect in my wife's death, and you need to know, first and foremost, that I've done nothing wrong."

"Why are you telling me this? This isn't an FBI case," the agent responded, realizing from experience that there was something else on Hall's mind. He wanted him to get to the point.

"I can't tell you my story over the phone," Hall responded. "We have to meet. Please keep this call confidential, except from Jill. I am pleading with you and your wife not to divulge my whereabouts to anyone, at least not until I know I'm safe. The reason will become clear after our meeting. I must have your word on this." John Rushly sensed the importance, the urgency in Marshall's voice. He thought about the request and concluded there was little to lose by meeting the man.

"Mr. Hall, I have no objection to this at all. Under the circumstances, it will have to be within a few days. If you are truly in danger, there is a jurisdictional matter I need to look into. I'll need permission from my own office and it will be necessary for me to contact the San Francisco Field Office before I become involved. Also, keep in mind, there are some who still may consider you a murder suspect."

"That's not a problem. I'm in Walnut Creek, about fifty miles northeast of San Francisco. I prefer not to travel. If you can arrange to come here, it will be better for me. This involves serious crimes, Agent Rushly." There was more fear than caution in his voice.

"If I can get clearance, I will be able to meet with you close to noon on Tuesday. I must advise you, Marshall, that as a Special Agent of the FBI and an officer of the court, if a federal offense has been committed, you may be arrested. Is that understood?" Rushly knew he was in the driver's seat. After all, the scientist had tipped his hand. It would not be difficult to track him down with the knowledge Marshall had already conveyed. They had already been on a long distance call that could be easily traced. Somehow he didn't feel Hall was trying to hide from the authorities, but he knew he should cover himself legally.

Marshall was silent for a moment. *The timing is perfect*, he thought. *Kimberly will be here on Monday.*

He took a deep breath before responding, "I understand, Mr. Rushly. This matter is much bigger than my wife's accidental death. The implications of what I have to tell you will astonish you. They are worldwide, and without trying to sound dramatic, could mean life or death for thousands upon thousands of innocent women." Marshall gave Rushly his location and they hung up.

On Monday, John would check into the illustrious career of

Marshall Hall, then meet him in California. John Rushly was a stickler for accurate information and thought that most times, it was far more valuable than guns and bullets. Before the meeting, he would acquire a staggering amount of information, both personal and business about the scientist and the firm he represented. He expected the jurisdictional matters would be worked out. He was right.

Kimberly was excited about seeing the man she loved. It was a two-hour drive from her home in Novato to Marshall's motel in Walnut Creek. The big question was her father. How was he involved in all of this? Her thoughts drifted as the miles brought her closer to her love. It had been so long.

Nearly missing the freeway turnoff, Kimberly dashed in front of another car and with tires screeching, made a quick right turn. It was only a few minutes to the motel. With her heart pounding in her chest from anticipation, she tapped quietly on the door of Room 212.

The embrace lasted minutes. At last, he had someone to cling to. The analytical persona of this renowned scientist had given way to a rush of emotions. The death of his wife, the funeral, the suspicions and the attempt on his life all seemed tolerable in the arms of his love.

"I love you," he whispered. Marshall paused, then looked out the window. "Kimberly, did you tell anyone you were coming here?"

"No one knows," she replied quickly, then asked, "Are you telling me someone actually is trying to kill you?"

"Yes, it's true. I'm meeting with the FBI. I'm in real danger. You must be careful. These people are capable of anything."

For the first time in a long time, Marshall was beginning to feel whole. He was determined to make things as right as possible. With Kimberly at his side and with the help of John Rushly, he was confident that this was his chance for a new beginning. He would take back his soul from those who would ruin and destroy him, all in the name of greed.

There will be casualties along the way, he thought briefly. He would level with Kimberly, even about what he suspected with regard to her father. There could be no secrets between them. With her aware of everything that had gone on, they would work it out together.

Everything else could wait until morning. He looked at her, tears in his eyes, feeling at once safe, yet vulnerable. He did indeed love this woman.

Carefully locking the door behind them, he reached over to turn off the light before taking her into his arms. As he felt her relax against him, he whispered quietly, "We can worry about what to do tomorrow. But for now, I'm just happy to have you with me."

Marshall Hall slept through the night, for the first time in weeks.

Chapter Four

Elizabeth Martin began to sense she was out of the loop. Closed-door discussions between Roger Maxco and Earnest Lasko, the corporate attorney, were becoming more frequent and more cryptic in nature. Several times, she heard Roger mentioning Julian's name in a raised voice, as if the scientist suddenly intimidated him. That afternoon, she went to the executive suite specifically to press Roger for more information. She was not expected. Receiving a deferential nod from Carol, the executive secretary, Elizabeth tapped lightly on Roger's door, then hearing the sound of his voice, opened the heavy mahogany doors and walked in.

"Do you have a few minutes?" Elizabeth asked. Roger Maxco was not a fool. He knew that catering to Elizabeth was important and he would continue to play the role.

"Come in, Elizabeth." He smiled warmly, getting up from his chair to greet her. "This is an unexpected pleasure. I thought you would be heading out early to get ready for your award presentation this evening." A woman's group was honoring Elizabeth for her sponsorship of outstanding high school graduates to attend Harvard Business School.

"I *am* ready," she smiled. "However, at this moment, I am puzzled and rather concerned that a more comprehensive report regarding Julian's research project has not been forthcoming. I understand this project has earthshaking ramifications in the medical world. A drug to *prevent* breast cancer! What I don't understand is why you've been so open about the topic for the last five years, and suddenly, when we're preparing to shoot it off to the FDA, you're silent."

Not one to mince words, Elizabeth leaned over the desk to be sure she had Roger's full attention. "Why the secrecy?" she asked quietly. She stood quietly, her manner suggesting she anticipated nothing less than a clear and direct response.

Turning away, trying to buy time, Roger looked at the beautiful skyline for a moment, stroked his chin, and then turned back to her. "Elizabeth, believe me," he cleared his throat, obviously uncomfortable. He knew he had to smooth the waters and could not let her see how furious she had made him by confronting him. "There has been nothing intentional here. The project has just become so highly technical and I didn't want to burden you. But I assure you, a full and comprehensive discussion is set for the next board meeting." *A decent try, Roger,* Elizabeth thought, but she wasn't sold.

Straightening up and using her nearly six feet of elegance to look eye to eye at her superior, she replied, "Please, Roger. Don't patronize me. You know better. I happen to know that this company's own researchers discovered this drug that's expected to save hundreds of thousands of lives. And suddenly you don't want to *burden* me?" She was beginning to get angry now. "Roger, listen carefully. As Chief Executive Officer and the third largest stockholder in the company, I think it's safe to say that I not only require some answers but also can approve, on the spot, the overtime necessary to get those answers. I don't care what it takes. I expect a full, detailed and comprehensive report on my desk by eleven o'clock tomorrow morning. Further, I expect to be kept informed, fully informed. Good afternoon, Roger." She turned and walked out the door, shutting it quietly but firmly behind her.

Her attitude belied the fact that Elizabeth Martin had been extremely attracted to the dashing CEO ever since his recruitment to the firm. In fact, she harbored a dichotomy of feelings—perhaps love, admiration, and rather disconcerting, an element of distrust. While her ethics were impeccable, she often saw him stretch the truth when presenting issues to the board. She had never thought those incidents important enough to call him on it. His phenomenal success in the industry and ability to take risks and make things happen were attributes she loved to watch.

Roger Maxco took a deep breath. He knew he had made a mistake in not giving pieces of information to Elizabeth over the last few weeks. But there had been so much happening, they were on the verge of total success or disastrous failure. He hadn't given her a thought.

Earnest Lasko, one of the Directors conspiring with Roger, had given him fair warning in the past. "Remember, Roger. That woman's extremely bright, but just as sensitive to her position and her power. You have to keep her informed. Otherwise, she'll start asking the wrong questions." That was two weeks ago. *Why didn't I listen to him?* Roger wondered.

"Carol," he buzzed his secretary, "Get Lasko. Tell him to drop whatever he's doing. I need to see him."

"Yes, Mr. Maxco."

Earnest Lasko was on the floor below and was on the phone immediately. "Hi, what's up?" Self assured with no scruples, Earnest had handled a major law case for Maxco-Litton, saving the company two hundred million dollars, firmly ensconcing himself in the firm. Roger had taken the lawyer under his wing and they had become close associates. They had been planning a financial rape of the company for some time, but had been sidetracked, thrown off course by recent events.

"Earnest, you were right. Elizabeth just left my office. Put your people to work tonight and see to it she has a doctored comprehensive report on the project by 11:00 a.m. Sorry."

"Thanks, Roger," came the terse reply. Perhaps we shouldn't let things slide this far in the future." The man was sleazy and disrespectful and his most prominent quality was that he didn't care who knew it.

"Your point is taken, Earnest." Roger sighed wearily. "It's got to be done, so get busy. I'll talk to you tomorrow." Roger hung up so he would have the last word.

The discovery of this life-saving vaccine would give Roger the opportunity of a lifetime. With inside information concerning timing of FDA approval of the drug, a windfall in stock profits could be taken at the expense of all other stockholders. A separate organization had already been created to purchase large shares of Maxco-Litton just before the news hit the streets. A week later, Roger, with the help of his personal lawyer, Michael Lowe, would arrange a massive sell off of Maxco-Litton stock. Knowing it would be only a matter of time before negative news of the vaccine would become common knowledge, they would take their profits before the stock plummeted. The giant pharmaceutical firm would plunge into disgrace and possibly bankruptcy. Roger would be gone.

It was an evil and despicable plan, giving the participants

lucrative golden parachutes. There could be tens of thousands of unnecessary deaths before the compromising information regarding the vaccine was exposed. With Marshall Hall dead and Dr. Julian Weitzel committed to the project, the conspirators were confident they would have time to perfect their scheme.

Weitzel was a tortured soul. He knew the repercussions of his silence would be disastrous. He also suspected that if he didn't go along with Roger Maxco, his daughter would be the next to be killed. *If they could kill Marshall so easily*, Julian thought, *they would not hesitate to murder Kimberly.*

The senior scientist did not set out purposefully to deceive his colleague. At first, he honestly believed his data was correct. The day before he submitted his final report, he noticed the flaw in his presumptive thinking—a vital recalculation was in error. This was in addition to the data that was not verifiable. Wanting to believe so badly, the good doctor ignored another calculation—the standard error of difference. He knew he ignored the standard deviations of the sample he used in his frequency distribution. He failed to divide the standard deviation by the total number of cases in the frequency distribution—a common statistical error. He opted to forget it and proceeded with the paper supporting Marshall Hall's original work. With two areas of concern, his conscience began to act up and he requested a meeting with Roger Maxco.

He was hoping beyond hope that these revelations might not make that much of a difference—he knew it could be corrected in time and adjustments made. Of course, Roger agreed. After all, the firm was entrusted with other people's lives. They had a responsibility to do it right. Both men, in their gut, knew better. Not only had statistical errors been made, but also the science of the interaction between chemical substances and living tissues had been compromised. When Weitzel came to his senses and formally stopped the project, Roger Maxco went ballistic. At that time, not realizing the potential danger to his friend, Marshall, Weitzel told Roger he was sure his colleague had discovered the errors and would also refuse to allow the project to go forward.

Jill Rushly was excited that her husband was becoming

involved with the investigation of the death of her friend. Jill now suspected there was more to the story of Joanne's death. *It may have been an accident,* she thought, *but Marshall Hall is holding something back.*

It was morning. John Rushly was catching a plane to San Francisco. He would rent a car and drive to his appointment in Walnut Creek with Marshall Hall. On the way to the airport, Jill couldn't help talking about her friend.

"John, I would give anything to attend this meeting. I can't help thinking about Joanne. I don't believe that her husband has told the whole truth."

"Reserve judgment," John replied. "By this evening, we will know a lot more."

"You're right, my handsome FBI agent." Jill said, smiling as she reached over to touch his face. "As usual." It was frustrating to Jill to not be able to take part in the investigation. It was not her jurisdiction.

Dropping him off at Phoenix Sky Harbor Airport, Jill's thoughts drifted once again to Marshall Hall.

"If you are guilty, you son of a bitch," she muttered, *"you have made a big mistake bringing my husband into the middle of this. He'll see through your scheme, whatever it is!"* She turned onto 44th Street and went north.

John Rushly had kept his promise. He had confided in no one. Other than Kimberly Weitzel, all other parties assumed Marshall Hall was dead. During the drive from the San Francisco Airport to the Best Western in Walnut Creek, the agent reflected on the information he had gathered the day before. The background of the wonder boy and the pharmaceutical giant had been a real eye opener. He thought hard. *This is one important and talented guy. If this meeting involves Maxco-Litton, it could get more than interesting. That's a four billion-dollar enterprise.*

It was just before noon when John's car pulled into the parking lot of the Best Western. Out of courtesy and caution, John called Marshall's room from the lobby.

"Mr. Hall. This is Rushly. I'm in the lobby."

"John, thanks for being so prompt!" the man sounded relieved.

"We can meet in my room, if you don't mind."

"I'll be right up," John replied.

The two men shook hands and seated themselves at a breakfast nook in the quiet suite. Coffee had been brought up to the room and was kept hot on the plug-in plate provided by the hotel. The drapes were opened slightly by Marshall and each man poured himself a strong cup of coffee.

"I know this is unusual," Marshall began, "but you will shortly understand the reasons for meeting under these circumstances. Do you have any knowledge about the company I work for, what we do?"

"Yes, I did some research on your background and that of Maxco-Litton. Impressive. You move in heady circles."

"John, I've been so fortunate—brilliant career, lovely wife, nice home, all the things a man could ask for. But I have made mistakes." He looked away, embarrassed, then continued. "My affair with Kimberly Weitzel wasn't planned. We worked late, so many nights. She never complained. We just grew closer and closer, over the last few years. It just happened. To complicate things, she's is the daughter of my closest colleague."

"Weitzel," Rushly responded, eager for the man to get on with the real crux as to why he was here.

"It wasn't right. I do regret it happening. To be honest, I love Kimberly." He cleared his throat, struggling with guilt. "My wife's accident has brought pain and heartache to a lot of people. But it *was* an accident." He looked directly into the agent's eyes. "We did have an argument, near the cliff. I was asking for a divorce. I had told her about Kimberly. She already knew." The widower lowered his voice, as if in a confessional. "I didn't tell that to the police. Truthfully, it may have contributed to her fall. If she had lived, I don't know what would have happened, with Kimberly and all. To complicate matters, I have discovered that her father has betrayed his profession, —and me. And that started a domino effect that led to the attempt on my life on the road."

John interrupted, his interest piqued. "Do you mean the close call you had in the water was not accidental? Someone tried to kill you?" He had perked up noticeably.

"Not only someone, John, but I believe someone in the company—possibly Maxco. He didn't do it personally, but I think he did hire two thugs to do the job. I am convinced of that. Further," he paused to take a breath, adding to the drama, "I'm afraid that insofar as Roger Maxco and his business is concerned, there is little difference between pharmacology and toxicology."

"Marshall, your story is taking on a hint of paranoia. Do you have proof that what you are saying is true?"

"I have evidence that Maxco-Litton along with others including Dr. Julian Weitzel are involved in the most hideous medical fraud ever perpetrated by a business entity on a civilized society."

With that statement, Marshall Hall began the long and detailed story that had brought the two men together, under such strange and unusual circumstances. Late that afternoon, after several deliveries of coffee and sandwiches, Marshall Hall finished relating the bizarre but believable details of his association with Roger Maxco and Dr. Julian Weitzel.

John Rushly later stared at his notes in disbelief. *My God*, he thought, *could this be true*? Marshall Hall was a convincing man. Further, he had given the FBI agent a definitive and credible description of exactly what was happening at the firm. Marshall Hall offered irrefutable evidence that a major crime was in the making. John struggled to understand the motivations of the people involved. The risks of being discovered and punished seemed to have had no affect on their thinking process. He wondered how the desire for money and power could ever become that strong to basically commit mass murder in such a heinous and bizarre way.

John needed time to absorb this incredible story. There would be meetings to be scheduled with the Director of the FBI and the Justice Department to determine an appropriate response to the potential threat. It was not only a matter of exposing their scheme, but the people involved needed to be put away. An elaborate plan would have to be put into operation—wiretaps, surveillance, and a continuing investigation to make sure no one who had participated in this despicable fraud would go free. *Most important*, he thought, shuddering at the probably consequences of this act, *the distribution of the vaccine had to be stopped!*

Chapter Five

Roger Maxco listened to the caller with utter disbelief. The incredulous news nearly stopped his heart.

"What in the goddamn hell are you saying?"

"Sir, we think Marshall Hall is alive."

The days following the attempted murder of Marshall Hall, the assailants were instructed to stay in the Bay area and report on activity surrounding the search and investigation. In addition, the leader Byron Storm was assigned the task of following the Weitzel woman. His vigilance had paid off. He had followed her to the hotel in Walnut Creek. The general demeanor of the girlfriend had convinced Byron he was onto something. Later, at the hotel, he had observed a different visitor—"handsome, official-looking guy," he said. That day, he got a pretty good look at the occupant of the room in question. There was little doubt in his mind—it was Marshall Hall! "Son of a bitch!" he had exclaimed aloud, before catching himself. "It's impossible!"

On hearing the news, Roger knew it wasn't impossible. The body had not been found. The visit by Kimberly Weitzel had cinched it. He believed. And now someone else was involved. "For now," he yelled impatiently, "leave the girl alone. *Finish* the job, Byron! You know how important this is, not only to me but to you!"

There was no doubt what Roger meant. *This time*, Byron thought, *I can't fail*.

The conversation was over but certainly not forgotten. Roger, visibly shaken, tried to stroll casually down to the office of Earnest Lasko. It was Lasko who had arranged the 'accident' along the lonely road into Bodega Bay. His earlier ties with a less sophisticated level of society had appealed to the corporate chief. Roger was assured that Byron Storm and his accomplice were the best around.

"I have news, Earnest," he was seething with anger. "I got a phone call. It appears that Mr. Hall is alive and well and is residing in a motel in Walnut Creek."

Blood drained visibly from Lasko's face as he dropped the file he was holding. He knew the implications. Wanting to believe it wasn't true, he responded. "This is ridiculous. Are you sure?"

The CEO responded, "Hall has been talking with Kimberly and another party. We don't know whom. It has to stop, now! I informed your friend that he has a job to finish. He agreed." The ringing of the intercom startled the men. "What is it Carol?" Roger barked.

"Mr. Maxco, there is an urgent call for you on line two—a man by the name of Byron. Shall I put it through?"

"Go ahead." Roger answered the first ring and listened to the caller, hitting the speakerphone button so Lasko could hear.

"Mr. Maxco, I have confirmed the name of the second visitor to Room 212. I have a source at the car rental agency. The man's name is John Rushly. This complicates matters. Get this! He's a Special Agent with the FBI."

A wave of fear and apprehension swept through the body of Roger Maxco. Within the past thirty minutes, his entire world had turned upside down. His reply to the caller was short and to the point.

"Keep me informed. Just finish the goddamn job!" Roger did not wait for an acknowledgment. He hung up the phone and turned to Lasko.

"We have a lot of work to do. I want you to call Michael Lowe—get him over here. Our project may need to be accelerated. It seems that the resurrected Marshall Hall has had a visit from the FBI. Fine! This is just fine!" He stomped over to the sidebar and helped himself to Lasko's best scotch.

A couple of hours later, the three men sat in an office with an atmosphere so oppressive, it could have been sliced with a knife. The conspirators felt so stifled with the weight of all this news, they needed more room and air to breathe. They adjourned to the conference room for further talk, taking the scotch with them. Each knew the other would rise to the occasion. This was a set back, they agreed, but not a total disaster. It was still early in the game and they had some interesting hold cards they were not ready to divulge.

In the private office next to the conference room, sitting quietly and unnoticed, Elizabeth Martin sat pouring over information she had been promised, data that someone, unbeknownst to her, had taken great pains to doctor. She was oblivious to the drama unfolding in the room next to hers.

John Rushly returned to Phoenix that evening. His wife was eager to hear all the news. They spent the evening sorting out the details. John had taken meticulous notes and along with the information he had gathered about Maxco-Litton, the pieces, although scattered, were falling into some kind of order. The two law enforcement officers, one off-duty, came up with a checklist.

- ✓ Joanne Hall dies in an accident while walking with her husband
- ✓ Funeral service with husband in attendance—cigarette issue
- ✓ Jill notified by Detective Staples that husband is a suspect—possible arrest to come
- ✓ Three days after funeral, husband (suspect) disappears in rain swept wash—car found
- ✓ A week later, Hall shows up in Walnut Creek. Calls Kimberly & Rushly
- ✓ Meeting with Rushly
- ✓ Alleged conspiracy involving nationally recognized pharmaceutical firm

"That's a lot to happen in so short a time, John," Jill commented.

"If you stop and think of what has happened between Hall and Maxco-Litton in the past six months," John replied, "it is astounding." John continued. "I have a meeting with my old friend Brian Brewer from the LA office tomorrow. He's attending a FBI conference at the Biltmore. I'm going to bring him in on this along with the bosses downtown. It should be an interesting day." *Yes,* thought John, *Wednesday at FBI headquarters in downtown Phoenix will be more than interesting.*

"John, I will be forced to live this investigation, vicariously," Jill interrupted her husband's train of thought. I can't take any more time away from the Department. You will keep me informed about everything having to do with this case, please?"

"Hey, you started it," John replied. "Besides, I will need your help with the local authorities in Bodega Bay. This Mike Staples is a pal of yours—right?"

"Michael and I are *very* close, John," Jill whispered, trying to look sultry. She only succeeded in getting a laugh out of him.

"I see," John responded, wanting to appear stern. "I intend to keep an eye on you two, along with everyone else involved. It should be a cozy investigation Ms. Rushly. Let's get some rest." He put his arms around her and pulled her close, loving the scent of her hair. "We both have a full day tomorrow."

As they started to walk up the stairs to bed, Jill had one more important thought. "John, do you think Marshall Hall is safe?"

"He's safe as long as Maxco doesn't find out he's alive," John responded, looking worried. "I notified the San Francisco Field Office to take precautions and keep the information under wraps. Hopefully, for the time being, that will be enough. In a few days, we may have to place him in protective custody."

Byron Storm was taking no chances. He and his partner, a bruiser known as Clinch, were making plans to finish the job they had botched on their first attempt. It was six o'clock in the morning on Wednesday. They had watched the entrance to Hall's room all night, and concluded there was no one else around. At 6:45, they would jimmy the lock, force the door and pump several shots into the sleeping scientist. They hoped the lock could be forced with little noise. Storm's Colt Python with a custom silencer would finish the job. Clinch would stand to one side as backup. He carried a 9mm Beretta.

The Best Western had several rooms that faced the parking area. Stairs and walkways were concrete with iron railings, and nearly silent when guests and visitors walked back and forth to their rooms. Hall's room was on a second level at the corner of the building. The staircase was just outside his door, a few feet to the left.

Unknown to the two hoodlums, an FBI surveillance team, two men in a dark van, had parked within view of the room. Their mission—to protect a possible government witness. The alert status given was seven on a scale of ten.

The two assailants had parked in an area that could not be observed by the office or the van. They walked the short distance to the bottom of the stairs to Room 212. It was quiet with no one in view around the parking area. They proceeded up the stairs quickly, quietly.

Sipping from a thermos of black coffee, the burly-looking agent behind the wheel of the van nudged his partner.

"Martin, we have company. Shit! I didn't see any vehicle. We have to move. Those guys are heading for Room 212. Keep your eye on the shorter one and stay to my right. Hopefully, they're guests. I'll call for backup, just in case." After notifying the dispatcher, the two agents stepped from the van and headed directly for the men who had nearly reached the top of the stairs.

"FBI!" shouted the first agent to reach the steps. "Turn around with your hands where we can see them! I say again, FBI. Stop and turn around with your hands up in the air!"

The still night air was shattered by the sound of three successive 9mm blasts from Clinch. His weapon had no silencer. The trained officers responded with four shots each from their service 10mm Glocks. Clinch was thrown against the rail by the force of six bullets that had found their mark.

Amidst the confusion and the sound of gunfire, Marshall Hall was wide-awake. He made the instinctive, though fatal, mistake of opening his door. Two shots from the Colt Python 357 literally lifted him into the air, then slammed his body back into the room. The magnum loads had entered his chest, shattered his heart, and severed his spinal cord. He was dead before he hit the floor.

Turning to help his partner, Byron Storm was hit four times by the two agents who were now half way up the stairs. One agent had sustained a flesh wound below his left shoulder. He was lucky. If he had moved to the left a few inches, he would have been killed.

It was over in seconds. Within minutes, police and FBI units were swarming all over the scene. Three men were dead. More importantly, Marshall Hall, chief witness against Maxco-Litton, was silenced. And this time, he would not reappear.

A formal investigation into the death of Hall and his reports of conspiracy by the drug company could now be opened. By 7:35,

John Rushly would be notified of the shooting and summoned to FBI headquarters. It would be a long day.

"Son of a bitch. Shit!" The agent listened intently as the San Francisco office related the details of the shooting. There were no documents found in Room 212. *He must have given them to Kimberly*, John thought.

"What's wrong John? Why all the swearing this early in the day. Who was on the phone?" Jill appeared from the bathroom, wearing a terry cloth robe and a yellow towel around her freshly washed hair.

John could hardly meet her eyes. She had just asked him if his witness had needed protection, and he had been so cavalier about it. John felt like hell. He had failed to protect this man who had trusted him with his life. Marshall Hall had trusted the FBI and they had let him down. John's mind raced ahead. It all happened so fast. *If only I had taken him more seriously*, he thought. *This man needed protection—not just surveillance.* He turned to face his wife, clean and fresh from her early morning shower. Her mood was about to change dramatically.

"It was our field office in San Francisco. Marshall Hall was gunned down at the motel this morning. The FBI was there and killed the two assailants. I let him down, Jill. He should have had one hundred percent protection."

Jill tried to be supportive while they were getting ready for work. "John, you did all you thought you needed to do. Agents were sent to cover him. You can't blame yourself." She tried in vain to comfort a visibly distraught John Rushly.

"Jill, I made a big mistake. His story was true. It deserved closer attention. Maybe I did what anyone else would have done, I don't know. But a good man willing to risk his life to save others is now dead. He trusted me. He came to me for help! I let him down."

"I'm beginning to feel a lot of empathy for him," Jill said. "If Joanne's death was an unfortunate accident, this man has been given a bad shuffle. Maybe his only weakness was infidelity. He has paid an awful price for that love affair, and for working with Maxco-Litton."

The couple had faced this kind of adversity in the past. But John was alone this time. It was his case. They briefly kissed then left for work. John's day would be busier than he had anticipated.

The late edition of the San Francisco Chronicle gave the shootout front-page coverage. It wasn't the banner, but anyone who picked up the paper couldn't miss the article. The lovely lady, sitting alone at the coffee shop, gasped when she read the headline, the cup of hot coffee spilling onto her skirt. Gasping for breath, Kimberly couldn't believe what she was reading:

> World Famous Scientist Killed by Gunfire
> Early this morning at a Best Western in Walnut Creek, renowned scientist Marshall Hall was gunned down by two unidentified men. FBI agents on the scene fatally wounded the assailants. Hall, a researcher for the pharmaceutical giant Maxco-Litton was pronounced dead at the scene. Authorities are silent and there has been no statement from Maxco-Litton. Hall's wife was recently killed in an apparent accident a few weeks ago in Bodega Bay. Police are still investigating that incident.

Sobbing uncontrollably, the distraught lady read the story over and over, hoping it was a mistake. Coffee shop patrons tried to comfort her, not quite knowing what to do. Unable to speak, Kimberly threw a five-dollar bill on the table and left. Upon returning home, she noticed the blinking, red light on the answering machine. With shaking hands, she pushed the button, then sat down, quickly, trying to make sense of what she was hearing.

There were three messages, one from John Rushly FBI, another from her father and one very special voice. That message was left at 6:00 a.m. She listened to that one first.

"Hi sweetheart, it's Marshall. I wanted you to know that I had a meeting yesterday with Rushly, and everything is going to work out. Call me when you get home. We have a lot of things to talk about. Remember that I love you."

The second message, this one from her father, was brief. "Kimberly, something terrible has happened. It's about Marshall.

Call me as soon as you get this!"

Emotionally drained and barely able to listen, Kimberly sat stunned, listening to the last message. "This message is for Kimberly Weitzel. Miss Weitzel, this is John Rushly. I am a Special Agent with the FBI. I met with Dr. Hall yesterday. It is important that you contact me as soon as possible. You may be in danger."

John left the phone numbers where he could be reached. Kimberly didn't wait to reason. She jumped up frantically, ran to the bedroom, grabbed a jet bag and began to pack. She would stay with friends, then call the FBI agent. She took the tape out of the answering machine and dropped it into her cosmetics bag. What else would Marshall do, she thought? She took a deep breath, inserted a new cassette and spoke into the machine. "You have reached 779-5555. We are unavailable at the moment. Please leave a message and we will return your call."

Marshall Hall had fallen in love with Kimberly, not only for her beauty, but for her street smarts, as well. Her father had always known his daughter had little interest in science. He knew she wouldn't be following in his footsteps, but had encouraged her independence throughout her life and had taught her to think for herself. He had taught her well. Kimberly was a survivor, having lost her mother to cancer when the girl was still a child.

I will survive this, she thought, struggling to zip her bulging suitcase.

Although Marshall had not had a chance to completely level with her insofar as her father was concerned, she knew he had uncovered something important, something he wanted to tell her. She shuddered at the thought that it might have had something to do with the murder of the man she loved.

Kimberly made sure there was nothing in the apartment anyone could trace. On her way out the door, she changed her mind about staying with friends. Not only might it endanger them, she realized, but also there was the privacy issue. Kimberly couldn't have anyone know where she was, anyone, that is, but John Rushly. But even that would wait. She planned to board a flight to Phoenix and stay at one of the popular Embassy Suites. Feeling the need to be out of the Bay area and to find out as much as she could about Marshall's death, Kimberly caught an early afternoon flight to Sky Harbor International. Her plane would land at three o'clock.

The agent was holding a conference with his superiors at the Field Office in downtown Phoenix. He instructed his secretary to notify him in the event that Kimberly Weitzel called. He began the meeting with a summary statement. Three administrative chiefs seated before him had already received bits and pieces about the San Francisco incident, complete with related background material. Ronald Kunz, Field Office supervisor and Maggie O'Brien, a senior special agent, flanked section Chief Fred Rowley.

"Guys," Rushly sighed, already weary, "it's been quite a week. I must tell you that new information is being gathered and sent to this office hourly. I alerted our people in New York to take an unobtrusive look at Maxco-Litton. In light of the information provided to me from Marshall Hall, I thought it would be wise to do a profile on their key executives. In addition, our agents are looking closely at Dr. Julian Weitzel. I left a message for his daughter in San Francisco to call me as soon as possible. As a precaution, I sent a team to her apartment this morning but she had left. Hopefully, she will get the message by remote, and call soon."

He stood up, then walked over to the desk directly in front of the staff, becoming more intense with every movement. Sitting down on the corner, he paused, making sure he had full eye contact before proceeding. "There is a lot of information we don't have. For one thing, the research data referred to by Marshall Hall is missing. Preliminarily, my notes taken at the Best Western in Walnut Creek will give us a good start. Ms. Weitzel may be in possession of more information. In my opinion, the seriousness of the allegations made by Dr. Hall demand a thorough and comprehensive investigation.

"You're aware this all started with the death of my wife's friend in Bodega Bay. The good news is that Jill has already established a working relationship with local authorities in the Bay area. It's a detective who's investigating that incident along with an earlier attempt on Hall's life. Since Hall's murder, the

California authorities have already stepped up their investigation. I'm going to request that I be assigned point on this case. While it means giving other cases a lower priority, for the moment, I believe that's a no-contest. I think there's something very big here. In my opinion, the potential ramifications of the alleged acts of Maxco-Litton are extreme. They're made far more sinister by the utilization of perverted science and the resulting cover-up. I'm sorry for the diatribe. *I really want this case!*" he finished, slamming his fist into his hand for emphasis.

Fred Rowley and the others all had complete confidence in their colleague and had become aware of Jill's talents in law enforcement, as well. Rowley was the first to speak. "I think all of us concur with your assessment of the seriousness of this case, John."

Maggie O'Brien nodded, interrupting. "Right! And taking into account that both Joanne and Marshall Hall are dead, plus Hall's assailants by our own agents, that's already four dead in two weeks!"

"It was Jill's friend, Hall's wife, which seems to be the one domino that started this drama," Rushly added.

Maggie continued, nodding, "Be careful what you wish for, John. This could be one dangerous and nasty assignment. I'm a little concerned about this becoming a one-man show. You're going to need a lot of support. Will you ask for it?"

Maggie O'Brien was a first class agent. In her forties, she was married and mother of four. She had been with the Bureau for twenty years and had earned the respect and admiration of everyone in the Western District. She was smart and very direct.

"Maggie, that's a fair question," replied John. "When I was given official standing with the Bureau during the inquiry into the International Church of the Apostles and their trained assassin, I made a few mistakes. It appeared on one or two occasions that I might have been something of a loose cannon. That's all changed. You may be assured that I'll handle this investigation by the book. I'll gratefully accept all the help I can get."

"You have my vote," Maggie smiled.

"You're the man, John." Fred Rowley said, the others nodding their approval. Fred continued. "It's your show, John. Keep us informed. This is a big one. Good luck."

The meeting was interrupted by an urgent phone call for Agent Rushly. He nodded in gratitude for their confidence, then took the call.

"Mr. Rushly? It's Kimberly." The low, soft voice sounded tentative.

"Yes, Ms. Weitzel. I'm glad you called. I am so sorry about Marshall."

Her voice sounded breathy now, and it was obvious she was nervous. "I am really scared. I left my apartment as soon as I heard your message and caught a flight to Phoenix. I'm going to stay at a hotel for a week or two. Am I safe? What is happening?" Obviously worried and distraught, and concerned not only for her own safety but that of her father, Kimberly was eager to be reassured.

"We're trying to sort this out, Kimberly. I need to see you right away. Give me your address. I'll drive over and we can spend some time together. I *promise* I'll keep you safe," he said more urgently than perhaps he should have, still feeling responsible for Marshall Hall's death. "Kimberly, did Marshall leave any papers or tapes with you? Anything at all?"

"He talked about a package. I think he was going give it to me the next time we met."

"Okay, don't worry about it." *Where was the information he needed*? he thought, struggling to remain calm.

"Mr. Rushly, I rented a car at the airport. I'll just drive over to your office."

"Fine, Kimberly, and please call me John. Let's see," he looked down at his watch, "it's already 3:45. We can meet in the morning, if you like. You must be tired. I don't want to push. Let's say ten o'clock at our downtown Field Office." Kimberly sounded exhausted. She would be easier to interview after a night's rest. John made careful note of her address, Embassy Suites, and assigned two agents to constantly survey the streets and neighborhood that evening. He doubted she was in any immediate danger, but this time wasn't taking any chances.

"That will be best for me, Mr. Rushly—John!" she corrected herself. "I'll see you around 10:00 a.m. And—" she hesitated, sounding worried, "I haven't been able to reach my father. Have you heard anything about him?"

"Not yet," John tried to sound reassuring. I'll have talked with the people at Maxco-Litton by the time you get here in the morning. Hopefully, I'll have some news at that time. You get some rest, okay?"

"Thank you, John. I'll see you tomorrow."

The agent knew Kimberly's father was the key figure in the drama that was rapidly unfolding at Maxco-Litton. But he needed to begin his investigation with a third party at the huge pharmaceutical firm. His study of the main players, all twelve Directors, would begin with the one person known throughout the industry for her impeccable integrity and high standards. With unquestioned credentials and a reputation for scrupulous ethics, as Maxco-Litton's Chief Financial Officer and a major stockholder, Elizabeth Martin would be contact number one on John Rushly's list.

Chapter Six

A sleazy, caustic Roger Maxco was chastising his partners in crime, Earnest Lasko and Michael Lowe. They looked at each other, uncomfortably, as the elegantly groomed executive turned on his highly polished wing tips to face them squarely, beginning his tirade with a touch of sardonic humor. "Those so-called professionals of yours, Earnest, have opened up a can of worms. The only consolation I can think of is that they are both dead and can't talk! Do you have *any* idea where this can lead?" His smile was more threatening than comforting.

"It's not all bad, Roger, Earnest said, squirming in the leather chair. "So Hall is gone and the men who killed him can't talk. Maybe we're better off than you think," he tried to smile, then thought better as Roger turned his attention on him.

"You make the perfect lawyer, Earnest. I'm glad you're on my side. I'll be counting on you to smooth this over with the other Directors. Elizabeth, for example, is going to need some massaging. She insisted on a detailed status report of Hall's project. Hopefully, you put that report together right—with a few important details left out. You can bet she will be taking a closer look in light of his recent demise."

"I'll take care of Elizabeth, Roger. I think she likes me." Earnest tried not to be put off by Roger's sarcastic chuckle.

"This all works for me, Roger. The project and Dr. Weitzel distracted her. Be glad she's not obsessed with the accounting problems and stock transfers. Look at the upside, Roger. *No one* seems to be concerned with the *real* issues!" His attempt at smugness failed.

Earnest Lasko, however, was absolutely correct. What was going on behind the scenes within the financial structure of Maxco-Litton was not only unsuspected but of critical importance. Therein lay the motivation and explanation of Roger Maxco's' dogged determination to destroy his own empire. The unscrupulous, illegal stock transfers and the mean-spirited sellout along the way of key executives who were getting too close to the truth, were only part of what needed to be kept secret. Roger Maxco, in his desperation to maintain status and control, had borrowed huge sums of money from questionable sources, and in so doing was forced to assign blocks of stock to interests not favorable to Maxco-Litton. Unknown to all but Lasko, his boss was nearly broke! With the advent of this new "miracle drug" and with Roger controlling the timing, his final stock manipulation scheme would bring him untold wealth, leaving Maxco-Litton in ruins. The Devil was hard at work.

"Let's not get too cocky, Earnest." Michael reminded his colleague. "Elizabeth is extremely bright—she could surprise us all. We've been lucky so far, but don't make any assumptions. And don't be afraid to check with me on the finer legal issues." The attorney still had reservations about this whole scheme.

"A point well taken," Roger said, "listen to this man, Earnest."

Elizabeth Martin had finished her review of the project information provided by Roger Maxco. Of course, she realized the information was skewed in favor of Roger and the lab work, but it was an impressive set of documents. Her private assistant had just served Elizabeth a cup of her favorite mint-flavored tea when the call came in. John Rushly was on the line.

"Who on earth is John Rushly?" Elizabeth asked her assistant. A shrug was her reply.

She took the call. "This is Elizabeth Martin, may I help you?"

"Ms. Martin, I am sorry to disturb you this morning. My name is John Rushly, Special Agent with the FBI. May we talk for a few minutes?"

"Of course, Mr. Rushly." Her curiosity was piqued, now. "How can I help you?" Elizabeth knew the death of Marshall Hall would bring inquiries from the authorities. She was somewhat dismayed as to why the FBI would be looking into his death, however. She had heard no details of the shooting.

"Ms. Martin, my call is official but be assured it is preliminary in nature. Our agents were involved in the Hall tragedy. Since he was a key researcher with your firm, we are naturally obligated to contact those who knew him."

This was a delicate call. His research had demonstrated that Elizabeth Martin might be the one person at Maxco-Litton John could trust and rely on. At least he thought her to be his best source for honest answers.

"I understand, Mr. Rushly," she answered with a voice bred in sophistication, "but I can't imagine how I can help you. We were not personal friends."

The bright and articulate executive was reading much more into his call, he thought. He hesitated for a moment, to check her comfort level. Surprisingly, she waited for him to respond. He smiled at the unspoken challenge.

"Ms. Martin," he continued unruffled. "There are matters of urgency having to do to with this case that I must discuss with you personally. Perhaps you could check your schedule. If you could find some time on Friday, I could take an early flight from Phoenix on Thursday and I could be in New York by late afternoon. Is the timing agreeable to you?" Elizabeth was smart enough to know this was not a simple request. Something big was in the works and John Rushly was closing this deal like a timeshare salesman.

"Yes, Mr. Rushly," she answered courteously. "I will make every effort to accommodate the FBI. We can meet late Thursday. Please, John, if I may call you John, ring my direct line from the airport, and we will arrange an appropriate meeting place. I prefer this rendezvous to be away from the executive offices. The press, you know." Everything that John Rushly had read or heard about this remarkable woman was true. He could sense her keen intellect and sophistication.

"Thank you, Elizabeth. Of course you may call me John. I do look forward to our meeting Thursday. And Elizabeth," he smiled through the phone at his quarry, "I do appreciate your cooperation." As he replaced the receiver, he realized that there was some kind of tension between them that he had enjoyed. *Wonder if she plays chess*? he thought, forgetting for the moment, the seriousness of the circumstance.

Elizabeth still held the phone in her hand. Staring out of the high rise executive suite over the New York skyline, she could only imagine what the agent had on his mind. She began to think the worst, becoming angrier by the minute. *So Roger has purposefully kept me out of the loop,* she thought, seething. *Rushly seems to know a lot about Marshall Hall. My God, what is he planning? The first time, Hall had an accident, didn't he? This time it was murder! A Special Agent of the FBI flying to New York—it must be quite a story. And how does Dr. Weitzel fit into all of this? What the hell's going on with our company?* A cold chill accompanied her fearful thoughts. She had invested her career, her life in this firm. "Tune in Thursday, Elizabeth." She whispered to herself as she marked the appointment down in her day-timer. "I can hardly wait to meet you, Agent Rushly."

Kimberly was on time for her ten o'clock meeting at the FBI office. Having parked underground, as instructed, she had taken the elevator to the main lobby. She was immediately directed to a reception area on the third floor. Dressed in a mauve-colored suit with a long, unconstructed jacket, she appeared to be quite elegant. Her large, dark glasses hid her obvious distress. Watching her enter from his glass-walled office next to the reception area, Rushly understood how a prominent scientist had become so incredibly attracted to this stately lady. Her classic demeanor spoke of a lifetime of pampering. It was obvious from her tailored clothing and gentle manner that she had come from money and breeding and yet, she spoke to the receptionist with a genuine sincerity that disarmed the girl and befriended her immediately.

As she pulled off her glasses, John noticed her bright blue eyes. It was hard to appreciate her sadness. She appeared confident and determined to survive. It was easy to believe she was the daughter of a world-renowned scientist.

He thought he had better make himself known before she became aware he was staring. He walked out to the reception desk and extended his hand. "Kimberly, John Rushly. Thank you for coming."

"Believe me, Mr. Rushly," she responded, "I'm happy to be here. I have so many questions."

The sight of the agent brought immediate relief, yet an element of realism to Kimberly, a realism that brought her shock to the forefront. She was sensing danger and was terribly concerned about her father. She knew it would take a lot of time to get over the death of the man she loved. She also knew questions to his death would consume her. She needed answers. She needed protection, and felt her father did too.

"Let's relax in my office, Kimberly. We have a lot of talking to do. Would you care for coffee?"

"Yes, that would be great." John's office was comfortable and she felt immediately at ease. A sofa and two chairs allowed for a less formal setting. John went to the sideboard and poured two large cups of steaming, black coffee. Unceremoniously grabbing a handful of Equal, four creamers and a couple of swizzle sticks, he returned to his desk, but not before noticing where her focus had been drawn.

"Is this your wife, Mr. Rushly?" Kimberly had noticed the photo on his desk.

"Yes," he smiled easily. His wife was easy to talk about. And pride always showed in his voice when he did. "Jill is a detective with the Scottsdale Police Department. We met on a case. We've just been married a year." He took a sip of his coffee and sat down behind the desk, pulling a yellow legal pad toward him.

"She is a lovely woman." Kimberly obviously wasn't ready to settle down, yet. He would have to be patient.

"I do feel safer now," she said throatily, opening three creamers and dropping them into her coffee. Stirring her coffee slowly, she looked up at him and said tentatively, "Between the Scottsdale police and the FBI, I should feel secure." It was more like a question.

"Kimberly, I am truly sorry about Marshall. I felt somewhat responsible for what happened. We had a very serious talk the day before. Based on his story, I assigned two agents to keep a lookout at the hotel. I'm afraid it wasn't enough."

"You can't blame yourself, Mr. Rushly." Her comment was both sincere and generous. "Who could possibly imagine what was gong to happen? I was so shocked. Shocked enough by his death, —but *murder*?" Our Research Institute has been nothing but dull! Always, dull! Nothing ever happens there! Now, it seems, there's all sorts of intrigue, but I just don't know anything. That makes it all the more, —unbearable!" Suddenly, without notice, Kimberly began to sob.

"Kimberly," he tried to comfort her by pushing a box of

Kleenex across the desk, then realized how ineffectual and juvenile that seemed. "I want you to know there is a full investigation underway into Dr. Hall's death as well as what's going on at the lab, if anything, and the accident that killed Hall's wife."

"Wha—?" She was obviously stunned. "Do you mean *her death* wasn't an accident?"

"I didn't say that—but that was the first thing that happened, leading me to believe that all of this may be tied together."

"I see." Kimberly fell silent.

John continued. "I am flying to New York on Thursday to meet with an executive from Maxco-Litton. Maybe I can begin to find some answers." He stood up to get more coffee, then remembered his most important question. "Have you heard from your father? We know he's in New York and working, rather than the Bay area. I received that information this morning."

"That's a relief," replied Kimberly, "I haven't heard from him for over a week. When we talked, he sounded anxious. He was overly concerned with my safety. It seemed strange at the time. There *must* be a connection between Maxco-Litton and Marshall's murder." Her eyes were bigger and bluer than ever when she looked at him, questioning.

John raised an eyebrow. "That's a very perceptive comment, Kimberly. What makes you think there is a connection?"

"My last conversation with Marshall skirted what was going on at Maxco-Litton. Marshall said enough to raise my concerns. He mentioned Roger Maxco—in his words, 'a hard case.'"

Kimberly thought about what she had said then remembered something her lover had told her several weeks before. "Another thing," she said, seeming to get into the investigation more, "Marshall was recently stressed over his latest project. He had told me that if the project weren't handled properly, a lot of people could get hurt, really hurt! I'm afraid I didn't take him all that seriously." Turning away from John, she reached into her purse for a cigarette. Lighting it, her hands trembling, she teared up again and John gave her a moment.

"Is there anything else you can remember?" his voice was more gentle, this time.

"You were right, John," she blew the smoke away from him,

re-crossing her legs and reasserting herself. "Marshall did want to talk about my father. I don't know what that was about. We never had the chance to have that conversation." She paused for a moment, changing direction, then asked, "What do you think is going on, Mr. Rushly?"

"Our investigation is just beginning, Kimberly. We do know there is something of a sinister nature taking place at the firm. I am not sure what it is, but it could involve your father." Watching her wince, he added quickly, "That doesn't mean he is guilty of any wrongdoing, Kimberly. But all of this evidently has to do with the project Marshall was working on. Your father was a collaborator, an integral part of that project. Has your father related any information to you that might help this investigation?"

"I can't think of anything else," Kimberly replied. "I plan to be here for a while and I hope to be talking to my father soon. Maybe something else will turn up." She paused, suddenly thinking of something else.

"Wait a minute! He did refer to the project using a code word. He said they used it when having lunch—when someone might overhear their conversations. He used the word Galen. I researched it, just for fun, and found it to be the name of an outstanding physician of antiquity—living in Rome. He produced about five hundred tracts on medicine and ethics. Anyway, if you run into it again, that's the name of the project Marshall and my dad were working on." She put out her cigarette and looked at her new confidante. She seemed weary and fearful at the same time.

"Kimberly, do me a favor," John said quietly, feeling that additional pressure would push her away. "Keep our meeting confidential—even to your father. I believe it will be in his best interest, as well as yours. I'm leaving for New York on Thursday, and will inquire about your father. Hopefully, I will be able to meet with him. I want to thank you for your cooperation. We'll see each other soon. Leave your address and phone number. If you notice anything suspicious in your neighborhood, call me—day or night!" He was determined to not let anything happen to this potential witness.

John and Kimberly exchanged phone numbers and the agent

made note of her hotel address. By the end of the week, John believed he would have more direction. Although still in its embryonic stage, the investigation into the death of Marshall Hall was beginning to take shape. Information was coming in each hour, adding clarity to the inner workings of Maxco-Litton and its top echelon. Unbeknownst to Agent Rushly, during that very interview, two other names had surfaced over the computer when checked against past white-color, criminal investigations—Earnest Lasko and Michael Lowe.

Chapter Seven

The voice was low and sinister. Roger Maxco had reluctantly taken the call. You didn't refuse a call from Charles Nitti, the most prominent name behind the Chicago mob, and Roger's private source for the massive loans that would finance his illicit stock manipulations. Weeks before, the two had come up with an elaborate code to assure his calls would be taken without divulging who was on the line. Picking up the phone, the executive tried to sound upbeat.

"Mr. Nitti, this is Roger Maxco. How can I help you?"

"I prefer that you do not use my name. We've discussed this. Listen carefully. We are distressed over the whole mess with Marshall Hall. The media's starting to get hold of this shit. Were you aware that your actions have already prompted an FBI inquiry? This is not good. We know this man Rushly."

"I can explain what—" Roger attempted to interrupt.

"I *said* just listen!"

Roger muttered an okay and Nitti continued. "With regard to *any other plans* affecting anyone's well being, call me first. We have our own people—*they're professionals*. Do you understand?"

"Perfectly," Roger replied.

"Once more, do not exceed your authority. There is now a question about the August funding. My people are nervous. We'll talk later." The caller hung up the phone.

Roger Maxco was understandably upset, more worried than he had been for a long, long time. Pressure was mounting. The August funding that was referred to was critical insofar as timing. Roger's scheme included the purchase of blocks of stock before the inevitable price surge after announcing their miracle cure. He was counting on Nitti and his friends. Without them, the potential profit from his scheme would be reduced substantially. Another worry he had ignored over the past few days was Dr. Julian Weitzel. It was time to address that issue and ensure there were no glitches. In addition, Roger Maxco's people had lost track of

Julian's daughter, Kimberly.

John's plane arrived on time and he hailed a cab to Manhattan. From a phone booth at JFK, he had arranged with Elizabeth Martin to meet at a trendy restaurant, The Blue Water Grill near 42nd Street and Times Square. John believed a quiet dinner would provide the logical setting to discuss Maxco-Litton. Expectations on both sides, whether real or imagined, would guarantee an interesting discussion. Both parties were looking for answers.

Elizabeth arrived early and arranged for a private table. She wore a smart, expensive Armani business suit, ivory on ivory, with satin stripes and perfectly matched accessories. Notably attractive, used to the seat of corporate power, she was confident and focused. There was not a hint of arrogance or any other negative trait one could attach to this striking figure.

Rushly, a dashingly handsome figure in his own right, was nevertheless equal to the task of meeting the third most powerful executive at Maxco-Litton. Knowing she had been written up in Forbes as a "Wall Street Mensa," and that he was no intellectual match, John Rushly had made his own mark in the world, and this investigation, in his mind, was nothing more than another complicated but solvable case. She was only an interview, nothing more.

As she watched him approach the table, Elizabeth made note of the agent's lean body and confident demeanor. His dark blue sport jacket, tasteful gray dress trousers and powder blue shirt with charcoal tie completed the package. Elizabeth loved good-looking, competent competition—this was her kind of social event.

"Ms. Martin, it's a pleasure to meet you. Thank you for meeting with me." He held out his hand. She took it warmly, smiling with a hint of flirtatiousness, a quality she had not exhibited for quite some time.

"Not at all Mr. Rushly," she found herself laughing quietly for some unexplained reason. "It is indeed a pleasure meeting a notable professional in law enforcement. Your work in dismantling The International Church of the Apostles was indeed impressive."

"You have done your homework, Elizabeth. Thank you for the compliment." He couldn't quite tell if she was making fun of him, just a little, but decided to let it pass. Nevertheless, since the two were now on a first name basis, they managed to order drinks and get through the first nuances of their first social encounter.

"I am inclined to believe you have done your homework, too, John." Elizabeth looked up over her Martini. "I noticed that someone pulled my Dun & Bradstreet yesterday. Was that the FBI by any chance?" she asked coyly, not at all like her. John nodded shyly. He had never anticipated the attention to detail this woman was capable of displaying.

"Well, let's agree the playing field is level. We both know a lot about each other, Elizabeth. My purpose for being here is this: I need to know more about the projects inside Maxco-Litton. In particularly, the project recently headed by Dr. Marshall Hall." John had decided it was time to begin the meeting in earnest. In an instant, Elizabeth was ready for game-set-match.

"John, if you don't mind, would you be kind enough to bring me up-to-date with your investigation of Marshall Hall's murder. I would feel more comfortable responding to your questions. You must realize there is an issue of ethics involved here. There are certain confidences that I must protect—unless, of course, there are mitigating circumstances." John smiled. The waiter approached them and their order was placed. The two decided on shrimp salads. They ordered coffee. The conversation continued.

"I understand, Elizabeth. There is not much to tell at this point. FBI agents killed the two men who had obviously been sent to assassinate Hall at his motel. Earlier, I had met with him. Based on our conversation, my investigation led to Maxco-Litton."

"Really!" Elizabeth was surprised that John had established so quickly a direct connection between her company and the murder. "Are you willing to fill me in on the details of that conversation?" A woman of tremendous loyalty to her company, she was not yet willing to believe there might be anything sinister in the dealings of her firm. She had been close to the inner circle for too long.

"It is necessary for me to use discretion, Elizabeth. There have been no arrests and my being here, although official, is preliminary in nature."

"You certainly have a way with words, John," she laughed lightly, shaking her head." Having ordered a light dinner with drinks and coffee gave the couple the required breaks with the sensitive subject, permitting them both time to think about their questions and responses.

"Is anyone at Maxco-Litton under suspicion, as yet?" she was becoming guarded. This company had been her life ever since college and a great deal of her stock portfolio had been amassed directly from the continued solvency of the company.

"Elizabeth, before I answer that question, allow me to make a general statement—a hypothetical scenario having to do with a major pharmaceutical corporation. Feel free to comment when I finish, okay?"

"Have at it, John. I'm all ears." She was playing again and he didn't mind it.

"Let's suppose that two brilliant scientists embarked on a major research project of a vaccine that, if successful, would propel them and their company to incredible heights—professionally and financially. The vaccine produced would save at least a hundred thousand lives each year. Let's say that FDA approval was just a few months away. What if one of the scientists discovers that the test data used by his colleague to support his original hypothesis was defective. What if a cover up begins between the scientists and the top executive of the company? Let's say that information is discovered that results in a death, a murder of the scientist that discovered it."

Elizabeth began to pale, her eyes glistening with a combination of horror and excitement. John continued. "Worse, FDA approval is going ahead. Lives are at risk. Not only does the vaccine not work, it could actually kill tens of thousands before the problem with the vaccine is discovered. Elizabeth," he paused for effect, "how does all of this strike you?"

Elizabeth Martin was stunned. She remained silent as she pondered what John Rushly had just related. She looked him straight in the eyes and gave him her reaction. "If I were a part of the organization you refer to, Mr. Rushly, I would do everything within my power to expose the fraud. I would see to it that anyone having anything remotely to do with such a despicable and reprehensible scheme be brought to justice and punished accordingly." There was a long interlude of silence. John Rushly had gotten the reaction he had predicted, the reaction he had hoped for.

A truly remarkable woman, he thought, once again admiring her beauty. "Thank you Elizabeth. That is exactly what I had hoped you would say. And now I will answer your question. Roger Maxco and Dr. Julian Weitzel are under suspicion."

Elizabeth took in a deep breath. Sadness and disappointment tore away at her stoic composure. To her, this was the worst kind of betrayal. A firm she had nurtured, people she had trusted and loved for years was on the brink of being destroyed—sold out by greedy and unscrupulous men with no sense of honor, decency or commitment to the humanity they had promised to serve. Her right hand pressed against her forehead while her left clung to the table for support. "My God," she shuddered, "my God, John!" The agent gave her time to absorb the impact of all he had said.

"Elizabeth, this is a time when we must look deep within ourselves for strength. I believe you have that strength. I believe you have the moral courage to see this through. I'll be with you all the way. What ever is going on here, we will find. Maybe I've gone too far. I could be off track, but I don't think so."

"John, I really like you," Elizabeth looked up at him, trustingly. "Your wife must be very proud. She is one, exceptionally lucky lady." Obviously shaken, her voice dropped and she asked, "Could we sit here awhile together, and just have a social drink? It looks as if we're going to be working together for the next few months. You've described an outrageous set of circumstances, yet to be proven, mind you, -" she tried to make light of it but didn't succeed, "—but you certainly have my attention."

"We can sit here as long as you like. And yes, I will join you for a drink. I'll be talking to Jill this evening, and I would like to tell her that you are someone she would be proud to meet, as well."

The dinner meeting had been more than John Rushly had expected. Arrangements were made for he and Elizabeth to meet again the next day, prior to John's departure. The Chief Financial Officer, turned sleuth, would begin to gather evidence. Her investigation, which would include a financial audit of Maxco-Litton, would be carried out with absolute discretion. An exhaustive look into the project known as Galen would begin immediately. Elizabeth would utilize her keen intellect and other resources at her disposal to honor her commitment to the FBI. She would make a complete and unrelenting inquiry into the affairs of Roger Maxco, Dr. Julian Weitzel, and anyone else involved in what she now believed to be a fraudulent and unforgiving white-collar crime scheme. She was hurt, deeply hurt and horribly betrayed. She'd been blinded by his charm, and had respected Roger Maxco enormously for what he represented, what he had accomplished in his few short years with theMaxco-Litton.

On Friday morning, close to the time John and Elizabeth were having their second cup of coffee and their second meeting regarding the alleged criminal activity at the firm, Roger Maxco, Earnest Lasko, Michael Lowe, and Dr. Julian Weitzel were in conference. The private get-together was taking place in the casually decorated conference room at the newly assigned laboratory of Dr. Weitzel near Lake Placid in upstate New York. The facility was a secure state-of-the-art, elaborate medical research laboratory, and a scientist's dream. In the conference room, there were thick, corduroy, over-stuffed chairs and a large game table, which would have seemed more appropriate for poker than quarterly million-dollar grant reviews.

At first engaging in small talk, Roger quickly proceeded to formalize the meeting with a non-agenda announcement. "There will be no comments today regarding the death of Marshall Hall. That's history. Today, it's important that we understand where we are and where we are going. I can tell you there is no turning back. Whatever the mistakes of the past, today we move forward. Before you say anything, I want to assure you, Dr. Weitzel, that we have no interest in harming your daughter. I know there were comments made concerning Kimberly, but they were in bad taste and uncalled for. That issue is at rest." He looked at the scientist long enough to know the older man had grown ashen in color, and he decided to change the subject.

"In your own words, Doctor, how is Galen proceeding?" In light of the call from Chicago, Roger Maxco was backtracking. He needed Weitzel on his side and he knew it would be stupid to keep putting out contracts for hits. He was sure the good doctor was in too far to bail at this time. The question remained, however, *would he cooperate? It would be difficult, but he could be replaced if necessary,* Roger thought.

"Well," sighed Dr. Weitzel, "I seem to have gotten myself into a lot of trouble. Marshall is gone, hopefully my daughter is safe, and my reputation is on the line with a terrible choice to make. Do I assist further in this dreadful charade or do I walk away? It appears that walking away could be—"

"I said no reference to Marshall Hall," Roger said firmly. "I mean it." Weitzel had wanted to say the word "deadly," but demurred.

"Sorry," Dr. Weitzel continued. "The timing is bad. To meet your deadline, Roger, certain compromises would be necessary. It would involve unethical and truly bad science. Further, in my opinion, there would be a window wherein the consequences could be deadly to a lot of people."

Roger, anticipating this statement had prepared a response. "That is not our intention. The time between the announcement of the vaccine and the surge in stock prices will be only forty-eight hours. Selling the stock and avoiding SEC snooping will take longer. Earnest ran the numbers. There could be a delay in shipping and that would reduce exposure. It's all very tricky."

"*Your* window, Dr. Weitzel," and he stressed the possessive pronoun, "could be limited to *weeks* if not days." Weitzel looked at the two executives with incredulity.

"Don't look so amazed," Roger stated blithely. "In our view, those are acceptable numbers. What do you think, Earnest?"

Lasko, over the past several years, had become cynical. Divorce, kids that didn't give a damn, continuing problems from his past legal wrong doings, had all taken their toll. Uncaring, unfeeling, a man who operated regardless of human consequence, he responded, "I see all of this as being acceptable, Roger." Turning threateningly toward Julian, he said quietly, "It appears to be somewhat of a problem for you, Dr. Weitzel."

"And somewhat of a problem for me, gentlemen," Michael Lowe said. "In my opinion, more time should be taken—in potential damage control."

Roger interpreted Michael's remarks as being for the benefit of Weitzel, who responded to Roger with all the dignity he could muster.

"I made an initial mistake," Weitzel said, "and I think it cost

Marshall Hall his—"

"Goddamn it, Julian, you're heading for deep shit!" Roger was losing his patience.

"Sorry again," replied Julian, "but I am not like you people. You are talking about killing a lot of people!"

"Well, fix the goddamn vaccine," Roger said. "But do it in time! Do you understand? Otherwise, we go with this. I don't want to have this conversation again, Julian."

The meeting was over. Roger, Michael and Earnest had originally planned an all-day conference. It had not been necessary. They had left the door open and a way out for Dr. Weitzel. It was a remote possibility. Perhaps the vaccine could be 'fixed.' If not, the three Maxco executives would deal with Julian. In the meantime, they would begin to formalize their scheme to greatly enhance their retirement plans.

The meeting between the FBI agent and the CFO had turned into a strategy session. It was decided that Elizabeth would report to John by phone or facsimile messages every two days. Elizabeth would communicate by call or fax from her home to John's direct line in Phoenix. They would meet in person as required. He would have her private number in her office, which no one answered, if he needed to reach her during the day.

Late Friday, John boarded his flight back to Phoenix. Jill would be waiting curbside at Sky Harbor for the 20-minute drive to north Scottsdale. Before leaving for the airport, Jill called her new friend at his home in San Francisco. Detective Mike Staples had just gotten home when the phone rang.

"Hello, this is Mike."

"Mike, this is Jill Rushly. How are you?"

"I'm great—a lot going on this past week. Guilty or innocent, Marshall Hall is dead. I understand your husband is heading up the FBI investigation. My office doesn't have much insofar as any ongoing investigation. Could you fill me in?"

"John's flying in from New York. Marshall Hall worked for a major pharmaceutical firm headquartered there. I should know more tomorrow. Is there anything else that might shed light on Joanne's death?"

'That's a tough one, Jill. With Marshall gone, it looks like the answers to our questions may have died with him."

"Mike, I'll let you know what I can. There will be a lot of information coming out but during the FBI investigation—most will not be shared. Of course, I have an inside track, but I do have to respect John's position."

"I understand, Jill. Let's keep in touch. There may be a lot to this case. It will be interesting to see if Marshall's employer had anything to do with Joanne's death."

"I hope it was just an unfortunate accident, Mike. That's my prayer. Call me if you learn anything. I'll do the same. I have to run."

"I'll do that, Jill. You take care. Listen, there is something else." He paused.

"What is it Mike?"

"The cigarette issue may not be important."

"What do you mean?" replied Jill.

"I looked into some of Marshall Hall's past habits including the brand of cigarettes he smoked. As near as I can tell, for the past ten years at least, Marshall Hall never smoked and when he did, years ago, he had never smoked the brand found at the murder scene." Mike Staples was proving to be more than the easy-going, rumpled-looking detective Jill had first met. He was perceptive, and was far more skilled than he let on.

"But he was smoking that brand at the funeral," Jill replied. "Anyway, you're right, there is a lot more to this case. Thank you for keeping me informed. I will do the same for you. Goodnight, Mike."

Chapter Eight

Roger picked up the phone in his private office, trying not to bristle when he heard the voice on the other end.

"Elizabeth, what can I do for you?" he asked smoothly, trying to sound warm. "I hope you received all the information you needed. There's no excuse for my not keeping you informed. Guess I was on overload." *She's the last person I need to raise a red flag with,* he thought.

"Yes, thank you Roger. Do you know where Julian happens to be? I tried his lab but one of his researchers said he didn't come in this morning. Is he in town?"

"I talked to Julian yesterday." *What's she on to, now?* he thought angrily. "He did mention he had a few personal details to take care of with his daughter. I'll make a few calls and see if he can be reached. He should be calling into his lab this afternoon."

"Let me know, Roger. I do want to talk to him. If you do locate him, would you ask him to call, please?"

"Of course, Elizabeth. I'll let you know as soon as I hear from him. Anything I can help you with?" *What was the bitch after?* he wondered.

Roger hung up, frustrated and angry, trying to figure out what his CFO would want with his head scientist. *If it has to do with the information I gave her,* he thought, *I need to know what's going on. I can't have her causing more trouble.*

While others were inquiring as to his whereabouts, the scientist in question was busy packing. No one had considered this obvious option still available to him. *I can simply disappear,* he thought fearfully.

Julian had decided he could not play a part in risking the lives of thousands of people, after all. These were the same thousands he had spent a lifetime trying to save, trying to cure. He was not a criminal and this was criminal activity. Not quite ready to alert the authorities, he needed time to sort out his thoughts, in particular, how to respond to Roger. First, he would contact his daughter and let her know what he was doing. He needed to make sure that she was safe.

Just as his thoughts turned to Kimberly, his phone rang. Unaware that she had sought temporary shelter in Phoenix, Julian looked at the Caller ID, panic-stricken. It was a 602 area code. Fortunately, his daughter was trying to reach him. Julian heard the ring, glanced at his caller ID, and wondered who could be calling him from area code 602.

"Yes?" he answered tentatively. If it were Roger, he didn't want his boss to know anything was wrong. He would just plead a flu bug and buy himself some time, he thought.

"Dad, it's me." She sounded relieved to hear his voice.

"I was just going to call you, honey. Where are you? Where is 602?"

"I'm in Phoenix—it's a long story. Dad, I have to see you. We need to talk. Can you come here?"

"Kimberly, I'd love to see you, too. A lot has happened. I need some thinking time, alone. I plan to be gone for at least two weeks. After that, I promise you will be at the top of my list."

"Listen Dad, I know a little about what is going on. The authorities have contacted me. They want to talk to you. I have a friend—he is with the FBI in Phoenix. Please come here. It's really important." She sounded more urgent, now.

"I am glad you're safe, dear. Tell your friend that I'm not going along with anything criminal. I just need time. I'll call you in a week. I love you. I have to go."

The call was a relief to Kimberly. At least she knew her father was alive and was not taking part in the nefarious scheme John Rushly had outlined to her. She would call John and let him know. *Where on earth is he going*, she wondered.

Julian was heading south and then west. He had never seen the Florida Keys and this was his opportunity. To avoid detection, he would drive the fifteen hundred miles in his new Ford Taurus, thereby eliminating airports, credit cards and rental cars. He had read about the Keys—informal, tranquil, shorts and tee shirts the standard dress, the perfect place to melt away, unnoticed, into the casual Bohemian environment of Margaritaville.

After three days, Roger began to worry. *Has he gone to the authorities?* He wondered. The company's private security people were having no luck in finding Julian. Roger stewed over the implications. *He's obviously hiding out, and will end up going to the authorities,* he thought, steaming. *The work is far enough along where he can be replaced. But what about the FDA?*

Swiveling around in his executive chair to face the glorious New York skyline, he made the decision. *It's messy, but it can be done. He has to be found. I'd better make the call.*

It was the private and secured line to the home of Charles Nitti. The time was 6:00 p.m.

"Hello." The voice was low and deliberate. On this line, names were permissible.

"Mr. Nitti, this is Roger Maxco. Good evening."

"What can I do for you?" the man never minced words.

"I am unable to locate Dr. Weitzel. We believe he is in hiding."

"How important is this development?"

"I have reason to believe it may be critical."

"I'll take care of it." The phone went dead. The contract had been sealed. It had taken a split second to mark a brilliant scientist for death. It was Nitti's turn to make a call. This man was one of Nitti's own professionals. His team seldom failed. The timing was right. The man known as Sweeper was home. That's who he was and that's what he did. No one needed to know any more.

"Yes?"

"Sweeper, you have a job. You'll have the information you need by noon tomorrow, usual place."

"Thank you." The dial tone prevented further discussion. There was never a need to discuss details. Sweeper had been retained many times in the past. His reputation was flawless. Once a job was set in motion, the end result was a foregone conclusion. Satisfied that the matter was taken care of, Charles Nitti began to think hard about Roger and the inherent risks involved by continuing his association with that firm. Once the Weitzel matter was closed, and everyone concerned had reaped all their mutual rewards from this project, there would be an important meeting with the Chicago group to discuss Maxco-Litton. Things were falling apart. The firm was becoming an albatross to the crime boss. He liked things neat and tidy.

Homestead, Florida—June 6, 1998

Although it had been several years since the devastation of Hurricane Andrew, Julian couldn't believe the remnants still left by the storm. Julian had just left the Florida Turnpike at Homestead for the two-lane road that meandered from Key Largo to the southernmost point in the United States—Key West. Julian had made no reservations, relying on the lack of tourism during the summer months. He paid no attention to the unusually high humidity. The sun was shining, there was little traffic, and balmy breezes seemed to make the world seem much simpler. Passing through Tavernier, Islamorada, and Marathon before crossing over the Seven-Mile Bridge on his way to Key West was exhilarating. It was only another fifty miles of delightful driving before he reached his destination. With the sun and warm air playing over his face, music playing and the sunroof open, he couldn't help daydreaming. His thoughts turned to his daughter. *I knew she would understand,* he thought, comforted by their phone conversation. *Now, at least she knows I am not a criminal. She is safe in Phoenix. I'll call her when I get settled.* Driving on down the chain of islands, he thought dreamily, *I should have taken her here as a child. It might have helped her deal with her mother's death. It's kind of like going back to the '50s.*

Dr. Julian Weitzel had spent most of his adult life stuck, by choice, in the sterile environment of a research lab. He had never been the adventurous type. This was a new experience for him and he wished Kimberly were along to share in this pristine beauty. Most of the drive was along the water's edge—the Atlantic Ocean on one side, the Gulf of Mexico on the other. He slowed to forty-five miles per hour as he drove through Deer Key. The speed limit was enforced religiously to keep motorists from killing the small deer that inhabited the island.

I haven't committed any crime, he thought. *Maybe it would be wise to contact Kimberly and have her inform her FBI friend as to my whereabouts.*

The drive from New York had worked magic. The last hundred and fifty miles from Miami had opened his eyes and cleared his mind. *Why should I do anything to further their evil plans? This is only a question of ethics. To hell with those people. To hell with*

Roger Maxco! He began to hum to the stereo. He was feeling better with every click of the odometer.

Driving into the center of Key West, Julian was brought back to reality. A cruise ship had disgorged three thousand guests, crowding the little town. They filled the streets and the small shops, but would retreat by evening. Julian knew he could easily find a Bed & Breakfast. He had noticed several in his travel guide. Irritated for a moment that he had left it in his house, he quickly picked up another while filling up his gas tank.

Driving down the street toward his destination, he noticed the Key West Sheraton, luxury hotel not too far from the water and still near the center of town. He wanted a few more people around so he wouldn't be conspicuous. He was given a room with an ocean view on the third floor. Facing the Atlantic side of the island, the room was nicely appointed with a queen-size bed. Best of all, the balcony was large enough to accommodate a morning breakfast. It was perfect. He was proud that he had the strength and courage to do what he had to do. He only wished he had done it earlier. Maxco-Litton now seemed far away.

That evening, Julian planned to stroll into the center of Key West and have a beer at Earnest Hemingway's old hangout—Sloppy Joe's Bar on Duval Street. The shorts and tee shirt were welcome a relief from the stodgy suit and tie he was used to wearing to attend senior staff meetings, which he hated. Any time Julian Weitzel had to spend away from his laboratory he considered wasted time.

This was a new side to the man, an existence foreign to him, and he found himself relaxing for the first time in his career. Since his wife's death years ago, his full commitment to his only love, pure science, had been a high price to pay. Revered by the scientific community, he had nearly lost the love of his daughter.

For Sweeper, the hired assassin, the scientist proved to be an elusive prey and a delicious challenge. There was no paper trail. Julian had evidently paid for his gas, food and lodging with cash. The search of his home, at first, had proved futile. In the trash, however, several travel brochures were found. Flyers from resorts in South Carolina and Florida had been casually discarded. This fact did not discourage Sweeper. He was sure there was something he was missing. A unique-looking card caught his eye, seeming out of place alone on the counter. It was a library card. *If you are going to disappear*, Sweeper thought, while helping himself to orange juice from Julian's refrigerator, *why not check out places at the local library?* He smiled at himself, feeling as if a tumbler to a safe had fallen into place. He loved the game of cat and mouse.

Sweeper was known for his uncanny attention to detail, patience, and persistence. An East Coast wise guy in the '60s, he had defined himself through years of experience as being the man who could be relied upon to carry out critical assignments. He left no evidence and never discussed the "assignment" again. He was absolutely discreet. His employers felt confident that their orders would be carried out without any trace back to them. There were never repercussions. Payment was made by a third party by crediting an account in an off shore bank. This eliminated any possibility of a connection.

Sweeper was an ordinary looking man in his mid-thirties. Trim with piercing blue eyes, he wore trendy but fairly conservative clothing. His sandy colored hair was always in style and he looked as if he had come from an upper middle-class home in the east, just a nice looking, ordinary man. A few select clients knew him by his one name, never by sight. There were no photos or artist sketches. He had been careful when leaving the mob life in New York City. Except for taking a couple of employer names with him, he had literally disappeared from the scene.

A check with the local branch of the New York Public Library revealed that Julian Weitzel had indeed been checking out resort destinations. A book entitled *The Florida Keys* had been returned two days before Sweeper had received his assignment. Only the librarian, while restocking the book, had touched it since its return.

Sweeper carefully rested the book on the table, looking for telltale signs of extraordinary wear. When lifting the book and thumbing through the pages, it appeared the section to the Florida Keys had been laid flat—opened and pressed flat so it would stay in place. One page, in particular, had a pencil mark on it by a paragraph describing in detail the small city at the end of that chain of islands—Key West.

It had been five days since Kimberly had talked with her father. She had called the FBI the next day. John knew the disappearance of Maxco-Litton's star performer was causing a lot of concern by those in charge. Reasoning that the release of the new drug could not happen without the support of Dr. Julian Weitzel, nevertheless, John felt strongly that Roger knew he couldn't count on Julian to complete the sinister plot. *What else did he have up his sleeve?* John asked himself. *Worse*, he thought, *Roger might be tempted to take Julian out of the picture, permanently.* The agent had already let one witness die by not taking this scheme seriously enough. He didn't intend to let it happen again.

John decided to quiz Elizabeth to see if the CFO knew anything about the scientist's disappearance. Had she talked to Roger Maxco? He dialed her direct line. It was four o'clock in New York. He was surprised to feel a flush of excitement when he heard her voice.

"Elizabeth Martin."

"I'm glad I found you in, Elizabeth. This John Rushly in Phoenix."

"Hello, John," she sounded pleased to hear from him. "I was thinking of calling you. I had a brief conversation with Roger this morning."

"Did you talk about Julian?"

"Yes, he's missing; did you know? There's absolutely no word from him. I hope nothing has happened. Roger has no idea where he is. I don't believe he is telling the truth." She held the phone away from her face briefly. The sound of his voice made her catch her breath.

"Elizabeth, I am worried. I need to ask you this question: Assuming the bugs are out of the proposed project and it has real merit, can it possibly be completed and submitted for FDA approval without Julian?"

"It could be, John. More time would be needed, however. Without Marshall Hall or Julian, it would take some really talented people to bring it up to speed. We can recruit that talent, most of it from Germany, but it would not be easy. To answer your question, John, it could happen—given time."

John was perplexed. "It appears to me that Roger's original plan as outlined by Marshall Hall can't be completed. Anyone new, starting at ground zero, running new tests and analyzing Julian's data would discover the flaws and stop the project. If that is true, what is Roger Maxco contemplating?"

Elizabeth replied, "John, you are absolutely correct. I never thought that far ahead. Now, I am more worried than ever about Julian. Can your people help?"

"Yes, yesterday I instructed our investigators to begin tracking Julian. Preliminarily, they are telling me he must have used cash and his own car to leave New York. At least we have the license number and description of his car. We should be able to locate him soon."

"That makes me feel better. I have nothing else John. I'll keep in touch. Let me know if you find him."

"Thanks, Elizabeth, I'll call you as soon as I have something."

Immediately, John alerted his team to contact the highway patrol in several states. John had little else to go on. He decided to make one more call. Without tipping his hand, he would let Roger know the FBI was vitally interested in the whereabouts and personal safety of the scientist. He hoped that might defray any unscrupulous plans Roger might have against Julian's life.

"Mr. Maxco's office. May I help you?" his secretary was always briskly efficient.

"This is John Rushly. Is Mr. Maxco in? My call is very important."

"Is Mr. Maxco expecting your call Mr. Rushly?"

"I can appreciate your trying to screen calls, Ms.—" he spoke curtly, then waited for her response.

"Carol, Mr. Rushly, you can call me Carol. I am Mr. Maxco's executive secretary. Sorry, I didn't mean to—"

"Carol," he cut her off. He wanted her to know he meant business. "I am with the FBI. I believe Mr. Maxco will take my call. I need you to put him on the line."

"Yes sir, one moment." There was a pause while Roger contemplated the nature of the call from John Rushly. Trying to appear confident, he picked up the phone.

"Hello, Agent Rushly, this is Roger Maxco. This call is quite unexpected. How may I help you?"

"Mr. Maxco, the Bureau is investigating the murder of Marshall Hall. I know the California authorities have questioned you but I wanted to check with you on something. It will only take a few minutes."

"Of course Mr. Rushly. I want to cooperate fully."

"Please think very carefully before you answer this question." John wanted the CEO to feel intimidated. "Do you have any knowledge as to the whereabouts of Dr. Julian Weitzel?"

"No," Roger couldn't help the slight tremor in his voice. Recovering quickly, he cleared his throat before responding. "We are all puzzled about his disappearance. He gave no warning about leaving. I suspect he has been under enormous pressure, personal problems I believe. We haven't heard a word."

"Mr. Maxco, the FBI is vitally interested in locating Dr. Weitzel. We are concerned about his safety. Hopefully, I can rely on you to let me know if you hear anything. I expect your full cooperation in this matter."

The call concluded with the usual platitudes from the executive. Roger was left, worried about what, if anything, the FBI knew about the Hall murder or the contract on Julian. John Rushly was satisfied that he had alerted Roger to his concerns. *Let's hope that call keeps Julian Weitzel safe*, he thought, *at least for now.*

Roger and Earnest were deep in conversation. Earnest was becoming somewhat skittish over the Weitzel situation.

"What is the plan for Julian? Do we know where he is, Roger?"

"He's gone Earnest." Roger preferred to keep his contracts to himself. "I don't believe we will see him again. We planned for this contingency. Don't worry."

"What about the call from John Rushly? He was telling you to keep your hands off Weitzel. What the hell does he know?" Earnest reached for a Cuban cigar on Roger's desk. His hands were shaking.

"Again Earnest, don't worry. Rushly can't know anything. We just have to adjust again. The project goes on. We may need to check our options."

The contingency plan was complicated but workable. A protégé of Julian had been studying the Galen project for months. He had taken meticulous notes and was privy to all of the research data that Hall and Weitzel had collected. More importantly, a second project was underway which was on a track parallel to that of the Galen project. It had been kept from Hall and Weitzel. In fact, Roger Maxco, Michael Lowe and Earnest Lasko were the only executives that had knowledge of this particular undertaking.

Tom Elliot, M.D., had been hired by Roger Maxco for one purpose—to provide a backup or contingency option to the Galen project. He had worked side by side with Marshall Hall and Julian Weitzel. They knew he had other duties including that of a troubleshooter for stalled or troubled projects. Incredibly bright, with impressive but tainted credentials, it was understood that Tom was close to the inner sanctum of Maxco-Litton. His authority was not to be questioned but he maintained a deferential presence when in the company of the two senior scientists.

Tom Elliot was fifty, and had never married. While enjoying an illustrious practice in cardiology at New York City Hospital, Tom Elliot had been sued for malpractice. The New York Board of Medical Examiners had found itself in the unenviable position of being unable to support one of its most respected and brilliant surgeons. A careless mistake during a heart bypass operation was so egregious that Elliot's position couldn't be logically supported.

One of the attending physicians described the operation. "In this procedure, a section of vein from the leg is sewn into the blocked coronary artery to form a bridge around the atherosclerotic region. In most recipients, the operation relieves the pain of angina. In many patients, it prevents a fatal heart attack. In this patient, it became apparent that a spontaneous contraction of an apparently healthy coronary artery, what is commonly know as a vasospasm, was the culprit. Elliot never anticipated the problem. In addition, he never checked with consultants who had conducted preliminary angiogram dye tests. Further, he failed to anticipate defects in the sinoatrial node or in the fibers that transmit impulses to the heart muscle. The patient died within ten minutes of Elliot's completing the bypass operation. Elliot was stunned. The fact that Elliot refused a simple drug test, post-op, sealed his fate. His ego just overtook his reason. In my medical opinion, he was on amphetamines. It was tragic."

Tom Elliot was unemployable except to Roger Maxco. Recruited into a new career as a researcher, Elliot was given new wealth and status with Maxco—Litton. The former cardiologist quickly became a loyal minion in the grand scheme of Roger Maxco. No one else in the company was sure what his role was. There were no questions. He always had an open and direct line to Roger's office. And the funding for the second project, the secret project, was hidden from the other Directors, including Elizabeth Martin.

Earlier, Elizabeth had tried to conduct a preliminary, independent audit of Maxco-Litton's books, including funding sources for research and inventory of pharmaceuticals. The board turned her request down, seeing no need for it. Finally, she made a request of the board to order a comprehensive internal audit of all departments and their respective, ongoing projects. Her request was again tabled, since most of the Directors believed it to be an unnecessary expense. Estimates ranged from ninety-five thousand to a hundred and thirty-five thousand dollars for such an extensive audit. Roger Maxco was relieved. He didn't care about the money. He had other things to hide.

Chapter Nine

Sweeper paid cash at the American ticket counter and caught a direct flight from New York to Miami, then a shuttle flight to the new airport in the unincorporated community of Marathon. Arriving at the terminal in Marathon, Sweeper was struck by the lack of tourists and particularly the lack of flights scheduled to utilize this elaborate facility. *It was obviously a government boondoggle,* he thought cynically, *since the terminal, with its closed shops, appeared more like a mausoleum than an airport.* The County evidently had money to spend and, with matching federal funds, it was obligated to complete someone else's dream.

Rental cars were plentiful and the drive to Key West would only take an hour. Sweeper rented a car with a sunroof and headed south.

He stopped at a Texaco station after crossing the Seven-Mile Bridge, picked up a Buddy Holly tape and a Coke. He was back on the road within minutes. With the sunroof open, the tape blaring "Suzie Q," he found himself wondering why he had gravitated toward this particular line of work. *I actually take life from people,* he thought, at once disgusted and proud of himself. *Hell,* he thought, *it's survival of the fittest.* Attempting to justify his profession to himself, he wondered why he seemed to have no conscience. *Although,* he reasoned, *he had never tortured anyone.* He hated people who hurt animals. When he was nineteen he had shot a man to death for kicking a small dog.

Well, maybe I do have a conscience, he thought. *Enough of this, Sweeper,* he interrupted his own thoughts—*It's time to concentrate on Dr. Julian Weitzel.*

This enigmatic character had gleaned little from his parents. Immigrants, hard working, and staunch Catholics, they sadly lived to see that their son never fit into the world they had tried to create for him. "He was a rebel *with* a cause," their priest had once said, —"his!" Billy, as he was known then, had always loved being independent and had absolutely no use for authority figures.

"The Pope," he once told his Catechism class on the first and last day he was allowed to attend, "was a huge crutch for those too weak to stand alone."

No one knew he was a homosexual. Having started out as experimental, he had grown to enjoy the alternative game of love. His affairs with young men were rare and discreet. At twenty-one, he dropped his last name and after his third kill for the mob, was simply known as Sweeper. From that day on, that was the only name he used with those who hired him. When queried about his profession, he liked to laugh and say, "I'm an independent contractor."

Key West was not an unfamiliar sight. A wealthy gay friend still owned one of the finest bed & breakfast facilities in the city. It was a converted mansion built in the 1940s. It was three blocks from Hemingway's home, which was now a major tourist attraction.

Sweeper arrived at four o'clock. He paid for a comfortable room, in cash, and decided to relax for two hours before dining. There would be no encounters, gay or otherwise. This trip was all business. He could sense he was not far from discovering the whereabouts of his prey. He had been in the business a long time. His instincts were perfect.

Tomorrow will be a good time to start my search, he thought. His one concern was that the Keys didn't provide a good escape route, in case of trouble. Authorities, with little effort, could easily block the two lanes of the Overseas Highway. Further, the Key West Airport was small and would be easy to monitor. In addition, a Coast Guard Station and Naval Air Station were close by. As he lay on his bed in the B & B, watching the ocean breezes moving the white curtains, he worried about the logistics, then fell asleep just like it was any other day.

Julian Weitzel had relaxed for three days and was already feeling restless. Having no friends in the area, he had exhausted the tourist attractions in two days. It was time to call Kimberly and give John Rushly the opportunity to make contact. It was 6:00 p.m. in Phoenix, three hours earlier than on the East Coast. Julian used his AT&T calling card.

"Embassy Suites. May I help you?"
"I'm trying to reach Kimberly Weitzel," Julian said.
"I'll ring that Suite for you, Sir—one moment." Kimberly answered the phone.
"Kimberly! Hi honey, I can't believe I caught you in. How are you?"
"Hi Dad. I'm glad you called. Where are you?"
"I'm in Key West, dear. It's wonderful here—balmy and lots of sun."
"Dad, John Rushly is worried. He thinks you are in danger. You must talk to him and tell him where you are. Will you do that?"
"That's why I called, Kimberly. I made a terrible mistake with Roger Maxco. But it's not irreversible. I want to talk to the authorities as soon as possible."
"That's what I was praying you would say." She seemed relieved.
"Kimberly, I need to know how I can reach Agent Rushly. Do you have a number?"
"A direct line, Dad. We've become friends. You'll like him—and his wife. She's a detective in Arizona." Julian jotted down the number and wished his daughter well. He assured her he would return home when it was safe, and that he would call the FBI the first thing in the morning.

Sweeper was taking no chances. At eight o'clock in the morning, after a lobster dinner and a night's sleep, he drove to the docks, a mile from the center of town. There was an impressive array of charter-fishing and pleasure boats, side by side in assigned boat slips. In the winter months, they would have been out to sea. A few were ready to welcome guests for chartered trips to the Dry Tortugas, a group of islands about seventy miles to the west. Some would cruise the Atlantic side heading north. At least twenty boats were available for special charters.

A 630 Sea Ray Super Sun Sport express cruiser caught the eye of the quiet, nice-looking man standing on the dock. The sixty-two foot hull could reach speeds of 34 knots. It had the accommodations of a small motor yacht. Sweeper doubted it was a charter boat. It was more than likely a wealthy Miami businessman's personal pleasure craft. The captain and one crewmember were stepping off the deck onto the dock.

"She's a beauty," Sweeper remarked casually. "Is she available for charter?"

"Of course," the captain replied, laughing a little, then adding, "for a very steep price."

"Name it," Sweeper responded.

"Are you serious?" replied the Captain.

"I need you to stand by *at the ready* for the next few days. At any moment, we could head directly for the Bahamas. I'll make it easy. Four days guaranteed at a thousand dollars a day. If we head out to sea, you can add another thousand for that day. Think about it. You might earn four thousand dollars just for sitting at the dock doing nothing. I insist, however, that this boat is exclusively mine during the next four days. Do we have a deal?"

"No drugs? No contraband whatsoever?" It sounded too good to be true.

"None," Sweeper replied, looking the Captain straight in the eyes, "only me and a small suitcase, which you may search once we're out to sea. If we have a deal, I'll give you two thousand dollars in advance, right this minute."

The captain shook his head, laughed amiably and stuck out his hand. "You own me and this boat for the next four days, pal. The owner won't mind at all. He is scheduled to be here in ten days. I've been instructed to take it on a shakedown cruise anyway, before he arrives. This is perfect."

The money changed hands quickly and Sweeper was confident that this transaction was good insurance. *As the captain said*, he thought, *this is perfect.*

In his suite at the Sheraton, Julian Weitzel dialed the number to the FBI Field Office.

"John Rushly."

"Agent Rushly, this is Julian Weitzel. Good morning."

For Julian, it was indeed a good morning. Although it was already eleven o'clock in Florida, room service had just brought breakfast and the table was set on the balcony overlooking the

Atlantic. In the distance, under full sail, several sloops were heading out to sea. He was finally learning to relax.

"Dr. Weitzel, I had hoped you would call today. Where are you?"

"I'm relaxing in Key West. Please call me Julian. This business with Hall and Maxco has been too much. I was so afraid for Kimberly, I guess I bent under the pressure, but it is time for a decision. I think she's safe."

"We need to talk, Julian, face to face. There is a lot going on. I need more information from you. Are you willing to work with me?"

"Yes, Agent Rushly, and I intend to cooperate fully. I drove to the Keys a few days ago. I can be back home in a few days."

"Julian, I believe you could be in danger. Why don't you leave your car at the airport? Fly to Miami and catch the next flight to Phoenix. Call me as soon as you have reservations. I'll have your car transported to your home. Are you willing to do this?"

"You are scaring me, Rushly. Is this really necessary?"

"I believe Maxco had Marshall Hall killed. You could be next. Don't take any chances. Stay around crowds if you can and watch your back. I'm going to have the Key West authorities escort you to the airport. One of our agents out of the Miami office will meet your plane. I'll be at this end and will meet you at Sky Harbor International."

"Okay," the man sighed, now more alarmed than he had been in days. "I'm a believer. I'll call the airlines and wait for the Key West police. Hopefully, I can leave this afternoon and be in Phoenix this evening. I'll let you know."

John was relieved. The two men said goodbye and John called the Key West Police Department. *At last,* he thought, *Julian Weitzel will be safe. He has a lot of damaging information about Roger Maxco and the company, and I want to know what it is!*

Sweeper had been checking all the major hotels. He was sure Julian was close. He spotted the Ford Taurus with New York plates at 10:30 a.m. It wasn't difficult determining which room the man occupied. Dialing any room then obtaining a correction from the operator usually worked.

At first, Sweeper tried to gain access to the room. On second thought, he figured if he were to complete his assignment in the parking garage, then leave the body in the trunk of the car, he would have more time to escape. A body in the room would be discovered too quickly and the law would have more time to create a massive search for the killer. He would be patient. The target would drive somewhere today, he figured. If not, plans could be easily changed.

Julian had confirmed a flight to Miami from the Key West Airport at 2:30. The local police had called and arranged to have a car meet Julian outside the main lobby of the Sheraton at 1:30. His connecting flight would leave Miami at 5:00 p.m. He would arrive in Phoenix around the same time due to the three-hour time change. Fortunately for his assassin, however, Julian decided to leave the hotel and drive to a local Walgreen to pick up a few items for the trip. It was 11:45 a.m.

The weapon of choice for Sweeper was a .22 Caliber Colt Woodsman, semi-automatic pistol. This particular gun was vintage 1950. If it were left behind for some reason, it couldn't be traced. With the custom silencer, a firing sounded like a loud spit.

Julian walked toward his car and looked around as the agent had suggested. He noticed the average looking man heading for another car and didn't believe anything was out of the ordinary. Abruptly, the man turned and walked briskly toward the scientist. Julian turned, starred into the man's face and couldn't believe he was looking into the barrel of a gun. With two split-second spits from the Colt, Dr. Julian Weitzel crumpled lifeless to the garage floor. It all seemed so simple to the assassin—almost like an after thought. Sweeper lifted the body, placed it quickly into the trunk and closed the lid. It was a ritual he'd repeated many times.

As he walked away, Sweeper muttered to himself, casually, "Sorry, Doc, nothing personal. You were in somebody's way." Whistling softly, he walked across the parking lot, turning away from the lovely Sheraton that had just lost one of its patrons.

A professional driving service would return the rental car to Marathon. There would be no suspicion there. All tracks would be covered. There were no flights out of Marathon that day and the four-hour drive to the Miami Airport could be risky. It was time to exercise his option and head for the Bahamas. Hailing a cab, Sweeper headed for the docks. It was a little after noon.

The captain was lunching on board. The Sea Ray 630 was

scrubbed down, fueled and ready to launch.

"Permission to come aboard Captain," he shouted, smiling.

"Yes, Sir!" They shook hands. "What's the plan?"

"We are leaving immediately. As promised, here is my suitcase—no drugs, no contraband."

"I see, no problem, Sir," the captain responded. Toss it down below and hang on. We are heading for Georgetown."

The roar of the 1080-hp 12V92's was reassuring. Effortlessly, the huge craft made its way out of the dock area into open sea. Temporarily on the Gulf side of the island, the Sea Ray would soon be on a course out into the Atlantic, crossing the Bermuda Triangle. It would be a three-hour trip. Sweeper was home free. There were direct flights from Georgetown to New York.

Mission accomplished, he thought smugly.

The agent had been waiting with some impatience for the call from Key West. He had instructed the local police to notify him as soon as Dr. Weitzel was safely in their care. It was five o'clock Phoenix time. The phone rang. "Yes?" John hadn't meant to sound so brusque.

"Sir, this is Sergeant Reynolds of the Key West Police Department. We are at the Sheraton trying to locate your man. He is not in his room and his car is parked in the garage. Has there been a change in plans?" Rushly felt the tension in his stomach. He had been very specific and Julian as well had sounded like a man ready to cooperate fully.

"Sergeant, did you take a good, hard look at his car? Was there anything suspicious?"

"We noticed the car, Sir. It was locked. Nothing out of the ordinary." There was a pause before the agent responded.

"Sergeant, have the car opened and search for any clues—including the trunk. I am not being paranoid, trust me. But I need you to check it out, okay?" John hoped his suspicions were unfounded.

"Yes sir, I'll be back to you shortly."

The local police had not taken the matter seriously. They were merely called upon to provide an escort for a witness. The sergeant was surprised when Rushly suggested they search the trunk.

Twenty minutes later, the phone rang again.

"John Rushly."

"You may not be paranoid, Rushly, but you sure called it this time. Your man is in the trunk, shot in the forehead—twice, with a small caliber weapon. We don't see much of this, but I can tell you it's a professional hit. I'm sorry sir."

The news couldn't have been worse. John had just spoken to Kimberly assuring her that Julian was on his was to Phoenix. He gathered his thoughts. He lost any attempt at trying to maintain his professionalism. "Goddamnit!" he shouted, pounding his fist against the wall. "Any witnesses?"

"No sir. No one saw anything. We don't have anything to go on. We could seal off the Overseas Highway and the Key West Airport, but we don't know what to look for."

"Sergeant, I know this happened in your jurisdiction. The victim was part of an ongoing federal investigation. Please alert your people that the FBI office in Miami will have agents in Key West by nightfall. We look forward to cooperating with the Key West police in this matter. Thank you for your help, Sergeant. I'll be in touch."

John dreaded what he had to do. He knew it was his job to call Kimberly. *How could she possibly deal with this*, he worried, *first Marshall, then her dad. And worse*, John thought, his fists clenched into two tight balls, *I have failed twice to protect a critical witness!* He began to reflect on the last conversation he had with the man that he now hated with a tremendous passion, Roger Maxco. "I suspect he has been under enormous pressure—personal problems, I believe. We haven't heard a word."

That bastard, John thought, *I know this was your doing!*

Chapter Ten

Charles Nitti sat alone pondering his relationship with Roger Maxco and the pharmaceutical giant Maxco-Litton. It had all started four years before when a former mob associate in Chicago referred Roger to Nitti. Roger was in trouble and needed cash—a lot of cash.

There had always been rumblings about the hard driving CEO ever since Litton took him in as a partner. His corporate performance had hushed the nay-sayers. Elizabeth Martin and Arthur Litton had encouraged the other board members to bring Roger on board. Elizabeth had studied the man's brilliant record with a competitor and realized he was highly aggressive and knowledgeable, just what the firm needed. Arthur Litton had agreed and it was a done deal.

Roger immediately renamed the company with Litton's blessing, cut costs and introduced an array of new and successful products. In his first two years at the helm, stock in Maxco-Litton had risen twenty-eight percent. His former employer remarked at a news conference, "Roger Maxco has the most brilliant business mind I have ever known, but you don't have to like him personally. He is arrogant and has a propensity to cut close to the edge. But I salute the bastard."

His assessment of Roger was closer to the truth than most people realized. There was a case of insider trading and a steep fine imposed by the SEC that was never brought out. In order to maintain his position within the business community, Roger personally paid the fine—nearly a million dollars. There were other repercussions. Many investors had to be reimbursed which took additional millions. Roger had resorted to borrowing from questionable sources. The price was high. Roger Maxco was now in debt to the Mob, thus the Nitti relationship.

Charles Nitti didn't worry about being repaid. All of Roger's assets, and in particular, stocks and options for future offerings, could not be sold or transferred without Nitti's permission. It was this situation that triggered the creation of the Galen project and prompted Roger to hire Dr. Tom Elliot. The murders of two prominent scientists, however, had not been included in the initial equation to which Nitti had subscribed. From Nitti's perspective, things were getting messy.

Confirmation of the Weitzel's 'check-out' came by phone. The call originated from the Bahamas, in Georgetown. The call took only a few seconds.

"Sir, the incident is settled. My work is complete."

"I understand," Nitti replied.

There were now serious questions by the Chicago group about the "August Funding" that Charles Nitti had referred to earlier. In fact, Roger Maxco was about to receive a most distressing phone call. Nitti had decided to call in all loans outstanding and to disassociate his group from Maxco-Litton. Nitti would give Roger ninety days to pay up and sever all ties.

Elizabeth Martin called an emergency Directors meeting. The meeting was scheduled for 8:00 a.m. on Thursday. The news that Dr. Julian Weitzel had been murdered in Key West had stung her sensibilities. She was in shock to think that two professional assassinations involving two top scientists in the industry, possibly in the world, could have been arranged by someone at Maxco-Litton. On Wednesday afternoon, Elizabeth had called John to let him know what she was doing. John was in his office. John answered his direct line.

"John, this is Elizabeth. I'm calling about Julian. Do you have any more details on what happened?"

"Elizabeth, our team in Key West is trying to sort it out. It was a professional hit. We have our suspicions but no hard evidence. We don't know who did the shooting or who gave the order."

"John, one reason I called is to let you know I have called a special meeting of the board for tomorrow. They stonewalled an audit I had proposed earlier. With this going on, I can't allow Roger or anyone else to jeopardize the financial stability of this company."

"What do you suspect, Elizabeth?"

"John, we both know murders are not committed in a vacuum. The Galen project was designed to create huge sums of cash. I need to know if there have been any illegal loans, stock manipulations, or anything else of a financial nature that could adversely affect our stockholders. It's my responsibility to protect them."

"Elizabeth," he responded excitedly, "you are absolutely right. The FBI has no authority to demand an audit of Maxco-Litton, but you do! I suspect you will have a fight on your hands. This may be a crucial issue for Maxco."

"I have considerable power and prestige with the other Directors and I intend to force the issue. Wish me luck."

"I do, Elizabeth."

"One more thing, John," Elizabeth asked. "Have you spoken to Kimberly? I met her once. She was charming. Is she okay?"

John sighed, rubbing his forehead with his fingers. "It was the toughest phone call I ever made. We think all the bases are covered and then you get slammed. Jill invited her over this evening. She really needs a good friend. Thank you for asking."

"I'll call you after the meeting, John. Thanks for listening to me. I could use a good friend, too. You know what they say, it's lonely at the top. With all this going on, it's quite scary around here." She tried to laugh but was unsuccessful.

"You have a good friend here, Elizabeth. I know how difficult this is for you. Please look upon me as someone you can trust and confide in. Call if you need to."

"Thanks, John. I'll do that. Talk to you tomorrow."

The agent loved his work—most of the time. *Damn*, he thought, *it's such a fight between decency and evil. It's hard to talk about people like Kimberly and Elizabeth and Roger Maxco in the same breath. Greed, hate, —well, the fight goes on. Stay with it, John,* he urged himself.

The phone interrupted John's train of thought. It was one of the Miami FBI investigators. John answered.

"Rushly, this is June Barker. I'm part of the investigative team in Key West. We do have new information for you. Do you have a few moments?"

"Yes, of course, June. What's going on?"

"We figured that a professional assassin would not use the Overseas Highway since it is two-lane and traffic tends to get congested easily. Further, there are forty-two bridges that are perfect for roadblocks. The highway can be closed easily and every car checked. Plus, the flights out of Key West are erratic at best. We think your man might have left by boat, so we did some checking around the docks."

"Hold on," John interrupted, "I want to close the door." Returning to his desk, he grabbed his legal pad. "This sounds interesting. Go on."

"I have some experience with boating in the area, so I began to hang out and talk to people at the docks. It seems there was talk of an unusual charter. Some man paid a particular captain a thousand dollars a day just to sit tight. The boat, a sleek 62-foot Sea Ray was described as being a real hot rod. Shortly after the murder, the boat was no where to be found. We contacted the owner. He was scheduled to use the boat later this month. He confirmed that his captain did charter the boat for standby and possibly for a short trip to the Bahamas."

John was getting excited. "You've done some really good police work, Barker. If you can locate that boat and the captain, we may have a positive identification of the killer."

"We're working on that." the agent replied, obviously pleased with the kudos. "The Nassau authorities have already been contacted. They are checking all flights out of Georgetown Airport. We anticipate the Sea Ray will be back in its boat slip in Key West, tomorrow.

"I'm a little worried about the captain," replied John.

"We thought of that. The only thing we could do was alert the Coast Guard and the authorities in Nassau. Maybe the guy thinks he got away clean. Do you know his profile yet? Maybe he won't kill unnecessarily. "

"For the sake of the captain," replied John, "I hope you are right."

Approximately four hours after the murder of Dr. Julian Weitzel, the Sea Ray by the name of "Big Deal" docked in the Bahamas. Sweeper had directed the captain to change course and head for the chief port of the Commonwealth of the Bahamas. Nassau was located on the northeastern coast of New Providence Island. With a population of two hundred thousand, it would be safer than Georgetown, he thought. The captain was trying to strike up a conversation with his quiet passenger.

"Sir, are you staying long in the Bahamas?"

"I'm not sure," Sweeper replied.

"If you were thinking of taking a flight, we could have docked in Georgetown."

Irritated at the questions, Sweeper responded, "Our business is concluded, Captain. Stop at the main dock in Nassau and head back to Key West."

"Yes sir, it's been a pleasure." The captain followed instructions, oblivious to how lucky he was. If they had been farther out to sea and the questions had persisted, he would have ended up as a tasty meal for sharks.

Sweeper felt safe in terminating the charter and melting into the multitude of tourists in Nassau. With a fake mustache and hair dye as a precaution, he considered boarding a cruise ship to Miami as opposed to a direct flight from Georgetown to New York. *Perhaps I should stay in Nassau for a few days*, he thought, *—maybe head for St. Thomas for a few days of relaxation.*

May 17, 1998

The board meeting of Maxco-Litton was about to convene as scheduled. Several Directors were apprehensive about what was going on and news leaks were appearing in various corners of the financial world. It was Elizabeth's job to squelch the stories and to regain the stature of her company by a complete and thorough audit. Roger Maxco called the meeting to order and deferred immediately to his CFO.

"Gentlemen, Elizabeth has felt it necessary to call this meeting. I turn it over to her, —Elizabeth?"

"Thank you, Roger. Thank all of you for responding to my call. You know me well enough to realize that I consider this meeting to be necessary. You will recall that not long ago, I suggested a formal, unscheduled audit of the entire financial structure of this firm. In fact, I proposed the audit in the form of a motion. It was turned down. That certainly was your prerogative." Elizabeth was polished and articulate, and did not display any hidden agenda. Her peers listened with respect as she continued.

"In light of the recent murders of our two top scientists, and the obvious speculation in the industry, as well as in the Federal Bureau of Investigation, concerning those deaths, it is absolutely imperative that we take immediate steps. We must re-establish, within the financial community our hard-earned reputation of integrity and financial stability.

I'm asking again for a show of hands for support of my original motion." Elizabeth paused, noting the majority of the board immediately raised their hands in favor of her motion.

"Thank you for your vote of confidence. I hereby declare that an independent accounting firm will immediately be appointed to conduct an unfettered and thorough audit of the financial structure of Maxco-Litton.

Elizabeth had won. Roger and Earnest sat in sullen though silent disapproval. Arthur Litton had given Elizabeth his unwavering support. She wasn't through. Looking around slowly, at the faces she had trusted and those who had trusted her, Elizabeth continued. "Thank you again, gentlemen. The audit will begin immediately. I will send a memo tomorrow morning stating this resolution and reiterating that all department heads are instructed to cooperate fully. If I may indulge you for a few minutes, I would like to comment on the current state of affairs here at Maxco-Litton.

"The FBI is investigating the deaths of Drs. Hall and Weitzel. The implications of their investigation could be significant. The fact that there is an investigation at all is creating a tremendous number of rumors and innuendo, all of which must be stopped. I am going on record today to advise each and every Director to remain absolutely silent with the press. Discretion is our only ally."

She continued, "You are to cooperate fully with the authorities." She noted Roger's scowl and turned to him as if questioning his motive. He looked away.

Undaunted, she continued, "We must operate on the presumption of innocence for all those who may be suspect. Hopefully, with the investigation complete along with the audit, all suspicions and fears will be laid to rest. That is my sincere desire. Gentlemen, if there are no questions, this meeting is over. Thank you."

Roger breathed a sigh of relief. Elizabeth had been straightforward but fair. He had not been singled out. The others knew she was right in her assessment. Elizabeth had come through once again. Her impeccable credentials and reputation had not only left the firm still intact, but her offensive posture may have significantly enhanced their position. Media aside, the board hadn't been instructed not to speak to the financial world. Her tack would be respected and perhaps save Maxco-Litton from further damage.

Roger now had some breathing room. The audit would take at least three months. There were to be no shortcuts. Elizabeth was given full authority to go outside the organization and retain the most prestigious and scrupulously independent accounting firm available. She would have to bid the process out, which would take weeks. It would take legions of CPAs to do the job that Elizabeth had in mind. Nothing would be left to chance. Every single stock transaction having to do with Maxco-Litton would be scrutinized along with each collateral loan deal. When finished, Roger thought, it would be his worst nightmare. He made a personal commitment, then and there, to bail out in sixty days. It was time for a strategy session with Dr. Elliot, Earnest, and Michael Lowe.

The conference room was empty. Elizabeth Martin sat alone watching, without really seeing, the New York skyline as it grew brilliant with stars above the tops of the buildings and artificial lights below. In deep thought, her mind began to wander. *You brought us so far, Roger. What went wrong? What were you thinking? What are you planning? How could I have misjudged you so? Tell me you're innocent and this is all a bad dream."* She stood up and poured herself a brandy, then sat on the corner of the conference room table where she had just won a victory that she hadn't wanted. Whispering into the night, she spoke the words she hadn't wanted to say, "My God, Roger, could John Rushly be right?"

Chapter Eleven

May 27, 1998

Roger Maxco was enjoying an after-dinner brandy in his study when his private line rang. The line was secure, reserved for only one person.

"Roger, I'm glad your home. Hopefully, you are relaxing." Nitti sounded more formal than usual.

What does he want? He never inquires about my health. Roger's heart started to race and he began to panic. *Something's wrong,* he thought. Taking a deep, quiet breath, he answered calmly.

"Good evening Charles. What has prompted this call?" He refused to play games with this man. He wasn't in the mood. He waited for the response.

"We have a situation, Roger. The people here are nervous. Allow me to be candid."

"Of course, Charles, please."

"The group has decided to disassociate itself from Maxco-Litton. The August funding is off. Existing obligations must be repaid. You're too hot right now, Roger. We don't like the FBI poking around and the "incidents" have disturbed too many people. Do you understand our position?"

There was a stunned silence before Roger recovered. *Time,* he thought, *I need more time.*

"Yes Charles, I do understand. It will take me a few months to liquidate and to sever our financial ties. However, I was counting on the funding in August. Can we discuss that issue?"

"I'm sorry Roger, but there is nothing to discuss. The funding isn't going to happen. Insofar as a time frame with respect to liquidating and severing our financial ties, you have sixty days."

Charles Nitti did not make casual statements. Roger knew there would be no funding and he had exactly sixty days to clean up his mess. Failure to do so would result in an unacceptable alternative.

He shuddered, struggling for composure.

"I understand, Charles. You may be assured your requests will be honored in a timely manner."

It was a facetious remark—Roger knew what Nitti had proposed was not a request but a clear and uncompromising demand.

"Very well. We understand each other. Have a pleasant evening." The call was over.

Well, Roger thought, *the bastard wants all the gravy but isn't willing to take the heat. Shit, I'm the one who's taking all the heat. Screw them! What I need to do can be done in sixty days—before these assholes get nasty and before Elizabeth's audit is finished.* Roger strode angrily to the bar, poured himself a double jigger of brandy and gulped it down. Looking up into his reflection behind the bar, he thought, *And screw the FBI! They haven't got shit!*

The strategy session with Dr. Elliot, Earnest, and Michael Lowe was set for Friday, the following day. They could work through the weekend, if necessary. Besides, Roger reasoned, there will be no interruptions. Michael Lowe, Roger's personal attorney, was essential in coping with the new developments.

A crony of Roger's from days past, Michael Lowe was a street-smart lawyer, with a unique talent for manipulating stock transfers. A CPA in addition to being an attorney, Michael had been indispensable in earlier transactions having to do with maneuvering funds from Chicago and skirting SEC disclosure laws. And true to form, being a close associate of Roger Maxco, he was completely devoid of ethics.

A week before, it had appeared there was plenty of time to maneuver and manipulate the Directors of Maxco-Litton—not to mention the FDA and the Chicago group. All had changed. Deadlines now were critical.

The laboratory outside of Lake Placid was elaborate by any standards. Under the direction of Weitzel and Hall, there was never a question of budget restrictions. What the scientists needed, they got. Stakes were too high to quibble over dollars. Tom Elliot was in his glory. Aside from ethical considerations, he truly deserved the status. His work was exemplary and he had wasted little time in adapting the work of the late scientists to further his own agenda.

The four men had agreed to meet in upstate New York in the large conference room next to the main laboratory. By 10:30 a.m., all were assembled to begin the most critical meeting of their careers. Trying to be lighthearted to cut the tension, Elliot remarked, as they were pouring their coffees and settling, "We should call this meeting, "How to manipulate stocks, scientific truth, ruin a pharmaceutical empire, and open your own golden parachute." His attempt at humor was met with silence accompanied by a dark look from Roger.

Trying to recover his social status with the group, Elliot quickly passed out report folders to each. They were marked CONFIDENTIAL WORKING DOCUMENTS. He had prepared something analogous to a term paper for his less sophisticated students. It recapped the work of Hall and Weitzel and outlined the original flaw in the raw data and mathematical conclusions from the senior scientist, the data that Hall had discovered. The meeting began with Elliot's comments regarding his work in progress.

"Gentlemen, we do have a vaccine of inestimable scientific value. At least, we are close. If Hall and Weitzel had followed through—that is backed up to the point before the compromised data was introduced, they would have seen how close they were to success. Are we there? Not quite."

"Do we have something we can sell, or not?" Roger barked. "Is there *anything* we can spring on the medical community that will lift Maxco-Litton to a place of prominence? I don't give a damn if the glory lasts a week. That's all we need. Am I right, Michael?"

Michael Lowe, aside from legal matters, was not familiar with the lab work at Lake Placid. He had been brought into the loop too late to bring himself up to speed on the total picture at Maxco-Litton. His research to date had concluded that Roger was in severe financial trouble. The obligations to Chicago were enormous and there was the matter of the unexplained murders of their two prominent scientists. Lowe did understand, however, the monumental importance of the work that had been done. Unfortunately, the company was under a microscope with the FBI currently conducting an investigation. He tried to respond as well as he could without antagonizing Roger.

"There is serious planning needed, Roger. First of all, I will need Tom Elliot to walk me through the new project, Galen II.

With that project clarified in my mind, my question to him will obviously be this: What is our credibility factor at this moment with the medical community and the FDA? Don't get me wrong Roger. Maxco-Litton, in spite of the present adverse publicity, is still a formidable and well-respected industry leader."

Sensing he had their attention, he leaned forward to make sure Roger would grasp the import of what he was saying. "However," he continued, "to move the stock higher, even for a short period, will require dramatic and significant news—news that will not only be impressive to the medical community, but also to the financial community. Remember—" he paused for dramatic effect, "that the stock *must be sold* before the inevitable! Any problems with the vaccine, and we know there will be, will send Maxco-Litton stock into a tailspin. We will need time. In any event, with the deadlines we are faced with to make this all happen, every second has to count. This *all* has to happen within weeks."

"That's only realistic, Roger," Earnest added, "but I'm more concerned about the audit and Elizabeth Martin."

"Don't worry about Elizabeth," Roger snapped. "I'll take care of Elizabeth!"

"In my opinion, Elizabeth *is* a worry, Roger. She's bypassed the bid process and already got independent auditors ready to swarm all over the goddamn place!" He let his irritation at Roger's comment be known.

"Sorry Earnest—"

"It's okay Roger. I thought she would be a concern."

"Forget her, Earnest—really. I'll take care of it. The auditors will take months to do their work, even if they uncover something. Months! Then weeks more to compile a formal report."

"Gentlemen," Michael interrupted, "let's split up so we can go over this report of Elliot's on our own, and have some lunch. We can resume this afternoon."

The four men decided to meet back at the laboratory at two o'clock. Dr. Elliot and Michael decided to find a quiet diner near the lab. Michael wanted to be brought up to speed on Galen II. Now part of the fold, Michael found himself impressed by the doctor-turned-research scientist. They hit it off right away. Both men were exceptionally bright and knew exactly what they wanted. Tom was convinced he had been screwed over by the establishment and wanted to screw it right back. Michael's attitude was no better. He considered life unfair in general and thought one should try to shape the odds in his own favor, no matter the consequences.

They chose a modest eatery close to the laboratory and settled into a lime-green, vinyl-covered booth, reminiscent of the 'seventies. Their dress was casual since they both felt the meeting would carry on into the evening. No one could have known by their appearance the impact these men might have on the world, as a result of today's meeting. The waitress, obviously new and a little nervous, spilled coffee in the saucer, irritating them both, and they motioned her away.

"Give us a few minutes. Okay?" Michael sounded agitated, then immediately apologized, not wanting to call attention to him. She poured the coffee, left two menus and walked away.

"I guess it is time to relax," Michael breathed a sigh and leaned back, trying to calm down. He was feeling too tense to be able to make decisions. There was a lot to decide today. Pouring cream into his coffee, he stirred it twice, lay the spoon in the saucer, and looked up at his new partner in crime. "Tell me about the project, Tom. It'll be faster than me trying to decipher this report. What's the bottom line? Do we have something real?"

"As I told the others, Michael, my work has paralleled that of Hall and Weitzel. The difference being that I was more conservative. Their work, although exceptionally brilliant, was hurried. I suspect that's when Julian ran into trouble. I guess after five years of research on one thing, when you come this close, your mind allows you to cut corners. He wanted to believe too hard. Delusion is not a word reserved for those outside the scientific community. I'm afraid he lost touch, just for a moment. And that's when it happened, the slip up on data and the math.

"However, we certainly do have something and it's real. I used their good data, manipulated the bad data which would take months for someone to uncover, and voila! We do indeed have a vaccine that will prevent breast cancer with few known side effects.

My tests confirmed what Hall had discovered—that certain drugs associated with high blood pressure and certain prescribed hormone replacement therapies could be dangerous when taken with this vaccine. This is my thought, however, and it's this that will buy us the time we need. I believe the FDA will not seriously challenge these tests simply because they will accept Weitzel's conclusions. It appears that Julian did pave the way to move us forward. The payoff is that with a modification of his data, we won't pay the price of lost time and further testing. From a medical perspective, we are premature in releasing the drug. However, in my view, the risks are acceptable. If it is put together in a professional and credible package, it can be sold to the medical as well as the financial community. Does that help?" Pleased with himself, Tom signaled the waitress to take their order.

"Whew, I guess so! What you are saying is that the risks are manageable and with the right kind of packaging, the medical community will endorse the vaccine and our public relations people can run with it."

"Yes, and if you have qualms about the drug, just let me say this—" Elliot's tone bore just a hint of a patronizing attitude, "Every single drug that goes on the market has a risk factor. They just don't play that up." Elliot knew that he had given Michael Lowe enough information to destroy him. The attorney, after all, was still an officer of the court. He intended to soft-pedal his confession as much as possible until he knew Michael was fully involved. Then it would be too late for the lawyer to back out.

"I understand, Tom. For the record, I think except for what I need to know, with regard to our legal position and helping to arrange the stock exchanges, from this point on, there are some things better left unsaid. I don't want to know about any potential criminal activity with regard to the marketing of high-risk drugs and manipulated data. That part of our conversation never took place. I'm in this deep enough, do you understand?"

And so the two came to a quiet but mutual consensus. One, a disgruntled but brilliant physician and scientist and two, a greedy lawyer who was willing to manipulate the stock markets but squeamish about causing possible deaths of unsuspecting women. All for greed.

The waitress brought their food, smiling with renewed confidence as they praised her for not dropping the heavy plates. Over Reubens, fries and two long neck bottles of Bud Lite, the two talked about golf, cars and their favorite vacation spots. They would join Roger and Earnest within the hour, ready to move forward.

The meeting concluded with everyone being brought up to date on critical elements of the plan and deadlines that were required to be met, in order to make everything happen.

The CEO made the parting comments. "Okay, I feel a lot better, our having all come to terms with everything we have to do. Elliot, get our publicist down to your office and have her write a press release. Once you and I have approved it, impress upon her that it is to be tabled with no copies floating around, ready for release in about forty-five days. When it's time, it will be released immediately. Make sure she understands this is absolutely confidential until that time. Leaks are not acceptable."

Turning to Michael, he said, "Lowe, I need the best of your legal mind at this moment. We will need all the paper work mapped out with the necessary contingency plans in the event of a glitch. Earnest, you and Michael will have to spend a lot of time together. Be ready for the drama. This medical news is a major breakthrough. The media and market will both go nuts. We cannot afford to become exhilarated with our own power, our own success. Every one is to keep a level head. We have the power to manipulate hundreds of millions in profit in a few hours, —and run! Have your lives in order, whatever you intend to do. I don't want to know. Now, let's get to work."

After the meeting, Roger asked Earnest to hang around.

"Let's go to the Sable Stable for dinner. We need to talk. Something's happened." What Roger had to share didn't need to be heard by the other two. Roger was always careful about the need-to-know aspect of critical information.

Settling into the back booth of the town's upscale steak house, with dark-mahogany wood throughout and photos of racing horses dotting the walls, Roger ordered a double Jack Daniels with water back. Earnest ordered a gin and tonic. He was getting nervous. Not wanting to press, he remained silent, knowing too well the volatility of his friend when pushed too hard or too fast. Small talk ensued until their drinks arrived and the waiter was instructed to leave them alone until called. The topic of conversation quickly turned to Nitti. The mob figure's phone call had shaken Roger to the core, and he needed to confide in his friend and colleague.

Earnest became visibly distressed listening to Roger relate the brief conversation. And although it would prove to be inconvenient and costly, Earnest was happy the association was coming to an end. Arranging the quick sale of stock had just taken on new meaning. It had been made clear that Nitti expected payment of his loans in full and within his time frame. This would be a great challenge for Earnest. As frightening as the consequences of not meeting the timeframe would be, Earnest was equally thrilled to have to perform such an incredible feat. Playing with money, big money was the greatest pleasure he had and he did it well.

"Roger, I'm a little concerned," he said quietly, needing to make his fears known without alarming his employer. There was a lot at stake, obviously the life of his best friend. "These people are not reasonable businessmen. Suppose we can't meet their deadline?"

"That is not an assumption we can even consider, Earnest. We *will* make their deadline!" Nitti is not only unreasonable, he is unforgiving." Roger continued. "You will be working closely with Michael and Elliot on this. They don't need to know about Nitti, but the stock deal is part of our total project. They just need to know how urgent it all is. Goddamn it!" Roger said, shaking his head. "It's been a long day. Let's get a big, thick steak and try to talk about something else. I'm exhausted."

Earnest saluted his friend with his gin and tonic, then drank it down. Beckoning the waiter, he decided to put responsibility behind him, just for the night. They had all absorbed a lot in one day, covered a lot of ground. The term 'critical deadline' had been used over and over during the day. It had lost its meaning. A few drinks and a steak dinner were just what they needed.

Three days of rest in Nassau had been too long. Sweeper contemplated his next move. He missed the excitement of 'the city that never sleeps'—New York. The FBI had alerted the Bahamian authorities that a man suspected of murder had been dropped off at the docks in Nassau. They were told he had made a hasty trip from Key West in a chartered Sea Ray 630. A description had been obtained from the captain after he had returned with his boat to the docks at Key West.

John Rushly was not hopeful. There were too many ways to leave the Bahamas undetected. But this was his best lead in solving Weitzel's murder. There were other avenues the investigation was taking, and the agent expected them to payoff.

A close look at all the Directors of Maxco-Litton had turned up an interesting fact. Gus Lanton had joined the firm at the same time Roger Maxco had taken over. Strangely, his background was illusive. Two of the other Directors had sponsored him and he was accepted with little challenge. He had no connection whatever to the company. Gus Lanton was from Chicago.

Placing a call to Elizabeth, John asked if the CFO had known anything about Gus prior to his coming to the firm. She knew little except that he had made it a point to personally befriend her from the beginning. She had made it clear that there was no opportunity for a romantic liaison but she would be available to assist him on a professional basis. According to Elizabeth, he honored her wishes. However, she said, he was vitally interested in knowing as much about the company as possible and never seemed to run out of questions. Feeling satisfied that Elizabeth had answered him matter-of-factly, John was ready to hang up when he was interrupted.

"John, do you have anything specific yet in Julian's or Marshall's deaths that would incriminate Roger Maxco?" This was a question she was almost afraid to ask and even more afraid to hear the answer.

"Only information given to me by Marshall. Obviously, it can't be corroborated. We are searching for a suspect in the Julian killing. He may be in the Bahamas, but we think he's from New York. The captain of the charter boat said the man casually mentioned New York City. I believe the motives may be found somewhere in the audit you have initiated. Other than that, although I know he is implicated, we have little to go on. I'm sorry."

"John, a meeting has taken place between Roger and one other Director. They met one of our scientists at Lake Placid. I learned that an old pal of Roger's, Michael Lowe, was at the meeting. He's a lawyer with a rather tarnished reputation, from what I understand. Perhaps that information will be of some help to you. Where do you go from here?"

"I'm taking a hard look at your Director friend, Gus Lanton. There is something about his background that doesn't make sense. He has strong connections with a group in Chicago—a disreputable group, I might add. He doesn't seem to fit the picture of a Maxco-Litton Director. He is—"

"Gus has no connection with Roger," Elizabeth interrupted him. "They barely speak. At least that's what it looks like."

"You're probably right. Gus has an agenda. I just have to find out what it is and if Roger is connected somehow."

"Feel free to call me, John. I'm really pushing this audit but it is going to take time."

"Thanks, Elizabeth," John replied, "and be careful. Don't ask too many questions. You'll tip them off. We will prevail—in spite of Roger Maxco. Talk to you later."

New Providence Island—The Bahamas

"Sir, I wish to see your passport. What has been your business in Nassau?"

Startled, Sweeper turned to the black officer, the crisp, white and black uniform epitomizing authority.

"Of course," Sweeper replied, handing the officer his passport, "I'm here just relaxing—heading home."

There was a definite resemblance to the description given to the Nassau authorities by the FBI. Except for the hair color and mustache, he fit the general description. The fact that he was alone and the hair color didn't look natural was enough to alert the officer. Sweeper had decided to board a cruise ship to Miami. He could gamble and mingle with the crowds on deck, easily blending in to the tourist population.

"When did you arrive in the Bahamas, Mr. Noble?"

"Oh, it's been over a week now."

"Do you have your transportation documents? Did you fly from the mainland?"

The questions were getting sticky. Sweeper knew the officer

was suspicious. He kept scrutinizing his hair and mustache. Sweeper was surveying the area. There were several people saying goodbye to loved ones preparing to board the cruise ship. Without disabling the officer, there was little chance for escape. They had moved off to one side during the questioning. The preoccupied crowd was about thirty feet away. The officer had a phone and nightstick, Sweeper noticed, taking a quick, professional inventory, —no other weapons.

"Yes, I flew over last week." He answered smoothly, moving into the personal space of the officer just enough to put the man on notice. "A copy of my ticket is in my bag. Would you like to see it?"

The sergeant was getting nervous. He was about to call for help when Sweeper made his move. Reaching into the bag, Sweeper had grasped the Colt Woodsman .22 before the officer could react. With precision and skill, Sweeper spun around and placed his weapon directly behind the sergeant's ear. There was a sound like no other—a small caliber weapon with a silencer—a spit, which no one heard. The hapless policeman, supported by Sweeper, was dead in a millisecond, 'walked' over behind a tall crate waiting to be loaded, and gently stowed out of sight.

This was not an afternoon for a cruise to Miami. The airport at Georgetown was probably watched. Sweeper headed for the docks.

It could be five hours or five minutes before the son of a bitch is found, Sweeper thought, his mind now in high gear. *Get out amongst the pleasure boats. Hitch a ride directly to Miami Harbor. Stay cool, but get off these islands!* Adrenaline was pumping and he knew he could afford to make no mistakes.

He was giving himself good advice. Once the officer's body was found, the entire Commonwealth would be on alert. He wasn't far from the pleasure craft that docked on the northeastern coast of New Providence Island. There were a lot of sailboats but they were too slow. He needed a powerboat with a greedy skipper.

Acting in a nonchalant manner, Sweeper approached a man in his early sixties. He was tending to his Carver 320 Voyager, a modest family cruiser built in 1994.

"Ahoy, "Sweeper shouted, "is your boat for hire?"

"I take a few people around the islands, friends mostly. I got no license to charge people." The man appeared interested, nevertheless.

"I missed my flight to the mainland. Could you take me to Miami Harbor? My sister is critically ill. She just went into the hospital. Otherwise, I would stay over and catch a flight tomorrow. I can sure pay you."

"Well, it's a few hours and the sea is choppy. I'd have to stay over one night. I don't know. It would take a lot of gas, too."

"Listen," Sweeper touched the older man's arm, gently. "I'm really in a bind. Suppose I just give you cash. Say five hundred dollars now and another five hundred when we land. That should cover all your expenses and give you some extra spending money."

"Okay, but we will have to leave right now. If the wind picks up, it could get nasty out there."

The boat was seaworthy, with all the latest GPS equipment. The Global Positioning System would assure a safe straight course for Miami. With twin 350—Crusader gas engines, the craft could do twenty-seven knots. It could be a fast trip.

"I will have to see all the money," the captain said, greed already creating a sense of power. Sweeper handed the captain five one hundred dollar bills and surreptitiously pulled a roll of large bills just far enough from his pocket to show the captain. He was careful to keep any onlookers from suspecting a cash transaction was taking place. Satisfied, the two headed over to the refueling station and immediately out to sea. Back at the cruise ship dock, all hell was breaking loose. Soon, the island would be sealed off.

It was late, but John's FBI people had strict orders to contact him with any new business relating to the murder. The phone rang at home. It was the Miami office.

"Agent Rushly, I know it's late. This is June Barker. I had talked to you before from Key West."

"Yes, June, what is it?"

"I received a call from the authorities in Nassau. One of their officers was shot earlier today. He was killed with a small caliber weapon. They believe it was our guy. Some people nearby came up with a description. Aside from the hair color and a mustache, it all fits.

The authorities are watching the airports, docks and cruise ships, and patrolling the streets. Unfortunately, there are a lot of ways to get out of the Bahamas unnoticed. They are really disturbed. This entire matter is getting more complicated."

"June, I have to tell you on my last case, we had the same thing going on with the Bahamian authorities. The last time, one of our agents was killed. This is bad news. Keep me posted. I'm sure he is trying to hitch a ride to the mainland. He can't stay in the Bahamas. It's too risky. Anything else?"

"I can tell you that this case is getting a high priority—two prominent scientists and now an international incident. You're on center stage, Agent Rushly. Let me know if I can help."

"Right, June. I'll call you at your office in the morning. If developments warrant it, I'll see you in Miami."

"Another thing, John. This may not work, but we are alerting the Coast Guard. He could be on the high seas. They can't stop every boat, but they can give us a heads up if they see anything out of the ordinary."

"Thanks again, June. I'll call you tomorrow. Goodnight."

John turned to his wife, Jill. "It's getting nastier, Jill. A sergeant in the Bahamian police force was found shot to death in Nassau. June Barker thinks it's our man from the Keys. I'm afraid I'll be spending more time away from Phoenix. No doubt the Director will be receiving calls tomorrow—the case is international now."

"Shades of your last case, John," replied Jill.

"*Our* case Jill," he reminded her gently. "It was you who finally cornered our man in San Francisco Bay."

"That's still hard to forget, John. I think of Dick Wolf often."

Jill could hardly forget the partner who gave his life to save her during a shootout on the Tiburon Ferry in San Francisco Bay. She reminisced with John for awhile, the subject eventually returning to where this case started—Bodega Bay.

"John," Jill continued, "do we know any more about the death of Joanne? Did Marshall Hall kill her or do you think it was an accident?"

"Your friend Mike Staples thinks he killed her. I don't know.

Will we ever know? Usually, in an ongoing case such as this one, something obscure comes to light. If her death didn't involve anyone else other than Marshall, we may never know."

"I promised Joanne we would know the truth." Jill remembered her promise made on the return flight to Phoenix.

"You might think about it this way, Jill," he said, reaching for her, trying to find a way to bring her peace and closure about her friend's death. "When Marshall was killed, Joanne may have learned the whole truth, after all."

"Wow," she said, smiling, looking up into his eyes before snuggling against his chest, "I never realized you were so spiritual, John. Sometimes you surprise me."

Chapter Twelve

For Kimberly Weitzel, the past few weeks had been absolute and total hell. The two most important men in her life had been murdered and no one had been arrested. Now, still temporarily housed at the Embassy Suites in Phoenix, she felt lost, disoriented, without purpose. Where was she to go? What was she to do? There seemed to be little hope in finding the peace and happiness that had been her goal for so long. Her faith shattered, her world devastated by loss, she knew she would have to reach deep within her soul to find the strength she needed to carry on. Suddenly there was a loud knock at her door.

Startled out of her reverie, she asked cautiously, through the door, "Who is it?"

"Federal Express for Ms. Weitzel," yelled the man at the door.

"Just a moment," replied Kimberly. She peeked through the keyhole to make sure there was a Federal Express truck outside and the courier was uniformed. She opened the door, slightly, holding her foot firmly against it.

"Sign here, please." Kimberly signed for the package and the driver left.

The package had made the circuitous trip from Lake Placid to San Francisco to Phoenix. Kimberly's friend, who had been housesitting for her, had forwarded her mail.

"Oh my god," she gasped aloud, "it's from Dad."

Unable to tear open the Tyvek envelope, she found a pair of shears and carefully cut away a quarter inch from the side of the package. There was a smaller envelope inside. Aside from miscellaneous documents and notes, Kimberly found a personal letter addressed to her. She read it aloud.

"Dear Kimberly,
 I am having a very hard time right now with Roger Maxco and the other 'power brokers' at the company. Some of the notes enclosed are from

Marshall Hall—some technical and some personal. Just in case something happens to me, I have enclosed copies of my reports to Roger including compromising information about the project named Galen. Please keep this material in a safe place. I will see you soon. You will hear from me but I prefer not to talk about this package on the phone. I know you'll understand.
    love you.
Dad

    Kimberly spent the next two hours reading the material Julian had sent. There was a personal note to Julian from Marshall Hall, which talked about his fear of Roger. He described threats made to him and Roger's veiled references to Julian as well as Kimberly. Other material was of a highly technical nature, about data analysis, which meant little to Kimberly. She began to reflect on the contents of the package.
    Threats against Marshall. Dad was also fearful of this man. Roger must have ordered them both killed. You're going to hear from me, Mr. Maxco, and you are not going to like the message, she thought bitterly.
    This package was what she had needed for direction. She would find the strength to fight this battle, to find out who killed Marshall and her father, and why.
    Kimberly's first inclination was to confront Roger Maxco but she knew better. This package belonged in the hands of the FBI. *John will know what to do*, she thought. She recoiled when she remembered how her visit to Marshall's motel room had helped Roger's men locate him. *Now*, she thought, *maybe I can help the FBI bring the bastard to justice. He has taken everything from me and he will pay.*
    There was one more important item in the package marked "Personal." Kimberly opened the large envelope that contained Julian's New York Life insurance policy for half a million dollars. She was sole beneficiary. Kimberly began to weep. The rest of his estate was left to his favorite charity—a farm near Lake Placid that served as a refuge for stray and wounded animals. The gift of two hundred thousand dollars would help them continue their work.

Kimberly vowed to use as much money as she needed to help bring Roger Maxco to justice. First, she would turn over the documents to John at the FBI office, then make immediate plans to move to New York City.

"Mr. Rushly, there is a Kimberly Weitzel on the line. Will you take the call?"

"Yes, Ruth, put her through."

"Kimberly, how are you? I have been worried."

"I'm fine, John. I received a package from my father. It had been mailed from Lake Placid and found its way to me in Phoenix. I am sure that his letter addressed to me and the documents included may be of help to you. I can bring them by."

"That's wonderful, Kimberly. Let's meet for coffee. There's a Coffee Plantation near the Biltmore on Camelback. You know it? I can be there in thirty minutes."

"I know right where it is. That's perfect John. I'll see you there."

Kimberly was hoping John would be available to share new information, but wasn't sure if she should tell him yet about her plans to move to New York City. She decided to keep that news to herself for the time being. He'd think it too dangerous for her to be so close to Maxco-Litton.

Kimberly was seated outside at a wrought-iron patio table when John arrived. It was nearly a hundred degrees and John suggested they move into the air-conditioning.

"Can't take the heat John?" she teased.

"I take too much heat, Kimberly," he laughed good-naturedly. "Today, however, I choose to control it by moving inside." He turned serious and reached for her hand. "How are you doing? I keep thinking of the pain you must feel. Suddenly losing two important people in your life is tragic."

"It's going to take a lot of time to heal, John, but I'm making progress."

Pensively, John looked at Kimberly, lovely in her bright summer dress. *What a strong lady*, he thought. *Some man will be very lucky someday*, John thought, *like I was to find Jill.*

"Kimberly, there have been some new developments. First, let me take a look at those documents your father sent you." John looked through the notes and pages of technical information. "I'll go through this back at the office. Wait a minute. This is a coffee shop—how about it?" John walked over to the self-serve counter and filled two large mugs with Hazelnut coffee, the flavor of the day. Rejoining her, he gave her time to settle in with her coffee before bombarding her with information. She was eager to know.

"John," Kimberly asked, "what's new in the investigation?"

"For one thing, it's become international. We think the man who killed your father in Key West then killed a police officer in Nassau. There is an intensive manhunt underway. He could be in Miami or heading for New York. We're not sure. There are several parts to this investigation. One of the Directors of Maxco-Litton, Elizabeth Martin, has ordered a comprehensive audit of the company. We believe that will tell us a lot. However, that's taking some time."

"I'm taking some time off, myself, John. I'll let you know when I land some place. There isn't much I can do here."

"Is there something else, Kimberly? You seem a little distracted."

"No," she replied, "I'm just worn out and need a change of scenery. I might take a week or so in the islands—St. Thomas, maybe. I'm not sure."

"That's a good idea," suggested John, "but keep in touch. I may need you."

John suspected Kimberly was not telling him something, but he shrugged it off. After reviewing more of the packet together, Kimberly answering all the questions she could, they said their good-byes.

"I'm going back to the hotel to pack," she said, "I'll call you in a few days," she said warmly. "Thanks for all you've done, all you're doing. Her eyes filled with tears and she turned quickly and walked to her rental car. She was scheduled for an early morning flight to New York. Her life seemed to have purpose again. John returned to his office to study the material, unsuspecting that this lovely girl fully intended to assist in this sordid investigation, whether she was permitted to or not.

The Carver 320 Voyager slipped into Miami Harbor without incident. The waves had been two to three feet high and the winds relatively calm. The dash to Miami had taken three hours. Just inside the harbor, the old man commented, "If you want to feel like you are something very small out here, take a look off the port bow."

About three hundred yards away, the awesome profile of a gigantic cruise ship appeared. It was heading further off to the port side but seemed like a mountain moving through the water.

"I see what you mean," replied Sweeper. "Sometimes it takes a man-made object to remind us of how insignificant we are."

Their boat pulled into the City Marina and docked just long enough for Sweeper to gather his bag, pay his fare and head for South Beach. The cabby was instructed to find a disco-type restaurant with lots of people around. That was no challenge. It was nearly midnight on a Friday night.

Sweeper felt safer being on the mainland. This was his turf—the trendy clubs where gays were readily accepted among the straight. Befriending no one, he had a meal with half a carafe of Merlot and retired to a small hotel close by. *In the morning*, he thought, *I'll take a cab to the Lauderdale airport and fly home to JFK—mission accomplished.* He was proud of himself.

Not realizing the irony, Kimberly Weitzel would arrive at JFK International Airport the same day as the man who had murdered her father. It was May 30, Saturday afternoon, 2:45 EST when her plane landed. Sweeper had arrived at the airport three hours earlier.

The Marriott, a few blocks from the World Trade Center, would be her home for the next week. She would rely on taxis for transportation. She wanted to be close to the World Trade Center—and the offices of Maxco-Litton. While settling into the comfortable suite, Kimberly began to thumb through the Yellow Pages. She called three of the listings under Investigators, but none gave her a feeling of comfort. She didn't know what questions to ask. *Wait a minute*, she thought suddenly, *what about the detective in Bodega Bay, Mike Staples. He's a natural, and he's already involved.*

Kimberly had not met Mike Staples face-to-face. Marshall had told her about the "persistent detective" working on his wife's accident. Mike had even called Kimberly once to ask about her relationship with Marshall. It was not a friendly call. Kimberly realized now that everything had changed. She wondered if he might be willing to take a leave of absence for a private job. She wanted someone she felt she could trust. *His superiors might go along with it since it is one of their open cases,* she thought, then chastised herself for her naivete'. *Oh, well, worth a try,* she thought, *besides, it might be wise to have an inside track on the Joanne Hall case.*

Her mind made up, she quickly dialed the hotel operator for long distance information. She dialed the sheriff's office in Bodega Bay. Listening to the ring, she looked at her watch and remembered she hadn't had dinner. It was four o'clock in the afternoon in California.

"This is Mike." He was the only one in the office.

"Detective Staples, this is Kimberly Weitzel. Do you remember talking to me about Marshall Hall?"

"Indeed I do, Ms. Weitzel. This is a surprise. How can I help you? Let's do first names, okay? It's more comfortable."

"Thanks, Mike. I'm calling from New York and I don't want to beat around the bush, I've been through a lot." He listened patiently.

"I know you suspected Marshall Hall of his wife's death. I may not be able to change that. But I've found that the death of my father in Florida is connected to Marshall's murder. I can convince you of that if you'll give me a—"

"You don't have to convince me, Kimberly," he interrupted. "I've been in touch with Jill Rushly and her husband. There are many unanswered questions, and the case just seems to be getting weirder with more and more complications. It's international, now. But once again, why the call to me?"

Kimberly explained all that had happened to her in the past weeks and about her meetings with John Rushly. She went on.

"I trust the FBI and particularly Agent Rushly. But I feel compelled to become personally involved. There are things I can do that I believe may move this along. I need your help, Mike, I need someone I can trust. I need you here. I'm staying close to the company that employed my father, close to the people responsible for this death. Also, I plan to go through my father's things at his office in Lake Placid and I want someone with me."

"Wait a minute." He laughed. "You're going way too fast! First of all, Kimberly, I understand what you're going through and I sympathize, I really do. But you're not equipped to investigate anything without putting yourself in extreme danger. Kimberly, I am not a free-lance detective. There is the matter of jurisdiction and time and money. Besides, you may be impeding a federal investigation."

"Mike, my father left me a lot of money. That's not an issue. Could you take a leave of absence? Mike, John Rushly was talking about you. From everything his wife said, you had a lot of training with the San Francisco Police Department before you moved to the Bay. Can't I hire you as a private investigator? Name your rate. Can't you take a vacation? You can do it if you want to. What do you say? I'll pay all your expenses and whatever else is necessary." She heard his breath intake and thought she might have stirred up some excitement that he had been missing in his years in Bodega Bay. Unwilling to take no for an answer, Kimberly continued, "John Rushly will understand. I'm not going to get in his way."

He laughed, "You're sure persistent. I need to think about this. It's come out of the blue. Give me your phone number. I'll call you tomorrow between eight and nine o'clock your time. Okay?"

"Please Mike. I need you here. I'll talk to you in the morning. Thanks for listening."

Mike said goodbye and pondered Kimberly's comments. A lot of people hired outside investigators when law enforcement agencies were working a case. *There wasn't anything wrong with extra effort,* he thought. *Maybe this would be interesting, after all. Things had gotten rather dull for him. Yes, I think I will talk to the Lieutenant. I've never been to New York.*

Kimberly knew that Mike Staples was more than interested. This had been his case from the start. I wonder what he looks like, Kimberly thought, remembering the warmth of his voice. *It sure would be nice to have some company in this,* she thought. She decided to order from room service and stay in for the night. Suddenly she didn't feel so alone.

The call from Mike Staples had been timely. With bated breath, Kimberly picked up the phone.

"Hello."

"Kimberly, this is Mike."

"Good morning. Have you decided?" She held her breath, afraid she wouldn't like the answer.

"I have, but I want you to realize the dangers and implications of what you are doing."

"Come on—"

"Don't interrupt. Listen carefully. Both Marshall and your father obviously knew too much about something that someone wanted to protect, at any cost. Really, this is a matter for the FBI. I know you have a personal stake in all of this but you could get hurt. I understand your frustration. The wheels of justice turn slowly; sometimes they stop completely. You and I may not be able to move them much faster. Before I accept your offer, you must agree to this one condition: If I see our investigation going sideways or sense imminent danger to you, we call it off. No arguments. Do you agree?"

"Okay Mike, I agree. Look, at least I feel like I am doing something for Marshall and my father."

"All right, I will be in New York tomorrow. It's slow here and they've been yelling at me to take vacation time for three years. Arrange for a room in your hotel, okay? In my opinion, this job is really about taking care of you. I know your mind can't be changed so I'm going along. Remember my conditions, —I call the shots and will abort the whole thing if I determine you are in imminent danger."

"I can't wait to meet you Mike. How will I recognize you?"

"I'm told I remind people of Colombo except I'm Irish, so I never understood it. Thick, unruly hair, and I don't own an iron. Guess that about sums it up."

He's got to be kidding, Kimberly said to herself, smiling.

Gus Lanton had been busy. He had been instructed to monitor the activities of Roger Maxco, to stay close to Elizabeth Martin, and to learn whatever he could about the pending FBI investigation headed by John Rushly. Further, he was coordinating the surveillance of Kimberly Weitzel along with other key players in the Hall/Weitzel investigation. Gus Lanton reported directly to the Chicago group—specifically, to one Charles Nitti.

The men in Chicago were leaving nothing to chance. Knowing that mistakes made by Maxco could seriously affect their organization, the planting of Gus Lanton, in light of current events, had indeed been a smart move. Gus had made arrangements to speak with Nitti that evening. It was the day Kimberly Weitzel arrived in New York.

"Good evening, Charles. Can we talk? This is Gus."

"Yes, of course, Gus. Go ahead."

"Charles, there have been some disturbing developments. First of all, Kimberly Weitzel, for some inexplicable reason, arrived in New York yesterday. She is staying at the Marriott near Carlisle Street. She paid for a week in advance. She made a phone call to the sheriff's office in Bodega Bay, California. That's where Marshall Hall was from. There was a call to her room this morning from that same number."

He took a deep breath before continuing his report. "Before she left Phoenix, there was an hour-long meeting with Agent Rushly at a coffeehouse in Phoenix. I do know the FBI would not allow a civilian to get involved in a murder investigation, but she handed him something, a package. You already know that she was having an affair with Hall and Julian Weitzel was her father. Kimberly may be a loose cannon." His report complete, he waited for the response. It came quickly.

"What the hell was I thinking, letting Roger Maxco run this show?" Nitti exploded. "Damn! There's a lot of shit going on. What the hell can we do?"

"Hopefully, Mr. Nitti, this isn't serious. If the detective from Bodega Bay shows up, that could be a problem. Unfortunately, we must protect Roger's interests until we get paid and our ties are severed with Maxco-Litton. The audit will take too long. He doesn't have much of a worry there. If a scandal erupts because too many people are poking around, that could hurt us."

"What's the good news Gus?"

"It appears the team—Roger Maxco, Earnest Lasko, Michael Lowe, Tom Elliot—have a program that will accomplish Roger's goals. I wired Lasko's office and Roger's, so between the two, I have a pretty good handle of what's going on. It's a matter of timing, now. You should know that Elizabeth and the FBI agent are cozy, at least on the phone. She is his inside contact. I believe it was Rushly who suggested she push the audit. There is no tangible evidence of any wrongdoing at this moment. As I said before, it's all timing. If Roger stumbles, we may have to cut our losses and split. There are a couple of other things I am looking in to but it's premature to discuss them."

"Well, as usual, Gus, you seem to be privy to all the important news. Keep me advised about the Weitzel girl. She could be trouble. Goodnight Gus."

As Nitti placed the phone back in its cradle, he began to think about his last conversation with Roger. *I hope he got the message,* he thought. *I really hope he got the message!*

Mike's flight was scheduled to land at JFK at 7:00 p.m. Mike had lived on the West Coast ever since graduating from college. After his wife was killed, he had become a happy bachelor and his disheveled appearance showed his total disregard for his looks. He had made a quiet life for himself away from San Francisco and was quite happy spending his off-duty hours fishing, sailing and roaming through bookstores and antique shops. But his passion was and always had been detective work. There was nothing he liked to read more than a mystery novel with action and suspense. That was his life. This opportunity had been impossible to turn down.

Kimberly had agreed to meet him at the gate, wearing a powder blue suit. She was polished and well groomed. She would be easy to spot.

Chapter Thirteen

"Has the world gone nuts?" The mobster paced his thickly carpeted study, turning occasionally to fire off a question to his informant. "What the hell is Julian Weitzel's daughter doing in New York with a numb-nuts detective from Bodega Bay? I understand Sweeper is back in the City, too. Throw in those stupid bastards at Maxco-Litton, and they might as well have a goddamned convention."

Gus Lanton had thought it prudent to arrange a meeting with his boss. Gus had no compulsions about spying on Maxco. His loyalties were set in concrete with the Chicago group. Christopher Santini and Tony Vittorio were also in attendance. Although not directly involved in the Maxco-Litton investments, Santini and Vittorio represented special interests that were affected by the role played by Nitti. Nitti was at the top of the food chain and wanted his more important subordinates to be fully informed of his activities.

"I know how you feel," responded Gus. "The fact that Kimberly has somehow enticed Staples to leave his job and come to New York raises an interesting question. I can't imagine this being sanctioned by the FBI. What the hell is John Rushly going to do with this maverick team?"

Christopher Santini spoke for he and Vittorio.

"Charles, are we insulated here? What's the exposure? Do we have more work for Sweeper or should he get out of the country? Is there a paper trail at Maxco-Litton?'

Everyone in the room took a deep breath. These were heavy questions and the crime boss knew that his men deserved clear and definitive answers. He thought hard before responding.

"I have given Maxco a deadline to clear his accounts. He has less than sixty days. Sweeper is beyond reproach—a professional. I may, however, ask him to leave the country, as a precaution. Insofar as another job for Sweeper, the answer is an unequivocal 'No!' Any attempt to silence the girl or her detective friend would bring the FBI and other authorities closer and they would come down hard.

"The paper trail issue depends on how clean Roger can cut loose. I'll see to it that he begins to cover our asses. Gus, bring Christopher and Tony up to date about what's going on inside Maxco-Litton. Before you get started, Gus, I'll have some food brought in. Gentlemen, lets take a short break."

The four men began to talk among themselves when Nitti rang for the maid. A few minutes later, the stout woman brought in a deli tray loaded with breads, meats, cheeses and condiments. Following closely behind was a young man who doubled as chauffeur and gopher, carrying a tray with a silver coffee urn and a bottle of brandy. The air began to fill with the drifting aroma of cigar smoke.

Gus waited until everyone had prepared their plates and sat down, then, with Nitti's encouragement, caught the group's attention again. "I have been tracking Roger's plan to bail out of Maxco-Litton. He is working closely with his accountant and a Director on the board, Earnest Lasko. The key player, in my opinion, is his personal lawyer, Michael Lowe. The technical and scientific support guy is a discredited doc named Tom Elliot.

"I have been able to develop a modicum of rapport with Tom Elliot. He is a strange character in that he doesn't seem to be interested so much in money as in pay back of some sort. In that respect, he is a little dangerous. Incredibly brilliant, it appears he has a vaccine positioned for release in a few weeks, not just the announcement, but the vaccine. The FDA hasn't even okayed it, so I don't know how he plans to do this. He also plans to publish in the Journal of the American Medical Association with the support of his friends in the FDA. He is introducing the findings in a co-authored paper by himself and Weitzel and Hall, a bit sticky in the medical community, considering the circumstances, but his ego demands it. But there seems to be something wrong with the vaccine that they're not revealing, so I don't know what good publishing will do, except find him temporary glory.

"Michael Lowe is setting up scenarios that will give Maxco-Litton stock a strong but temporary boost in the market. At this point, Roger will sell off his shares and take care of his obligations to our group. He is trying to mitigate his anticipated losses due to the absence of our August funding. I haven't figured out exactly what he has in mind.

"There is something else going on at Maxco-Litton. I don't know what it is but it's extremely important. Roger has set up a private and secured line and takes a lot of calls from overseas at strange times of the day. I wasn't able to wire that phone. I've determined, from reviewing phone records from my source at the phone company, that these calls are coming in from all over the world. In the past few months, he has made arrangements to travel extensively, but not through the normal company travel services.

"Here is the clincher. We know that Maxco is one of the brightest managers in the corporate world. Inventory control has been the key to Maxco-Litton successes. They have always managed to keep the flow of goods in direct proportion to demand. Enormous savings result since you eliminate the need for warehousing and the concomitant need for personnel."

"Damn it Gus—slow down, do we need those big words?" Nitti was trying to ease the tension that was building. The men laughed, he had succeeded.

"Sorry Charles." Gus continued, undaunted. "I obtained documents that indicate there are huge stockpiles of certain drugs that are not allocated for normal retail outlets. It doesn't make sense. I'm not talking about a few hundred thousand dollars in inventory—from what I can see, it could be into the hundreds of millions. It's not only the vaccine but a lot of other drugs. Without approval of the vaccine, they must have gone ahead and manufactured it anyway! It's ready for distribution."

"This is news to me, Gus. What else?"

"I'm not sure, Charles. So far, there has been no need to concern you, but with all this other business—Kimberly and the detective, calling in loans and stopping the August funding—it's becoming more important. Roger Maxco has something up his sleeve in addition to the Galen II project."

"What the hell is—" Nitti interrupted again. This sounded like more bad news.

"Don't get worked up, Charles," Gus responded, "I'll get a handle on this. I'm as concerned as you are. Give me another week. We will have some answers."

"I don't like any of this," Vittorio commented. "I'm glad you pulled the plug. This Maxco bothers me."

"I think we are all in agreement," Nitti agreed. "We extricate ourselves from the firm at the earliest possible date. In the meantime, we monitor our friend Roger, along with the Weitzel girl and the detective. Gus, you're the point man. Stay on it."

It had been a long afternoon. The four men finished cigars and drinks before leaving. As Gus Lanton rolled away from the isolated mansion in his '98 Black Cadillac, he thought to himself, *What the hell is Roger Maxco's next move? What's the son of a bitch up to, now?*

John listened intently to the excited but clear voice on the line. It was his FBI contact in Florida, Agent Barker.

"John, we have a tentative ID. The man in Key West and Nassau may be an illusive hit man who goes by the name of Sweeper. He is a professional assassin and until now has been virtually unknown. The tip came from a reliable source in New York. Our people are comparing artist sketches and checking the story from end to end. We think it's for real."

"June, it sounds as if we're getting somewhere. Do we have any prints—anything that will give us a positive ID?"

"Our source goes back a long way and he has held onto a weapon that was used in a New York killing in 1987. He claims we can lift a print off the gun, which will give us what we need. The New York office will call you, but I wanted to give you the breaking news."

"Does the source have any idea who the man may be working for now?"

"He may. By tomorrow this time, we could have an answer to that question. I wish I could work with you on this case, John."

"June, you are working with me. This is a real team effort. Thanks for calling. Let's keep in close touch. I really appreciate what you are doing."

"Thanks John. I look forward to meeting you in person."

"That won't be long, June. I have a feeling we will meet each other soon."

With the phone replaced in the receiver, John's thoughts turned to Kimberly. *I'll call her friend to see if I can track her down. She should know what is going on.*

John dialed her home number in California. A young woman answered immediately. Explaining who he was, John asked where he could reach Kimberly.

"I've been working with Kimberly since the death of her father. Is she still in town? Do you know where she can be reached?'

"She's talked about you several times, Agent Rushly. I guess I can tell you where she was headed. I don't have an address or phone number. The last thing I know is she bought a ticket to New York."

There was a stunned silence as John tried to absorb that information. He thought of pressing for more, but knew there would be nothing else that Kimberly would have told her friend.

"Thank you. You have been helpful. If you do hear from her, tell her it is important that she contact me." John Rushly leaned back in the soft leather chair behind his oak desk and tried to contain his worst fears. *What in the hell is she doing in New York? She can't go after Roger Maxco on her own. She knows better.* Buzzing his secretary, John fairly shouted his orders.

"Carol, get me the Field Office in New York City."

"Yes Sir, right away. Mr. Rushly, —your wife is on the other line. She says it's urgent."

"Okay, hold the call to New York."

"Hi Jill. What's going on?"

"John, I just heard from Mike, you remember, the detective from Bodega Bay. He has taken a leave and has joined Kimberly Weitzel in New York. My God John, what are they doing?"

"I just heard myself that Kimberly went to New York. This is crazy. What the hell are they up to? Mike should know better. Jill, I was just about to call our New York Field Office and alert them. I don't believe Mike and Kimberly realize how dangerous these people can be. And worse, Julian's killer may be in New York."

"I wanted you to know, John. Hopefully they won't carry this too far."

"They shouldn't be in New York at all, Jill. I'll call you later. I want to talk to our people and see what we can do. I'll be home around six. Let's go to Annie's for dinner."

"It's prime rib night!" they both said together, laughing. No matter what they were working on, together or alone, they loved their special nights out. It helped them get away from the stress of their jobs.

Taking a deep breath, obviously calmer now, John repeated his initial request to his secretary, his thoughts turning once again to Kimberly and New York. *She thinks she's going to investigate on her own. Why did Mike Staples join her? What an amateur! He does know better.* John couldn't believe what had transpired. He kept thinking about the potential consequences.

Kimberly had informed Mike of her appearance so thoroughly he teased, "This sounds more like a blind date than a meeting for sleuthing." They both laughed. Mike's description of himself was accurate.

The speaker in Terminal 8 blared, "Miss Weitzel, pick up a white paging phone." The announcement was repeated twice. Mike's flight had arrived twenty minutes early, a first for JFK, and Kimberly was twenty minutes late, not a first for her. Having missed each other at the gate, he had walked away to buy a magazine. He didn't like having her name blared across the terminal but there was no other way.

"Yes?" she responded to the page, unsure as to whether she should answer.

"What a relief!" he laughed warmly. This is Mike. I'm near security at American. Where are you?"

"Where I am supposed to be detective," she responded wryly, "—at the gate!"

"Okay, stay there and I'll find you."

"Yes, Sir!" she replied pertly, her throaty voice breaking into a chuckle.

The stunning lady approaching Mike Staples was breathtaking. Mike did a double take and could barely speak her name.

"Kimberly?"

"Mike Staples, what a pleasure. You described yourself perfectly." She laughed heartily, taking his hand. "I'm happy to meet you. You're quite a handsome man and don't worry," she teased, feeling safer this minute than she had for weeks.

"Worry about what?" he couldn't help but notice a taunting smile on her lips.

"I travel with a steamer, you don't need an iron."

"Well, thank you." He blushed, not knowing quite how to take her. "May I suggest you look lovely? Do I have to learn to dress for New York?" Following her through the terminal, he noticed that she was wearing Jill Sander perfume, a scent he would never forget. It was the only luxury his late wife had allowed herself.

"You don't have to learn anything, Mike. After dinner, I'll get you settled in your room and bring my steamer. I don't want you calling attention to yourself. We'll be messing around at Maxco-Litton upstate. Their labs are very exclusive and I mean to introduce you as a friend. I don't want them to know who you are. And, well, if you were with me, no disrespect intended, but—"

"Somehow, Kimberly," he grinned, "I can't think of anyone's hands I'd rather be in, but Kimberly, as far as pressing my clothes?"

"Yes?"

"Not gonna happen," he grinned, opening the taxi door for her.

She answered his remark with a smile that dazzled him, completing throwing him off guard. Mike Staples was quite secure with who he was.

"This is a special occasion, Mike. I was sure you wouldn't eat the airline food. My thought was we should have a nice dinner, my treat, of course, discuss our arrangements and I'll fill you in on what I know so far, then we can retire to the hotel. You'll want to rest from the trip." She blushed suddenly, adding as an afterthought, "Of course, you have your own room."

"Of course," Mike replied stoically. He started to grin, but was determined to not let her know how much he was enjoying her discomfort.

Both were surprised with the instant rapport that had developed between them. The fact they both were single and around the same age and very attractive, in their respective ways, made their first encounter quite a pleasant one.

In the cab ride to The Calico Kitchen, an intimate Italian restaurant not far from their hotel, Mike remarked, "John Rushly knows we are in New York together. I know you wanted to keep this quiet but he should be informed as to our progress, if not our plans. It's the right thing to do, and safer. Overall, it will serve our purpose if I'm allowed to stay in the loop, even as an outsider. I wasn't able to call and tell you."

"I understand, Mike. We couldn't have kept it secret anyway. You did the right thing."

Dinner offered them an opportunity to learn more about each other. Both were aware that this had to be a trusting relationship. Once again, Kimberly agreed to follow Mike's lead. She was grateful to have him on her side.

"Kimberly, there are certain things we can't do, things that would jeopardize the FBI's work. We don't want to be in a position where we might impede Rushly's investigation. As a matter of courtesy, not to mention covering our asses, pardon the expression, I will be calling him in a day or two."

"Mike, I feel bad about John. He probably thinks I am crazy or just stupid. If you could smooth things over a little, I would feel a lot better. I know you're right."

"I believe we are going to do just fine," he said sincerely. "I'm going to enjoy working with you."

"So what's our first move," she couldn't keep from blushing and made an instant promise to herself to get over this rush and get down to business. "Where do we start?"

"We concentrate on Roger Maxco. I'm with you as a friend and you need to know the status of your father's work. In addition, you have a right to all of his personal effects—not only at his home but at the laboratory. With any information we gain from this and from observing Roger's reaction to our aggressive inquiry, we will have plenty to work on next week. It should be interesting. I plan to keep Rushly informed since he will be more willing to reciprocate with what he knows. I'm sure he'll feel better once I explain to him my position, knowing that I am looking out for you."

Kimberly was impressed with Mike's grasp of the situation. *This man is an enigma,* she thought. *Why Bodega Bay? There's a lot to learn about him.*

Mike spent the evening talking more about his personal life than he could have imagined, all about his wife's death, the fiasco they called justice, and his move away from San Francisco to get away from the criminal element and a system that had betrayed him. Taboo subjects in the past, he opened his soul to this new lady in his life. For the first time in years, Mike Staples felt he was becoming romantically involved. He wasn't ready to show those feelings, but they were there—hidden deep below the surface. He wondered. From his point of view, this was all very strange. *After all*, he thought, *other than a few phone calls and dinner, I hardly know her.*

The new companions finished dinner along with a lovely bottle of Cabernet Sauvignon and took a cab to the hotel. They would chart out the course for the next week and the first order of business would be to pressure Roger Maxco to turn over Dr. Julian Weitzel's papers. In so doing, Mike Staples knew that his investigation would be well under way. And whatever they uncovered, at least at this point, would be shared with Rushly. He looked forward to making contact with Jill's husband.

The CEO was working overtime. He was faced with the repayment of hundreds of millions of dollars to the Chicago mob and the approaching timetable to announce the new vaccine, which would immediately drive the stock to new heights. If that plan went awry for any reason, Roger had backup—his most grandiose scheme to date. He had manufactured and stored billions of dollars of drugs and the vaccine, ready for the market—the black market. The Russian Mafia was waiting in the wings to receive it. They would distribute the drugs and vaccine at their discretion. Roger Maxco and his colleagues were ready to bail. With this plan, it didn't matter if FDA approval was not forthcoming. Maxco and his group wouldn't care. They would be long gone.

Gus Lanton had been right. The Inter-Office Memo was supposed to have been shredded. It had been faxed from Krasnogorsk, a major city northwest of Moscow. Roger's secretary had left the document, momentarily, next to the main shredding machine. Gus quickly retrieved the paper and substituted a harmless document, which he began to shred. Roger's secretary thanked Gus for completing her job. She thought nothing of it. It was a lucky break. He retreated to the privacy of his office.

It was a cryptic message. The knowledge that Gus had regarding the warehouses and huge stockpiles of merchandise helped to make sense out of this urgent message. Gus began to read the fax to himself.

FACSIMILE TRANSMISSION
TO: RMML:
Expect shipments. Transfer of funds ($1.4 billion) to be confirmed upon receipt of goods including new vaccine. Must have shipping documentation in hand to take simultaneous possession Moscow, Paris, Krakow, Berlin and Amsterdam. Confirmation of destination codes by utilizing invoice numbers 2136789—5697654—3769245—4793654—4509123 in precise order. All verified 7/27/98. Initial transfer of funds ($200 million) 7/1/98 contingent upon acknowledgment via prior encrypted codes to this number.
LK

Gus placed the document in his brief case and pondered its implications. It was clear that Maxco was playing a more expanded game than anyone could imagine. *He is setting up Maxco-Litton to take a hard fall*, he thought, pleased with himself for uncovering the last cog in the wheel. *Wow, drug inventories could end up on the black market. He plans to dump the vaccine before FDA approval. This is his backup! What an ambitious and dangerous plan.*

Roger's office door was slightly ajar when Elizabeth gave it a light tap and stepped into the room.

"Elizabeth, what a pleasant surprise," Roger said. "It's been a while. Is the audit moving forward?"

"Yes, Roger, as you know, that will take some time. I did want to ask you a question. There seems to have been a glitch in our report generated by the mainframe computer regarding the inventory control program. Do you have any knowledge of unusual amounts of inventory being stocked and held in our warehouses?"

"I did receive a report yesterday from one of the technicians," he replied. "It appears that we are temporarily overstocked in some quarters due to computer malfunctions. Your information is correct. In my opinion, it will be corrected shortly and we will be making adjustments in production. We should be back to normal in ten days or so."

"How is Tom Elliot progressing with the Galen II project? With all this going on Roger, you've been extremely busy."

"I appreciate your concerns, Elizabeth, but I can assure you that there is nothing going on that is not being handled." His voice was becoming more brisk. *What is she after?* he thought, irritated at the interruption.

"That's reassuring," Elizabeth responded. "I guess all this business about Marshall and Julian still has me puzzled. Have you come up with any thoughts?"

"I understand the FBI is working on the case. It's best to leave these matters in the hands of the authorities. I have no theories, Elizabeth. Do you?" She was getting to him. He stood up and turned away from her, reaching for the water pitcher. He took ample time to fill his glass, doing his best to not appear ruffled.

"No, Roger, I don't feel qualified to comment on these issues. Well, thank you for your time. You will apprise me of any significant development?"

"Of course, Elizabeth," Roger replied, "I will keep you informed."

The conversation had not been comfortable. Elizabeth was not her usual self. She was asking too many questions. Roger was particularly disturbed that she was looking into inventory control. No one knew about the stockpiling, no one. Jack Drummer, the production supervisor, didn't know enough to ask questions, the workers didn't care what they were producing. They were paid too well to ask questions. And the warehouse manager did just what he was told. *What does she know?* he pressed his fingers against his temples, trying to alleviate the stress.

"Carol," he shouted, "get me Tom Elliot on my secure line." After a few moments, Carol buzzed Roger.

"He's on the line, Mr. Maxco." The response was almost immediate.

"Tom, listen carefully. I want you to go ahead with final preparations on the new vaccine. I need as much as I can get. Complete the formula and have it in the hands of Jack Drummer, my production supervisor by the end of the week."

"But we don't have FDA—"

"Forget about the FDA. Just have it ready for Jack. Is that clear?"

"We can't distribute it without FDA approval," replied Tom.

"It's not going out through regular channels Tom. I have my own distribution system. I'll explain later."

"I don't have a handle on the side effects data. The report's still too sketchy."

"What the hell is this, Tom. All of a sudden you are Mother Teresa? Do your job—this isn't new to you. Are we on the same page or not?"

"You caught me by surprise, Roger. There's no problem. I'll have the documentation by week's end." By the time he had finished speaking, the phone had gone dead.

"Carol, get me Jack Drummer."

Jack Drummer was an old friend of Roger's from the days before Maxco-Litton. An experienced pharmacist and production manager, he had been with Roger at the last company. He was the only one who knew the story of Roger's questionable past. Roger knew he could trust him as long as the money was there. It was a convenient partnership.

"He is on the line Mr. Maxco."

"Jack, this is Roger."

"Yes, Roger. What's going on?"

"I know we are set with the our current stock of inventory. Included in the shipments will be the new vaccine. Tom Elliot will be in touch by the end of the week. Gear up for production—one hundred thousand vials in each shipment. We can sell as much as we can produce. But I need it yesterday!"

"Yes, Sir. We'll give double-time and have round-the-clock shifts. No problem."

"Good!" Roger slammed the phone down and swiveled around in his chair, looking out at the city he nearly owned. "There!" he muttered. "It's done, no more pussy-footing around! I'll make every goddamn deadline! The bastards!"

The weekend brought relief to all those under pressure at Maxco-Litton. It was only temporary relief to Tom Elliot, Jack

Drummer, and the rest of Roger's staff assigned the task of producing more vaccine with a newer formula. Although this cancer vaccine had been modified to keep the risk factors manageable, it still was not perfected. And since the formula had changed, actual production would be no small task. The allocation of resources to Roger's pet project would not be easy to keep confidential. Other related matters were already drawing the attention of Elizabeth and Gus Lanton.

The gathering storm was punctuated by an early morning telephone call to Roger's office.

"Mr. Maxco, Ms. Weitzel is on the phone. I have her holding. Do you wish to take the call?" Roger was stunned. *Why in the hell is she calling me*? He gathered his wits and agreed to take the call.

"This is Roger Maxco."

"Mr. Maxco, this is Kimberly Weitzel. I'm Julian's daughter. You do remember Dr. Weitzel." It was a facetious remark that set the tone for the conversation.

"Of course I do, Kimberly. He was our most valued employee. You have my condolences. I am sorry for your loss."

"I thought I would see you at his funeral. You must be extremely busy." Roger was no longer interested in superfluous banter.

"What can I do for you, Kimberly?"

"Mr. Maxco, I have friend working with me to help settle my fathers business. It is time to retrieve his personal effects. Hopefully, his office has not been disturbed and I can take possession of his personal things. I have scheduled Wednesday to accomplish this. Perhaps you can arrange for my entrance into the building at Lake Placid? And to his office, please. I hope you will accommodate me?"

"This isn't much notice, Kimberly. Our lawyers will need time to review our position with respect to Julian's effects, etc."

"I don't understand. I am entitled to all his personal effects. What are you talking about?"

"Kimberly, Julian signed an Employment Agreement, a Confidentiality Agreement, and a Non-Compete Agreement. Surely you realize that most of his writings belong to Maxco-Litton. Insofar as his personal effects, I can certainly arrange to have those items delivered to you."

"Mr. Maxco, I insist on seeing my father's office. Please inform your people that I will be in Lake Placid Tuesday evening and I will be at the laboratory on Wednesday morning. I don't think at this sensitive time at Maxco-Litton, you want the media breathing down your neck."

He understood her meaning and responded curtly, "I will have one of the board members meet with you, Kimberly. His name is Earnest Lasko. He is knowledgeable and should be more than helpful. Please ask for him at the reception desk. Shall we say 10:00 a.m. Wednesday?"

"Thank you, Mr. Maxco. I look forward to meeting with Mr. Lasko. Good day sir."

"Let me know if there is anything else I can help you with, Kimberly. I'm sure we can satisfy your requests. Goodbye."

"Son of a bitch," Roger muttered as he hung up the phone. *This damn broad shows up now. Shit!*

"Carol, call Earnest and have him meet me in my office. It's important. And get Tom Elliot on the phone."

Roger's brain was racing ahead trying to determine what she had in her head. What was she looking for? Roger's thoughts were interrupted.

"Mr. Maxco, Earnest is on his way and Tom Elliot is on line two."

"Roger, this is Tom Elliot."

"Tom, you are going to have a visitor on Wednesday. It's Julian's daughter. I want you to stay with her as long as she hangs around. I'm sending Earnest there to help you. Don't allow her to talk to any of the staff. She will be collecting her father's personal effects. Has any of that stuff been disturbed?"

"No, Sir," Tom said. "I have kept his office pretty much as it was. Of course, I have removed notes and documentation that pertain directly to the project. There are still several less important files there. Shall I clean out all the Maxco-Litton material?"

"Tom, before Kimberly arrives, I want you to put all of the less important material back in Julian's files. Make it look as though nothing was disturbed. Earnest is good at this sort of thing. Let him assist you. Make sure his personal files and private artifacts are in their proper place. In other words, make the office look as though we have respected his position and left things as they were, awaiting final disposition. Do you understand?"

"Yes, I will get his office ready right away. I'll keep some material out and act as if I'm reluctantly giving it to her. I'll make her feel as if we have nothing to hide."

"That's the idea, Tom. Let me know how the visit goes. She may have one other person with her. Give them a royal tour. I need to keep her in check. I'll talk to you on Wednesday."

Roger Maxco considered himself a master of deception. He wondered, though, *I may be underestimating Ms. Kimberly and her friend. They probably have a specific plan. Well, they can also be dealt with. The stakes are too high to stop now.*

Chapter Fourteen

John Rushly had finally received positive identification of the shooter. The fingerprint obtained from the gun turned in by the FBI informant, from a New York killing in 1987, did in fact match the prints found on the Sea Ray. Photo identification removed all doubt. June Barker had called and said, "As we suspected John, his name is Sweeper."

The manhunt was on with a predictable response. Through his well-organized underground, Nitti had already learned of the FBI's success. From his offices in Chicago, the mob boss made arrangements to contact his illusive, suddenly less valuable employee. Within two hours, contact had been made. Nitti cleared his throat.

"Are you aware of the situation?"

"Yes."

"It's important you leave the country. You know who to contact."

"Too risky. I'll sit tight for a few weeks."

"If you think you know best. Don't make any mistakes." Nitti's voice showed that he didn't like being challenged.

"There's no problem, Sir. Thank you for calling."

The conversation ended. Nitti had confidence, nearly absolute confidence. In the event there was a capture, Sweeper would strictly adhere to an unbreakable code of silence. However, with Nitti, there was always a backup plan. *He may have to go*, Nitti thought.

The crime figure was a little relieved that Sweeper had decided to stay in the United States. He hoped there would be no need to silence him. In the back of his mind was a recurring thought. *I might need him for a more important job.*

The Bodega Bay detective was calling Rushly to inform him about Kimberly's scheduled visit to her father's lab.

"Agent Rushly here."

"John, this is Mike Staples calling. I wanted to bring you up-to-date on some information and to assure you that Kimberly is safe."

"I have been worried, Mike. What's going on?"

"She spoke to Roger Maxco yesterday, a less than cordial conversation. However, Roger did agree to allow Kimberly to meet with a member of his staff at the laboratory in Lake Placid. She wants to pick up her father's things. I'm going with her."

"I still think it's a bad idea for you and Kimberly to be poking around New York." John knew no amount of convincing would discourage the two, and decided to make the best of it. He continued, "I received word today that her father's killer is an illusive assassin by the name of Sweeper. We believe he's in New York. Hopefully, with this information, you can convince Kimberly to leave. This case could blow wide open with serious repercussions. You must understand that Kimberly Weitzel is in danger."

"She is a determined lady, John. Believe me, I think you're right. If I can't convince her to leave, I am not going to let her out of my sight."

"Mike, you know that an experienced assassin has the edge. There is little you can do if there is a contract out on her. As a precaution, I'm having a photo sent by courier to your hotel. It should be there shortly."

"That will be helpful, John. I'll do what I can. Thanks for the information."

"Once again Mike, you people should not be this close to Maxco-Litton. We believe that Maxco is in serious trouble with other factions. Preliminary reports from a corporate audit tell me that Roger is in a desperate situation. He's getting pressure from other sources. Believe me, this is an explosive situation. *You must get Kimberly out of New York.*" He emphasized the words. He didn't want to lose another witness.

The agent was not at liberty to give Mike all the facts. He was receiving constant substantial updates from Elizabeth convincing him that there was new urgency in the investigation.

"I know you are right, John. Let me talk to her this evening and I'll get back to you. I'm beginning to sense we are in over our heads."

"You call me tomorrow, Mike. Promise?"
"Yes, definitely. Talk to you later, John."
John was beginning to feel the investigation taking on a life of its own. He kept glancing at his checklist. There was another notation to add to the growing list.

- ✓ Accidental death of Joanne Hall
- ✓ Attempt on the life of Marshall Hall
- ✓ Discovery of sinister plot—Maxco-Litton
- ✓ Murder of Marshall Hall—assailants killed by FBI agents
- ✓ Murder of Dr. Julian Weitzel in Key West
- ✓ Killing of Bahamian police officer in Nassau by killer of Weitzel
- ✓ Ongoing audit of Maxco-Litton by Elizabeth Martin
- ✓ Other players identified in medical scheme by Roger Maxco—Earnest Lasko, Tom Elliot and Michael Lowe
- ✓ Rumors of Chicago underworld figures connected to Maxco-Litton
- ✓ Weitzel's assassin identified—Sweeper traced to New York City
- ✓ Kimberly Weitzel and Mike Staples join forces and move to New York

I'm afraid of where this is headed, John thought. *The time frame is creating an explosive situation. It's time to put Roger Maxco on notice. With Kimberly now very much at risk in New York, I have no choice.* He began pacing the office, trying to think.

John Rushly was moving into a determined and aggressive posture. The stakes were too high to wait for events to unfold. He picked up the phone and dialed the private number of Elizabeth Martin.

Elizabeth had just reviewed some of the documents forwarded to her by the independent accounting firm. Although the major pieces to the puzzle were not in place, there was a disturbing trend. The telephone interrupted her thoughts.

"Elizabeth."

"Hi, it's John." He sounded intense. "How are you?"

"I'm doing okay, John. I hear that Kimberly is in town. Is she okay?"

"That's what I'm calling about. We've identified Julian's killer, at least the shooter, not the person who hired him. The man is known as Sweeper and he has been traced to New York. I am worried about Kimberly and her detective friend, Mike Staples."

"What can I do, John?"

"I want a formal meeting with Roger. I prefer that you arrange the time and place. It will be official in nature. He is a suspect in both murders. I didn't want to tip my hand at this point, but our case is developing rapidly. He needs to know he is under investigation. That might prevent any further violence, at least slow it down until we can get a handle of this case."

"This will be disruptive to the company, John. As a senior board member, I may have to recommend that he step down until his name is cleared."

"That's your call, Elizabeth. We don't have sufficient evidence to formally charge him. It may be easier to keep track of him if his position with the firm is left undisturbed. Once again, that's up to you."

Elizabeth thought of the consequences of a showdown with Roger. After a few moments, she realized that John was right.

"John, you've made an important point. Until he's formally charged, there will be no call for Roger to step down. I'll talk to him this afternoon and set up a meeting. Are you coming to New York?"

"Under the circumstances, I believe that is best. It will give me a chance to meet with you and to speak with Kimberly. Call me later and confirm the date. Tell him I want this meeting no later than Friday. That will give him two days to think about what he is involved in. It'll put some pressure on him."

"John, while you are here, we need to discuss the audit. I have some preliminary information that looks like trouble. I'll put together a synopsis and see what you think. I—"

"Yes?" he sounded warmer now, less hurried.

"I'm looking forward to seeing you again. Look for my call this afternoon. Thanks for calling, John."

"Elizabeth, please be careful. I'll talk to you later."

Now it was Elizabeth's turn to wonder what was happening.

So Roger is now a formal suspect, she thought, stunned. She could hardly believe this man whom she had admired so much could have done something so horrendous. *My God, Roger, what have you done to yourself—to the rest of us? You are destroying the company and all it stands for. Damn you!* Elizabeth buzzed Roger's private line.

"This is Carol. May I help you?"

"Carol, this is Elizabeth, please inform Roger that I must see him before he leaves this afternoon. Is he there?"

"Ms. Martin, Roger will be back shortly. I'll give him the message."

"Please tell him it's urgent."

"May I tell him what it's about?"

"Yes, you may. Tell him it's urgent." Elizabeth disconnected the call.

Sweeper was not comfortable after his brief conversation with Nitti. His finely tuned killer instincts sensed the cryptic message in his boss's voice. It was something he would keep in mind. There was no immediate threat to his wellbeing. But he had no illusions. He lived in a world of predators without scruples.

Maybe it would be better to leave, his mind wrestled with indecision. *I don't need money. What's keeping me here?* Sweeper answered his own question. *I want a normal life—maybe somewhere less chaotic—I'm finished with the gays. Goddamn it. I want to be straight*, he thought. *I was doing it for a kick; it's not a kick anymore.*

Sweeper had been fighting this battle since he was fourteen. It wasn't until he had passed thirty-eight that he became frustrated with his life style and longed for a more conventional existence. There was a girl he had met several weeks ago, and he hadn't been able to get his mind off of her. Due to his profession and his current status of hiding out, he hesitated in making the first move.

She operated a bookstore on Third Avenue in Lower Manhattan. She had invited him to stop by anytime. He would walk the thirteen blocks from his apartment and drop in for a chat. "We'll see," he muttered, preparing to leave the apartment. "It's a start."

Of course, he struggled with himself while getting dressed. W*hat do I really have to offer someone—a life of romantic adventure? I don't think so. What the hell are you thinking of Sweeper*? He chastised himself, speaking clearly to his image in the mirror, "You're a goddamn paid assassin who's lived most of his life as a homosexual—not exactly a classic start for romance and a normal life!"

The walk was uneventful except for his shattered nerves. Approaching the bookstore, Sweeper almost turned around and gave up. Then, in a burst of resolve, he walked into the small shop and noticed her behind the counter near the cash register. No one else was around.

"Hello there," he said. "Is the invitation to stop by still okay?"

She smiled prettily. "It's still open. How have you been?"

"Okay," replied Sweeper. "I did want to see you again. I have been on a job, out of town, you know. Anyway, I thought we could have coffee or a drink after you close. What do you think?"

"I think that is okay. Why don't you come by at six this evening?"

"I'll be here. It's Nancy, right?"

"Right!" she seemed pleased he'd remembered. "And you are Richard?"

"Yes, Richard." *This month it's Richard*, he thought.

"Great Richard, I'll see you at closing."

Sweeper had met Nancy at a record store two months earlier. She had an open face and a pleasing, decisive look about her—light brown hair, brown eyes, and a sweet, genuine smile. He was taken with her but still wondered, in his heart of hearts, if a relationship with a normal woman would last. He was never sure if his gay tendencies were part of his psyche' or part of his thirst for adventure. Regardless, today he was ready for a nice diversion. There was something about Nancy. Walking out of the shop, he thought happily, *this lady could be my turning point!*

Excited by his brave new attempt to change his life, Sweeper decided it was time for some new threads. There were lots of trendy shops nearby. He instructed the manager of one store to deck him out in "cool, upbeat, GQ clothing." The results were pleasantly surprising. Walking out of the store, he had the look of a successful author—soft cotton shirt with matching tie, sport jacket with taupe-colored, pleated slacks, and black Italian loafers. Looking in the mirror that reflected Sweeper's new image, the shop owner commented, "Sir, that is one handsome outfit. You really look collected. Congratulations." Sweeper thought, *He should be congratulating himself on the sale—$1475!* He paid in cash, astounding the clerk who was careful not to say anything, as if this happened all the time.

Satisfied with his new persona, Sweeper made his way back to his apartment to while away the afternoon.

Nancy Johnson was not a New Yorker. She had come to the city twelve years earlier, attended New York City College in Library Science and dreamed of opening her own specialty bookstore of first editions. After six years as an assistant, she bought out the owner, changed the name to The Mystery Hour, and began looking for a mate, precisely in that order. She had divorced her first husband six years before, at age thirty.

The man she knew as Richard had intrigued her from the beginning. *He has that self-assured, yet vulnerable look,* she thought. *There is something important going on inside this man. I want to get to know him.*

Richard returned at the appointed time. Closing the store, the nice, average-looking couple meandered three blocks up the street to a small Italian bistro. The conversation was slow and deliberate, not as natural as they had expected.

"Have you been married, Richard?"

"No," he answered simply, then added, "The right woman never came along. You?"

"Once." She blushed, nearly wishing she hadn't asked him. She didn't want him to think she was being pushy. She took a deep breath, smiled up at him, and continued, "It was several years ago. He was addicted to gambling. For two years he tried to quit. It ruined our relationship and destroyed us financially. I don't know what finally happened to him. I never saw him again."

Richard grinned. The conversation was becoming more relaxed.

"Richard, I have to tell you. I really like the transformation. You look incredibly handsome."

Damn, she has my number, he thought. *These clothes and me must look out of place.*

Noticing his dark look, she hurried to correct herself. "I shouldn't have used the word 'transformation.' But it's such a change from earlier. You look great, believe me."

"I guess I'm a little self-conscious. I needed a change. They feel great. Thanks for the compliment."

It was nine-thirty before they reluctantly gave up their table and walked out into the cool night air.

"How about lunch tomorrow, Nancy?"

"You're on, Richard. I have an employee coming in at 11:30. Anytime after that will be fine."

"Let's get a cab. I'll drop you off and then go home."

"I like that Richard—no pressure. You're a sweet man. Thanks for a lovely evening."

Sweeper arrived at his apartment around 10:00 p.m. A dark Fleetwood Cadillac was parked a half block down the street within view of his front door. It seemed unusual, and Sweeper decided to investigate. He casually entered his apartment, then climbed out a back window. Moving stealthily down the block, careful to stay out of sight, he approached the Cadillac from behind. He saw that the driver's window was open. Slipping quickly up behind him, he growled with an animal instinct, "There is a weapon with an armored piercing bullet aimed at your gut. Tell me what you are doing here and who hired you? Keep your hands on the wheel." Sweeper noticed the man was alone.

"Hey, I don't know nothin'. What the hell are you doing?" Nervous, the driver heard the distinctive "click" of the hammer being cocked, ready to fire.

"One last chance. What're you doing and who hired you?"

Having been briefed on the man he was hired to watch, the driver decided to tell the truth. He was not willing to gamble with his life. "Okay, Mr. Nitti gave me the job. He wanted you to be safe, that's all."

"Thank you. Tell Mr. Nitti that I don't want anyone watching me. The next time, there will be no warning. Do you understand?"

"No problem, Pal. Look, it's just a job. I didn't mean nothin' by it."

"Move it. And consider yourself sufficiently warned. Nobody follows me without consequences. If I were you, I'd find another zip code."

Sweeper knew that Nitti was just being cautious and keeping his options open. *But it was a careless act and not too bright,* Sweeper thought, angrily. *Nitti will get the message,* he thought.

That night, Sweeper thought for hours and hours. *If it were possible to move and take Nancy with me that would be acceptable. What am I saying?* He'd catch himself daydreaming and bring himself back into check. *I don't even know her. Am I turning into a hopeless romantic? Besides, she has her own dream, The Mystery Hour. I must be crazy. We'll see what happens tomorrow.* He tossed and turned all night.

The morning came with a slight drizzle and cloud cover. It was refreshing, but a heady day for Sweeper. He had dreamed he and Nancy were madly in love until she found out what he had been doing the past years. He awoke in a sweat.

I'm going casual today, he thought, his hands shaking as he stood before the mirror trying to tie his necktie. "All right, goddamn it," he spit, giving up after the third try to make the ends come out straight. He cursed to himself, "Get a grip, you stupid bastard!" *What had this woman done to him,* he thought helplessly.

It was nearly noon when he dropped into the bookstore. There were two customers but Nancy's assistant had arrived so Nancy was free to go.

"Right on time, Richard." She smiled happily. "By the way," she teased, "how come you have so much free time? Are you independently wealthy?" The questions had already begun, as he knew they would.

"I am financially comfortable—no debts." His voice showed his irritation.

"I guess that sounded nosy, sorry." She hated herself for putting him on guard. *When would she learn?* She vowed to be more cautious.

"No, I have no secrets, Nancy. Not from you." He relaxed a little. "You need to know that I'm not a bum."

Lunch was delightful. This time, Sweeper found a gourmet French restaurant that featured light but tasty fare. They sipped on a bottle of wine from the vineyards near the Normandy coast.

"I'm feeling a little tipsy, Richard," she giggled. "Forgive me for being so forward, but I must tell you that I find you extremely attractive. I could easily fall for you."

There was silence as Richard savored each word. He took a long drink from the crystal wineglass before reciprocating. He wanted to enjoy this perfect moment.

"Nancy, I feel the same way. It's been a long time since I've felt anything for anyone."

"For me, too, Richard. But you and I seem to have a real connection, don't we?" she reached across the table and took his hand without any embarrassment.

"Nancy," he said softly, "I must let you know that I may have to move. I don't want to leave—it's my position. I know it's presumptuous of me—you with your store and all—but I think we might have a chance at a life together." He began to stumble, realizing this was totally absurd yet knowing he had never been more sincere in his life. *My God,* he thought, *what is this? I've never felt like this. What the hell am I doing?*

"Wow!" She laughed nervously, pulling away from him. "Why don't you tell me what you really feel?" Look, Richard, I appreciate what you're saying but, —it's taken me a long time to build my dream, from scratch. And in time, I may be willing to give it up, but not after two dates." She was at once flattered and confused.

"I'm so stupid at this, Nancy. What a dumb ass! You're absolutely right. We barely know each other. I didn't mean to push."

Both were enamored with each other and the outpouring of emotion had brought them even closer. Calling her assistant, Nancy asked if she could handle the store for the rest of the afternoon. They went back to her apartment, as if in some romantic dream. There was no hesitation and fewer reservations. They both were surprised at the intensity they felt and easily expressed without knowing each other. Later in the evening, they sat in front of the television and had leftover pasta from Nancy's fridge.

Reeling from all that had happened, Sweeper started to apologize. "I have been pushy, Nancy. God, I don't want you to get the wrong idea. I'm just so attracted to you!" Taking her hand to his lips, he whispered quietly, "There' is no need for me to move immediately. The job can wait."

"Let's talk about it in a few weeks, Richard. I'm afraid we'll

ruin a good thing by moving too fast. Okay?"
"You're right, Nancy. We'll take our time."
There would be no gentle lovemaking that night. Mutual respect and consideration once again had given way to lust. *I've never felt like this before*, Sweeper thought, feeling more fulfilled than he ever had with a man.

Chapter Fifteen

The meeting between the FBI agent and his adversary had been set for Friday at four. Elizabeth had been surprised at Roger's reaction. He had stated in no uncertain terms,

"Elizabeth, I have nothing to fear from the FBI. They are mistaken if they believe I have had anything to do with two brutal murders. It's a ridiculous assumption and I am anxious to clear my name."

John notified Mike Staples that he was meeting Roger on Friday and wished to see Kimberly later that evening. Mike agreed, and they arranged to have dinner together. Kimberly was eager to see John and report on the trip made to Lake Placid.

The twin towers of the World Trade Center gives one a feeling of admiration for what man is able to create, John thought, standing on the sidewalk in awe and remembering his dramatic impressions from Ayn Rand's *The Fountainhead*. He shuddered to imagine what the CEO was capable of destroying. He had met briefly with Elizabeth, then was shown to her employer's outer office. Carol, Roger's secretary, offered John coffee and stated very efficiently that Mr. Maxco would be available in a few minutes.

Dressed in a dark gray, single-breasted suit, John's appearance was professional but understated. His manner was cool and efficient.

"Mr. Rushly, what a pleasure, I'm Roger Maxco." Roger emerged from his private office, appearing smiling and confident. The two men looked each other over, neither ready to tip his hand.

"Maxco, thank you for taking the time to see me." The two men retired to Roger's office. The CEO led the way to the burgundy leather chairs in the corner of his office, giving the appearance of a less than formal meeting.

"I felt there was little choice, John—if we may speak on a first name basis." Maxco had bristled at the agent's obvious omission of his courtesy title.

"Yes, of course, Roger." John's eyes were direct, intense, and he showed no signs of backing down. He had met too many men like this. The entrapment of white-collar criminals had become his specialty.

"Elizabeth informed me that this meeting was official on your part. How can I assist you, John?"

"I'm sure you are aware that the FBI is investigating the murders of Marshall Hall and Julian Weitzel. In addition, we believe Weitzel's killer was also responsible for the death of a policeman in Nassau. The man has been identified and tracked to New York."

"Excuse me, John, but what have I to do with all of this?"

"I'll be frank, Roger. Certain papers recovered from Marshall Hall, together with notes taken during a personal interview I had with him, point to improprieties on your part that could have given you motive to order these killings. Of course, you are under no obligation to offer any comments, certainly not incriminating statements, regarding these matters."

"This is outrageous!" Roger sputtered, standing up to face his accuser.

"If I may continue, Roger—" John refused to get ruffled. He knew he had the upper hand. Without waiting for the reply, the agent continued. "I am here for one purpose today. You are aware that Julian's daughter is in New York. In fact, she recovered certain documents from her father's office at Lake Placid. Let's say you should take the following statement, off the record, as good advice: Whatever you are planning with Maxco-Litton, do not risk the lives of any innocent people. Kimberly Weitzel is not to be harmed. Do you need me to repeat that?" His eyes had become daggers. *I refuse to lose another person to this sleazy bastard,* he thought angrily. He hadn't expected to feel the intense hatred that he was feeling toward this man.

"I am afraid I must stop this nonsense, Mr. Rushly. The tone of your comments along with the fanciful innuendo is not acceptable. Unless I am under arrest, this meeting is concluded. I take offense, Rushly, at your statements.

"Take all the offense you want," John replied, allowing himself to laugh out loud at the pompous ass. "But let me remind—"

"No, let me remind you, Mr. Rushly," Maxco interrupted the agent. "I rescued this firm and prepared it for the twenty-first century. Maxco-Litton has saved the lives of millions of people through our flawless research and the manufacture of new products. How dare you make these outlandish statements."

"I agree, Maxco," John stood, staring his enemy in the face. "This meeting is over. I see through you, Sir—and I don't like what I see. Good day."

John Rushly had made his point. Roger Maxco was on notice. The FBI was investigating him and the push for an indictment was on. Neither man moved. The heat in the room became oppressive as Roger began to sweat. John looked into Roger's eyes as if to confirm his resolve to bring this man down. Roger had not imagined the stinging verbal abuse to which he had been subjected to by the powerful and convincing presence of John Rushly. John nodded slightly as he turned and left the room.

A shaken Roger Maxco, as if he were a robot given a specific order, walked jerkily to the credenza and poured himself a double scotch, neat. The world of Maxco-Litton, as he knew it, was closing in—he had been ill prepared for this onslaught.

"Mr. Rushly," Elizabeth found him by the elevator, "was the meeting productive?"

John turned in her direction as she came closer, taking a second to admire her pristine elegance. Still ruffled from the emotion of the meeting, he took a moment to respond. "Yes, Elizabeth, it was. I believe Roger Maxco knows, in no uncertain terms, exactly where I stand. The conversation was not by the FBI manual," he laughed. "But I believe he got the message."

"Can we meet later?" Elizabeth replied. Her question was personal.

He hesitated, a warning bell going off in his head. She was so sophisticated, so beautiful. He cleared his throat, feeling a little discomfort, "I'm having dinner with Kimberly and Mike Staples. You could meet me for breakfast at my hotel, if you like. I have to leave around 10:30 in the morning."

"Okay John. I'll meet you at eight." Her innate poise carefully concealed the disappointment she felt.

"See you then, Elizabeth."

The elevator doors closed between them and John was alone with his thoughts, thoughts of the sleazy CEO he had just confronted. He had learned early in the game that people under pressure make mistakes. And Roger was no exception. Other matters going on in Roger's life compounded the pressure—and the FBI knew about most of them. The connection with Nitti and the pressure of an impossible deadline to repay a massive amount of money, the audit that threatened to bring down the company before Roger was ready, the timetable for the production of the black market drugs to the Russians, all made Roger Maxco nervous, very nervous. The FBI was becoming more aware, but pieces were still missing.

And now, there was another matter that John Rushly was looking into—the sudden disappearance of Earnest Lasko. The superficial story told by unsuspecting Maxco-Litton employees to FBI undercover agents in the cafeteria was that he had a nervous breakdown and his family had taken him home to Kansas. It didn't make sense. John's preliminary investigation confirmed that his family in Kansas had not heard from him in months. He had literally disappeared.

Mike and Kimberly were seated and having relaxing, before-dinner drinks when John appeared.

"Mike, I don't believe we have met. I'm John Rushly." Kimberly stood up and hugged her protector. She hadn't seen him since Phoenix.

"I'm glad you're here," she said. "Sorry if I've caused you any trouble, John. Mike has been filling me in on your conversations."

"Right now, we seem to be safe. That's the main thing. I have been worried Kimberly. The case is turning ugly. I had an unfriendly chat with Maxco this afternoon. I wanted to let him know that he is a prime suspect in the deaths of Marshall Hall and your father. He got my message loud and clear."

"Give John the package, Mike." Kimberly had made copies of all the documents she was able to retrieve from her father's laboratory.

Mike handed the manila legal folder to John. "John, while Kimberly was being escorted through the lab, I managed to glean a few choice papers from a file cabinet *not* set aside for our visit. The reception in Lake Placid was well planned. I knew there wouldn't be much original material they would give us. Anyway, the papers I am referring to seem to be technical in nature but they refer to the FDA. Your people may be able to make sense of them."

"Good work, you two. Now, you're fired!" Everyone laughed, but they knew what John was suggesting.

"In other words," Kimberly responded, "you want us out of New York."

Just then, the waiter took the orders and all three, as if they were having a social dinner, finally relaxed.

"A lot of things are happening on several fronts with Maxco-Litton," John said, carefully buttering a hot roll. "It's in the hands of the FBI and other agencies now. You have done your part, Kimberly. It's time to go home and let us finish. I can assure you that each and every person who had anything to do with the deaths of Marshall and your father will be prosecuted. There is a lot more to do, but in time, I want you to stay safe, and that doesn't mean in New York! There's only so much we can do," he said, gesturing at Mike with his butter knife, "to protect you. Don't worry, we'll get the job done."

"Yeah, yeah," she mocked him gently. "What a speech, John. Okay, we'll go back to California. Incidentally, John," she blushed, hesitating. "Mike and I have found that we kind of like each other."

"You know, Kimberly," John laughed easily, "I kind of suspected that. It must be the cop in me." Mike looked a little sheepish, then reached over affectionately to touch Kimberly's hand. *It's good to see Kimberly having fun again*, John thought.

"I feel that I need to clear the air, for some reason," she continued. "You both know that I loved Marshall. It wasn't right, but it happened. John, Mike and I have mutual respect for each other. Everything's on the up and up. That means a lot to me, now. But I want to thank you for what you are doing. I know it's your job, but I have felt your understanding and compassion for me. I appreciate it more than you know."

"You're very welcome, Kimberly, but your steak's getting cold." He smiled warmly.

Mike Staples was a happy guy. He knew when he first met Kimberly that he was hooked. Raising his glass of Samuel Adams, he said, "To good friends—forever."

"To good friends!" they responded.

The next morning, Elizabeth arrived at John's hotel and called his room. He answered on the third ring.

"Good morning, John. I'm downstairs. Are you awake?"

"Yes, Elizabeth, just finished shaving. Order coffee and I'll be right down."

John hurriedly finished packing since he would check out after having breakfast with Elizabeth. He would take a cab to the airport. Dressed casually for the trip, he matched Elizabeth for Saturday morning dress.

"Good morning, Elizabeth. You look relaxed. First time I've seen you in slacks. You look nice. Have you ordered?" He shouldn't have said anything that personal, he thought. He really loved his wife, but this woman was so elegant, just so perfectly poised, it was hard not to be attracted to her.

"Coffee's here." She poured for him, then looked into his eyes. "I thought I would wait for you to order." A perky waitress stood by waiting for her cue. John ordered the Spanish omelet and Elizabeth ordered a poached egg on wheat toast. Elizabeth continued. "Well, how was the meeting with Roger, John?"

"Not really my style, Elizabeth but I had to make a point. I wanted to make sure that Roger wasn't too cocky about his scheme with the FDA and the killings. He is on notice. I want him to think before he acts. My main concern was Kimberly. She could be in danger, not to mention you."

"Me?" she replied. "Why me? He doesn't know I'm helping you, I've been very careful to keep our conversations private."

"Let's face it, Elizabeth, this audit of yours is already causing trouble. There's motive in those numbers. You could be an important witness for the government."

"Are you sure Roger is in that deep?" There was still a longing by Elizabeth that there really wasn't a strong case. This company was her life.

"Too many circumstantial pieces fitting together along with

some hard facts—like the financial manipulations. You know that, Elizabeth, what with—"

"It's so pat John—are you sure?" she seemed unable to grasp the import of what he was saying.

"This isn't like you, Elizabeth. Am I missing something?"

"No, you're right John. It's just that Roger has done so much for the company. He never seemed as if he could be an evil person."

There was something different about Elizabeth this morning, John thought. Maybe she is sorrowful about Roger—definitely something different.

"On Monday, Elizabeth, would you fax me the latest reports dealing with Roger's stock purchases and sales. I am particularly interested if any assets have been pledged."

"I should be able to get that out by midmorning John. That will be about 2:00 p.m. your time."

"Hey, look at this food. Are you sure an egg and toast will be enough for you?"

"John, you're a very smart man—handsome and smart. I hope we can remain friends."

"I don't see any reason we shouldn't," John remarked. He was reading something else into that statement.

John ordered a cab, terminating the breakfast meeting. They shook hands and went their separate ways. *This lady is in some kind of trouble,* John thought. *She is so bright and strong. I'm sure she can handle whatever it is.* John's thoughts turned to Phoenix and Jill. *I'll be home soon sweetheart. Whew! Close one!* He threw his bag into the trunk and got into the back seat for the ride to the airport.

Nitti had received the message from his lookout that Sweeper was not happy he was being watched. The message didn't matter. The inner sanctum of the Chicago group, consisting of Nitti and two other Mob bosses, had made their decision. Sweeper would leave the country, one way or the other. Arrangements had been made for an extended European vacation. This time, there would be no choice for the paid assassin. He was, after all, an employee. He would do what he was told.

"We are in agreement," Nitti said. "Any reservations?"

"Do we meet again in the event he refuses?" It was a legitimate question for the others since Nitti would be the one to issue the order to terminate Sweeper should he not choose to leave the country.

"There will be no need to meet again regarding this matter. He will leave or he will be taken care of."

The network of informants Nitti had cultivated over the years had provided startling facts relating to the FBI manhunt and investigation of Maxco-Litton. It was decided there was little choice for the Chicago group other than encouraging Sweeper to disappear. Nitti concluded the meeting.

"That arrogant bastard." Roger was directing his comments to Michael Lowe. "He thinks he is so goddamn smart. He repeated Rushly's words to his lawyer, " 'I have word that the assassin hired to do the Weitzel job has been identified. The FBI is conducting a massive manhunt.'— John Rushly is smart, Michael. Let's not underestimate him. My concern is with the people who hired this Sweeper or whoever he is. They are probably nervous about that situation."

"Shit! Suppose they catch him and he talks. Are we insulated?" Michael knew that sooner or later they all could be implicated if people started to talk. "Be glad there is no one to tie us to the Marshall Hall incident," he said.

"Some incident," replied Roger, but what about this Sweeper?"

"That's Chicago business—it's their problem, not ours." Michael was attempting to calm Roger, but decided to offer his opinion with respect to related matters. "It's important we keep things on a fast track. Is the !ab responding? What about Elliot?"

"At least it's weeks, now, not months. He's coming through. Meantime, regarding drug production, there's too much warehoused. It's showing up on paper because of our computerized inventory system of bins in the warehouse. Goddamnit! We set it up for efficiency, now it's too efficient. We can't hide product, anymore." He was pacing now. "I have to cover the inventory surpluses. Elizabeth is getting suspicious. You're right, all of this has to happen soon. Time is running out.

Speaking of the surpluses, Gus Lanton has been looking into a few items that really are not his business. I want you to do a background check. Remember, he came into the firm when I did, basically an unknown. I never took the time to figure out just where he came from. I was too busy rebuilding the firm." Roger stopped to sit down and light a cigar. It always relaxed him.

"You may be getting paranoid, Roger." Michael leaned over the table by his leather chair to pour a hot, steaming mug of coffee. "Gus seems to be a competent but rather benign member of the board. Let's not start looking under rocks for communists."

"Okay, Michael," Roger said, "anyway, check him out. He can't do us a lot of damage—the stuff he looks at is normal paperwork. I can't have anything screw up the initial transfer of funds—that's two hundred million dollars. Those inventories must be ready for simultaneous shipment. We have forty-five days!"

"Any qualms from Tom Elliot?" Michael asked.

"No problems," replied Roger. "He has assured me there were no production problems. The vaccine will be ready and the shipments will be on schedule. Those are his exact words."

"We need to keep it all moving, Roger, but don't make any waves. We have the FBI, Elizabeth, Nitti and his gang and a guy named Sweeper to worry about. Stay focused. Okay?"

"I understand, Michael. Do your part—my job will be done."

"Incidentally, Roger, what about Kimberly and the California detective. Have they left town?"

"They think they found what they wanted. I don't see a problem. I suspect they're leaving."

"Just observe," Michael suggested, "we need to keep a very low profile. We don't need any unnecessary attention. You're the boss, Roger, but listen to me on this one. John Rushly is watching you closely. My information suggests he really likes Kimberly. I think he feels responsible for not getting to her father in time."

"Right, Michael. Thanks for the suggestions. But remember who's in charge. That's it for today. Keep me advised. You stick to the legal matters, I'll take care of the rest."

Michael Lowe was used to Roger's caustic behavior, especially when stressed. The meeting was over with one parting comment. Michael couldn't resist. "Be sure you do, Roger. The stakes are high." He walked out before the CEO could have the last word.

Chapter Sixteen

For three full days, Sweeper and Nancy were lost in a whirlwind of passion, something neither of them had known before. By the end of the fourth day, Sweeper had moved his few meager possessions into Nancy's apartment. Although an ardent relationship from the start, there was a measure of caution due to their respective independence. During their first dinner as a live-in couple, Nancy's remark said it all.

"Richard, the respect we have for each other's personal space will make this work. Most men I've found aren't interested in sharing a life with an independent, career woman. It takes quite a man, a secure man, to handle this."

"And quite a woman, a secure woman, to accept a man on face value, a man she knows little about. I won't disappoint you, Nancy. We'll make it work." As if on cue, they both got up to clear the table. He was already enjoying the domestic, quieter side of life. *It just wouldn't bother me at all*, Sweeper thought, while stacking the dishes, *if all the drama and trauma were behind me. I really like this.*

At nine o'clock, Dan Rather was doing a promo of an upcoming story and updating an earlier report— "prominent scientist, Dr. Julian Weitzel had been murdered in Key West and was the subject of an ongoing FBI investigation." The anchor mentioned the New York firm, Maxco-Litton. Nancy was surprised when Sweeper angrily jumped up and abruptly turned off the set.

"Hey, what's that about?" Nancy asked, obviously irritated. "We could have our first fight. I'm a fan of Dan Rather—besides, that was a New York story."

"I just wanted to look at you, undisturbed. Sorry." He made no effort to turn the TV back on.

"Well, relax," she responded, smiling. "Easy does it, okay?" She felt a sense of discomfort, but decided not to press. *Did he move in too soon?* she thought.

The past week, with its visit from Charles Nitti's goon, had nearly been forgotten. But his dark past lurked in the recesses of Sweeper's mind. The next morning, Nancy had left for her store. The quiet and solitude gave way to thoughts of what had been and what could be.

I can't erase what has been, thought Sweeper. *Maybe the time will come when Nancy and I can move forward and not be prisoners of years gone bye. I'll take today and let things unfold.*

It didn't take long for things to unfold. Usually, when there was a new job for Sweeper, there would be a brief message left for him at his favorite antique store in Greenwich Village. If urgent, the message was relayed to an answering service and held for Sweeper. He decided to check for messages.

"This is 7201. Do I have any messages?"

"Yes, sir, please call CN. It's dated 6-6, sir. That's all."

The timing is not right for a new assignment, Sweeper thought, *maybe it's something else. Shit, he left the message yesterday!* He walked outside to a pay phone so there would never be a record of the call to Nancy's apartment.

The Chicago crime boss picked up his private line, sensing who the caller was even before checking the Caller ID.

"Yes, it's quiet here, go ahead."

"I am responding to your call. By the way," Sweeper said cheerily, "I hope you are not disturbed by my last communication."

"That was understandable," Nitti replied gruffly. "Something new is in the works. It's time to leave. They are too close. You agree?"

"I need time—a few weeks."

"Not acceptable—three days."

There was silence between the two men. Sweeper gathered his thoughts, realizing this was a direct order.

"All right," he responded stiffly, "three days."

"Good luck. Let us know where you can be reached. You know where to go?"

"Yes, I'll be in touch. Good bye."

Sweeper had never been in a position of confrontation with his employers. It had never mattered. Now there was Nancy. He would spend the day trying to figure out his next move. *Whatever it is,* he vowed, *Nancy will be a part of it. How to explain this,* he wondered.

The Command Center in New York, that had been set up to coordinate the search for Sweeper, was in high gear. There was an electrical tension in the air. Fred Rowley had been with the FBI in the New York Field Office for three years. Young and inexperienced, he was still one of the most dedicated agents in the office. He made the call to the Phoenix agent.

"Agent Rushly, we wanted you to know that we think Sweeper was spotted four days ago. We followed up the lead and discovered that your man left his apartment abruptly. There is not a trace. We don't believe he has left town—just moved. He was seen in the company of a lady the day before yesterday— unidentified. I wanted to keep you apprised."

"Good work, Fred. Keep in mind that he has other things to worry about, aside from the authorities. He can't be popular with his employers right now. They obviously know about the extra murder of the cop in Nassau and know he has been identified. We have seen to that."

"Good work! What did you do? The young agent laughed. He loved this business.

"Our mole in the Bureau has been identified, but he doesn't know it. We gave him the information that we wanted out—it works perfectly. Think we'll keep him as a mole." John laughed and was glad his colleague could appreciate their tactic.

"I get it. Yes, I would say there are others vitally interested in the whereabouts of our man Sweeper. We'll keep that in mind."

"Thanks for the call, Fred. Incidentally, Kimberly Weitzel and Mike Staples are supposed to be leaving New York tomorrow. That should be a relief to you guys."

"Definitely," Fred replied. "We're observing them just to be safe. I'll get off the line, John. Anything else?"

"No, thanks for calling, Fred. Talk to you later."

On Tuesday, June 9th, one day before Sweeper's deadline to leave the country, Sweeper decided to delay his conversation with

Nancy. His plan would not solve any long-range problem but it would buy him some time. He waited in the apartment for her return from The Mystery Hour.

"You look wonderful as usual. How was your day?"

"Having fun, waiting to come home to you—not a bad life!" She kicked off her shoes and walked into his arms.

They settled for an early dinner at home. Sweeper had bought wine, and had chopped vegetables for stir-fry. He prepared dinner, as she perched herself on the barstool, sipping White Zinfandel and watching him. Trying to sound as natural as possible, he approached the subject carefully.

"Nancy, I have to go away for a few days. It's an account I've been working on for a while. I didn't think it would pan out, but the people in San Francisco are excited to get it going."

"San Francisco?" she asked. What's going on, Richard? You're not married or something." It was the "something" she was worried about. This was a little too sudden in light of what had been going on.

"Hey, no! Don't be silly!" he laughed, trying to allay her fears. "It just came up. It may be a real break for me."

Sweeper had referred to his healthy commissions, independent contracts and out of town trips, but had naturally failed to mention the exact nature of his business. Locating clients for publishing houses was his story, and seemed quite nebulous to Nancy.

"What exactly do you do, Richard?" She hated herself for being suspicious, but sensed something out of place. An intelligent woman, Nancy had never been taken in by anyone.

"I'm a kind of broker," he explained, "like I receive commissions when book publishers sign on with someone I sent them. It's not complicated. You just need a lot of contacts. Most of my business is done in either San Francisco or New York, sometimes in LA if I get someone a screenplay deal. Those are the largest contracts." He hoped he sounded convincing.

The explanation was becoming more plausible. Nancy wanted it to be plausible. Since she owned a bookstore, she was familiar with various publishing houses and thought she might be able to understand his business better if they could discuss it.

Taking a sip of wine, she asked thoughtfully, "Do you do any business with Ingram, Richard?" Ingram being the largest book distributor in the world, Nancy thought she might have found some common ground for discussion.

This wasn't going at all well for Sweeper. He had painted himself into a corner and chastised himself for being so stupid to start a subject he knew absolutely nothing about.

"Not really, Nancy. I don't actually order books for anyone—I'm just a finder for the publishers."

"Don't the publishers go through agents." She kept pressing, now totally confused. "Are you a literary agent?" She sensed something was wrong, and not with her questioning.

"I mainly work for the vanity press—self published books. The author pays for all the services. Are we finished with the twenty questions now?" He made no move to camouflage his irritation, knowing she would stop.

It was the first hint of real tension between them. Although Sweeper certainly hadn't passed the test, Nancy's emotions were deep enough that she chose not to press the issue further. She would do anything at this point to prevent losing him. "I'm sorry, sweetheart." She backed off with a smile. "All of this came so soon—I'll miss you terribly. I was concerned—you are kind of a mystery, you know." Still uneasy with his cryptic responses, Nancy was determined not to go any further.

"I guess I'm the sorry one, Nancy. I'm not use to being grilled."

"You take your trip and have fun. Get some work done and make some money. I love you for it. Whatever you do is fine with me." She hoped she had smoothed over the edges.

Turning to the refrigerator for a second bottle of chilled wine, Sweeper breathed a sigh of relief. Nancy was fine and Nitti would be satisfied for awhile. He knew if they were watching him, a trip to San Francisco would not meet the conditions set during the phone call. "Leave," meant leave for Europe. He would have to take great care.

Setting the table together, they were quieter than usual. *What a lousy feeling*, reflected Sweeper, *lying to the woman I'm falling in love with. Lies and deception. When will it all end? She doesn't deserve this; she doesn't deserve me. How long can it go on?*

Watching her gracefully place the cloth napkins beside the plates, he thought, wistfully, *Maybe I could get a job with a real publisher—that would make it okay. I can tell the others that I am no longer available—for any job. If they won't let me go, I'll kill them. Wait a minute; the killing ends here and now.* Noticing that she was behaving a little more tense than usual, he reached out and pulled her gently to him. Breathing softly into her hair, he surrounded her with his arms and it felt so good.

"Are we okay, Nancy? I don't want anything to ruin this."

"Yes," she looked up, her eyes misty and loving, "we're okay."

June 10—New York City

"Sir, he boarded a flight to San Francisco. I can't tell if he has any connecting flights."

Nitti listened closely to the caller before responding. "Don't lose him. If he stays any length of time in San Francisco, you know what to do."

"How long?"

"It's Wednesday. If he isn't on an international flight by Saturday, game's over."

"Yes, Sir, I understand"

Sweeper had been careful, but for the time being, had overlooked the slim ordinary looking man in 12-C. He fit in too well with all the other passengers. The flight was nearly full. A pawnshop in Chinatown had been alerted that a slight gentlemen identified as Louis would pick up the special order on Thursday. It was a small caliber handgun with a silencer—not registered and not traceable.

Leaning back in his seat as the 707 climbed to thirty thousand feet, Sweeper once again contemplated his life. *What's this accomplishing except buying a little time to try to come up with a plan? What will I do about Nancy?* He was so distraught, he did something he never did on a flight, because it took the edge off his caution. He asked for two bottles of Scotch and downed them both.

Now more mellow, he found himself remembering his favorite Sinatra song. Humming ever so slightly, he mouthed the words as he looked out at the puffy clouds, "…sorry for you, she has no sister—just a tomboy in lace, that's Nancy with the laughing face…"

Several hours later, suitcase in hand, Sweeper took a taxi from the airport to downtown. He rented a suite off Union Square, a converted apartment—now a timeshare that rented by the week. Louis, his yet undiscovered, appointed assassin checked himself in close by at the exclusive Regency House, two blocks away. It was vital that Louis remain inconspicuous. He was warned that Sweeper's mind worked like a television camera, always panning the 'audience'—never forgetting a face—precisely focused. Louis had made one mistake, a mistake Sweeper never would have made on a job. He had followed his target to the baggage claim, left, and hailed a cab.

Louis had no baggage.

Sweeper was suddenly on full alert. It took him only minutes to find out where the slight, ordinary man was staying. Best of all, he believed his man was not aware that he had been detected. As usual, the more professional, experienced assassin had the advantage.

The owner of the pawnshop in Chinatown had been expecting the man from Chicago. The weapon was picked up at two o'clock on Thursday, exactly as planned.

I still have tonight and Friday to enjoy San Francisco—Saturday's a workday, Louis thought.

Louis wasn't the only person working overtime on the Sweeper case. The FBI had been alerted that a man answering his description was seen leaving the San Francisco airport. Further investigation revealed that his flight had originated from New York. John Rushly was notified immediately, along with his colleagues in the Bay area.

Nitti in Chicago had received word from his source in the FBI office in D.C. that Sweeper had been spotted in San Francisco. This was not good news. Turning to his lawyer and Maxco-Litton informant, Gus Lanton, Nitti expressed his concern.

"This may not be worth pursuing at this time, Gus." He was referring to the contract, already set in motion.

"In my opinion, Charles, the Saturday deadline should be called off. Can you reach Louis?"

"Not unless he calls—it's on auto pilot."

"Kind of like a launched missile—"

"I don't like that analogy, Gus."

"Sorry, Charles. I just don't want anything unnecessary or reckless going on. We have a handle on Roger Maxco—maybe Sweeper is not such a problem to us."

"Not now, but If the FBI gets to him, he could be," replied Nitti.

"I'm not sure he would tie us in, Charles. All of this may be for nothing. Is there *any* possibility of reaching Louis?"

"None," replied Charles, I told you—it's on autopilot. That's the way we operate. It's safest. Contact of any kind is dangerous during an operation like this. Once you commit, it's done."

"I guess the best we can do is wait."

Saturday, June 13—Union Square—San Francisco

It was sunny and cool in the City by the Bay. To Sweeper, there was a sense of drama in the air. For Louis, his orders were clear—to take out his quarry. The FBI, in contrast, was searching for the same man, with little luck. Their goal—to capture a killer.

All Sweeper wanted was to be left alone. He needed time to sort out his dilemma and come up with a plan. How could he possibly leave the country when he had just found someone to finally make him happy? His thoughts of Nancy would have to be set aside, at least for now. Today, he would think about one thing—survival.

What is wrong with those people? he wondered bitterly. *Years of reliable service and it come to this—saving myself from them. There is no loyalty among this element. This is it. Nancy will have to come with me. We can live in Zurich or Lucerne. If only I could reason with this guy—the man who has been ordered to kill me. Damn, will it never end? The killing must end, here, today. I promise you Nancy.*

A gay activist rally had been scheduled for 11:00 a.m. on Saturday. There would be huge crowds surrounding Union Square—a perfect opportunity for a professional killing. Sweeper knew his man would use the rally to complete his work. It was as if they both were trained from the same manual.

On Thursday and Friday, exactly at noon, Sweeper had walked to the center of Union Square to feed the pigeons. Saturday would be no exception. The shot would come from behind the bench—a small caliber with a silencer. That was the script—but Sweeper would modify that scenario by turning the tables. A Newsweek magazine with a small mirror inside would give Sweeper the edge. It was 11:30 a.m. In his suite, preparing for his daily walk to the center of Union Square, he thought to himself. It will be split second timing—it has to work. He dressed conservatively in khaki trousers and a white shirt with the sleeves rolled up precisely two turns. *Average,* he thought, *I must look average.*

It was time. Crowds of people, mostly gay activists, were filling the Square. He would share a bench with two elderly ladies. Predictably, Sweeper noticed the slight man off to one side, pretending to read a newspaper. As he walked about sixty feet behind Sweeper's bench, he stopped.

The Newsweek prop was working. Louis slowly began his merciless march to the area directly behind what he thought to be the unsuspecting target. Step by step, closer and closer, now only fifteen feet behind the bench, Sweeper could see the newspaper lowering, the newspaper that concealed the weapon. *Timing, Sweeper, timing—three more seconds,* he thought to himself.

In what appeared to be a surrealistic, slow motion scene from a bad movie, Sweeper spun and fired his .22 caliber long rifle load into the forehead of the astonished assailant. The man crumpled to the ground, dying, as his brain shut down. Casually, quickly, Sweeper melted into the noisy crowd, a gentle smile on his face. No one realized the drama that had unfolded within six feet of the park bench. It was all over in less than four seconds.

Sirens were screaming and wailing as police and rescue made their way through crowded streets on the way to Union Square. Local police and FBI were almost immediately on the scene trying to sort out what witnesses couldn't accurately describe. Since the man killed had no identification on him, but was well dressed, he was immediately suspected as being an assassin. He was too well dressed to be homeless. His face was not known to local law enforcement or the agency.

Having happened within hours of Rushly's bulletin, the FBI concluded that the shooter had been Sweeper. The two elderly ladies sitting on the park bench had described Sweeper perfectly.

They had been having a discussion about whether they thought he was gay. They couldn't decide. The entry wound affirmed a professional hit. The bullet would be removed from the man's head and sent to ballistics—that would take time.

Sweeper decided not to leave town for a few days. Today, Saturday, would be a dangerous time to be out and about, he concluded. He had food on hand, a TV and reading material. I'll just stick around the apartment, he thought. It will all cool down. He decided to call Nancy.

Nancy was just closing her store when the phone rang.

"The Mystery Hour."

"Hi, I miss you. And you know what I've decided?" He spoke as if it was an ordinary Saturday afternoon.

"What?" she laughed, delighted to hear his voice.

"Nancy. I love you."

"Oh, Richard," her voice softened. She had waited a lifetime to hear those words from the right man. "I want you back here, Richard. That's an order!" *She sounded so happy,* he thought. *I really want to make this woman happy!*

"It will be a few days more, sweetie. The job is more complicated than I thought. I may have to spend some time in Europe. How would you like to travel overseas for a few weeks? You could get your assistant to run the store, couldn't you?" *God, he missed her.*

"Richard, you know I can't stand to feel pressured. This is still really sudden. When you come home, we'll talk about it, okay?"

"Fair enough," he couldn't disguise his disappointment. "I can hardly wait to see you."

"What are you doing when you're not working?" She tried to change the subject. As much as she felt for him, she needed time to think.

"Just sightseeing and buying you presents. There is some business that I can take care of over the weekend. I need to be here Tuesday and Wednesday. Is that okay with you? But think about Europe."

"Just get back here as soon as you can. I don't know about this Europe thing. It's a little sudden and it's not that easy to arrange management for the store. Like I said, Richard, we can talk about that later."

"I'll call you tomorrow, at home. I love you"
"I love you, Richard." *There! She'd said it. That was the first step,* he thought. He was getting closer to persuading her. The call was over but Sweeper's internal struggle began. *How can I possibly subject her to this kind of life?* he wondered, wrestling with his conscience. There were untold and unending risks inherent in his dangerous world of intrigue and murder. Sweeper knew it would never end.

FBI Crime Lab—San Francisco—

"We did a rush on the ballistics—it's our guy, Agent Rushly, no doubt about it. He may have left town by now, but we don't think so. Our profiler believes he will stay put for a few days at least, til things cool down."

The Bureau in San Francisco was on full alert. This was John Rushly's case but he couldn't be everywhere at once. He was becoming frustrated. "Thanks for the update. It sounds like self-defense—if there is such a thing when two assassins square off. I suspect he will take a car to an airport other than San Francisco. Keep an eye on Oakland and Sacramento. We might get lucky. If something appears imminent, call me - day or night!"

"Yes, Sir, we sure would like to nab him for you. The agencies have a pool, San Francisco, New York, Miami and Phoenix."

"You do that," Rushly laughed, glad to ease the tension for a moment. "I have plenty of other items to address in this case. I need a lot of help. Be careful."

"Sir?"

"Gambling's illegal." Rushly hung up, laughing.

He had been busy reviewing the latest reports from Elizabeth and other tips that were coming in. Someone in the organization of Maxco-Litton, concerned about massive amounts of drugs being stockpiled at certain company warehouses, made certain the information reached the CFO. Earlier, Elizabeth had confirmed with Roger that inventory control was a problem. She passed along to John the explanation that Roger had given—"an errant computer program."

John was also concerned about the Galen II project. What was its status and how did it relate to the stockpiling of drugs? He couldn't figure it out. John had promised his superiors that no unauthorized drugs would leave the Maxco-Litton laboratories. FDA approval was absolutely necessary.

"There are to be no chances taken with respect to contaminated or questionable drugs," the Washington Bureau Chief stated. "Nothing is worth that kind of risk."

"I agree, absolutely," John responded. "I won't let that happen under any circumstances. We have people watching the warehouses, Sir."

Deciding it was time to check in with Elizabeth again, the agent dialed her direct line. He was thrown to hear a man's voice answer her private line, and spoke before he realized what he had done. "Elizabeth Martin, please. This is a personal call."

It was too late. Both men on the line knew what had happened. Roger had got caught answering Elizabeth's private line and now he knew the FBI had the number.

"Damn you, Roger" John heard Elizabeth's angry voice in the background. "Don't ever pick up my private line again. Please leave my office." John had never heard her angry and listened admirably as she chastised her own boss, with a poise he never thought possible in an angry woman.

"I'm sorry," her voice came on the line. She sounded concerned. "This is Elizabeth Martin."

More embarrassed by not thinking, and being caught by Roger than angry with her, John couldn't help himself. "What the hell is he doing picking up your private line," he asked angrily. "Sorry, Elizabeth, it sounds like I called at the wrong time. Goddamn it, I let him know who it was!" *How stupid*, he thought, *to tip my hand this late in the game.*

"I can't imagine why he picked up my phone, John." She said soothingly, obviously aware of his distress. "Maybe he's getting paranoid. Usually, he never comes in my office much less using my phones. This is distressing. I'm sorry you got caught in the middle."

"My concern is for you, Elizabeth. The man is dangerous."

Trying to pass his warning off, Elizabeth changed the subject. "Tell me, John. What's happening on your end?"

"It seems like everyday there is something going on with this case," came the exhausted reply. We tracked Julian's killer to San

Francisco. There was an attempt on his life but he won, —this time. We have another body, however, —in Union Square, no less."

"Are you sure this is all related? Are these awful people fighting among themselves?"

"Our assessment is that the person or persons who ordered the killing of Dr. Weitzel were afraid the assassin was near capture. We believe there was an attempt to silence him. He obviously knows too much about this entire sordid affair."

"What can I do, John?"

"Elizabeth, I'm concerned about this inventory matter. Something smacks of black market distribution and I cannot put my finger on it. Do you have any further information?"

"There seems to be a shroud of secrecy that has descended over that entire subject. I'm pressing, but keep getting stonewalled. I don't buy the computer-glitch explanation."

"What about Galen II?" he asked. "Have you heard about that project? Particularly its success and promotion date?"

"Do you suspect the two issues are related, John? That project is under wraps, too."

John's suspicions were confirmed. The stockpiles of inventory and the Galen II project have something in common.

"Yes, Elizabeth, I do. It may be time for another showdown with Roger. What can you do?"

"It would be daring, but our bylaws allow an override of authority in cases like this. Security could be called in and all inventories frozen subject to completion of the audit. It would be a last resort John. A major fight would be triggered—possibly work against me. He is, after all, my employer."

"That's too risky Elizabeth. Do this for me. Fax a list of your major distribution warehouses along with identification of drivers and trucks, which would be involved in a major rush to move goods—especially to airports. Can you do this?"

"Give me a few days, John. It's possible. What exactly do you suspect?"

"I need more facts, Elizabeth. I'm not sure—my suspicions are tentative. I just want to be ready if something major happens. While you're at it, fax me what you have on Tom Elliot. Give me any updates you can glean from that laboratory and Galen II."

"I'm taking notes. God, I'll be glad when this is over! So many good people have invested in Maxco-Litton. I want justice—at the same time, I want to keep this organization intact. It seems I've worked here my whole life."

"We'll keep working together, Elizabeth. That's all we can do—one crisis at a time."

"I wish there were humor in this," Elizabeth replied wistfully, "I surely do. Thank you, John. Is there anything else?"

"Not today. I'll look forward to receiving the information. Thanks again. Call me if anything comes up—day or night."

"I feel more secure knowing you're looking out for me. By the way, say hello to your wife for me. She's one lucky lady. I look forward to our next talk."

John was still convinced he could monitor the activities of Roger Maxco with the help of Elizabeth and his other sources. One of his associates, Brian Brewer, had remarked, "This is ready to blow, John. Toss in the Chicago connection and you have the potential for real fireworks. I don't know enough about this Sweeper fellow, but he sure knows how to survive. I suspect they had their best man tracking him. Watch your back."

What was the Chicago connection? John puzzled. *I would like to meet the man in charge!*

Hundred upon hundreds of documents obtained by Elizabeth, over the past several weeks, were beginning to complete the picture. Layers of corporate and private partnership entities clouded the identities of the real players. *Ultimately they will be uncovered*, John reasoned

Chapter Seventeen

Rather than telephone Charles Nitti, Gus Lanton showed up in person at the mobster's Chicago office. He had been in New York when he learned of the San Francisco fiasco. Obviously, he reasoned, the *second* best hit man in the country was dead, because Sweeper was still alive and probably well aware of who ordered the hit. In normal circles, Gus thought, this activity is known as a backfire. *For Charles Nitti*, he thought, *it could be a conflagration.*

"What is it, Gus? I thought you had to be in New York?"

"I have been in New York and I'm back with disturbing news."

"You should have called. I don't like people showing up here, unannounced. What's up?"

"The wrong man was hit."

The normally cool and collected Charles Nitti grimaced at the news. Not wanting to appear too anxious, he asked quietly, "Where's Sweeper?"

"The authorities are searching the Bay area for Sweeper. They have a body—but it's Louis. He was found in Union Square. Nothing can be traced here, but I'm sure there are items on his person and in the hotel that will be of interest to the FBI."

"I'll be damned! You were right. The risks were too high. I have never fucked up like this before. How vindictive is Sweeper? If he's smart, he'll leave the country."

"Charles, past performance suggests he will remain rational—he doesn't believe in revenge for the sake of revenge. He's a philosophical guy. However, he's not stupid. He'll want you to know he didn't appreciate the attempt. If he can hurt you, he probably will. Then again, if he really is involved with this girl and wants to be left alone, he may leave the country and hope for the best. I think that's your best way out"

"If there is anyway to get that message to him, do it." Gus had his boss's full attention. "This shit has to end. It all started with Roger Maxco. Get back to New York. Find out how close we are to ridding ourselves of this mess. You have full authority to confront Roger Maxco. I want that son of a bitch out of my life."

"I think you are right, Charles. There's no need for me to play games any longer with Maxco-Litton. He might as well know who I am and who I work for, that we're right on his ass. Don't worry, he will be out of your life—one way or another."

It was getting late and the two men decided to have dinner before Gus left for New York. They would work out the details over drinks.

"Remember Gus," Nitti said, gritting his teeth, "I want it made clear to Roger that our business relationship is totally severed by the deadline I set last month. He has eight weeks from today. That's it."

"I'll see to it Charles—July 20."

Sweeper decided to leave San Francisco on Tuesday morning. He rented a mid-sized sedan under an assumed name, then drove south to Burbank—a one-day trip. He took a red eye on America West to Phoenix, then the next morning, caught an early, non-stop flight from Phoenix to Boston. The remainder of the trip was by rental car and he drove directly to Nancy's apartment. Changing his appearance slightly and leaving town at the busiest time gave him additional anonymity. It was around four in the afternoon when he arrived home. He expected Nancy to come home from the bookstore around six.

The extended and complicated trip had given Sweeper time to think, and to sort out his situation. It all became painfully clear.

It was obvious that Charles Nitti had acted out of self-preservation. He did not feel the need for revenge. It had been a business decision, that's all. Besides, he thought, any reckless behavior on his part would place Nancy needlessly in danger. *The authorities will be focused on my being captured. There is no doubt I must leave the country.* He paced the apartment, stewing over the decision he had to make. *I may have a week at the most before they close in. I'll marry Nancy if I have to, but she'll have to understand that we must live in Europe for a few years. There are no other options.*

Nancy saw the rental car and held her breath. *He's back*, she thought, *God, I missed him!* She ran up the steps, taking two at a time, laughing all the way up. "Richard, are you home?" She left the door open and raced into the front room. Their embrace was long. "Oh Richard, I missed you so much—promise me you'll never leave again," she said breathlessly.

"Nancy," he said, his voice choked with unexpected emotion. "I've never loved anyone as much as I love you. I don't want to let you go."

They whiled away the evening with talk of the store, future dreams and Richard's trip, with obvious details omitted. After a nice, quiet dinner and wine, Richard broached the subject he dreaded.

"Nancy, listen closely, I must talk to you about this."

"You're scaring me, Richard. Please tell me you're not married."

"Nothing like that, believe me."

"What is it? Tell me."

"Within the next few days, I have to leave for Europe. I want you to come with me, — to live."

"This is sudden Richard. What can be so critical that you have to leave right now?"

"I need your trust on this one, Nancy. Look, you don't have to drop everything immediately. Take some time to sell the store or find a manager. You can join me in a few weeks. How does that sound?"

"You just asked me to trust you, Richard. Now I'm asking you to trust me. Be honest! I can take it. Nothing could be so serious as you're making it out to be. I love you. Why are you doing this?"

As he poured a fresh glass of Cabernet Sauvignon, he wondered if this would be the end. *I've come so far*, he thought, *I love her so much.*

"You're right, Nancy. It's these international clients. They're insisting I be close to their operations in Zurich. It's such a rare opportunity, I hate to let it pass by."

"Richard, I don't want you to sacrifice your dreams for my bookstore. How about a compromise?"

"I don't know, I—"

"Richard, tell them you accept the position but need several weeks to put things in order. That's reasonable enough. What do you do for them that requires such an immediate departure?"

"But I, Nancy, please understand—" he was stumbling all over his words. He loved her so much, he nearly found himself telling her the truth.

"I do have someone in mind for the store," she responded, saving him from self-destruction. "She could manage it for a few months, with an option to purchase. I'll tell you what? I'll take care of that end, and you keep your people happy. We could probably leave in less than a month. What do you say?"

Richard knew he had stretched the line as tightly as he could. If he refused Nancy's reasonable proposal, it could be all over. Reluctantly, he put the best spin on it and agreed.

"You're the light of my life, Nancy." He grabbed her, holding her fast against him. He was so relieved, she mistook his relief for passion. "God, Nancy, I really love you. We'll do exactly as you say. It's a great plan. I may be gone a few days now and then before we leave, but at least I'll be in the country and within reach until you're ready to go. Fair enough? Besides—" he whispered in her ear, her soft hair brushing his cheek.

"Besides what?" she asked gently.

"We'll have time to get a ring for you. You're not going to Europe single."

"Oh, Richard, I—" but tears interrupted her reply.

Roger Maxco was conferring with Michael Lowe when Carol buzzed his office.

"Mr. Maxco, Gus Lanton is calling. He wants a specific appointment, for this afternoon, if possible. What should I tell him?"

"Hold on, Carol." Roger turned to Michael.

"What the hell does Gus Lanton want? I *never* talk to him!" His voice showed an edginess that had recently become the norm in the executive office.

"It may be nothing, Roger. Relax. Keep the troops happy—give him his lousy appointment." Michael shrugged off the question and helped himself to a stale doughnut.

"Shit, there's a board meeting at the end of the week. What does he want now?"

"Roger, it's no big deal—see him," Michael replied, his impatience showing.

"Carol, tell him to come at four o'clock today."

"Yes, Sir."

Gus was under strict orders by Nitti to see Roger Maxco at the earliest possible time. He was looking forward to the meeting. It would be nasty, but interesting.

"Damn it, Michael," Roger ranted on. "What else must I contend with today? I got word there was a shooting in San Francisco that supposedly is tied into the FBI investigation of Julian's death. What the hell is that all about?"

"I suspect, Charles, it had more to do with the Chicago group than us."

"What the hell are they doing? Can you find out more about this? Those bastards are putting the squeeze on me and now they're shooting their own people. Goddamn it! If I had sixty days without people interfering from all parts of the globe, this whole thing could be over."

"I'll see what I can find out," Michael responded quietly, trying to keep his boss calm. Do you want me to be here for your meeting with Gus?"

"Let me handle that inconvenience. You look into this San Francisco matter."

At 3:30, Roger returned to his office. He didn't like surprises. What did Gus want? Roger decided to check with Elizabeth. He rang her direct line.

"Elizabeth here."

"Sorry to bother you. This is Roger."

"Yes, Roger?"

"Do you know anything about Gus Lanton wanting to see me in private?"

"Not a thing, Roger. He usually keeps to himself. I barely speak to him. He didn't say anything?"

"No. Anyway, he will be here shortly. I was just curious. Thanks Elizabeth."

"No problem, Roger. Let me know if I can help, okay?"

"Sure. See you later."

"Wait a sec'," she replied. Quickly cradling the phone into her shoulder, Elizabeth turned to the man in her office. "Gene, is there anything going on with the other Directors that I should know about?"

"Nothing other than most of us are becoming disenchanted with Roger," he responded in a low voice, laughing a little, "But only you know that. I guess there's nothing else."

To Roger Maxco, the man now sitting in front of his desk looked like a different person.

"Gus, this is quite a surprise," Roger spoke smoothly to his mysterious board member. "I don't believe we've talked much, certainly not alone. What can I do for you?"

Confident, focused, authoritative, Gus had taken on a new persona. This was the real Gus Lanton.

"First of all, Roger, I must confess to you that my position at Maxco-Litton has been a subterfuge."

"Excuse me?" Roger felt his stomach turn upside down.

"Yes, Roger, a charade if you will. My purpose here has been to monitor the activities of Maxco-Litton on behalf of my employer."

"What the fuck are you talking about?" Roger screamed, not caring who might hear him.

"What I am trying to tell you, Roger is that I represent Charles Nitti and the Chicago group. My tenure here at Maxco-Litton has been a sham—designed to watch you and keep track of our investments."

"This is a fucking outrage—" Roger grabbed a marble paperweight, flinging it haphazardly across the desk. It missed its mark.

"Stay calm, Roger." Gus said calmly, completely unruffled. "It's in your best—"

"Don't talk to me like this, you goddamned traitor! You're fired! Do you hear me, you son of a bitch? Fired! Get out, you—"

"You don't want to do this Roger," Gus interrupted quietly, irritating Roger even more. "I can't be fired and you know it." Gus had taken charge. Rising steadily to his feet, he looked down upon Roger Maxco and continued, "Listen closely, Roger—look at me!" The hate, rage, and frustration seethed within the man seated. Gus continued. "We are on to your entire scheme including the stockpiling of drugs and the vaccine. We don't give a shit what you do with your crap—you will pay us off and take us out of this cauldron of shit. Once again, Roger, listen closely—I'll say it once—It all ends in precisely eight weeks Roger. Excuse me," he smiled mockingly, it's seven weeks and six days. Mark your calendar Roger. I believe that's all I have to say. Now, I will adjourn this meeting. Meeting adjourned, Roger—seven weeks and six days—July 20."

During Roger's tirade, Carol had called security and Elizabeth Martin. Carol had never heard such language and seen such violence spew out of the mouth of her boss.

"Roger, are you all right?" she asked tentatively. "Are you okay? —Roger?"

"Leave me alone, Goddamn it," shouted Roger. His secretary backed away from the door, ashen.

Gus had just passed Elizabeth in the hall. He said nothing, his face focused and stern.

"Roger, let me in." She tapped lightly on the door. There was silence. Suddenly the door to Roger's office opened. A security guard, having caught up to Elizabeth stuck his head through the door, holding her back long enough to ask the CEO if he were all right. He was waved away. A hoarse, quiet voice finally came from within the inner sanctum.

"Come in Elizabeth. Shut the door."

It had been some time since Elizabeth had seen her employer and colleague out of sorts. Disillusioned, flushed, nervous, obviously stressed, Roger poured a straight double shot of Canadian Club. He gulped it down his throat in seconds. After a few moments, he gathered his thoughts and seemed back to his old self, calculating and determined.

"Roger, what is going on? What happened in here?"

"I just couldn't take it. It seems our quiet Mr. Gus Lanton works for one of our competitors," he lied smoothly. "He's an industrial spy!"

"I don't believe it," Elizabeth said, shaking her head.

"Believe it. He came here to make a deal—a joint venture if you will—on the new vaccine. The bastard has a lot of information." It was important for Roger to keep the real reason for Gus's visit confidential. *This is the perfect cover*, he thought, *it's logical—Elizabeth will believe it.* He was instantly proud of himself for recovering so quickly.

"No wonder you were upset!" She found herself believing him, even feeling some compassion for him. "This is bad, Roger. What else does he know that could hurt the company?" She poured him another drink and handed it to him. He was calming down, now, becoming more himself.

"I have no idea. It wasn't a friendly meeting."

"No kidding!" What do we do about it?"

"Let me handle it. I'll do a damage assessment and let you know—it may not be as serious it appears. For now, let me get back to work. I need to send an Inter-Office Memo immediately restricting Gus's access to all Maxco-Litton business."

"I will leave everything in your capable hands, Roger," Elizabeth said. "Maybe you should take some time off—at least the rest of the day."

"Yes, after the memo. Goodbye Elizabeth."

Roger was thinking hard about Gus's last words. *They have cut the time—seven weeks and six days,* Roger thought, beads of sweat breaking out on his forehead. *They screw up in San Francisco and I pay for it. Those bastards—I'll have the last word—I'll fix those sons of bitches. That goddamned Gus Lanton is history—he's gone!*

In contrast to Nancy and Sweeper's doomed love affair, Kimberly Weitzel and Mike Staples were becoming more involved then either had expected. They decided to stay over in New York a few more days to see the sights.

"Let's forget about these people, Kimberly, about Roger and the others. Let's have some fun. I think your conscience is still bothering you over the fact you were in love with a married man. Throw in the fact that his wife was killed, and that's a serious prescription for guilt. You need to take your mind of all this."

"Do you still believe he killed his wife?" Kimberly was searching, below the surface. She wanted to know what Mike thought, as a law enforcement professional.

"We may never know, Kimberly. I guess now I'm on the fence. The answer to that question may have died with him."

"I'm going to believe he didn't do it," Kimberly responded.

"Enough," Mike said, taking her hand. "Let's talk about us." Their walk continued down 75th Street with its quaint shops—antique stores, coffee shops and bookstores.

Tugging at his arm, Kimberly steered Mike into the bookstore tucked between a newsstand and a Baskin Robbins.

"Mike, this looks interesting, The Mystery Hour. How appropriate for you! You should like this." They walked in and began to look around. The shopkeeper approached.

"Welcome to my shop, I'm Nancy."

"Hi, we're visiting from the San Francisco area. I'm Kimberly Weitzel and this is my friend, Mike Staples."

"Can I help you find something?"

"Just browsing, thank you," said Kimberly.

"Where did I hear the name Weitzel? A photographic memory served her well in the book business. Curious as usual, Nancy had already recalled the Dan Rather story. Then she remembered.

"The news story—the scientist."

"That was my father," replied Kimberly.

"Foot in mouth, that's me! You can see why I specialize in mysteries. I am sorry. Forgive me?"

"There's nothing to forgive—it was news. My father's death is still a mystery. Someday, it will be solved."

"I'm sorry, Kimberly." Nancy felt chagrined and wasn't sure how to apologize. "I never meant to—"

"It's understandable that you would be curious," Kimberly interrupted, sensing the young woman's discomfort. "Thank you for your concern. We'll just look around, if you don't mind."

"Of course, let me know if I can be of any assistance."

Trying to be helpful, Mike kept the conversation going.

"I suppose someday there will be a book written about this case." Then, turning to Kimberly, he changed the subject, "How about something to eat?"

"I'm ready, Mike. Let's go." Kimberly turned to Nancy and briefly took her hand, saying, "We enjoyed your little shop."

"Come back," replied Nancy, "I promise to just talk about books."

That evening at home, Nancy couldn't help talking about her day. She spoke to Richard.

"Remember that news story about the scientist murdered in Key West?"

"Vaguely," Sweeper replied cautiously.

"Well, I totally embarrassed myself today. His daughter was in my store."

The statement landed like a bomb. Sweeper stood staring at her, frozen in place.

"What do you mean? Tell me exactly what you mean." His demeanor had changed instantly.

"I'm telling you that Kimberly Weitzel was in my store with a friend today. Isn't that wild?"

"What were they doing in your store?" Sweeper stared at her blankly, careful to mask the emotion he was feeling.

"Just browsing, what do you do in a bookstore?" She had noticed a change in him. She didn't like it when he shut her out. "They were from San Francisco. Can you imagine? Millions of people in New York City and these two walk into my store."

"So they walked into your store," Sweeper tried to control his voice. "Did they ask you any specific questions—like about your personal life?"

"Why on earth would they be interested in my personal life, Richard? What's going on? You look worried."

"I just—"

"You're upset! I can tell. There's something about Weitzel. First, you turn off the news. Now you want to know if this Weitzel girl is asking about our personal life. I don't get it, Richard, and I'm tired of being kept in the dark." She looked at him expectantly, waiting for an answer.

Sweeper had made a mistake. He had unintentionally aroused her suspicions.

"Look, Nancy. It's not important. It doesn't matter. As you said, it was just a coincidence. It's of no concern to me." Sweeper had covered his concerns the best he could. He hoped Nancy accepted his comments as genuine.

Later that evening, as she sat alone in the bedroom, brushing her hair, her queasy feeling wouldn't go away. She began to wonder. *What do I know about this man? Did all of this happen too fast? Who is Richard Baxter? I'd better slow down until I find out.*

Just then, Richard peeked into the bedroom, smiling. "Are you okay?" he asked.

"It was a difficult day, Richard. I have a really bad headache. I'm going to take something and go to bed. You can stay up and watch TV, it's okay." It was not okay. Something was wrong. Nancy could feel it in her bones. *I'll look into this tomorrow,* she thought.

Hoping her suspicions were unfounded, Nancy Johnson hesitated before calling her friend, Norman Gould. Norman, a private investigator, was a steady customer at the store.

"Norman, this is Nancy. Can you talk for a few minutes?"

"Sure, Nancy, what's up?" He sounded pleased to hear from her.

"Hopefully, nothing, but I'm concerned about Richard. I want to be sure everything is okay."

"What do you mean? Do you think he's married or something?"

"No, it's something else—you may think I'm stupid."

"Not these days, Nancy. You're being smart. What's bothering you?"

"He takes unexpected trips and suddenly wants me to move with him to Europe. That alone doesn't bother me. But a few days ago, he turned off a newscast I was watching. It had to do with the Dr. Weitzel, the scientist who was murdered in Key West. Yesterday, the man's daughter shows up at The Mystery Hour—probably a coincidence. It was Richard's reaction to her visit that has me puzzled. He grilled me about it. Really was disturbed about her visit. It was too much. Do I sound paranoid?"

"Just cautious," Norman replied. "Since you have no contact with his family and you're living together, I suggest we take a look. Fax me what you know—name, places he has been, profession, job information—anything you can think of, no matter how insignificant it might seem."

"Norman, can you look into the Key West incident? I'm curious. It was Dr. Julian Weitzel who was murdered. His daughter's name is Kimberly. Her friend's name is Mike Staples. I hate to bother you with this but I need to feel safe. I really think I love Richard. I want this to work."

"Fax me the information, Nancy. I'll get right on it. And don't feel like a spy—this is just being smart. If everything is okay, it will be a good thing for both of you."

"Thanks a lot, Norman—call me at work."

Back in the apartment, Sweeper pondered his situation. *She's concerned and rightly so,* he thought. *Suppose the visit to the store by Kimberly was not a coincidence—too close! It's time to move on. I was a fool to think my life could be normal. God, I can't stay in New York. And what about Nitti? It's getting dangerous for Nancy!*

With time running out, Sweeper began to make plans to leave New York. The big question, he hadn't answered. What to do about Nancy Johnson?

Chapter Eighteen

The call from Key West was totally unexpected. The Rushlys were having lunch in their Scottsdale home when John's cellular rang. Few people had that number. Caller ID proved it to be his office. Smiling at his wife, John shook his head. They had hoped to have a quiet meal together. A moment their conflicting schedules rarely permitted. He answered tersely, hoping his caller would be discouraged from any lengthy conversation.

"Agent Rushly," the efficient dispatcher's voice came on the line. "You have a call from Sergeant Reynolds, Key West PD. Do you want me to take a message or patch it through?"

"Patch it through, Beth—it must be important." There was a brief moment's wait, then a click.

"Rushly, this is Sergeant Reynolds—do you remember me?"

"Yes, Sergeant, you were very helpful. What can I do for you?"

"It may be nothing, but it seemed strange to me. A P.I. by the name of Norman Gould called from New York with a fair amount of questions about the Weitzel murder. I gave him your name. He was asking specifically about the killer who had been identified. I thought you should know. I'll give you his number in New York."

"This may be important, Sergeant—thank you for thinking of me. Let me jot that number down." He repeated it after the sergeant. "Okay, anything else?"

"That's it, Sir—hope it helps."

"Thanks for calling."

Jill had been listening intently and couldn't wait to hear the other side of the conversation.

"What was that all about, John?"

"A New York P.I. made an inquiry with the Key West police. It may be nothing but it has me curious."

"Naturally," replied Jill, you are one curious guy." On her way to the sink, she sauntered up to him, pretending to be sultry and suggestive. "By the way," she said in her poorest imitation of a low, sexy voice, "how are you and Elizabeth Martin doing? Is she still *cooperating*?" and she stressed the word.

"Elizabeth is fine," he laughed, grabbing her and placing her squarely on his lap. Ruffling her hair, which she hated, he smiled, then regained his serious nature. "She has a big job on her hands. I'm worried about her safety."

"Has she hit on you, John?" There was no mistaking the too casual tone. "You talk about her in such glowing terms."

"Listen, you," he took hold of Jill's arms and made her face him straight on, "this guy is absolute business with other women, all other women. I know exactly what I have at home. You are the one and only in my life, and don't you forget it." He leaned up to her lovely face and kissed her forehead before brushing the hair out of her eyes, the hair he had just messed up.

"Just checking, sweetheart." Then she said mischievously, as if she couldn't leave it alone, "But is *she* all business?" She got up and poured them both a cup of coffee.

"It's interesting," he said thoughtfully. "She never mentions her personal life—I don't know if she has any. She's smart and attractive. I would think she would be taken."

"And how about Kimberly and my friend Mike?"

"Now, I turn the tables. You've lost out on that one. I think they're in love."

"What? My Mike in love with someone else? Damn!" She came back over to sit on his lap and he wished that they both didn't have shifts to complete. Kissing her lightly on the lips, he thought, casually, that they weren't going to get much sleep that night. Somehow, he didn't think it would matter.

"Okay, Jill—we're even." He picked her up off his lap and patted her fanny before finishing his coffee. "Time for me to go about my business and call Mr. Norman Gould in New York. He may have a lead on Sweeper. Who knows?"

"And time for me to return to my duties with the bad boys. I'm glad we could sneak away for a nice lunch at home. See you tonight, handsome."

John headed for his office to make several calls. His priorities were Norman Gould, Kimberly and Elizabeth, in that order. He wanted to make sure Kimberly and Mike had left New York. Then he would comment on the documentation Elizabeth had faxed to his office.

It was four o'clock in New York when the P.I. picked up his phone.

"Gould Investigations, may I help you?"

"This is FBI Special Agent John Rushly in Phoenix. Is this Mr. Gould?"

"Yes, Mr. Rushly, I was about to call you. You must have talked to Sergeant Reynolds in Key West."

"Yes, I did. May I ask the reason for your inquiry into the death of Dr. Weitzel?"

"I'm checking out something for a friend. She is worried about the guy she is in love with. It seems he travels a lot and becomes very distressed when anything about this case comes up. I heard that the perp had been identified. Can you help me on this?"

"The case is under investigation by the Bureau, but we certainly welcome new information. Our man is trim, five feet ten, clear blue eyes, nice looking but rather ordinary. Clean cut. We tracked him to New York, then San Francisco, and back to New York. Tell me about the boyfriend."

Norman read the description and other details he had been furnished about Nancy's Richard. "One more thing, Agent Rushly, Nancy's store was visited by the daughter of the victim. Her name is Kim something. I don't know if that means anything, but I thought you should know."

John Rushly sat in stunned silence. He did not believe in fortuitous circumstances. Quickly gathering his thoughts, he carefully outlined his plan to Norman Gould.

"Norman, listen carefully, your friend Nancy could be in immediate danger."

"Oh, shit! What have you got?" Norman had been hoping Nancy was mistaken about this whole thing.

"Listen, I need your help. We have to act fast. Where is she now?" John's voice reflected obvious concern.

"She owns a bookstore. It closes at six. She's there right now." Norman sounded as if he were near panic.

"Gould, listen to me. Do not phone her. She may become alarmed and call him. When you get to her store, tell her you have spoken with me. As a precaution, I want you to escort her directly to your place. Do it now. She is not, under any circumstances, to return to her apartment, not for clothes, not for so much as a toothbrush. Give me your address."

All of a sudden, the obscure private detective from New York found himself in the middle of an FBI murder investigation. He jumped at the chance to help his friend and to assist the investigation. He gave John his home address and phone number.

"Look, this is just a precaution," John felt the hairs on the back of his neck stand up. He knew this was the call he had been waiting for. Clearing his throat, he said, "I'm sending an agent to your home. When he arrives, I want you to insist on identification and have the agent give my name as a reference. Don't let anyone else in. Is that absolutely clear?"

"I understand," Gould said, shakily. "Rushly, do you think this is your man?" Norman was still hoping Nancy was not in danger.

"It could be. If it is, he is a professional trained killer. Stay out of his way. Now I want you to leave and pick up Nancy and take her directly to your home. Now! Any questions?"

"No, Sir, I'm leaving now."

"An agent will be at your home when you arrive—don't take any chances. I'll be in touch. And, Gould?"

The response came shakily. "Yes?"

"You just may have saved your friend's life with your inquiry."

John Rushly had a gut feeling that this was real. Kimberly knowingly or unknowingly was too close. John buzzed his assistant.

"Gene, get me on the next flight to New York—call our New York Field Office. Maggie O'Brien was just transferred there. I need her right away."

"Yes, Sir, right away." It took only a few moments.

"Maggie is on the phone, Sir."

"Maggie—John Rushly, I need your help."

"What is it, John?"

"Norman Gould—I need two agents at his apartment—protective witness—it's a friend of his, Nancy Johnson. She may be living with the Weitzel killer, without her knowledge. Make sure both Norman and Nancy are safe and keep twenty-four hour surveillance on Gould's home. I'm on the next flight to New York. Have a car at the airport. I'll let you know the flight number and time. Maggie, this is happening as we speak. Norman is picking her up at a bookstore on 75th Street. It's called The Mystery Hour.

To be safe, send a car to the store. Maggie, have the agents at the store and at Gould's apartment, mention my name. That's Gould's cue that our agents are for real."

"I'm on it, John. Don't worry." Maggie noted Norman's address and phone number, immediately dispatching two cars—one to The Mystery Hour, the other to Gould's home. John's assistant interrupted.

"I'll be there soon, Maggie," John said, "gotta go."

"You're all set, John. Your ride is outside. The flight leaves in forty-five minutes. The federal agent on board already knows you're en route and that you'll be packing a piece. He'll meet you at security."

"I'm on my way. Keep in touch if anything unusual develops. Call the plane, if necessary. Be sure to notify Maggie—flight number and arrival time. Thanks. Oh—"

"Sir?"

"Would you mind calling Jill and telling her I'll call her from New York? We were planning on a quiet evening at home. So much for that," he laughed.

"No problem, Sir, she always understands, being in the business."

"Thanks, Gene." *Yes,* he thought, *Jill always did understand, but I'm going to make this one up to her with a long honeymoon that has been postponed far too long...as soon as this case is over.*

Norman Gould's heart was racing. Luckily, he found a close parking place and headed for The Mystery Hour. He paused briefly before entering the store. There were two customers and a man standing by the counter.

Oh, shit! That could be him, Norman thought. *Okay, stay calm—let him finish his business and leave.*

It was 4:45 and Norman knew Nancy would keep the store open until six. *It is him,* he thought, nearly gasping with fear for his friend. *Leave for God's sake,* he said to himself. Sweeper was kissing Nancy—telling her something sweet, no doubt. *Good, he is leaving—alone.* Chills ran down his spine. *This is the last time I'll do PI work for a friend,* he promised himself. *It's too damn nerve-racking.*

Norman waited until Sweeper was out of sight before entering the store.

"Nancy—"

"Norman, what are you doing here? God, Richard just left! What if he'd seen you!"

"I know, I know. Nancy, close the store. We have to go. Right now!" He grabbed her arm urgently, to let her know how important this was.

"What—?"

"Please, Nancy. We have to go. Now!" Norman politely asked the two customers if they could return another day. "We have an emergency," he said. At the same time, an official looking sedan double-parked and two men approached the front door. One of the men approached Norman.

"Sir, I'm Special Agent Harris with the FBI. Are you Norman Gould? We are here at the request of John Rushly."

"Thank you—I was afraid you might be someone connected with Richard." Norman turned to Nancy just as she started to ask questions.

"What's going on, Norman? Damn it, tell me now! This is scaring the hell out of me." She could not believe the words that followed her request. In a state of bewilderment, she began asking more questions.

"Who is he? What proof do you have? Do you know for sure?"

One of the agents pulled an artist sketch and a photo from a file folder.

"Is this the man you know as Richard, Ms. Johnson?" Her heart sank and the queasy feeling in her stomach became physical pain.

"Oh, no—my God, no —" She couldn't finish the sentence. Nearing collapse, she was helped, half carried, half dragged to the car.

"Mr. Gould, we will meet you at home. This lady is in protective custody. Do you have room at home for one of our agents? I want someone inside your home as well as outside."

"Yes," replied Norman, "I have three bedrooms. We'll work it out. I'll be right behind you. By the way, you missed your man by five minutes."

Nancy had barely glimpsed the artist sketch and photo but she knew it was Richard. Reading the caption, "International

Professional Assassin—wanted in the death of Dr. Julian Weitzel—armed and dangerous" dashed her hopes and dreams. The ride to Norman's home was a nightmare come true. She sat, stunned, as she left these men taking over her life.

Oh, Richard, she thought, her heart screaming at her for ripping it in two, *I love you so much! But I can't love this man—a killer. What in God's name have I done?*

John was notified onboard the 707 as it headed for New York. Remembering a previous case where another vulnerable young woman barely escaped with her life, he thought, *Thank God she's safe!*

As John was flying east, the interview in the FBI car continued, "Ms. Johnson, can you tell us what plans were made between you and Sweeper before he left the bookstore?" The FBI agent knew this was a devastating turn of events for Nancy but the answer to this question was critical.

"Sweeper? I'm sorry, give me a few moments. I am really confused and upset."

"I understand," the agent responded. "I need you to try to let us know as soon as possible. This man is extremely dangerous. Remember your visit from Kimberly—he murdered her father."

Nancy thought she was going to be sick.

As she arrived at Norman Gould's home, she found herself torn between her feelings for Richard and her contempt of his alter ego's evil and despicable life. Nancy decided to give the agent what he wanted to know. *He deserves to be caught*, she thought. *God I'm so embarrassed—how could I have been so naïve, so stupid?*

"We are supposed to meet at Club 57 at six thirty. We were planning to have a casual dinner and talk about our future. We were planning to, —planning to, —go to Europe. That's all I know." She began to cry.

"Thank you, Ms. Johnson—I know this is hard. Believe me, it was the right thing to do."

They had one hour. The agent was patched through to the downtown office in the Federal Plaza building.

"Maggie, Special Agent Harris. We have the Johnson lady in protective custody at the home of Norman Gould. She is supposed to meet the man we know as Sweeper at Club 57 at six thirty."

"I'll set it up from this end," was the reply. "You stay with Ms. Johnson, along with the other agents. I want her safe at all costs."

Maggie O'Brien was a true professional. She had worked with Rushly in the Phoenix Field Office before being transferred to New York. She had forty-five minutes to initiate an elaborate plan to capture her man—Sweeper. She intended to do it.

Early evening hours at Club 57 were considered to be a quiet respite from the clatter of Upper Manhattan. From six to nine, it was a favorite among romantics for gourmet dining and soft music. Later, it became loud and rowdy. Maggie O'Brien was meeting with management along with eight undercover agents in a quick briefing and strategy session. Two agents were to be waiters that evening, one a bartender and the others, customers supposedly waiting outside for entrance. Three of the agents were female. It was decided that Sweeper would be arrested before he was seated. Maggie was giving last minute instructions.

"The last thing we want is for a civilian to be harmed. Sweeper stays in the reception area. Under no circumstances will he be allowed near the other customers. Jenson, Hardy and I will make the arrest—in the foyer. The rest of you have your positions and assignments. In case he gets back outside, that's covered. We want him alive. He may or may not have a weapon. But take no chances. If necessary, take him down. Any questions? He could be here any moment."

The agents moved toward their assigned places. Management was nervous but was assured all would be over in a few moments.

At 5:40, ready to take a cab to Club 57, Sweeper decided to stop by the bookstore to pick up Nancy. Perhaps it was instinct, perhaps not. He often changed plans merely as a precaution. Predictability was not his style.

"About a half block, driver, that's it, The Mys—"

"What did you say, pal?" The cab had stopped just opposite the bookstore.

"It's closed. Lights out—no one there. It's close to six. She must have left early for the restaurant. Damn." He found it difficult to hide his disappointment.

A Ford Ltd. that was parked down the street moved closer to

the cab, the driver trying to get a look at the passenger.

"Move it!" shouted Sweeper. "Step on it, let's go!" Sweeper spotted the Ford. The two men in suits looked out of place. The Ford was caught at the light in cross traffic.

The Kimberly thing! He thought frantically. *Someone put it together. Shit! Nancy knows!*

One of the agents shrugged and said, "That could have been him."

"Call it in. Alert our people at the restaurant. I think it was our guy."

Sweeper barked orders at the cabby. "Find a pay phone, driver—about three miles east."

Sweeper waited until 6:20 before calling Club 57.

"Club 57."

"Yes, I made reservations for Johnson. Has my party arrived? Nancy Johnson."

"Just a moment, Sir." An agent had taken the call.

"He made us. No chance to stall or get him here. What's the call, Maggie?"

"Tell him Ms. Johnson is here—in the restroom, and that his table is ready."

"Sir, Ms. Johnson is here. She is unavailable at the moment, the ladies room, you know. Your table is ready."

"Thank you," Sweeper responded, "I should be there in fifteen minutes. Please let her know."

How stupid did they think he was? he wondered. He hadn't made reservations, and if he had, they would have been in his name, not hers. He knew it would only take a moment for them to realize their mistake.

He knew it was over. It would be difficult to leave town and he didn't have a prayer of talking to Nancy. *She's in protective custody*, he thought. *God, I love her so much! If only we had left the country. Too late now—take care of yourself.*

There was only one man who could help Sweeper leave the country, but he would never turn to him, now. He was the man who tried to have him killed—Charles Nitti.

Chapter Nineteen

Roger Maxco was becoming paranoid to the extreme. In his mind, everything and everyone was against him. Sitting in his office, he found himself muttering, "John Rushly and the FBI, Charles Nitti and the Chicago group, their spy, Gus Lanton, even Elizabeth with her audit—they are all enemies. Seven weeks and change, indeed! Fine, I'll have the last laugh!" Picking up the phone, he quizzed his secretary, "Carol, is Michael Lowe in the building?"

"He's at the laboratory in Lake Placid, meeting with Dr. Elliot. Do you want him on the phone?"

"Yes Carol, let me know when you reach him."

Michael Lowe was the only man Roger thought he could trust. He needed to consult him about an important matter. It was dangerous, he knew, but Roger had to have the upper hand and was contemplating a discrete challenge to Charles Nitti. In his mind, he needed to take the offense. Nitti was closing in too fast.

Michael Lowe was on the phone in a matter of minutes.

"Michael, I have an idea. You may be able to help."

"Yes, Roger," Michael replied, "what can I do?"

"I want to locate this Sweeper fellow. You and I know that Nitti has tried to distance himself—more accurately, tried to eliminate their man. Sweeper must be distressed and need help. He may be able to help us, depending on what he knows. Do you think he is in New York?"

"I don't advise this, Roger. This kind of activity is out of our bailiwick."

"It's an idea I have for backup, in case of emergency. Try to reach him, okay?"

"He's the subject of a manhunt, Roger. The last word I have is that he narrowly escaped capture a few days ago. In fact, your FBI buddy John Rushly is back in town. Sweeper was tied in with some lady—it backfired. There is a way to reach him—if he is still in town."

"Do it."

Roger was insistent. He had not forgotten the humiliating meeting with Lanton, Nitti's spy.

"It's against my better judgment Roger, but I'll see to it. It may take a few days."

"Do it, Michael. Goddamn it, just do it!"

Sweeper had been forced to find an obscure, small apartment near Prospect Park in Brooklyn. All his personal items—clothing and toiletries had been left at Nancy's apartment. An overwhelming sense of loss and depression enveloped every nerve and muscle. He had never felt so alone and desperate. Never before in his entire, chaotic life had he experienced the natural and complete love of a woman. He was desolate and empty, and blamed no one but Charles Nitti.

Word reached Sweeper through an elaborate series of cryptic messages left at previously arranged drops. He was to call a private number, cleared by a friend, at any time. The prefix was New York, not Chicago. Dejected and dispirited, he dialed the number. It rang twice.

"Michael Lowe."

"I was told to call this number—the code is 708."

"We know your situation. I represent someone at odds with your former employer. My client has an issue that you may help to resolve. Further, he can assure you safe passage to anywhere in the world. Is this of interest to you?"

"Yes. I must talk directly with your client. Tomorrow morning—eight o'clock."

Michael provided Sweeper with Roger's private line. He didn't like what he had arranged, but that was Roger's business. What that business was, he didn't want to know.

Sweeper was intrigued. *At odds with your former employer*, he thought, and *assures safe passage to anywhere in the world. There may be a marriage here*, he thought.

Michael immediately called Roger.

"Roger, you will here from you man tomorrow morning, eight o'clock."

"Thank you, Michael, you have done me a great service. I'll

keep you informed."

"Please don't, Roger—I don't want to know what you have planned. Just be careful. You're not the only one involved."

"You're far too cautious, Michael. Sweeper may prove extremely valuable to our cause."

"Let's leave it at that, Roger. Goodnight."

"Goodnight, Michael."

Maggie O'Brien met John's plane at La Guardia. By the time the plane arrived, the hunt for Sweeper was in full swing. The trap set at Club 57 had not worked, but Nancy and her P.I. were safe and in protective custody. The next morning, John Rushly was driven to Gould's to meet Nancy. After cursory introductions, he began the conversation.

"Nancy, I want you to know we all believe you have an extraordinary amount of courage. I know this is a very difficult time."

"I don't feel heroic, Mr. Rushly. I betrayed the man I love." It was obvious the woman had not slept.

"You didn't betray anyone, Nancy," John said. "You were protecting yourself from a man who deceived you, a man who allowed you to love him when he had nothing to offer you. You need to remember that every moment he chose to be with you, he put your life in jeopardy. Sweeper, the man you knew as Richard, was a dichotomy. The man you knew may have been kind and considerate, even incapable of violent acts. The man you didn't know, the very same man, is a cold-blooded assassin—a man who kills professionally, for money. You were taken in and cannot be faulted. Nancy, this man betrayed you in the worst of all scenarios—his world is death and madness—you could never live in that world."

"You sound as though you have experienced this before, Mr. Rushly." Nancy's voice was weak, her emotions spent.

"Yes, Nancy, I have. You are not alone and you did the right thing. After Sweeper murdered Dr. Weitzel, he killed a policeman in Nassau. May I ask you a few questions? It may help our investigation."

"Go ahead, but there's not much I can tell you."

"Maggie said you mentioned that Sweeper was planning a trip to Europe. Could you elaborate?"

"He had come back from San Francisco and seemed agitated. The plan was for me to either go with him to Europe or join him there later. He wanted to go right away but said I could join him in a few weeks. I was upset, so he conceded that he'd wait and we'd go together." Nancy's stomach churned as she recalled their conversations, knowing now that she was ready to marry and run off with a killer.

"Nancy, are you convinced he is trying to leave the country?"

"After this, Mr. Rushly, he will leave as soon as possible."

"Did he have any friends, or call anyone other than you?" asked John.

"There were numbers he called—more like picking up messages. At least once a day he would go out and make a call."

"What about your phone?"

"He seldom used it—I never thought about the tracing thing. Am I really that naive?" Suddenly, without warning, she broke down.

"You're not naïve, Nancy." John replied, "You had absolutely no reason to suspect him of anything, anything at all. You're a sensitive and very honest woman. It's pretty obvious you love him. Why would you consider such things? Remember, he is a professional—secrecy and deception are his stock in trade."

John thought for a moment, then continued his questions. "We picked up one interesting number from your phone records. Is this a number that you may have called?" Nancy studied the number.

"No, that number is not familiar to me," Nancy said.

"We found this notepad with an indention of the word Nitti. Does that word or name mean anything to you?"

"I remember him muttering that name when he got back from San Francisco. He was really upset."

"The name is Charles Nitti—a Chicago underworld figure. Sweeper knew him, possibly worked for him. Can you think of anything else, Nancy?" John asked gently.

"I'm sorry, my mind is not that clear. Maybe tomorrow." Nancy was showing the strain and John decided to call the next day.

"Nancy, I'm really proud of you. Don't be hard on yourself.

You have suffered a loss and you need time. I'll call you tomorrow, okay?"

"Thank you, Agent Rushly. You've been very considerate. Will I be able to go back to my store soon?"

"We'll talk about it tomorrow. It's possible. Your safety is more important. Although, I believe he did love you—he just didn't know how to put it together. I don't believe he wants to harm you. More important, at this juncture there is no reason he would."

"I don't believe he would harm me—I don't believe he would."

"I'll call you in the morning, Nancy. Try to relax this evening. This will all get better each day, I promise."

John was recalling his experience with another young woman who was involved with an international assassin, and she had survived. Nancy was no exception. Maggie and John drove back to the Field Office. There was still no word on Sweeper's whereabouts. The airports, bus terminals, and car rental agencies had all been alerted. Local and state police were cruising the streets and highways with photos of Sweeper. John decided to stay in New York for a few more days, at least.

At precisely eight o'clock the next morning, Roger picked up the phone on his private line. "This is Roger Maxco."

"I was instructed by Michael to call this number. Are we secure?"

"Yes, state of the art. You're Sweeper. From what I know, we have a mutual interest—Charles N.," Roger remarked.

"I have no further interest in Mr. N. came the reply. I do have an interest, however, in leaving the country. Can you assist?"

"My firm has personnel and goods leaving for every country in the world, every day," Roger smugly replied. I can arrange your departure with ease and discretion—guaranteed." Roger knew he was using the right bait.

"And what can I do in return, Mr. Maxco?"

"I won't bore you with details. I'm buying time. Let's say I want Nitti's operation to suffer—a monkey wrench in the machinery, so to speak."

"What is the name of the monkey wrench?"

"Very good—and direct. Gus Lanton works for Nitti and for me—he seems to have his loyalties out of order. He is in New York and due to visit our laboratory in Lake Placid. I can have a complete package—times, dates,—everything on Mr. Lanton, delivered anywhere you wish. Do we have a deal?"

"With the package, Mr. Maxco, include all the details arranging my departure. And don't cross me. You know I can bury you *and* your precious firm."

"That is exactly why all of this will work," replied Roger, "we're two of a kind."

"Have your delivery man at the entrance of the Stillwell Avenue Transit Station at noon on Friday. The white package will have an eight-inch long piece of black electrician's tape across the front. Make sure he holds it so I can see it clearly. Yes, we have a deal."

"Noon Friday. White package—black tape. Goodnight."

Sweeper didn't give a damn about Charles Nitti or disrupting his organization. He was convinced Maxco would deliver on his promise—getting him out of the country. For that, Gus Lanton would be dispatched.

I must talk to Nancy, Sweeper thought. Maybe someday she could forgive me and join me in Europe as we planned. *What am I thinking?* He shook his head. *She must despise me now. This is my cross, my burden—for all my deeds.*

Like a slap in the face to Maxco-Litton, Gus Lanton scheduled his visit to Lake Placid to confer with Tom Elliot about the Galen II project. To the staff at the laboratory, he was just another Director checking on their progress and surveying the operations. Roger took no steps to interfere with Gus's visit—his plan was already in motion. Elizabeth was surprised. She questioned his motive in the hall outside the offices.

"Roger, that man should be arrested instead of being allowed to visit our facility at Lake Placid. What were you thinking?"

"Gathering evidence, Elizabeth. Just setting a trap. Let me handle this, I know what I'm doing." Roger appeared smug and confident.

Not satisfied with his answer, she pressed him further. "He's already confessed. You have witnesses! What more do you need?"

"I told you—"

"Yes, Roger, you told me, but you didn't explain. Don't forget I'm a major stockholder and I've built this company up to the point where you could take it on and make it a success. But I'm a viable part of the team, and I don't want this man on our property. Is that clear?"

"Damn it, Elizabeth, listen to me. I'm setting him up for a criminal trespassing charge, among other things. Industrial espionage is still illegal, you know. He'll be there at two o'clock tomorrow. Stay out of it."

Uncharacteristic of her normal poise, Elizabeth stormed off to the ladies room, wondering what Roger was up to. *I'll fix his ass*, she thought. *At 5:00 p.m. Tuesday, Gus Lanton will officially be relieved of all duties and ordered to vacate the premises. It will be by my executive order as an officer of the board,* Elizabeth thought to herself. *That order will be impossible for Roger to challenge or to change. This is a typical Monday,* she thought, becoming less enchanted with her CEO every minute.

The three-mile drive leading into the Institute compound was, except for shift changes three times a day, an isolated two-lane road. Sweeper used the weekend to finalize his plan. He would position his car just off center, blocking the road two miles from the electric gate. Gus Lanton's Chevy Blazer would have to stop. He would probably offer to assist the troubled motorist, thinking it was a stranded employee, Sweeper figured.

It had rained the night before, and rinsing the air had given way to a fresh-smelling Tuesday morning. Sweeper was on his way to Lake Placid. The papers included in the package he had picked up at the Stillwell Avenue Station included detailed escape plans that would take Sweeper safely to London, and ultimately to Zurich. Roger Maxco had kept his part of the bargain. Now, it was up to Sweeper to keep his.

While waiting for his prey, Sweeper reread the letter he had composed for Nancy. A contact in Iowa would mail it in hopes of confusing the authorities.

My Dearest Nancy,

I know there is no explanation acceptable to you for what I have done. Regardless, Nancy, you must know I love you. I always will. Because of you, I curse my deeds—because of them, I have lost you. I pray to a God that I don't believe in, if only—if only.

You must know I would never have harmed you. I am just a mercenary, fighting battles for other people, perhaps not justified in your world but not so different from nations and their wars. It's been going on since the beginning of time.

I never thought there would be a place in my life or in my heart for love. I had never thought it possible, until you. Please believe that I love you. I wish it could have been different for us. Perhaps, someday, I will call you. Perhaps, someday—

With all my love—
Your Richard

Gus was completing his work at Maxco-Litton. One last visit to the lab, a report to Charles Nitti, and then to say a final goodbye to Roger Maxco, perhaps a mock toast to his miserable life. He was nearing the lab when he noticed the car ahead. It was blocking the two-lane road. *It must have spun out*, Gus thought, noticing the road was muddier than usual due to the rain. *It must be someone from the lab.*

"Need some help?" Gus yelled, pulling alongside the stranded motorist.

"Yes, sorry for the roadblock. It stalled on me. Maybe you could help me move it to one side?"

"I'll pull over. Heading for the lab?" Unaware of any danger, Gus smiled amiably.

"Yes—delivering materials."

Gus parked and walked over to the stranded motorist. "What are—?" Gus looked at Sweeper's hand in amazement.

He never knew what hit him or why. Sweeper advanced directly toward him, with outstretched hand that held a .357 and fired four magnum loads into the chest. Thrown back by the force of the bullets, his heart exploding, Gus Lanton collapsed. He was dead before he hit the ground. That's how Sweeper liked it.

To confuse authorities, this attack was not vintage Sweeper. He had never used a .357 Magnum and had never shot anyone in this manner, head on with multiple blasts.

The crime scene was left in impeccable order—no prints, no identifiable tire tracks, and no other clues. Sweeper was ready to begin his initial steps to leave the country.

At 5:00 p.m., employees were beginning to leave the laboratory compound. Tom Elliot would be working late. He would begin to wonder what had happened to his late afternoon appointment with the member of the board. A lab assistant, Mary Liebowitz, noticed the car off to one side of the narrow two-lane road. Slowing, ready to assist a colleague in trouble, she gasped at the sight. He lay face up, close to the left shoulder of the road. Mary stopped her car and hurried to the victim, his massive wounds apparent. Having worked earlier in her career as a trauma nurse at New York County, she was able to assess the damage within a split second. Although his chest was one large, gaping hole, she knew he had been shot several times. There was no sign of life. Struggling not to vomit from the horrific sight, she grabbed her cell phone and dialed 911.

"911, what is your emergency?"

"This is Mary Liebowitz from the Maxco-Litton Institute on Route 7. I'm six miles off the main highway. A man's been shot. His car is here. Send police and the coroner."

"How do you know he is dead?" The 911 operator was not about to send a coroner for a live patient. She would be the laughing stock at the precinct. Somehow the caller seemed too together, in such a critical moment, and she wondered whether this was a prank call from a college student.

"Trust me," Mary replied, taking a deep breath to calm the nausea. "He's dead. I was a trauma nurse. This man has suffered massive injuries. I'm sure he has no heart left, at any rate. It's been blown through his back."

The dispatcher seemed to take notice and the pendulum swung

the other way and she bulleted questions at Mary. "Units are on the way. Is there anyone else around? Are you in danger?"

"It appears to have happened a few hours ago." Mary was finally back in the groove of her nursing experience, and ready to report the obvious without emotion. Quickly scanning the man's body and the scene, she said, "The blood is drying and there are other signs. A few leaves have blown onto the body. It's been here for a couple hours, probably. There's no one else around."

"I have an ETA of eight minutes, Ma'am. The police have requested that you back away from the body and remain in your car, to protect the integrity of the scene. Thanks for your help."

"I understand." Mary said, glad to be relieved of the burden. It had been a long time since she had been exposed to such violence, and it always helped to be in a sterile environment and have other professionals around. She was suddenly feeling very exposed and vulnerable.

"Mary?" The dispatcher interrupted her thoughts.

"Yes?"

"Please leave your phone line open until they get there. I want to be sure you're safe."

"That won't be necessary. I can hear sirens in the distance. Thanks again. I'll stay here to answer questions, if they need me."

A State Highway Patrol car was first on the scene followed by local police, then an ambulance. Officer Curt Mantis saw Mary get out of her car and wave to the officer.

"Officer, I'm Mary Liebowitz from the Maxco-Litton lab. I'm the one who found him," she said pointing at the body. "He's been shot several times—massive wounds. My best guess is that he's been dead a couple hours or more." She received a snide, patronizing look from the officer, as if he didn't appreciate a layman's assessment of the scene.

"Did you see any other cars when you stopped?" he asked coldly.

"No, I had just left the lab and this is what I found."

"Do you know the man? Does he work for Maxco-Litton?"

"I don't recognize him. Actually, I haven't really looked at his face. He may work out of the New York office, I don't know. I didn't touch the body. I didn't look for identification."

"Ms. Liebowitz, I'll need to see your driver's license—you

may be an important witness. If you don't mind, stick around and give your statement to the local police. Thanks for your help."

Two detectives had already arrived from Lake Placid. They had been having a bite to eat at the café down the road when they were paged. They talked to Mary, searched the body, and discovered several documents confirming the victim's name and employer. Pete Hunter, one of the detectives, commented to his partner.

"Jake, you know we did receive word from the FBI to report any incident related to Maxco-Litton. Also, we have this Sweeper guy on the loose, but this doesn't fit his M.O. Who are we supposed to call?"

"The name's in the car, Pete—it's a New York City contact—O'Brien I think. Just a minute." Jake found the name and phone number. He placed the call.

"FBI Field Office, how may I direct your call?"

"Maggie O'Brien, please. I'm calling regarding the Maxco-Litton investigation. I'm with the Lake Placid Police Department."

"What is your name sir?"

"Detective Monroe—Jake Monroe."

"One moment, please."

The telephone was picked up immediately, as if she had been waiting for his call. "This is Maggie O'Brien, what's happening, detective?"

"Ms. O'Brien, we are investigating a murder about three miles from the Maxco-Litton lab on Route 7. The man killed is an employee, according to his papers. He's on the board of Directors. We haven't called Maxco-Litton, yet. Our department is responding to your formal request to apprise the FBI of any incident involving that company."

"We are indebted to you, detective." She sounded breathless. This is extremely important. One of our agents, John Rushly, will be in contact with you. Please, do not contact anyone at Maxco-Litton until Agent Rushly has had a chance to discuss this with you. He will need a detailed report of your findings at the crime scene. Are there any witnesses?"

"A lab employee discovered the body on the shoulder, just off the road. There's still no one else around. It's kind of isolated here. We do have the profile on this Sweeper fellow—doesn't look like his work. This was messy. Really messy, and hostile. Not a clean shoot. They blew his chest away."

"Thank you, Detective. Rushly will contact you shortly. Do you have the name of the victim?"

"Gus Lanton."

"Thank you for your cooperation."

"I'll be waiting to hear from Rushly."

Maggie O'Brien grabbed her notebook to track down John Rushly. He was in New York and kept his cellular phone active. She dialed the number.

"John Rushly."

"John, this is Maggie O'Brien. One of the Directors of Maxco-Litton has been murdered—Gus Lanton."

"I'll be in the office in minutes—anymore details?" John could taste action and was getting the scent of Sweeper. He knew he was nearby.

"John, it happened near the lab at Lake Placid. You can call a detective who is on the scene. His name is Jake Monroe. He said the job was messy—not Sweeper's style. The seas are getting rough, John."

"It appears that the life expectancy of a Maxco-Litton employee is lessening by the day," John said, wryly. "Any witnesses?"

"A lab assistant found the body. That's all. Nothing else."

"Thanks, Maggie, I'll call the detective. Give me the number."

Maggie O'Brien gave John the number, then alerted other agents that Sweeper may have been involved in yet another killing. The Highway Patrol and local police were also put on alert. John wasted no time dialing the detective.

"Detective Monroe."

"Detective, this is Agent Rushly, I understand you have a murder on your hands—could you fill me in?"

Monroe gave John all the details, including the fact that he had reached someone at Maxco-Litton, "an Elizabeth Martin."

"She said she knew you, John, and would be talking to you soon. That's about it. We found no evidence at the crime scene. It was a violent shooting, but professional, regardless. Absolutely nothing of value was found at the crime scene—nothing to help us. Nothing removed from the wallet, and his Rolex is intact. We have secured the victim's car. You can see it at the impound."

"Regardless of the method of operation, Detective, I have a hunch our man Sweeper had a hand in this. He's hot right now, and must be very thorough. Sounds as if this was a pretty thorough job," he said, grimacing.

"It wasn't pretty," agreed the detective. "I wish I could be of more help. Call me anytime."

"Is it Jake?"

"Yes, Sir."

"Thanks, Jake, I'll be in touch."

John speed-dialed Elizabeth's private line.

"Elizabeth Martin." She sounded shaky.

"It's John, Elizabeth. It appears that our look at Gus was justified. He was found shot to death on the road near Lake Placid." Elizabeth couldn't believe what was happening.

"That's terrible news. Son of a bitch. We need to meet, John. I'm really scared."

"It's about time, lady," John said, pretending a gruffness he didn't feel. She had been so instrumental in getting him information and reports, she seemed to have been made of steel. "I'm glad I stayed in New York. Elizabeth, I'm near the Metropolitan Museum of Art, not far from Rockefeller Center. How about some coffee?"

"I'll be there. I can't leave this office too soon! I should be there in about fifteen minutes. Where we met before, on 57th, okay?"

"I'm leaving now," came the response.

John's cab headed south to 57th Street. Elizabeth dropped everything, praying that Roger either was too busy to notice her whereabouts or perhaps had left the building. Her face muscles were strained and tense, causing the receptionist to look twice as the normally elegant and poised woman marched out of the building without her attaché.

John and Elizabeth felt strangely calm and removed from the onslaught of violence that seemed to be surrounding them as they carried their coffee out to the patio near the sidewalk. Temperatures were in the low seventies—a delightful summer day. Geraniums had been planted along the wrought iron fence enclosing the patio. The tables were comfortably shaded with multi-colored, canvas umbrellas. It was a pleasant setting. The conversation was not.

"What in God's name is going on, John? It's beginning to feel like everything is out of control."

"Roger Maxco may be out of control, or his friends in Chicago," John replied quietly, careful not to be overheard. "What happened in the office, Elizabeth? What about your conversation with Roger, and the tie to Gus Lanton?" Elizabeth gave John a blow-by-blow description of the office incident.

"It's hard to sort out Roger's motives, Elizabeth. At this point, I'm firmly convinced that we are dealing with an unpredictable and paranoid personality. I'm convinced that Gus's killer was Sweeper, the same man who killed Julian Weitzel and the cop in Nassau. But how did he get into the middle of Roger and Gus Lanton? I can't figure that out."

"John, I have to stop this madness. I may not be able to arrest anyone but I can sure slow Roger down. I have been talking to Arthur Litton. He's been my mentor since day one. He's not active but he can help. He keeps such a low profile, but he is really distressed about all this. He can be trusted, John. The man is as close to a saint as you can get. With his help, Roger can be stopped."

"Stopped from what?" John replied. We have no proof of his involvement in these killings."

"There is plenty of circumstantial evidence, John, and while that's not enough for you to prosecute, the firm of Maxco-Litton does not need solid proof. With the preliminary reports from the audit and the fact that he is a suspect and being investigated by the FBI—that's enough for Arthur. We can retire him, John. What do you think?"

This was a tough question. The agent knew a lot more about the activities of Roger Maxco and his contacts than he was permitted to divulge. The Drug Enforcement Agency and the Internal Revenue Service were now a part of his ongoing investigation. He held in his hands extremely sensitive information, information with potential worldwide repercussions. He couldn't apprise Elizabeth of this new, startling information—it would have to be shared only on a NEED TO KNOW basis. Carefully, he couched his answer in less-than-specific language.

"Elizabeth, in my opinion, Maxco-Litton should conduct itself in a reasonable and prudent manner. In other words, if you, as a prominent Director, and Arthur Litton, as co-founder and owner, see fit to replace or to mitigate the influence of one of your top people, then you should do just that. Your responsibility is to run the organization properly. It's a management decision, not a legal or FBI matter."

"Are you sure you are not in the diplomatic service, Mr. Rushly," Elizabeth replied sardonically, stressing the *mister*.

"Okay—caught. I just have to be careful, Elizabeth. There are things that I can't discuss with you. But I can give you a broad brush-stroke of advice."

"I do understand, John. I just feel so alone. This man has disrupted my career and a company I helped to build. I am resenting his power and have absolutely no idea how much damage all this fall out is going to cost our stockholders, perhaps the life of the firm itself."

"That's understandable—but don't take any unnecessary chances, just to get back at him."

"He can destroy our entire company, John. He could *knowingly* destroy a four billion-dollar company! It makes me sick."

"Until we have solid evidence for an indictment, Elizabeth, Roger could very well cause a lot of damage. Perhaps you should clip his wings, if that's possible to do without endangering yourself. It may slow him down."

"Thanks for the coffee and conversation, John. Maybe someday soon, we will be able to talk about something more pleasant."

"I believe we will, Elizabeth. Stay strong. You're a remarkable woman."

"So why are all the remarkable men taken, John?" It was the first flirtatious remark she had made toward him. John didn't respond. He reached over to squeeze her hand, and then they parted. He felt he had been paid a real compliment. *One could easily love that women,* he thought, watching her walk away in her Armani suit, gliding gracefully, even comfortably, atop two-inch heels. *She is truly unique.*

Chapter Twenty

Newark, New Jersey—Maxco-Litton Airport Facility

"Listen closely, you fucking bastard! At this moment, your life has no value—it's about to end. You have one slim chance." Sweeper could not contain his wrath. He had boarded a 707 for a direct flight to London—a Maxco-Litton chartered jet carrying emergency drugs ordered by a London hospital. His cover was perfect—a pharmacist under the firm's special dispensation to accompany the shipment. Just three minutes prior to departure, however, the flight was mysteriously cancelled. Sweeper found the nearest phone. In a rage, he dialed Maxco's private line.

"What! Why are you calling me here? Everything has been arranged. What are you talking about?" Roger was furious at the interruption. He didn't need any more problems, least of all with a trained killer.

"The flight was cancelled."

"That's impossible." Fear and apprehension enveloped Roger.

"Listen, Maxco, you son of a bitch, —in the past two weeks there has been an attempt on my life, I lost the woman I loved, the only thing in my life that ever mattered to me, and now you and your goddamned doublecross. Think hard, Maxco, and listen carefully—unless you perform, *I will kill you*. If that's not possible, I'll see to it you spend your remaining days in prison. I'll personally make your life a living hell! Now, fix it!"

"God, I promise you this was not my fault! I promise you—faithfully—I'll get you out of the country! Give me twenty-four hours. You will have a chartered jet—I promise." Roger was truly panicked. He had been naive dealing with the likes of Charles Nitti—this day, he knew he was in mortal danger. Sweeper was a gifted killer.

"Twenty-four hours—I'll be close to this hangar and your plane. Don't even think about failing, Maxco. I have nothing more to lose." Sweeper hung up the phone. He was smart enough to know that something had happened on Roger's end. *The bastard didn't even know*, Sweeper thought. *Someone tripped him up—and me.*

Sweeper had promised himself one other call. The professional, cold-blooded killer dialed the number with trembling hands.

"The Mystery Hour."

"Nancy—" he thought his heart was coming up through his chest into his throat. "Nancy. Don't hang up—please. It's me." The silence was thick with emotion.

"We have nothing left, Richard—you've taken it all. I can't talk, now." Near tears, Nancy held the phone, speechless. The hurt and pain all rushed back in an instant. She suddenly realized it had never left.

"I never deserved you, Nancy, I know. But I do love you. You have to forgive me."

"I can't give you absolution, Richard. You are two different people. I forgive Richard for lying, but not the other for killing. It's over." The overwhelming sense of loss and sadness allowed Nancy to place the phone back on the receiver. She closed the shop and went home. The emptiness was everywhere.

Sweeper slumped into a near-fetal position on the floor of the Maxco-Litton hangar. For a brief moment, he contemplated suicide. He could not remember feeling so alone, so desperately alone. "I'll kill them all," he muttered under his breath. "I'll kill them all—Maxco, Nitti—the sons of bitches, I'll kill them all!"

Roger was busy tracing the order that had not only cancelled Sweeper's flight, but also all scheduled flights under his direction. It didn't take long for him to identify the source—Elizabeth Martin.

He stormed into her office, not realizing there were other Directors in her office, sitting around her conference table. "What's the meaning of this?" he screamed wildly. "Who the fuck do you think you are?"

"Roger, have you gone mad?" Elizabeth demanded coolly. "I'm in the middle of a conference. What the hell has come over you?"

"*You* have come over me, Elizabeth! Explain these memos you have sent, without my authorization, to our distribution centers."

Flinging the memos across her desk, he stood before her glaring. She got up from her desk, walked across the room and closed the door. The other Directors were silent. Returning to her executive chair behind her executive desk, she faced him in her most elegant, executive manner and ordered Roger Maxco, her boss and Chief Executive Officer, to "sit down." Her tone was not to be questioned.

"You want an explanation, Roger. This is my version: Dr. Marshall Hall is dead. Dr. Julian Weitzel is dead. Gus Lanton is dead. And you, sir, are under investigation by the FBI. You may be culpable in these murders, Roger, I don't know. But it seems you are bent on destroying this company. I can't let that happen.

"Furthermore, the audit is turning up some very strange accounting practices, not to mention the inventory problem, which you promised to fix. Arthur Litton and I, subject to a formal hearing by the board, are relieving you of your duties. For lack of a better term, your management of Maxco-Litton has temporarily been suspended."

"You can't—"

"I *have*—"

"Goddamn you, Elizabeth—you have no authority. Arthur doesn't have the authority. He—" Roger was trying to tell Elizabeth something else but stopped.

"Don't swear at me, Roger. You brought this on yourself. Your tirade with Gus Lanton has been of great interest to the authorities and I am sure you will be receiving another visit from the FBI. I have tolerated your ego and blatant disregard for morality and ethics long enough. This is Wednesday, Roger. Friday, you are to have your house in order. The lawyers are coming in and there'll be an emergency meeting of the board that day at 11:00 a.m. You're invited to attend, but it won't be pleasant."

"You've turned on me, Elizabeth. I'll have a court order by Friday. I'm running this goddamned company!" Roger turned, nearly frothing at the mouth, slamming her door on the way out. Elizabeth took a deep breath before she turned to face the three Directors sitting quietly watching the theatrics. "I'm glad that's over," she said, regaining her composure. "Round one—he's not going down easy." They all nodded in agreement.

Roger raced to his office to call Michael. Filling in the details, he could hardly contain his rage. He thought of Sweeper—life and death—the man had to be flown out of the country tomorrow.

"Maybe this is a good thing, Roger. Slow down. I'll have a meeting with Elizabeth and Mr. Litton. We need to put something constructive together—something positive for the company to take their minds off Gus. Besides, they can't tie you to that mess. Please don't tell me you had anything to do with it, Roger—I don't want to know. Stay at your office. I'll be there by six. We'll get this under control."

"I guess I really need your advice, Michael—I've moved too fast. I need a favor."

"What is it, Roger?" his colleague was losing patience. Roger had become a loose cannon and this man didn't want to go to court over this mess.

"There's a friend of mine that has to leave the country tomorrow, even this evening, if possible. Can you help? Elizabeth has temporarily clipped my wings—literally."

"Well, lest you forget, Roger—you have more corporate jets than American has, what about the Lear you have sitting by for emergency shipments?"

"They're grounded, Michael. Elizabeth took away my car keys, temporarily," he said sarcastically, trying to make light of his critical situation. He didn't want Michael to know why he needed the plane or whom it was for.

"I'll get to work on it—where is he?"

"He's at the facility at Newark—at a hangar, ready to go."

"Okay, I'll be back to you in a few hours."

"You're a lifesaver, Michael." Roger wasn't using a play on words—he meant it literally.

John Rushly had temporarily lost track of Kimberly and Mike. He was sure they had left New York. Had he not known they had stayed and were tracking down their own lead found among her father's papers, he would have issued an all points for them. Things were becoming more disjointed, more dangerous by the minute.

During their visit to Julian's laboratory, they had uncovered an inter-office memo relating to the assignment of certain stock options by Roger Maxco to a company called Alliance Enterprises. At first, Mike Staples had thought it unimportant. In fact, the original was included among the papers turned over to the FBI. But on their way out of town, Kimberly mentioned the memo, suggesting they stop in Chicago on their way back to California. The address for Alliance Enterprises was displayed prominently on the letterhead, they agreed it would not be a difficult lead to check out.

They were staying just off the Loop on Lake Michigan and decided to take a cab to Alliance Enterprises the next day. That evening, the new lovers enjoyed a quiet dinner at their hotel. Over poached salmon with dill and rice pilaf, they discussed their plans, both naïve to any danger that might be related to their visit.

"We'd better get some sleep," Mike said, finally. "Tomorrow, we have a mission—who or what is Alliance Enterprises and what connection could they possibly have to your father's death?"

Charles Nitti sat in stunned silence trying to comprehend the murder of one of his most valuable employees. Christopher Santini and Tony Vittorio were sitting across the desk from Charles when the telephone rang. Christopher looked quizzically at Charles.

"What happened, Charles? you don't look so good."

"Gus Lanton is dead—murdered."

"It doesn't make sense," replied Tony. He was one of ours—no threat to—."

"A threat to Roger Maxco," Charles interrupted.

"He wouldn't dare. He's—." Christopher was visibly disturbed by the news.

"The word you're looking for is *insane*—Roger Maxco is nuts," said Nitti. "My guess is he offered Sweeper a way out of the country, and the price was Gus. I may be wrong, but I don't think so."

"If it's true, Charles, there is no trust. This guy could bring us all down."

"That's not all of it," said Charles.

"I'm getting word that the Russians involved are worried. Roger has a backup scheme. The shipments that Gus found out about are scheduled for simultaneous delivery in July. It's a

Russian Mob deal. Roger gets two hundred million dollars on the first of the month. We get a big piece of it. Now he has some of his Russian friends wondering what the hell is going on. The FBI is getting too close. This killing of Gus is going to cause a lot of problems, a lot of problems."

"Are we out of control on this, Charles?" asked Tony.

"Not yet," replied Charles, but time is running out for Maxco. If he doesn't deliver, the Russians will kill him. If they don't, I will. We made a big mistake trusting that guy. Have our people in New York confirm Roger's responsibility in this. I want hard evidence. Then we act."

The three men continued their conversation when Nitti's phone rang again. It was a local call—the warehouse address of Alliance Enterprises.

"What!" he barked into the phone. All he needed was more bad news.

"Sir, we had two visitors to the warehouse. They came into the distribution office and started to ask a lot of questions. They said a Dr. Julian Weitzel had given them the address—thought we might be holding some of his personal stuff. It sounded fishy except the girl identified herself as Kimberly Weitzel — she had ID with her. The guy with her was a friend—name of Staples."

"Where are they now?" Nitti said, nearly disbelieving what he was hearing.

"They tried to look around, but I made 'em get out. I told them we do import and export, never heard of her father, and to leave the premises. That's it."

"Okay, you did fine, fine. Let me know if they return."

"Yes, Sir."

"Maybe it is out of control," Nitti said, turning back to his goons. "What the hell is Kimberly Weitzel doing here? Goddamn it, we're being connected to all this shit."

Trying to plug the holes, Nitti directed Christopher and Tony to find out what they could about Gus's murder. The loss simply meant no further inside information would be forthcoming from Maxco-Litton. *Who else can I approach?* he wondered. *Why doesn't someone just plug Maxco and clean up this mess!*

"I guess that was a dead end," Kimberly said, everything

looked normal to me, Mike."

"It may have looked normal, Kimberly, but it wasn't. The guy was hiding something. For sure, he was not running an import-export business. There was nothing going on, no activity. I'd like to know who owns the building. Let's check with a title company—the ownership is a matter of public record."

"You're the detective, Mike. Let's do it."

Checking the local Yellow Pages, Mike found the address for Chicago Title—it was just a few miles east. It only took a few moments once they reached the customer service desk. The clerk came back with a copy of the Deed.

"The Deed indicates the property is owned by Alliance Enterprises, Inc., a Delaware corporation."

"No help there. Where do the tax bills go?"

"A law firm in Delaware. They probably represent the owner."

"Looks like they have that covered," Mike said. "They are definitely hiding something."

"We tried, Mike," replied Kimberly, maybe John can find out more. We should give him this information."

"You can have a copy of the Deed. That's the best I can do."

"Thanks for you efforts. You've been very helpful." Getting back in the car, Kimberly and Mike decided they had had enough of coast-to-coast sleuthing. It was time to return to his home in Bodega Bay. From there, they would contact John Rushly.

It had been nearly seventeen hours since Sweeper had threatened his adversary's life. He had been holed up in a clump of canvas tarps, piled in an unobtrusive, little-used corner of the hangar. Still there was no word from Maxco. Michael Lowe had run into one problem after another in trying to arrange a flight for Sweeper. There was, however, some new activity at the Newark facility. Elizabeth and Arthur Litton had arranged for a company Learjet to be flown from Newark to JFK. The executive jet would take Arthur from JFK to the airport at Ft. Lauderdale, Arthur Litton's hometown and private retreat.

Sweeper had dozed off—he awoke hearing the excitement.

"Kevin, let's get this lady fueled. We're heading for JFK then Ft. Lauderdale."

"You got it—should be a good flight. Pilot Matt Ray had instructed the mechanic to "top it off." Kevin was nearly finished when Sweeper stepped out from his hideout, twenty yards from the refueling truck.

"Who is that, Kevin?" the pilot said. Both men were curiously watching the man approaching. He was carrying a small bag.

"Hello!" Sweeper shouted, smiling casually. "Mr. Maxco said I could get a lift." He was now standing only ten feet from the plane. The refueling was finished and Kevin, the mechanic, looked at the pilot and shrugged.

Matt Ray climbed out of the cockpit to walk around the plane for a visual inspection.

"Hello, I'm Matt Ray, the pilot. I haven't received any instructions to take on any passengers. Do you have written authority?"

"My name is Sweeper. You can call Mr. Maxco's office."

"I'm sorry, Sir, I have instructions from Mr. Litton and Ms. Martin that Mr. Maxco's authority here has been temporarily suspended—office politics, I guess. Anyway, there's nothing I can do, sorry."

"I see," said Sweeper, "in that case, let me see if I can find my ticket. Never losing eye contact with the pilot, Sweeper swiftly pulled the .357 from his bag. "Gentlemen," he said politely, "the three of us will be leaving now. Don't argue. I'm a desperate man." When they hesitated from shock, he lowered his voice. "If you don't move now, I'll shoot your friend, is it Kevin?"

"It's your show, pal—let's go." Matt Ray had been an F-16 pilot in Vietnam—shot down twice. He turned to Kevin and said, "Get in Kevin, and don't worry."

"Good thinking, Matt," Sweeper said. "You guys play along and no one gets hurt. I don't like your boss but I have nothing against you two. Let's head out."

"Where are we going?"

"Head for England—I need to figure out the best place to land."

The pilot's face had turned chalky. Struggling hard to keep his composure, he looked Sweeper right in the eyes and spoke calmly.

"Sir, this plane is a Learjet 31A. It has a top speed of 533 mph and a maximum range of 1,266 nautical miles. It's designed for short trips within the continental United States. Believe me, I'm ready to go—except over the Atlantic Ocean." The pilot sounded sincere. He had reached into the door pocket and brought out an operating manual giving specifications of the aircraft. He handed it to Sweeper.

"It looks like you're right, Ray. Suppose we head south to Miami or Ft. Lauderdale."

"That will be close," replied Ray. "Without headwinds and at a speed of 450 mph at 45,000 feet, we could make Jacksonville—possibly Ft. Lauderdale. Certainly no further." Ray knew that flying at 45,000 feet would attract attention, possibly from a military aircraft. He didn't mention that fact.

"Okay, let's go. Kevin, I'm going to tie you into your seat—sorry. I don't want to be distracted from where our pilot is going. Ray, no radio communication and no tricks. I have little to lose."

The Learjet 31A lifted into the air and headed south. The radio crackled with questions and warnings, all too late. Sweeper was impressed with the accommodations—a private lavatory, plenty of headroom, and beautifully trimmed leather executive seats. A feeling of euphoria and sadness swept over Sweeper. He was away from the danger of New York, but leaving Nancy too.

"How do we land without involving airport security and the police, Ray?" Sweeper asked?"

"We can pretend we have a mechanical failure—that we need an emergency runway. That's the only way we can make an unauthorized, non-scheduled landing. I would worry more about Maxco-Litton reporting a stolen aircraft," he responded, his composure intact.

"Maybe we'll get lucky," Sweeper said. "They may not miss the plane for two or three hours."

"When we land," Ray said, "Kevin and I can pretend we are the only ones on board. That will give you a chance to escape. I don't want any shooting. I'm not going to alert anyone until later."

"Very smart, Ray, but not a good plan. I need to get out of the airport. Kevin and I are the mechanics, okay? That's the story." Ray nodded and carefully charted the course before switching to autopilot.

"Where the hell is my jet?" Arthur Litton asked, confused.

"We don't know, sir. It took off from Newark and disappeared."

"Did it crash?"

"No, Sir—it headed south—out of sight."

Arthur grabbed the phone and called Elizabeth.

"Elizabeth, Mr. Litton is on the phone. Can you take his call? He says it's urgent."

"Yes, Marcie, put him through."

"Arthur, what's going on?"

"It appears that my jet has been stolen. It's gone—no word from the pilot."

"I wonder if this has anything to do with Roger—I'm calling the FBI. John will know what to do."

"Let me know what's going on, Elizabeth. I'm going back to the apartment. I was looking forward to the Lauderdale trip."

"Be glad you're not on that plane, Arthur. We don't know what could be happening right now."

"Be careful, Elizabeth. Call me later."

Elizabeth wasted no time. According to Maggie O'Brien, John was on his way back to the office.

"Ms. Martin, what is your emergency? Can I help?"

"Maggie, one of our company jets has been hijacked from the Newark facility. It was scheduled to pick up Mr. Litton at JFK and fly him to Ft. Lauderdale. There is not a sign of it anywhere—no crashes reported. I called the FAA—they're looking into it. They have the jet ID numbers—it's a Learjet 31A."

"I'll inform John as soon as he comes in. In the meantime, let me follow up with the FAA. I'll make sure other airports and commercial flights have this information. What is the range of the aircraft, Elizabeth?"

"I'm not sure. It's only used for short trips—1,000 miles or so, I guess."

"I'll get back to you," Maggie replied.

Maggie O'Brien contacted the FAA to try to determine the status of the aircraft. They had notified other airports and alerted commercial pilots to be on the alert. John called Elizabeth the minute he got back into the office. He was laughing.

"Elizabeth, it seems there's never a dull moment at Maxco-Litton. I understand you have now lost a plane."

"And I'm losing my mind, John. I know Roger has something

to do with all of this. Mr. Litton and I relieved him of his duties—he went berserk. Now, Mr. Litton's private jet is missing. It left Newark for who knows where."

"I have a strong hunch the man who killed Gus Lanton is on that jet."

"Whoever he is, John, he has our pilot and mechanic. They're both missing. What can we do?"

"I was handed its specs as I got in, Elizabeth. I understand it will have to refuel. It's been off the ground an hour and a half. That means it will have to land in an hour. We're hoping a commercial or military jet will spot it. How high can that jet fly, Elizabeth?"

"Arthur said it could cruise at 50,000 feet."

"They'll probably stay within the normal altitudes so they won't be noticed. Does Roger have anything to say?"

"He's in denial John, he's really screwed up."

"If our passenger wants out of the country, he will stay close to the East Coast. Maybe he's heading for Florida. I'm going to alert the Miami Airport. He could take a flight to Europe from there with no problem."

"John, the original flight plan was from JFK to Ft. Lauderdale—he might try to land there."

"Okay, Elizabeth, let me get to work. I'll be calling you."

"I'll keep your cellular number handy, John." She hung up and sighed, exhausted from the continuing stress. *When was the last time I did a normal day's work around here?* she asked herself, irritated with the toll this was taking on company business.

"Change of plans, gentlemen." Sweeper stood behind the pilot, making sure the gun was visible to him. Ray, head for the new County airport at Marathon. It's midway down the Florida Keys."

"That's crazy," Ray responded angrily. "We don't have enough fuel."

"I don't give a crap! That's where we're going. You'd better start conserving, slow down if necessary." Sweeper was in no mood to be challenged.

"You're talking two hundred miles beyond our range! Are you crazy?"

"Yes, Ray, I am crazy. If you try to land anywhere else, I'll shoot us all. Believe me, I've had a very bad week."

"We are on course for Marathon," Ray responded, adjusting the computer, "—in the Florida Keys." He shook his head, knowing better than to argue.

Sweeper knew the risks. With only a two-lane highway out of the Keys to the north, he could become trapped. However, he reasoned that the Miami and Ft. Lauderdale airports would be swarming with FBI. They would never suspect him to land in the Keys. The airport at Marathon had been helpful before, in tracking Julian Weitzel. It was an unusually quiet facility, a county and federal government boondoggle.

I can hitch a ride north in a small sailboat—they will never find me because they won't be looking, Sweeper thought. *In a week or so, I'll fly out of Miami Airport.*

"Stay at fifty thousand feet, Ray. I don't want anyone to see us. Start your descent farther down the Keys. Where are we now?"

"North of Orlando—heading straight for Marathon—about forty minutes away."

"Good work, Ray. Don't screw up."

"In twenty minutes, we'll be on fumes," Ray reported nervously. "It's going to be close, very close."

"Land at Ft. Lauderdale! We're not going to make it," Kevin shouted, losing his cool for the first time.

"Shut up, Kevin—Ray will land the plane and we'll all be safe." Sweeper was nervous, too. But with a broken heart, he really didn't care at this point.

"Then what?" Kevin shouted, "Then what?"

"I'm letting you go, no problem. Ray, you make sure there is no trouble with the Marathon people. It's pretty sleepy there—tell them you are parking for several hours. Okay?"

"Then what?" Ray parroted Kevin's concern. He knew he and Kevin were witnesses.

"I'm going to tie you both securely, bust the radio, and sooner or later they'll investigate. I have no reason to hurt you guys. Just get us on the ground."

The fuel-warning indicator came on 110 miles from their destination. Ray had started his descent. They were outside the flight patterns for commercial jets but could be tracked by radar. It was time to contact the Marathon tower.

"Marathon tower—this is private Learjet 31A requesting clearance for landing. We will need non-emergency mechanical service. Do you read?" Ray was instructed not to mention the real emergency — low fuel. That would have brought emergency vehicles and police.

"Learjet 31A—you are an unscheduled flight cleared for landing—do not disembark. Your persons and cargo will need clearance. Acknowledge with flight origination and destination."

"Roger that, no problem. ETA twenty minutes. " Ray conveniently did not answer the question of departure. He wanted to arouse suspicion.

"What the hell do they want?" shouted Sweeper.

"They want to know where we came from." Ray shrugged, tapping the fuel gauge.

"Tell them," Sweeper replied. "Make something up, Houston or someplace."

"Okay, let's hope it matters. We could flame out any second."

"Marathon, point of origin, Houston—ETA eight minutes."

Tension mounted as the sleek jet made its final descent into the Marathon airport. The fuel warning had gone verbal—"Low fuel emergency. Low fuel emergency."

"That means we're cooked in minutes," Ray said, sweat breaking out on his forehead. "I'm going in—we have one pass, that's all." Ray was cool but knew how unforgiving airplanes could be. His life could end any second. He had been given clearance. Kevin, sweating with fear, closed his eyes. Sweeper seemed unconcerned.

"Touchdown," shouted Ray.

They taxied to a predetermined place on the field away from the main terminal. The idea that Sweeper proposed would not work. Personnel from the airport were required to isolate any unauthorized or unscheduled touchdowns. Fortunately for Sweeper, the crackling voice over the radio gave him seconds to plan his escape.

"Sorry, fellows, you have to stay on the plane. Customs people won't be here for forty minutes. We don't have the authority or the staff present to check you out right now." Sweeper grabbed the mike and began to talk.

"We understand. Our mechanic is really sick. I'm opening the door. Do you have a place where he can lie down? Our air is out"

"Okay, one person off the plane. We'll send an escort out there. He can rest in the terminal."

Sweeper seized the opportunity and disabled the radio. Ray and the mechanic were tied securely—and gagged. Sweeper removed the coveralls from Kevin and an identification card, one without a photo. He stepped from the plane and leaned against the wing, waiting for his ride.

"Not feeling so good?" said the driver,

"Not really," replied Sweeper.

There was minimum security at the airport. Flights had been reduced dramatically upon the new terminal's opening three years before. Marathon was more of a community than a town, unincorporated. A few new chains had opened to service the surrounding area—K-Mart and Home Depot. Several small marinas and boatyards catered to the tourists and offered refuge to sailors and powerboat people just hanging out for the summer.

Sweeper pulled his .357 from under the coveralls and stuck it into the ribs of the driver.

"Listen carefully, your life depends on it."

"Son of a bitch, what is—."

"Shut up and listen. Get on your radio and tell the others I am really sick, that you're taking me to the local hospital. Make it good." Sweeper cocked the .357 for effect.

"Ahhh, Ron—this guy is pretty sick—I'm heading for the hospital. I'll call you from there—gotta go."

The car headed out of the airport onto the Overseas Highway and turned left heading toward Key Largo and the Miami area. The frightened driver was pleading for his life.

"Let me out—the car is yours. There's no one around."

"Good idea," replied Sweeper." The driver was ordered to pull off just below the bridge at Plantation Key.

"Go for a swim, pal, that'll will slow you down. Leave your clothes."

Grateful for the chance to get out alive, the sweaty driver took off his clothes and ran into the Gulf side of the island. Satisfied that he would be preoccupied for a time, Sweeper raced ahead. It would be necessary to abandon the airport car. At Key Largo, fifty miles southwest of Miami, he made his move. An airport shuttle van was leaving for the Miami International Airport—it was a private service not connected to any of the hotels. He paid the fare and tried to relax. It was sixty miles to the airport.

The Miami office of the FBI was on full alert. Maggie dialed the New York number.
"FBI, New York Field Office."
"John Rushly, please. It's urgent." John was motioned to the phone.
"John Rushly."
"Here we go again, John. This is Maggie. I'm in Miami. Your friend Sweeper is on the loose. He's back in the Keys." The Miami office had received a call from the Marathon airport personnel.
"He's trying to get out of the country, Maggie. Have you alerted all the airports in South Florida?"
"All airports, bus terminals, rental car agencies, and the highway patrol have been notified. It's a massive effort, John. We are worried—the guy is desperate—we know what he is capable of doing. We also have the Coast Guard patrolling the Gulf and Atlantic side of the Keys. He may be trapped. Just below Homestead, we have blockaded the Overseas Highway. In our opinion, John, we think he may be between Key Largo and Homestead."
"Just a suggestion, Maggie—he may double back. I would set up a roadblock at Marathon. He may try to make it to Key West— he could get lost there."
"You're right, John. I'll get right on it."
"I hope he can be taken alive. He could bust our case wide open. Call me with any new developments, Maggie. Oh, shit, Maggie, I'm coming on down to Miami. I have a hunch. Call my cell phone."
"I'll look for you, John. Are you renting a car?"
"Yes, Maggie, I'll have time to take care of that in the air. Where will you be?"
"I'll be at the checkpoint in Homestead around seven o'clock this evening."
"There is a 2:00 p.m. flight available to Ft. Lauderdale. I can

make that and drive to Homestead. That will burn up five hours. I'll see you there."

"Great, John. Finally, face to face."

This is close, John thought as he hung up the phone. *This guy can bury a lot of people. I do need to be there.*

Chapter Twenty-one

News filtered through to Roger's contact in Krasnogorsk that parties, not exactly friendly to the Russian Mafia's purposes, were scrutinizing stockpiles of drugs in the warehouses of Maxco-Litton. A partial, although an unsatisfactory explanation had been obtained from Michael Lowe and passed on to Roger's Russian contact in New York—Alexis Kardonoff. The exchange of words took place at Timothy's Coffeehouse off FDR Drive along the East River. It was ten o'clock on Saturday morning. The two met for the first time. Michael was apprehensive.

"Mr. Kardonoff, I'm Michael Lowe, Roger Maxco's attorney."

"Thank you for meeting me, Mr. Lowe. I don't like phone call in matters that are sensitive." Stocky, with a fat face and thick eyebrows, he spoke with broken English. *He could be a Russian spy straight out of a novel*, Michael thought, taken with the man's air of mystery.

"Mr. Maxco wanted me to assure you that he has the entire matter regarding the inventories under control. One of the Directors had ordered a comprehensive audit of all Maxco-Litton activities. It's turning out to be a minor interruption. We are still on schedule."

"Not minor for your friend Sweeper - yes?" Michael tried to hide his surprise too late. The mention of the name was totally unexpected.

"Forgive me, Alexis, I'm afraid I do not understand your comment." Remembering Roger's request for assistance in taking someone out of the country, it all began to register. *Could that have been Sweeper?* Michael thought.

"Come now, Mr. Lowe, you must be aware that your superior was to transport a very important individual out of the country. Our sources identified him. We understand he was quite upset. We worried about that. This man could be disruptive."

"Yes, I do remember. Roger did handle that matter."

"Perhaps not very well," Alexis added. "Getting back to our

problem, Michael, this Director, Elizabeth Martin, she is your problem." There was a threatening tone to this comment that sent chills through Michael's body.

"Elizabeth Martin has great usefulness to our firm. She is under control. Roger wants to keep her safe." Michael tried to impress the Russian—hands off.

"I understand," replied Alexis, but we are available to solve these kinds of problems. We want you to know that."

"That won't be necessary." Michael reiterated, "That won't be necessary."

"Well, in summary, you see no delay in our shipping date? Remember that the initial transfer of funds is conditioned upon absolute certainty on your part that you can deliver. An error would be devastating."

"We are absolutely sure that there will be no delay—you may pass that along to your people in Krasnogorsk."

"Thank you for the coffee, Mr. Lowe. I'll pass along the information, and your comments regarding Ms. Martin. Good day."

What in the hell are we into? thought Michael. *These people will wipe out anyone in their way. They make the Chicago group seem tame. I wish we could go back to the stock deal. Too late to get out—better let Roger know there is no turning back.*

The driver of the airport shuttle was straining to see what was causing the holdup. Traffic was at a standstill. Sweeper was trying to determine if there was an accident up ahead or a roadblock.

"Driver," Sweeper said sternly, "can you get on your radio and find out what the problem is?"

"Way ahead of you, pal," the driver replied, "I'm just getting the word now." The driver was using headphones. "There's a major roadblock just this side of Homestead—could be a two-hour delay. They're looking for someone—sheriff cars, local police and the FBI. I can turn around, folks, and let everyone out—you'll have to decide." There were moans about missing flights and several passengers stated they wanted off.

"I'll pull over at the Circle K ahead. Those of you who want refunds and are getting off, give me your names and addresses. I have no cash on board."

The van stopped in the parking area of Circle K and Sweeper stepped out. He went inside the store, purchased a cup of coffee, and walked outside near a crowd of people. He looked at his watch, trying to appear casual. It was 6:00 p.m.

I need to head back toward Key West—this is no good. Sweeper was thinking fast, starting to panic.

He walked to a small marina where a few fishing boats were docked. Conversing with one of the boat captains, he learned more about what was going on.

"—a lot of excitement," commented Sweeper.

"It's a big show," replied a burly looking fisherman from one of the boats. "They're trying to play it down—but it's big."

"What do you mean? What the hell is going on?" asked Sweeper.

"We intercepted Coast Guard messages. There is a real manhunt going on. Shit, even the Coast Guard is looking for this guy—they almost boarded our fishing boat."

"Now they're all over the goddamned roads," shouted the captain. "How the hell are we supposed to get home?"

"Unless you're heading back toward Key West, forget it—no one's getting through up around Homestead—that's what I hear," said the fisherman.

"Is there a motel on this side of the island, one with a boat dock?" Sweeper inquired.

"Islamorada," shouted the captain "Reasonable, too."

"How far?"

"About eight miles."

"I'm stuck—no car—no motel. How much would you charge to take me over there?" Sweeper didn't want to appear too anxious.

"How about twenty bucks?" asked the captain. "I might as well do someone some good today."

"I'll give you thirty, Captain, it'll save me a lot of trouble." Sweeper decided to lay low for a day or two.

The fishing boat stayed inside the reef, which was offshore about four miles. It was a little tricky since it was possible to go aground.

"How much longer?" asked Sweeper.

"Not far, pal—we have to take it slow."

John Rushly had landed at Ft. Lauderdale Airport, rented a car and arrived at the roadblock just below Homestead. A command center had been set up by the Miami FBI, and Maggie O'Brien was in charge. Some traffic was getting through but it was slow. Each car, van and truck was searched.

"Maggie, it's good to see a familiar face. Damn, I hope were on to something. Let's get this bastard."

"As you can see, John, we have our hands full."

"It looks like you have things under control Maggie," John said. "Have there been any sightings of Sweeper?" The electricity between them was evident. They both knew they were on a manhunt and sensed that they were very close to their quarry.

"We think he's somewhere near Key Largo—a private airport van operator gave us a description that fits. We have been systematically checking all public transportation. We got word on this last lead about thirty minutes before you arrived."

"Maggie, I'm going to head toward Key Largo. Are agents in the area?"

"I'll drive down with you, John. We took your advice and set up a roadblock just above Marathon. I have agents standing by at the Marriott in Key Largo. We can communicate with both roadblocks and everyone in-between. "

"Let's go." John, Maggie, and one other agent, Gene Harper, headed down the Overseas Highway. Each could feel the excitement and tension mounting as they closed in on their prey. They passed over the drawbridge just to the northeast of Key Largo. Biscayne Bay was off to the left as the car exceeded the fifty-five mph speed limit. The sultry evening air prompted Maggie to turn on the air-conditioning. It was close to ninety degrees with an equal percent of humidity—nearly tropical.

"This is your best chance—I doubt he's found a way out."

"I hope so," replied John. "He is extremely resourceful. He's disappeared into thin air more than once. This time I'm not going to lose him."

"Rushly, I understand it's important to your case for us to take this man alive." Gene Harper had been with the FBI for twenty-three years. At fifty-five, he was in remarkable condition and an expert marksman.

"Not at anyone's expense," replied John. "It may be possible—

but he is cornered and faces multiple murder charges. If he can be disabled without risk, that's preferred to an all-out shooting. I think—"

Maggie interrupted. "John, that's the Circle K where the van driver last saw Sweeper—lets have a look. How about a cup of coffee?"

"Excellent idea, Maggie." The hair stood up on the back of his neck. *We're close, goddamn it,* he thought. *I can feel it.*

The convenience store was crowded. Everyone seemed thrilled to be experiencing a real manhunt. No one was concerned about the possible danger. John approached the counter with Maggie and Gene. Each had poured a cup of coffee from the pots on the burners. John paid for the coffee and showed the clerk a photo of Sweeper.

"Have you seen this man today?" John said, "I'm Special Agent Rushly—FBI." He flashed his badge.

"He was here just a couple hours ago," replied the clerk. "Kind of an ordinary looking guy but he seemed a little agitated and was acting nervous."

"What do you mean?" asked John.

"He asked me if anything was going on, heading the other way, away from the excitement. He seemed real intense, that's all."

"Was he walking back toward Marathon? Did you see a car or anything?" Maggie wanted to know.

"I didn't see a car or anything. He just walked out. That's all I saw."

John was satisfied. "Thanks a lot. You've been a great help."

The motel dock was in sight. The captain was careful to keep the fishing boat in between the red and green markers.

"Red right return!" shouted the captain.

"What does that mean?" asked Sweeper"

"If you're returning from the open sea, you have to make sure the red markers are on your right," he explained. "If not, you can go aground or worse."

Just as the captain was lining up to the markers, two hundred feet away, a Coast Guard small cruiser flashed its lights. Out of the muggy twilight, a bullhorn sounded.

"This is the United States Coast Guard. Heave to skipper—we'll toss you a line. Cut your engine." At the same time, a powerful searchlight pierced the heavy air. It wasn't dark, but the light was still effective.

"I'll be damned," cried the captain, "son of a bitch! Never been stopped by the Coast Guard in my life."

"Captain, you're not stopping now." Sweeper had already gone into action "Head for the dock. Your life depends on it." The .357 Magnum pointed at the captain's head was a good persuader.

"Holy shit—what is this?" The captain was shaken. Sweeper answered his question.

"This is a .357 Magnum aimed at your head. Now move it."

The diesel snorted and now under full power, the boat headed for the dock.

"I can't see the goddamned markers. We're going too fast!" the captain shouted.

"Head for the dock and don't slow down," Sweeper insisted, waving his gun.

"United States Coast Guard—You are ordered to stop your engine. The small craft used for shallow water rescue was no match in size to the escaping fishing boat.

"Where the hell are they going?" the Coast Guard officer asked.

"They can only end up on the dock, Sir—they can't escape."

"It may be a hostage situation. Follow them in—slow." "Sailor," the officer shouted to another seaman, "bring the M-60 on deck—also some small arms. Radio operator—get me the FBI. This may be their man."

The fishing boat slowed as it approached the dock.

"Ram the dock! Whatever you have to do! Don't slow down—hit the shore or the dock, but don't slow down!" Sweeper knew his only chance was to hit the earth running. He needed to distance himself from the Coast Guard as fast as possible. He knew they were armed.

"Okay, okay—don't shoot! Screw it—we're going in!" The captain prepared to ram the docks and cut his engine. The weight of the fishing boat shattered planks and posts. Sweeper leaped to the dock and ran toward the motel. Shouts and threats from the Coast Guard filled the night air.

"You in the fishing boat, raise your hands and face the light—don't move! Stop! Coast Guard!" The officer was shouting at Sweeper who was disappearing into the scrub pines. Shots rang out—the officer was firing his pistol into the air. Sweeper was out of sight.

"I have the FBI—they're in Key Largo—patched through to their mobile." The seaman was excited. The officer grabbed the mike.

"Go ahead, this is Rushly, FBI—what do you have?"

"He's on foot, Sir—Lazy Palms Motel—ten miles below Key Largo. He came down the coast - commandeered a fishing boat. The captain of the boat is here, but he can't talk right now, Sir. He's throwing up over the side."

"Stay right there—we're on our way—ten minutes."

"Yes, Sir," replied the officer. "He may be on the road—trim guy wearing a dark jacket."

"Let's make that five minutes, Maggie. Hit the red light—no siren. Gene, keep a sharp eye. My guess is that he'll try to hijack a car."

Sweeper was running hard toward the main highway. The hot humid air was taking its toll. He burst in front of a slow moving Ford Thunderbird. Tires screeched—the driver swore out loud.

"What the hell are you doing? Are you fucking nuts?" Just in time, the driver locked his doors. The car in back didn't stop in time. A Cadillac slammed into the rear of the Thunderbird. The road had widened into two lanes heading each way. The Thunderbird was heading west toward Marathon. Traffic heading towards Homestead was moving at ten miles per hour.

"There's a problem up ahead, John. Looks like a wreak. I'm pulling over." Maggie had seen the Cadillac that had hit the rear of the Thunderbird. She stopped off to the side on the shoulder with her red lights blinking. A County Sheriff's car was heading the other way and stopped. Someone yelled, "Look out, he has a gun."

Traffic had stopped in both directions. It was nearly dark. A passenger in another car ran up to the Sheriff's vehicle.

"He's in the store across the highway, Officer! He's got a gun! He's in the gift shop next to the kite store."

John and the two other agents were signaling the Deputy Sheriff pointing toward the gift shop. John shouted, "Get around in back, Sheriff—stay put!— FBI." John had held up his ID. Maggie was on the phone calling for backup. Shots rang out—loud.

"Sounds like a cannon," Gene said nervously. Adrenaline was pumping in all of them.

"Too many civilians here. Gene, try to get those people in the line of fire out of their cars. Make sure they take their keys." Fortunately, another patrol car had appeared and was already taking care of the traffic problem.

John advanced toward the gift shop, taking cover as he got closer. Maggie was a hundred feet away, moving steadily toward the shop.

John began to shout. "You, in the shop, come out with your hands raised. This is the FBI. You are surrounded—come out and clasp your hands over your head."

Suddenly Maggie yelled out a warning. "Look out, John, a side door—he's making a break for it!"

"Stop! FBI—stop!" John shouted at the suspect whom he couldn't see clearly. Sweeper turned to fire.

Maggie took a stance and fired three shots—Sweeper was down. "He's hit, John." Maggie moved closer. "John, I can't see—can you see his hands? He's down in the brush."

"Okay, Maggie—be careful. Wait, I see his hands—no gun." The second shot had caused Sweeper to drop his weapon. He lay in the dirt unconscious—looking quite harmless. *Just an ordinary looking man,* John thought. John cuffed him and felt his pulse.

"He's alive. We need a chopper—an ambulance will never get through."

"I'm on it, John," Gene replied, "we have an ETA of twenty minutes—it's Coast Guard from Key West."

"How 'bout a paramedic? Our man has a serious head wound." John was determined to keep Sweeper alive.

The Sheriff's Deputy was trained for medial emergencies. He dressed the wound as best he could, from the First Aid kit, and covered Sweeper with a blanket.

"Nothing else we can do, Sir. He needs a trauma team, now."

The helicopter whirled overhead—cars were moved out of the way to allow a landing on the Overseas Highway. Medics rushed toward Sweeper—started an IV and loaded him. John jumped on board.

"We're heading for Miami General," the paramedic said to the agents, "we can land on the roof." He jumped in and gave the thumbs up sign to the pilot. "Let's go."

"Lift the roadblocks," ordered Maggie. "Let's move this traffic. Gene, we need to go. I want to see John at the hospital. I hope Sweeper makes it—touch and go. I hated to shoot him. I had no choice."

"That's right, Maggie," Gene said, "you had no choice. Be glad it's over. At least no civilians were hurt."

"Thank God," replied Maggie. That's only the third time in my whole career I've had to fire my weapon at a suspect. I hope he lives."

The news had spread faster than a Florida wildfire. All the networks and wire services carried the story.

AP Wire Service 6/29/98 10:00 p.m. EST: Florida Keys—A fugitive sought by the FBI for multiple murders was captured in a hail of gunfire tonight in Key Largo. The man was allegedly shot several times by an FBI agent. He was airlifted to a Miami hospital—we have no report on his condition. An FBI spokesperson has confirmed that the wounded man is a suspect in the murder of Dr. Julian Weitzel. Weitzel, a research scientist employed by Maxco-Litton, was found dead in the trunk of his car several weeks ago.

Charles Nitti was having a late dinner and watching the news. Pausing, with the fork halfway to his mouth, he thought, *I hope he's dead. He'll be impossible to get to, now. They won't let him out of their sight!*

Roger Maxco was at home. Michael Lowe had stopped by with the details.

"Is there any word on his condition, Michael?" Roger asked, already worried that Sweeper might talk and incriminate him.

"The security is tight, Roger. He's surrounded by FBI agents. No one is allowed on his floor without special clearance and a police escort. It's a lockdown. Absolutely no information is being released. The hospital media spokesperson has been issued a gag order."

"That goddamned Elizabeth and her special orders! He could have been in Europe by now, —shit!" Roger was anxious for news about Sweeper's health.

"Michael, our friends in Russia are wiring funds on the first. We need that two hundred million. It will keep Nitti quiet. Damn, we are so close."

"They are worried, Roger. I didn't like the tone of the meeting with Alexis. That group will stop at nothing. The Russian even mentioned Elizabeth." Michael had failed to mention that part of the conversation before the Sweeper news.

"That bastard!" Roger sputtered. "Elizabeth Martin is my business. What the hell is wrong with those people?" For some reason, the Elizabeth issue hit a nerve. She had once respected him, he thought. He couldn't remember exactly when he lost her respect, but if anyone were to deal with her, if would be him.

"I was more than clear, Roger. I told them in no uncertain terms that she has great usefulness to our firm and that she's under control. That you want to keep her safe."

"I'm glad you did, Michael. I know she's been a pain in the ass, but I don't want her involved in this. She doesn't deserve to get hurt." The sudden compassion seemed out of character for Roger. Michael looked at him inquiringly.

"Nothing will happen to her, Roger," he said, trying to assure his boss. "They're not stupid. The money will be sent. But I can tell you this. If we don't perform, all hell will break loose. At this point, there are no options but to proceed, with or without Sweeper."

"I want you in Miami, Michael. We have a medical connection there. Find out what's going on at the hospital."

"Fair enough. I'll find out what I can. Take care."

Michael Lowe wasn't comfortable with the turn of events. He was now seeing the CEO as deranged—brilliant, but strangely out of focus. He wondered if they could pull off such a complicated scheme. *Stock manipulations are one thing,* he thought, *but this business with the Russians is something else.* As he drove home, he lowered his window to smell the warm summer air—he could feel the humidity, oppressed by events out of control.

You're in too deep, Michael, chastising himself, —*conspiracy to commit murder, illegal sales of drugs, SEC violations, depraved indifference to human life, obstruction of justice—there truly is no way out. Our plan has to work. There's no time for a deal. I wonder if Tom Elliot and the others realize what we are into?*

The scene at the hospital was one of organized chaos. Security was tight. John and Maggie were standing by for any update on Sweeper's condition. His head trauma was serious, but he was alive. They would have to wait. Hours later, one of the chief surgeons finally appeared.

"Agent Rushly? I'm told to speak only to you."

"Yes, I'm John Rushly. Doctor—this is Maggie O'Brien of the Miami field office."

"I'm Doctor Stanowski—Chief Surgeon. I'm afraid I have little to report."

"What's his status, Doctor? Is it possible for us to see him— talk to him?"

"I'm afraid not—he has extensive brain damage from the gunshot wound. Right now, he is in a coma. There is disruption to the cerebellum."

"Meaning?"

"The cerebellum coordinates voluntary movements by fine-tuning commands from the motor cortex in the cerebrum. The cerebellum also maintains posture and balance by controlling muscle tone and sensing the position of the limbs. All motor activity, from hitting a baseball to fingering a violin, depends on the cerebellum. Our man is completely dormant—we have a lot of tests to conduct. And hours to wait."

"What about the coma?" John asked.

"The coma resulted from decreased metabolic activity in the brain, which may be caused by cerebral hemorrhage and inflammation of the brain. He may have permanently damaged nerve tissue—we're waiting for the results of the electroencephalogram—EEG. Sorry, we'll just have to wait and see. He may come out of this in days, weeks, or maybe never."

"Thank you, Doctor. By the way, we're sorry for all the security—the man is a professional assassin and could be an important witness. There are a few people hoping he doesn't recover, people who would probably try to see to it that he doesn't. We would like to keep his condition confidential—could you alert your staff? It's important to their safety that we keep a low profile on him.

"Yes, of course, Mr. Rushly, but it could be difficult. He is getting medical attention from a lot of people. I can't guarantee that his condition will remain secret."

"Just ask them to do their best, Doctor. Thank you for the report. The news isn't good for us, but we appreciate your cooperation."

Maggie O'Brien shook her head. She felt so responsible. "I'm sorry, John, I would have shot him in the leg, but I didn't have much time."

"Be glad you didn't get hit, Maggie. You had no choice. This guy is a trained killer. No one can fault you for this. Think of it this way, you got him off the streets!"

"It's late, John. What do you say we go for a drink? My treat." Maggie was grateful she was working with John Rushly. He was solid as a rock. She was exhausted from days on end of searching for the elusive bastard that lay twenty feet from her, clothed in nothing but a bed sheet, with tubes entering and exiting every orifice in his body.

"You're on, Maggie. I have a feeling I'm going to permit myself one giant, fucking hangover tomorrow morning." Nodding at the hospital bed, through the glass, he added, "Besides, he's not going anywhere. Let's get the hell out of Dodge. I just want to call Jill on my cell phone, on the way, do you mind?"

The nursing director and ICU staff was briefed once again on the need for confidentiality regarding their star patient. Satisfied that security was in place, the two FBI agents headed for a quiet hotel bar to relax and replay the scenario that had finally brought the man known as Sweeper to the end of his professional career. It had been a long and grueling day.

Chapter Twenty-two

Wednesday, July 1—New York City

The wire transfer of money came through as promised by "K"—Roger had complied according to his instructions, "...acknowledgment via prior encrypted codes."
Of course, Roger reasoned, *the shipments must be timely and complete—in the air no later than July 27. If something goes wrong,* he thought worriedly, *money would be irrelevant.*
He knew that Elliot and members of his team were working overtime, as were the packagers. The plant was in full swing and not one soul on the line knew what they were creating or preparing for shipping. Maxco-Litton paid too well to ask questions. No one wanted to rock the boat. Roger retrieved the fax from his locked files. He read it carefully once again, as if he hadn't memorized the entire thing.

> Transfer of funds ($900 million) to be confirmed upon receipt of goods including new vaccine. Must have shipping documentation in hand to take simultaneous possession Moscow, Paris, Krakow, Berlin and Amsterdam. Confirmation of destination codes by utilizing invoice numbers 2136789—5697654 — 3769245—4793654—4509123 in precise order. All verified 7/27/98. Initial transfer of funds ($200 million) 7/1/98 contingent upon acknowledgment via prior encrypted codes to this number.

At the laboratory in Lake Placid, Tom Elliot was running into unexpected problems. The models created for the vaccines were not living up to his expectations. Something was drastically wrong.
What the hell has happened? Tom wondered. The test batch, thought to be the last step in the painstaking process, had become

contaminated. *Damn,* Tom thought, *this could put us back a month!* He called his staff in and they decided to go back into the research and testing program. It would take a week. *We have that much time*, Tom figured, *—no need to alert Roger.*

The Gallen II project, as originally conceived by Drs. Marshall Hall and Julian Weitzel, had become a sham. There was no longer any pretense that FDA approval was forthcoming. Along with the stock manipulation scheme, it had given way to Roger Maxco's self-serving and despicable deal with the Russian Mafia.

Roger, in the meantime, was successful in obtaining a temporary court injunction to stop Elizabeth and Arthur from relieving him from command of the Maxco-Litton empire. The healthily bribed judge's "opinion" read, in part:

> "While there may appear to be questionable improprieties, it is the opinion of this court that the petitioners have not met the required burden of proof for malfeasance in office. Mitigating circumstances suggest that Roger Maxco may be unfairly singled out due to a pending FBI investigation. Therefore, this court sees no legal basis in preventing Mr. Maxco from continuing his duties as Chief Executive Officer of Maxco-Litton."

Elizabeth was sitting in her office, Arthur Litton across from her. He rarely came into the City anymore. He had come in just for this ruling. Elizabeth couldn't believe what had happened. "No wonder Simpson went free! My God!" she said angrily, tossing the flimsy piece of paper across the desk at her mentor. "What do they want?"

Arthur Litton seemed equally taken aback. "Stay on this, Elizabeth—you have my absolute and continuing support."

"Thank you, Sir—I'm going to need it. I need to call John. You can stay if you wish."

"I'll be getting along, Elizabeth. I am not as young and spry as the rest of you. I can't tolerate all this intrigue. Call me if you need anything. My wife came in for some shopping. We're going to lunch, then home."

Elizabeth had not talked to John since the episode in Key Largo and his long vigil at the hospital in Miami. That was yesterday.

She didn't know where to reach him. *The New York office can track him down*, she thought.

"FBI, how may I direct your call?"

"Special Agent John Rushly," Elizabeth asked, giving them her name.

"Mr. Rushly is on assignment in Miami. I can give you their Field Office number, if you wish."

"Could you contact him and have him call me at my office?"

"Yes, Ms. Martin. I will notify Agent Rushly of your call."

Elizabeth was terribly disturbed by the court's decision. In one instant, she had lost all leverage. *If this man they call Sweeper talks*, thought Elizabeth, *that may end the stranglehold Roger has on the company*. The ringing of the phone alerted her.

"Elizabeth, this is John. How are you?"

"God, that was quick!" She laughed. "How are you, John? I heard there was a gunfight. It's all over the news. Is he talking?"

"He's still in intensive care, in a coma. It's not good news. The doctor doubts he will be talking soon, if ever. What's going on with you?"

"The news here is just as bad, John. A judge reversed our order to oust Roger. He's back and I'm more concerned than ever. Do you have *anything* else we can use? Any new evidence?"

"We keep sorting it out, Elizabeth. I cancelled my trip home. It looks like I'll be in Miami or New York for the next few weeks."

"Your poor wife. Wonder if she regrets marrying someone in law enforcement?" Remembering that Jill Rushly had chosen the same career, she laughed. "I forgot, John. How stupid is that?"

"It's okay," he said wryly, "maybe we'll both get out of the business and have a honeymoon some year."

"Listen, John, Roger was in such a good mood, yesterday. I don't mean that lightly, I mean he was walking on air! He kept saying, 'it's July first, isn't it?' and grinning. Does that mean anything to you?" In spite of all the chaos and the court thing, Roger appeared somewhat settled. It was rather disarming."

"There's nothing significant about the date to me, Elizabeth. Of course, we don't know what Roger is up to. I think he's one of the sleaziest people I've ever met." John thought about the date, but nothing came to mind.

"John, I can control the situation here only to a limited extent.

Roger has the authority he needs insofar as inventory and shipments are concerned."

"Elizabeth, do you have people you can trust at the warehouses and airport distribution centers?" John needed a backup—against what, he didn't know.

"I may be able to plant some trusted employees, John. What should we be looking for?" John's idea for backup was taking shape as they spoke. His mind was clear.

"This is what you need to do. One, make sure you have at least one person that you can trust at each warehouse and airport distribution center. Two, have him report to you any unusual amounts of drugs stockpiled or ready for shipment. Three, they should notify you immediately of any activity indicating that a shipment is imminent. That's my suggestion, Elizabeth. It will give us more eyes and ears. We have to stay one step ahead of this guy. I have a feeling he's playing with some sort of deadline. In the meantime, Sweeper may awaken from his coma and give us more information."

"I made notes on everything you said, John. You're right—I'll get started right away. I know you're busy—I'll let you go. Stay in touch, —please."

"You're on point, Elizabeth. You be careful." As he hung up, he wondered if he should leave her at the firm for the time being, or just pull her out for her own safety. *What the hell is Roger up to?* he thought for probably the hundredth time.

Charles Nitti received the call he had been waiting for. Tony Vittorio had a contact close to an insider at Miami General. Security was such that the woman, a circulating nurse in O.R., demanded $10,000 to pass on details of Sweeper's condition. She was paid in cash with a sack of small bills left at the Miami bus terminal and within twelve hours, had given all pertinent information over the phone. It was passed on to Tony. He called Nitti.

"Charles, this is Tony—finally, some news."

"I hope it's good for us and bad for him," replied Charles.

"Sweeper took one in the head—he's in a coma—doesn't look good. According to my source, the prognosis is that he may never recover. At least, he's not talking,—probably never will."

"What a relief! Has Maxco been informed?"

"Agent Rushly has spent a lot of time at the hospital. We know he is in contact with Elizabeth Martin. That means he knows a lot about Maxco-Litton and Roger Maxco. I'm sure Rushly is getting his information from Elizabeth."

"I have more good news, Tony. If you see Santini, fill him in. The Russians made their initial payment to Roger—we have two hundred million. It's a start. If he screws up with the Russians, we won't have to worry about him. He'll be dead. But we won't be out that much." He continued, his voice steady, "Tony, we need to initiate Plan B. Do you understand?"

"Yes, but under the circ—"

"Doesn't matter," the mob boss interrupted gruffly. He could pull out of it and we could all be in trouble. You know Roger Maxco would sell his own mother if he could get a deal with the FBI."

"It won't be easy, Charles. It means another Sweeper. Any ideas?"

"The guy we used in Miami in 'ninety-six, —he's been low key—gambling debts, needs cash." Charles had been in contact with Neil Polatski for a week in anticipation of taking out Sweeper, possibly Maxco, too. Known in international circles as Pollack, he had once been employed by the Bosnia Serbs. Always behind the scenes and a master of disguise, not even Interpol had been able to get photos of this elusive assassin.

"Expensive operation," said Tony.

"A million," Charles replied, "—but worth every cent."

"It's your show, Charles—probably good insurance. Suppose Roger tries something?"

"Have a talk with Roger—hands off! Make sure he gets the message. This is not the fucking amateur hour, although, after everything that's happened, I sometimes wonder. Remember Marshall Hall?"

"How can we forget, Charles? Don't worry, he'll get the message. I'll call you later. Let me know if you need me."

Charles Nitti made the call he had hoped would not be necessary. But Sweeper was alive and frighteningly vulnerable to the authorities. He couldn't take the risk—he dialed an international area code and number. That call was forwarded to an another. Pollack answered.

"Yes."

"This is Chicago—I am depositing to the numbered account—half now, the balance in ten days. Did you receive the packet?"

"Yes, the terms and conditions are acceptable."

"Ten days?"

"Yes—goodbye."

I regret this action, Charles thought, *but these things are necessary. I never knew Sweeper. Well, what can I do?* He reached over his polished mahogany desk to the humidor and selected a Cuban cigar.

It was mid-morning on Tuesday when the phone rang. The shop had no customers. "Mystery Hour—this is Nancy."

"Nancy, this is John Rushly, it's good to hear your voice and know you are back at the store, and safe."

"It's been tough, John. I want to thank you for your concern." She waited for him to talk, hating herself for anticipating the news, any news, of the man she knew as Richard.

"Nancy, Sweeper has been captured. I'm sure you've heard the news, but we wouldn't release his name. He was shot by one of our agents and is near death in a Miami hospital. It's terrible news but I wanted to be the one to tell you."

"My friend told me about the capture and that he was in the hospital—nothing else. Is he going to die?" A flood of tears and a rush of emotion unexpectedly came over Nancy. It was difficult to separate the two personalities, Sweeper and Richard. She still needed time.

"I'm sorry to bring this all back to you, Nancy. I know it's hard." John felt her grief, doing his best to comfort this special lady who had had the misfortune to fall in love with the wrong person.

"I know it's necessary, John—but I have to know. I'm going to remember this man as the person I loved. And I have said goodbye to him, John. I needed to know he had been captured. Thank you for thinking of me."

"Nancy, you call me if you need anything, okay?" It was not an idle comment. John was genuinely concerned.

"Thank you, John. I'll keep your card. Good luck." Having been open just an hour, Nancy Johnson placed a closed sign in the window and went for a long walk.

Sweeper lay quiet and still, under watchful guard. The Floor Nurse was just finishing her rounds. Sweeper was last on her list. She checked vitals and concluded there was no change from the hour before. *I wonder what he is thinking*, she pondered, his wrist in her hand. *Maybe he isn't thinking about anything—maybe he can't.* The nurse was wrong. Sweeper was thinking intensely, thinking about Nancy and the concept of redemption. It was just that his body didn't seem to function with his thoughts. Sweeper was, for all outward appearances, a vegetable.

Nancy, I did it for you—I didn't shoot the lady cop—enough killing. I couldn't give up—too painful living without you. I'll never leave here—that's okay. You're safe. Where is the white light? he wondered, looking around in his mind's eye. *No angels for me. Nothing's fair—just good luck, bad luck, no luck. I'm ready.*

In the city of Krasnogorsk, worlds away from the hushed, sterile environment that was now Sweeper's home, Alexis Kardonoff conferred with his Paris and London subordinates in the Russian Mafia. It was a conference call on secured lines. The subject: Maxco-Litton, specifically Roger Maxco. Kardonoff opened the conversation. The other men on the line would listen—they would make no comment except to acknowledge what they had heard.

"Gentlemen, my voice, it is clear?"
"Yes."
"Yes."
"Good. Maxco has received his initial payment. I believe the simultaneous shipments will be timely—July 27, 1998. However, it is necessary that the shipments are doubled and the time accelerated. Demand from our South American sources has exceeded original estimates. In fact, prices have risen. This is a two-billion-dollar undertaking. With the chaos and uncertainty surrounding Maxco-Litton, there will be no other opportunities to

duplicate our order. I want your men, at each warehouse and airport distribution center, to scour their locations for additional inventories on hand. I will apprise Roger of our intentions. Report your findings to me no later than July 11. I will be demanding delivery on July 20. He will have no choice. The FBI is too close and there is the matter of an assassin in protective custody. Our dealings with Maxco-Litton are coming to a close. Have I been clear, gentlemen?"

"Clear."

"Clear."

"This conversation is over."

There was no doubt in the mind of Alexis Kardonoff. He had sensed, during his conversation with Michael Lowe, that the entire operation could be in serious jeopardy. The implied threat to the wellbeing of Elizabeth Martin was purposeful. This was the last act of this international drama, he hoped. *One more telephone call to you, Roger Maxco—to keep you, as the Americans say, honest.* Alexis timed his call to coincide with Roger's usual arrival time at his executive suite in the World Trade Center. It was precisely eight o'clock EST.

"Mr. Maxco, you have an international call on line two. Strange accent. I don't yet have a name. Shall I take a message?"

"No, Carol, I'll take it."

"This is Roger Maxco."

"Roger, this is Alexis Kardonoff. How are you?"

"I'm fine, Alexis. Let me pass this call through another line, security, you know."

"Yes, Roger, I understand. My line has been swept—no problem."

Roger dreaded calls from Kardonoff. Usually, they only occurred when there was a problem, especially when deals had been made but not completed.

"Go ahead, Alexis. What can I do for you?"

"New information reaches us, Roger—not good. We understand there are problems with the FBI, not to mention your creditors. The warehousing and inventory documents we have received do not reflect readiness on your part. There is conflict in your organization. All of this, Roger, makes us nervous."

Roger was seething with disgust over this Russian telling him what had gone wrong. *What does this bastard really know?* thought Roger. *I'm the one on the front line? Without me, the whole goddamned deal would fall apart.* Before commenting, Roger tried to regain a modicum of composure.

"I understand your concerns Alexis, but these matters are under control. There is reconciliation at Maxco-Litton—"

"I interrupt you, Roger—there is no reconciliation. You have court problems with others, Elizabeth Martin—Arthur Litton, the board of Directors."

"You don't have all the—"

"I do have all the facts, Roger. Do not interrupt—listen to me. We have people within your organization. They are in your warehouses, laboratories, and airport distribution centers. Because of your problems, Roger, we are moving the shipment date from July 27 to July 20. We cannot give you more time. Incidentally, you had better check with your man Tom Elliot. He is having unexpected difficulties. We know a lot, Roger. Do not underestimate us—is big mistake." Kardonoff waited for a response, adding a few more words of advice.

Roger responded before he was finished. "You are pushing. That's not our deal. I don't like it." Roger's tone reflected what he felt. *This foreign son of a bitch*, he thought. *You may get more than you bargained for.*

"Roger, how can I say this? Our organization has *billions of dollars* at stake. Do you know what that means? I will answer for you. We will do everything necessary to bring this transaction to a successful close. If we are betrayed or you do not perform, no one will be spared pain and agony—even death. I'm sorry to be so blunt. Do your job, Roger. July 20, that's the date. I hang up, Roger." Kardonoff's broken English was no hindrance to the delivery of his message.

Roger Maxco was stunned. He had never been threatened in such a manner in his entire, sinister and inauspicious life. *What the hell is this Tom Elliot business?* he thought. *Talk about a pact with the Devil—these bastards are more than dangerous!* The main issue with Roger was the eighteen days left to produce, stockpile and ship drugs and the vaccine.

Elizabeth Martin was busy reviewing her notes from John's call. She began to make the necessary calls. It would take several hours to cover all the bases, but she had many friends throughout the pharmaceutical firm. Satisfied that personnel was in place and each person she confided in knew exactly what to do over the weeks ahead, she left her office and walked to West Broadway. She was heading for a small café called Gourmet Croissanterie, three blocks from the second tower of the World Trade Center. It was 1:30 in the afternoon.

A black 600 Series Mercedes pulled up and two men quietly recommended that she get into the back seat. She had no choice.

"This is kidnapping, you fools—who are you?" From Elizabeth's point of view, she didn't appear to be in danger. The men were well dressed and very polite, insistent, but polite. The man in the back seat was dressed impeccably in a dark suit, striped tie, and seemed to be Russian. The car remained at the curb.

"Ms. Martin, my name is not important. Please accept my apology for this intrusion. I need a minute of your time. You will be free to go." Resigned, Elizabeth shrugged as if to say, "Go ahead."

"Ms. Martin, our people have a financial interest in Maxco-Litton. We are not shareholders, but we have a special arrangement with Roger Maxco. We need your help."

"What is going on with Roger? What do you mean?"

"Ms. Martin, you don't have to do anything—that's the point. Give Maxco the free reign he needs to complete our business. Do you understand?" Elizabeth was beginning to feel the intimidation and to fear for her life. The Russian gentleman was making his point.

"I believe I do understand," replied Elizabeth.

"Good—then we are finished. You see—there is no problem. Let him do what he needs to do, Ms. Martin. To do otherwise could be fatal."

His last words fell like an anvil. The stalwart and composed Elizabeth Martin was shaken. The massive sedan sped away— Elizabeth didn't notice the diplomatic plates. She turned abruptly and returned to the sanctity of her office in the World Trade Center. Lunch was not a priority. She would confront Roger Maxco.

Chapter Twenty-three

Charles Nitti had spent half a million dollars needlessly. The assassin known as Sweeper was pronounced dead by Dr. Stanowski, the attending physician, at 8:20 a.m. July 3, 1998. The man never regained consciousness. The FBI was notified immediately and Rushly was both relieved and disappointed. Sweeper would have provided insight into Maxco's scheme, whatever it was. It would continue to be a source of frustration for the agent, and he felt that time was running out. Pollack had completed his plan to finish Sweeper but his services were not needed.

"Look at it this way, Tony," Nitti said to one of his hired hands, "I didn't waste half a mil-, I saved it."

"We're getting lucky, Charles." His boss's logic was clear and Tony agreed. "We have two hundred million dollars and Sweeper is gone. If Roger performs, we'll be home free. If he doesn't, we will only lose money. It'll be Roger who will have to escape the Russian Mafia. Good luck," he said snidely.

"By the way," Nitti said, taking a long satisfying draw on his cigar, "I've collected another piece of good news."

"Yeah? What is it, Charles?"

"The Russians have moved up the date on Maxco—only seventeen more days, that's it. Roger is scrambling." The men smiled at each other, knowing Maxco was no longer their problem. The Russians would have him well in hand.

"More good news," Tony replied. "The sooner the better. Well," he stood up and stretched, relaxing for the first time in a long time, "I'll leave you to your stogies and brandy, Charles. It's been a long but productive day. Take care." They both felt the pressure lifting and were glad the relationship with the insipid Roger Maxco was nearly over.

At least for now, the Chicago group would be content with the news of the day. Sweeper had been forever silenced, a significant amount of money had been returned from Roger Maxco, and the

Russians were in control of the time schedule for the final payments. Nitti could only guess at the astronomical profits within the grasp of the Russian Mafia—he estimated that a two billion-dollar transaction was in the works.

Roger Maxco was ecstatic about the news. He had received the call from Miami with a sigh of great relief. The news from Tom Elliot was not quite so exhilarating, however. With some prodding, the doctor admitted he was having last minute problems with the vaccine. In the middle of his phone conversation, he promised to work day and night to resolve the issue.

"I know this is disturbing to you, Roger, but it's not a disaster. Everyone is working twelve-hour shifts, then returning. In three weeks, it could all be—"

"Goddamn it, Tom—" Roger exploded, fear taking over reason, "we don't have three weeks! These shipments must be positioned to go, *no later than the* nineteenth! Do you understand? That's fourteen days from now!"

"I thought we had more time, Roger." Elliot had lost one promising career from screwing up. He wasn't about to lose this one, at double the prestige and the money. "Don't worry, Roger, I'll make it happen."

"There isn't any choice, Tom. You have a chance to get back at the establishment and make a lot of money at the same time. Failure means it's all over. I mean *all over*. Call me mid-week with some *good* news. Goodbye."

Tom Elliot had been too optimistic with his boss. In reality, he had real concerns. The vaccine was still ineffective forty percent of the time. There would be no FDA approval; he knew that. Roger didn't care. But the vaccine would be sold in foreign countries and millions of people would believe it would be one hundred percent effective. Many individuals would forego critical tests, thinking they were safe, only to be stricken with cancer. But it would be too late.

God, there is still the risk to people with heart problems and interactions for women taking common prescriptions for PMS and other female maladies, Tom thought, wrestling with his conscience. *If I can't fix all this, thousands—eventually millions will be affected.* He knew that the black market that began in this warehouse, the very drugs to be shipped overseas would return via the same route to be put into the hands of unscrupulous companies and passed onto the consumers here in the United States.

Ten minutes later, Elizabeth walked into Roger's office, in a daze. Appearing disheveled, she had a look on her face that Roger had never seen before.

"Elizabeth, what is it? Are you ill?" Elizabeth reached up with shaking hands to tidy her French twist. Strands of hair were slipping out of its normally pristine style. She walked over to Roger's credenza, opened a cabinet door and brought out a bottle of Absolut. Silently pouring a double shot of vodka, she waited until she felt the sting changed to smoothness, going down her throat before she turned back to face him.

"Are you ill, Elizabeth? What's wrong?" She walked toward the window and looked out at the dramatic skyline, then turned back to look at him, carefully.

"Is it all worth it Roger? Is it all worth it?"

"Elizabeth, make sense. What are you talking about? You don't drink during the day. Hell, you hardly drink at all! What in the hell is going on?"

"Not much, Roger—only that through your Machiavellian plot, whatever it is, somehow you managed to have my own life threatened."

"That's nonsense!" He went pale and stood up, clutching the desk. "Who threatened you?"

"Your friends, Roger—the people you do business with, whoever they are."

"Who were they? What did they say? What do they look like?" He was practically spitting at her; he couldn't get the words out fast enough.

"Like foreigners, maybe Russian," was the reply. "They had thick accents."

"What! I don't believe it." *I told them to leave her alone, goddamn,* he thought, unable to conceal his wrath.

In truth, Roger did believe it. He went on. "What happened, Elizabeth? Exactly what happened?" Elizabeth described her ordeal. There was no mistaking her fear.

"I'm not making this up, Roger. How in god's name did you

get involved with these people?"

"I don't know what to say," Roger said, adding, "I'm sorry."

"Sorry," replied Elizabeth. "You're sorry. That's it?"

"Look, I got into trouble—I needed a lot of money. I—it was all for the company, the stockholders, I—"

"No more lies, Roger." she said, cutting him off. "I want the truth. My life is on the line. You tell me the truth right now or I'll make your life so damned miserable—"

"Okay, okay—let me have a drink. Make sure the door is closed all the way. Tell Carol we're not to be disturbed." Roger was thinking fast, he needed time. This was a new development, Elizabeth in mortal danger. Elizabeth sat down on the leather couch in the corner of the office and Roger began to pace, making up lies as he went along.

"It's true that I owe these people a lot of money. They want me to pay them off in shipments of certain drugs—it's not illegal, exactly, I just couldn't let anyone know about it. I didn't realize they were so touchy. When they heard about the audit and your court action, they panicked. See? You kind of brought it on yourself." Seeing her instantly bristle, he thought better of his tactic and backed off. "I'll straighten this out, Elizabeth. Don't worry." Lies and deception were so ingrained into Roger's psyche his statement didn't seem like a lie to him at all. He waited for Elizabeth to respond.

"My God, Roger, you are dragging this firm into an abyss—it's worse than Hell!"

"That's chaotic logic, Elizabeth," he responded quickly, irritated to be scolded by her. "Don't be so melo—"

"And that's oxymoronic gibberish, Roger," she interrupted him angrily. "Listen to me! Anyone looking at this firm over the past eight weeks could only reach the same conclusion. We are the goddamn Titanic, Roger, and we're heading toward an iceberg. Whether it's an abyss or an iceberg, Roger, the results are the same. The life of this company is in danger, and now, thanks to you, so is mine. My question is, and it's a valid one, just what are you going to do about it?"

"I promise you, Elizabeth, you're in no danger. In a few days, everything will be back to normal. I'll have a face-to-face meeting with these people. I won't let them hurt you."

"That's reassuring, Roger," Elizabeth snapped at him. "Is that what you promised Marshall Hall and Julian?" Her remarks were biting. "In the meantime, you won't mind if I alert the FBI. I believe it is a crime to drag someone off the streets against her will and threaten to kill her."

"You're overreacting, Elizabeth. Don't aggravate the situation. Give me time to clear this up, okay?"

"I am making no promises, Roger. I advise you to take care of your illicit business quickly. Time is running out. I won't let you destroy Maxco-Litton. That's a promise!"

"Thank you, Eliz—" but he was cut off.

"Don't thank me, Roger. I didn't agree to anything. Just do your job and try to stay out of trouble. I'm watching you. Now I am beginning to wonder what happened to your accountant, Earnest Lasko. Where the hell is he, Roger? He seems to have dropped off the face of the earth and no one's mentioned him for weeks!" Elizabeth shook her head angrily, as if she couldn't even comprehend all that had happened, then she turned and walked out of the executive office. Roger intertwined his fingers, sat thoughtfully for a moment, then decided to have another drink. He didn't want to think about Earnest Lasko.

What is wrong with those people, he thought. *They are sitting on a gold mine and want to make waves by scaring Elizabeth. If only there was a way to deal with these bastards—after they give me what I want. At least they had nothing to do with Earnest.*

Elizabeth had made no promises to the boss she used to admire. Her life and the life of the firm she had helped nourish her entire career outweighed any feelings for him. She decided to apprise the FBI of the incident. She wanted protection.

Kimberly had followed the news of Sweeper's capture with great interest. *At last*, she thought, *some measure of justice for my father. If I only knew for sure who hired this man.*

Upon her return to Bodega Bay with Mike, she began to thoroughly enjoy developing a serious relationship. She felt her life was regaining meaning and order. They had moved in together and were already talking about becoming engaged.

Lieutenant Lewis Ramsey had requested a meeting with Mike

three days after he had returned from the East Coast. The lieutenant had uncovered new information regarding the Marshall Hall case. They talked about everything that had transpired, including the capture and death of Sweeper in Miami.

"This case has taken many twists and turns, Mike," said Lieutenant Ramsey. "Now there is new information that may preclude you from staying on the case." Ramsey knew this was not going to be a pleasant subject for Mike.

"What do you mean, lieutenant? I don't understand."

"Your relationship with Kimberly Weitzel—."

"Wait a minute," Mike said defensively, "that's my business!"

"I wish it were your business, Mike, but there is a problem. Several months prior to Joanne Hall's accident, Marshall Hall had been making substantial deposits into Kimberly's checking account. You know they were having an affair. Mike, this doesn't look good."

"That's ridiculous! I'm sure the money can be explained. It doesn't mean anything." Mike tried to justify what Ramsey was suggesting. He was caught off guard.

The lieutenant continued, "Mike, you're a detective and a damn good one. You know better than to brush this under the rug. Even you suspected Marshall of pushing his wife off that cliff. Now we find his girlfriend had been receiving a lot of money from him over a period of several months. Only two weeks after her death, Mike, Hall deposited nearly three hundred thousand dollars into her account. You can't ignore that kind of circumstantial evidence."

"You suspect them both? You think they planned it?" He was nearly choking with fear. It was hard for Mike to detach himself.

"Look, in addition to that lump sum, there were systematic deposits made—from five to ten thousand dollars every two weeks, going back months before the accident. It's suspicious. We have to question her."

"Okay, you're right," Mike said, "but let me do it."

"No way, Mike," replied the lieutenant, "you're too close."

"Lieutenant, she hasn't been accused of anything. It may be innocent. I promise you I'll be objective. You will have a complete and objective report on your desk in the morning. Please." His plea was sincere.

Reluctantly giving in, Ramsey continued. "You and I know there could have been a conspiracy to do away with Joanne Hall. Detach yourself, Mike and get the facts. It may hurt, but they will come out because of you or in spite of you. You have one shot. It better be good."

"Thanks lieutenant." He was relieved. "I really appreciate this. Believe me I need to know as much as you do—even more. I'll see you in the morning."

Mike was nearly paralyzed with fear. Thoughts shot through his head like rapid-fire. *There must be a logical explanation for the money. Maybe Marshall just wanted to squirrel away a few bucks—a guy thing. But what about the three hundred thousand dollars? That was the exact amount of the advance they had uncovered that Marshall had gotten from Maxco-Litton. Why did he need that money, with all the other cash he was giving to Kimberly? Could she have been blackmailing him?* He shuddered to think of it. Then he began to think about the New York trip, about Chicago and their sudden relationship. *Maybe she went to New York knowing that I would join her—she could keep tabs on the investigation of Marshall Hall and still locate her father's killer. Maybe pretending to fall in love with me was just to get me to back off. Stop it!* he thought, fighting with his own suspicions. *You don't know a thing. Talk to her!*

Kimberly was home when Mike arrived around dinnertime. The ranch-style house was alive with dark-green, neatly trimmed hedges and an array of wild flowers. A local gardener had taken meticulous care when the two lovers were away. Since their return, Kimberly had been busy redecorating and buying new furnishings. That morning she had traded her '96 Explorer for a new Eldorado Touring Coupe—candy apple red. It was in the driveway.

"Wow," Mike said, "is that your new car?" Mike's stomach seemed to jump into his throat.

"What about me?" asked Kimberly, smiling teasingly. "How about a 'Wow' for me?" She laughed, throatily.

Embracing her perfunctorily, he thought about how to address the money issue. "Kimberly, we need to talk. It's serious." He took her gently by the arm into the kitchen, seating her at the harvest table. "The lieutenant has some questions about your relationship with Marshall Hall. I told him I would rather take care of it with you. I don't want you to have to go in to the office." She looked at him quizzically, not comprehending the seriousness of his demeanor. "I'm sorry, honey," he struggled, loving even her vulnerability at that moment. "I have to keep everybody happy."

"Incidentally," he said, trying to change the mood by reaching into the refrigerator for an open bottle of white Zinfandel. Pouring two healthy glasses of wine, he continued, "I love the car—expensive huh?" He was terrible at masking his feelings and Kimberly reacted at his obvious ploy.

"God," she sighed, taking a sip of the California grape, "I hate to get back into all of this about Marshall." Looking up at him trustingly, she smiled a little, "Go ahead, Mike. Let's get this out of the way. Then you can drive us into San Francisco and we'll have a nice dinner."

"It's the money, Kimberly. Where did it all come from? The best hotels in New York and Chicago, all the expenses, the renovation of the house when we returned, gardeners, a new wardrobe, and now, a top-of-the-line El Dorado? That takes a lot of cash. A whole lot of cash!" The answer that came wasn't the one he wanted.

"So what's the big deal?" She had been too quick to anger. "Didn't I mention that my father had a large insurance policy with me as the beneficiary?"

"You mentioned it in passing, Kimberly—that's all," replied Mike. He was hoping she would volunteer more information. He sat quietly. It was a tactic he often used with criminals. Unable to stand the silence, the guilty would often confess out of discomfort. He hated himself for using it with the woman he loved.

She began to speak, slowly, softly. "He left me half a million dollars, Mike. That buys a lot." Kimberly seemed more self-assured with her simple, plausible explanation. She was beginning to become quite irritated. She looked up at him, her bright eyes nearly daring him to go further.

"Damn it, Kimberly, what else? Is there anything else?" Mike had to press, hoping for all the details voluntarily. He didn't want to ask her about Marshall's large deposits in her account.

"What is wrong with you, Mike? That's it—a half a million dollars—isn't that enough?" She was protesting—hiding something and Mike knew what it was.

"You need to explain the money you received from Marshall Hall, Kimberly." His voice broke with emotion. "The law knows about it. I had hoped you would include that information in your explanation." Mike was already distressed. Having to grill her was depressing him. *Better me than the lieutenant,* he thought sadly. Kimberly looked away, angry with him for not trusting her. Tears welled up in her eyes, but she refused to let him see them. Finally, she turned slowly and defiantly toward him, determined to confront him.

"You want to dredge it all up again? All right, Mike. You tell your precious lieutenant that Marshall Hall and I did indeed have a torrid love affair. We were deeply, passionately, hopelessly in love. If he had an insurance policy on his wife, I didn't know it. He was preparing to leave her and thought she would take everything he had. He was depositing money in my account periodically to protect it. He asked Maxco-Litton for an advance so he could offer her a cash settlement in exchange for an uncontested divorce. He was going to tell her the night she died. But in case it backfired, he wanted the money in my account. That's where all this is coming from. When they both died, I was left with all this cash. I want it gone. I don't want any ties to him, any longer. I wanted to start a new life with you. Daddy's insurance just added to the problem.

"Marshall loved me, Mike. We would have eventually married. He hadn't slept with his wife for years. He found out several years ago that she had been continuing to see a stockbroker from San Diego she had worked with for eight years before her marriage. That's why she never cared about Marshall's hours and why she supposedly visited her father in southern California so often. When Marshall confronted her about it, she laughed at him. Since his priority was his career, they never bothered getting a divorce."

Pausing, she poured a second glass of wine. Taking a deep breath and raising her glass challengingly, she looked him square in the eyes. "Our affair doesn't sound so sordid now, does it? Did you get all of this? You and your boss can digest all of this information and then arrest me if you want, that is, if you can arrest someone for falling in love and receiving money, accidentally. If he hadn't died, most of that money would actually have gone to his wife. Now, Mike, get out. I want to be left alone." Her defensive and caustic tone sickened him. *How could I have doubted her? What a goddamn fool!* he thought. There was nothing left to say. He turned and walked toward the front door.

"We'll talk tomorrow, Kimberly. I can't even tell you how disgusted I am with myself right now, but you could have told me about all of this before. I think it's best I stay somewhere else this evening." Mike meandered down the front cobblestone walkway passed the gleaming Eldorado and the fresh smell of azaleas. He didn't look back.

Back on the East Coast, Elizabeth Martin had regained her composure and was contemplating her next move. Not satisfied with Roger's weak explanation, she had simply retreated into the deep recesses of her mind, trying to imagine if it would ever be possible to return to a normal and productive life.

Guilt besieged her. *Shouldn't I have seen this coming?* She was consumed by doubt in herself, something she was not used to. *Why was I so blinded by Roger's talent for business to look the other way until it was too late? Have I contributed to this madness? Roger has betrayed all of us, the Directors, the stockholders, the firm. It was my firm, too!* she thought, tears of remorse springing to her eyes. *People have been killed—others threatened. Oh, Roger, why? Please fix it before it's too late!* She begged him silently.

The ringing of the phone interrupted her thoughts. Having fallen into the throes of depression, she was grateful to be brought back to reality. It was John Rushly.

"This is Elizabeth," she answered haltingly.

"Hi, this is John. Can you talk?"

"Yes, John—I'm alone."

"Elizabeth, is Michael Lowe one of your Directors?"

"He's Roger's personal attorney. Why do you ask?"

"One of our agents spotted him at a coffee house on FDR Drive with a Russian by the name of Alexis Kardonoff. Our sources tell us this guy is connected. Have you met Michael Lowe?"

A Russian, she thought fearfully, remembering her abductors. A chill ran down her spine. "I have met him a few times, John. This

Russian connection is interesting. Earlier today, I was ushered into the back seat of a black Mercedes and given some advice."

"What are you talking about, Elizabeth? This sounds serious. Give me the details."

"I was on my way to lunch—walking toward Park Place. A sedan pulls up and two men 'suggest' I get into the back seat for a talk. I was so stunned, I didn't even think to fight. The gentleman seated in back was polite, very intimidating, and—Russian. I was strongly advised to permit Roger to finish what he needs to do without interference. If I didn't cooperate, the man said, in these words, '... to do otherwise could prove fatal.'"

"I'm sorry you are in the middle, Elizabeth. Now you understand how dangerous this is. I want you to back off, now." John didn't want to suggest this approach, but his integrity gave him no choice but to advise her to do so. Elizabeth, however, had been pushed too far and responded predictably.

"You know I can't do that, John. There's too much at stake. I'm afraid we can't even comprehend where this is going. But all of it has to stop. Roger needs to be watched more than ever. Just give me some protection—I would like to be able to walk to lunch without the threat of being kidnapped."

"That's not a problem. Look, I'm going over to the photo lab to pick up some pictures of our Russian friends. I want you to look at them. It will help if we know exactly who it is we're dealing with. Let's meet in the morning. What's good for you?"

"Let's keep it simple. There is a Starbucks at Beekman and Park Row. How about nine o'clock?"

"That's perfect, Elizabeth. I'll be outside your apartment at 8:30 a.m.—personal transportation, courtesy of the FBI."

"Great—no cab. I'll be outside right on time. I'm going home, John—it has been a long and difficult day."

"I'm sending a car to take you. I want them to check out your apartment and secure you for the night, okay? Keep my numbers and your cell phone handy, and call me if you see anything out of the ordinary. I'll see you in the morning."

"Thanks, John." Her voice broke and she realized how grateful she felt, how long it had been since she felt really safe.

John Rushly knew that with these players in the game, the stakes had been raised once again. There was a hint of desperation in the actions of the Russians. *This must be much bigger than I originally anticipated*, thought John. *Shit! I may be in New York until this whole thing is finished. I miss my wife.* He decided to call home, just in time. Jill was becoming concerned.

It was four in the afternoon, Scottsdale time. Jill was in her office when John called. He called her extension directly.

"Jill Rushly."

"Hi, sweetheart. It's your husband, the other Rushly." He found himself smiling, just having heard her voice.

"My wayward husband, I might add. You need to come home. I've forgotten what you look like." She was only half teasing.

"Believe me, Jill—I would like nothing better. Everyday something comes up, serious stuff. This case is heating up. It just keeps getting bigger. I expect any day for it to end up with a White House cover up."

"Maxco-gate," she responded, laughing.

"Jill, Elizabeth Martin was forced into a sedan today and threatened. Too damn many innocent people are being wrapped up in this. I don't know how I can protect them all."

"What are you saying, John? Is she all right? John, how long are you going to be in New York? What if I join you for a week? Would we have evenings together or are you still on a twenty-four hour schedule. I miss you terribly." Jill's cases lightened in the summer. She knew she could take a week or two. She waited for John to respond.

"I'd love that so much, Jill. I miss you, too, and this can go on for several more weeks. But since Sweeper's death, my twenty-four hour schedule has lessened. I'll make time to be with you, honey. I really want to hold you. I'm tired and discouraged."

"My sweet love," she said softly. "John, have you seen the commercial where a harried mother tells her two little girls she can't take them to the beach because she has to meet a client and the little girl says, 'When can I be a client?' The mother grabs her cell phone and off they go to the beach."

"Okay, Jill," he nodded, understanding. They had been apart too long this time. "You can be my client. When can you be here?"

"Let's see," she said, back to business. Pulling her day-timer toward her, she responded quickly, "Today is July 7th. How about if I arrive Monday, the 13th?"

"I can hardly wait—you can meet Elizabeth Martin."

"I'm looking forward to that, John. You have certainly told me enough about her." Her comment didn't go unnoticed and he winced.

"We're good friends, honey, but she is now in danger. And we're not playing with the bubble gum set. Looks like assassins and the Russian Mafia. It's a big show. This case not only involves the FBI but is starting to involve the Federal Trade Commission, the Justice Department, also the Drug Enforcement Agency and the IRS."

"You be careful, Agent Rushly," she replied happily. "I couldn't live without you. Incidentally, are you eating okay—and what about sleep?"

"Jill, you can take good care of me when you arrive. I'll call you tomorrow to make sure the department will let you go. I know how valuable you are. I love you."

"I love you, too, John. I'll see you soon." John wasn't crazy about Jill being in New York only because there was always the chance of danger. But he couldn't wait to see her.

"I can't wait," replied John. I love you!" Hanging up the phone, he suddenly felt better. *I want my wife by my side*, he thought, *isn't that what it's all about? Yes, you fool,* he answered himself, *that's what it's all about.*

Chapter Twenty-four

Michael Lowe was sitting alone, engaged in deep thought. He knew the authorities were building a case against Roger Maxco and those closest to him. As a street-smart lawyer, he had no illusions. The Security & Exchange Commission violations over the past year alone were enough to send him away for years. Worse, the CEO could possibly connect him to the murder of Gus Lanton. Deep down, in the depths of his gut, he was convinced that Roger's scheme with the Russians was doomed to failure. He thought long and hard.

Maybe this is it; we've gone too far, he thought hopelessly. With the Russians involved, he knew no one would be safe. He had heard about them threatening Elizabeth. That was just too close to home. *The Gus Lanton murder was a mistake* he thought, *it just served to satisfy Roger's thirst for revenge. I wonder what the FBI really knows? How much does Elizabeth know? It's time to sound her out. She could still be a valuable asset, just in case. Maybe she could act as a liaison between the FBI and me? What is this—what am I thinking—that's admitted jail time. Do I have a choice?* He was torn over what to do.

This was heady stuff for the usually over-confident, egocentric attorney. Although he had no family to consider, psychologically, prison was not an option for him. *I could talk with Elizabeth to find out exactly what she knows,* he thought, trying to come to some sort of conclusion. *That's it!* He had decided. *I'm going to find out as much as possible and see what options are out there.*

He caught Elizabeth completely off guard. Having met with Roger at eleven o'clock, Michael walked over to Elizabeth's secretary and announced himself.

"Ms. Martin, Mr. Lowe is here. He says he would like a word with you. Shall I set up an appointment?" Elizabeth suddenly remembered that John had asked about Michael. *Perhaps it would be wise to see him,* she thought.

"Ask him to come in. I have a few moments free." She laughed at herself realizing that the only business she seemed to be conducting lately was to stay alive and keep the firm going.

"Hello, Elizabeth," he said smoothly, smiling. "Thank you for seeing me."

"Of course, Michael, come in. Have you been meeting with Roger?"

"As a matter of fact, yes. I thought it might be productive if we talked a little—about Roger and Maxco-Litton." The bright and tenacious lawyer was no match for Elizabeth. Having met casually a few times, he didn't really know the extent of her brilliance. Even without notice, she was immediately ready for him.

"Mr. Lowe, as Roger's attorney, I know you can not speak freely about certain matters having to do with his recent aberrant behavior. I suspect any conversation we have will be limited. Regardless, I have agreed to see you. What can I do for you?"

Michael looked at her as if she was a sparring partner and they were playing for a championship. He couldn't help himself from smiling. *I'll bet she's a chess player*, he thought wryly, enjoying her stance.

"Yes, there is certainly the matter of confidentiality. And of course, I am obligated to work in my client's best interest. But frankly, I'm concerned about the FBI investigation. I understand you are in contact with an agent by the name of Rushly. Is there any information you would be willing to share regarding his inquiries?"

"I suspect you are asking the wrong person," she responded coldly. "Perhaps you should contact Agent Rushly." Michael Lowe had underestimated Elizabeth. Her appraisal of him and his questions were more than insightful.

"I agree. Agent Rushly would probably be the person to whom I should direct my questions. I'm looking for a way to help Roger—and of course, the firm, indirectly. You may be more interested in that objective than John Rushly."

Well what do you know? Elizabeth thought. *Perhaps the little weasel's real interest is in talking to John. He wants to make a deal.* She smiled at him as if she were looking straight through him.

"In my opinion, Michael, Roger has gone too far. I understand he is indebted to some unscrupulous people, the Russian Mafia, it seems. Do you know anything about that issue?" Elizabeth was determined to keep control of the conversation.

"I understand he approached them for a loan." Michael didn't know what to say. He knew she was laying a trap for him.

"You needn't be so coy, Michael. I understand you have met with one of the Russians personally. Would you be willing to share with me information from that meeting? That's not privileged information, at least not so far as your client's concerned." Elizabeth had completely turned the tables and Michael felt himself losing control of his anger.

"It seems you are well versed, Elizabeth. I'm afraid our meeting has been unproductive. I certainly can't divulge a conversation I have had with a client."

"You're telling me this particular Russian, Alexis Kardonoff, is your client? Well Michael, I'm not sure it was him, but one of Roger's Russian friends forced me into a car yesterday and threatened my life. I suggest you reappraise your client list and advise Roger he's in bad company." Michael Lowe seemed to shrink in the woman's presence. She was way out in front and he realized how formidable she could be.

"You're quite a lady, Ms. Martin. It seems I have underestimated your depth of knowledge regarding Roger Maxco and his activities. I would like to keep the communication lines open. There may be a time when it could prove beneficial to you—and to the FBI."

"I believe that is a good idea, Michael. Thank you for coming to see me. I have enjoyed our conversation. Good afternoon."

A reflective and beaten lawyer left the executive suite and the building. He knew she would pick up on his last statement. Michael was now seriously considering the possibility of making a deal with the FBI. Timing was everything. *If I delay too long,* he thought, *the opportunity will be lost. I get the feeling from the bitch upstairs that they are really close to blowing this wide open. It may already be too late.*

Far from the executive chaos and political intrigue of New York, Jill was about to make a call to her friend. She and Mike hadn't talked for some time and Jill was curious about John's remark that he and Kimberly had become romantically linked. More important, Jill wanted to follow up on the investigation of Joanne's death, still intending to keep her promise. Mike's residence line had been disconnected, and had a forwarding referral. Glancing at her watch, Jill dialed the new number. It was 7:30 p.m.

"Hello?" The woman at the other end of Mike's phone had obviously been crying. Kimberly was sitting by the phone, in the hopes Mike would call to apologize.

"This is Jill Rushly, I'm trying to reach Mike Staples. Do I have the right number?"

"Mrs. Rushly, this is Kimberly Weitzel. Mike isn't here."

"Kimberly, its been awhile. How have you been? You've been through so much, my deepest sympathies for all your loss. I understand you and Mike are seeing each other. I couldn't be happier. From what I know of him in such a short time, he's a very special guy." When the response was slow in coming, Jill added, kindly, "How are you doing,?"

"You probably should call Mike at work tomorrow, Jill. We've had some problems today, and I don't know where to reach him." Kimberly was somewhat ruffled about the personal comments. She had only met Jill Rushly when John brought her to his home. She resented the intrusion into her personal life.

"I'm sorry, Kimberly. I hope this isn't serious. Can I help in anyway? John's in New York for awhile. I'll be going to see him soon." Kimberly gathered her thoughts.

"I shouldn't have been so sensitive, Jill, sorry. I'm sure Mike and I will straighten this out tomorrow. I appreciate your call." It was apparent that Kimberly wanted to free the line in case Mike was to call.

Respecting her wishes, Jill didn't press any further. "Take care, Kimberly. I'll try Mike at his office. Goodnight."

The tenor and tone of Kimberly's voice and comments suggested that this was not just a lover's quarrel. Jill was concerned for Mike. The next morning at 8:30, Jill called Mike's office.

"Just a minute, Detective Rushly, he's coming around the corner with his coffee. I'll transfer you to his desk." The receptionist informed Mike that Jill Rushly was calling.

"Hey, Jill? How's my new buddy? Where are you?" he asked, genuinely glad to hear from her.

"Hi, Mike," she laughed easily. "How are you?"

"I've been better. I was going to call you later—it's been an emotional roller coaster for me. Kimberly and I had a few problems. I made the mistake of listening to my head instead of my heart. I think I fucked it up, Jill." He was eager to confide in the friend he'd made, finding that he could talk to her more easily than anyone at the office.

"I'm sorry to hear that, Mike, but according to her teary voice when I called the house, I somehow don't think you screwed anything up permanently."

"You think?" he asked, surprised.

"I think," she responded, smiling. "I know relationships take a lot of work, Mike, especially when you're in law enforcement. It's just a different breed. John and I have a great one because that's the frame of reference for us both, but regardless, it's worth it in the end. Do you want to talk about it?"

"It has to do with the case, Jill. There were unanswered questions about Kimberly. I forced her to answer some pretty tough questions. I should have backed out of it and let the lieutenant ask them. I should have just sat back and been supportive."

"What questions, Mike? She certainly can't be a suspect." Do you want to talk about it?" Mike related the details of the deposits made into Kimberly's account, the lieutenant's demand for information and the inquisition that created the gulf between them.

"Mike, listen to me. You weren't just doing your job. You were trying to protect her. Sometimes, we get into that gray area and can't get out. But you're right, you're too close, Mike. You shouldn't be working on this case at all, in any capacity. But you've evidently got a really special girl there, according to John. You need to step back, let the lieutenant or whomever take over the case and get your relationship back on track." She was glad she had called.

"I guess I just jumped the gun, Jill. Too much time in Vice. It just hit me all at once. All this stuff about the new car, the furniture, and all the other trappings. Shit, the rest of us work all our lives and never have enough. I guess the circumstances of her getting it just made both of us uncomfortable.

"Mike," Jill asked quietly, "what are you still doing on the phone?" she laughed.

"You're a good friend, Jill. You're right, I'm going to see Kimberly."

"Call me Mike—let me know what's going on. Take care."

He didn't even bother to put the phone back in the cradle, but pushed the button to click off, then on. Dialing quickly, he took a deep breath. She answered on the first ring.

"Hello?"

"Sweetheart, Kimberly, please let me apologize."

"Mike, you have nothing to apologize for. I thought about it all night. It would have looked horribly suspicious. I should have just been more open about it from the beginning. I just didn't want you to think I was a gold digger."

He laughed, "There's absolutely no way I'd think that, Kimberly. Not if you're in love with a cop!"

"When can you come home?" she sounded so snuggly, as if she were still half-asleep.

"How about if I pick you up at noon and we'll go to the Sea Gull for lunch, okay?"

"Okay, Mike."

He sat at his desk smiling, all morning, filling out paperwork, and waiting for lunchtime. His lieutenant seemed satisfied with the answers Kimberly had given to Mike.

Jill was torn. No sooner had she hung up from making airline reservations to go visit her husband than the phone rang. It was Renee. In just three minutes, Renee had talked Jill into meeting her in Bodega Bay for the weekend to help her dismantle the house, clothing, and furnishings. She had found a buyer for the estate and hadn't touched anything since both her parents' deaths. Jill couldn't say no. She would have to postpone her trip to New York. Beside, she thought, it would give her a chance to see Mike and Kimberly. Insofar as she was concerned, the case of Joanne's death had to be put to rest. She had to find out, once and for all, if it had been accidental or by calculation.

She decided to stay at The Victorian Lady, a local bed &

breakfast. It gave her the willies to think of staying in Joanne and Marshall's house. *No wonder Renee' sold it,* she thought.

Mike was thrilled to hear back from her. He looked forward to seeing the spunky lady detective again. *Besides,* he thought, *she can see Kimberly. I know they'll get to like each other.*

One FBI agent, stranded in New York on a case, however, was not so happy. He missed his wife terribly. He cautioned her to stay within jurisdictional boundaries as far as Joanne's death was concerned. "This is their case, Jill," he said, "I know how inquisitive you can be," he laughed, knowing she had a thirst for crime solving he had rarely seen even in the most career-oriented detectives. And remember," he said protectively, "Marshall Hall, dead or not, was a catalyst of this much larger picture. Keep me informed of anything unusual, okay?"

Jill headed off to Bodega Bay to dismantle a house and poke into an old mystery. John sat in New York, disgusted with a case that had already exasperated him in more ways than one.

John and Elizabeth drove to Starbucks at Beekman and Park Row. It was 9:15 a.m. The trendy coffeehouse was filled with both tourists and professionals. Many had spilled out to the patio area where colorful umbrellas, glass-top tables, and wrought iron chairs with deep cushions welcomed the patrons. Plentiful greenery and pink and white petunias added to the casual ambiance. They ordered coffee and croissants.

"This is pleasant Elizabeth. Hopefully the rest of your day will be as nice."

"You're dreaming, John." She smiled broadly. "Another visit from Michael will take care of that idea."

"Michael Lowe—I ask about him and he suddenly shows up at your office. I wonder if he is psychic?"

"Whatever he is John, he is one troubled man."

"What do you mean?"

"In my opinion, based on his questions and demeanor, he may be up to his ears in trouble. He asked about you. I may be wrong, but that meeting may have been his opening volley, with our Mr. Lowe trying to make a deal with the FBI."

"Really?" John was surprised that the lawyer would begin any repartee with Elizabeth.

"Yes, John. I must say, he did realize that he was outgunned," she smiled again, "—but he is no fool. He is hedging his bets."

"Do you think Roger has any knowledge of this?"

"Absolutely none. This guy hasn't made a decision. He may decide to bet on Roger."

"You're really in the middle now, Elizabeth. How does it feel?" John knew the danger and wanted reassurance that Elizabeth was prepared to face whatever the investigation uncovered.

"John, I'm sensing that whatever is in the works will unravel quickly. I don't believe Roger has much time to do whatever it is he has planned."

He thought carefully before responding. "Elizabeth, I'm trying to get a court order to place a hold on all drug inventories designated for overseas shipments by Maxco-Litton. The DEA is very concerned. So far, the judge isn't sympathetic to our cause. We still need more evidence, but without tipping our hand."

"Michael may be your answer, John. If the Russians are concerned about me, you can imagine how nervous Roger and Michael are making them. A little more pressure from the Russians may push Michael your way."

"You should be very careful, Elizabeth. My agents can't watch you every minute."

"I'm pretending to let Roger have more slack, John. I'm sure I'm being monitored in some way. That may take the heat off." She paused, suddenly remembering something. "Didn't you say your wife was coming to New York?"

"Something came up," he smiled sadly. She had to go to the Bay area."

"I'm sure you're disappointed," Elizabeth responded, pretending not to feel the lump in her throat.

"Yes, I was looking forward to being with her. This is probably best, though. I have a lot to do and it could get dangerous."

"It will be easier for you to look out for me, John. At one time, I thought I could depend on Roger. Now I know that isn't possible."

"That's too bad. Roger is such a waste of talent—he could be capable of doing so much good."

"I know—it's hard to understand."

He sat back, stirring his coffee, absentmindedly. It was good to just sit and relax for a few minutes. "Before I became a full time agent with the FBI," he said, "I was a commercial real estate broker in Phoenix. I learned a lot about talented people. Some of them, a few, always felt the need to come in through the back door. It seemed strange to me—the front door could be wide open but some people just don't care. It's like a disease. They could accomplish more by being absolutely honest—but they choose to be devious and self-serving."

"That sounds like Roger. Its frustrating, John."

"We're not going to change much sitting here, Elizabeth. Let's go to work. Call me later today. I may have a chat with Lowe. Maybe a little more heat on Roger is in order."

"That's your department, John. You know what you're doing."

It was a short drive to the World Trade Center. John dropped Elizabeth within view of the front doors. They touched affectionately and John headed for Upper Manhattan. *What a lady*, he thought, watching her enter the revolving doors, *what a lady!*

John headed for the FBI Field Office at 26 Federal Plaza. His temporary office was on the twenty-third floor. He knew there was nothing illegal about a pharmaceutical company having extraordinary amounts of drugs available for shipping. However, it was illegal to ship them out of the country before licensing, especially to questionable and unapproved sources.

Further, there was the matter of the cancer vaccine. The application for FDA approval had been dropped by Maxco-Litton. That meant one of two things to John. One, that the research had determined the drug ineffective and they didn't want to spend anymore time on it. Two, that the drug was effective but dangerous. If that were the case, Maxco-Litton was not only producing the vaccine, but also willing to sell huge amounts of the vaccine on the black market.

Maybe it's time for a talk with Lowe, John thought. *He might be the weak link in the Maxco-Litton conspiracy. Yes, time to act—those shipments could leave the country anytime.*

There was a certain amount of protocol involved when attempting to reach the attorney of someone you are investigating. It was necessary for John to arrange for a third party to plant the idea of a meeting. If Michael were to contact Rushly of his own volition, there would be no question as to the propriety of the meeting. And the logical person to drop a subtle suggestion to Michael, John thought, would be Elizabeth.

Actually, the Chief Financial Officer-turned-sleuth was way ahead of the pack. She had already left a message on the attorney's personal voice mail.

"Michael, this is Elizabeth Martin. I hope you didn't interpret our meeting as being confrontational. My concern is the welfare of Maxco-Litton. I do suggest you contact Mr. Rushly to learn more about the difficulties Roger may be facing. I'm sure he would appreciate hearing from you."

Elizabeth was satisfied that the cryptic and subtle nature of her message would fall on receptive ears. She also knew that whoever heard the voice mail could not take offense, at least outwardly, at her suggestion. That afternoon, she let John know what she had done. He was impressed.

In San Francisco, Jill had arranged to meet Mike. In fact, Mike offered to pick her up at the airport. They drove into the city and decided to have dinner at Amelio's, an upscale Italian restaurant on Powel Street. It was 7:00 p.m. Kimberly had stayed at home.

"You have good taste, Jill, this looks expensive."

"It's my treat, Mike. I'm so glad to be here. I thought maybe Kimberly would be with you." The couple was shown to their table and given time to continue their conversation. A waiter was never out of eye contact.

"She's fine, we're fine." His eyes sparkled. "We had a long talk before I left. If only she had leveled about the money earlier, it would have looked a lot better to the lieutenant and I wouldn't have had to push her so hard. Water under the bridge, or whatever. Guess we learn as we go, there's no perfect manual for relationships, is there?"

A waiter interrupted asking if they would care for a drink before ordering.

"Coffee, please," Mike said, "I'm driving. Jill asked for a wine spritzer and water with lemon. The waiter left.

"Anything else in the investigation on Marshall's death—or Joanne's? And is Kimberly okay with my being here?"

"Not really. She knows you were close to Joanne and that you are looking for answers."

"Oh, shit, I didn't even think of that! No wonder she was a little chilly toward me on the phone. Poor kid."

"Right now, she feels everyone is against her. I don't blame her." Mike put down the menu signaling the waiter. Suddenly they were famished. Jill ordered egg plant parmesan and Mike ordered alfredo fettucine. Both were brought garlic bread and a salad. Changing his mind about the drinking, Mike ordered a carafe of the house Chianti. "We may have to stay all night, Jill," he laughed, meaning nothing by it.

"Should I make it a point to meet her, Mike? I have a feeling you and I will be close friends and I want Kimberly to feel secure with that."

"I know she really likes your husband, Jill, and I'm sure she'll warm up to you."

"I don't know what help I can be, Mike. I'll be here for a few days, helping Renee with the house. Maybe we can come up with something that will clear the air. I'm here as your friend and strictly as a sounding board. I won't get in your way."

"I'm glad you're here, Jill. I'll talk to Kimberly. Maybe we can all have lunch together."

"That would be great, Mike. I'll be busy at the house tomorrow. Let's get together on Tuesday. I'll need a break from manual labor and you'll have time to talk to Kimberly, how does that sound?"

"That sounds fine, Jill. If something comes up tomorrow, I'll call—where are you staying?"

"You know The Victorian Lady? It's the B & B just past the church on the way to Petaluma. Here is their phone number. Anyway, you'll be dropping me off there. In the morning, Enterprise is bringing a car over."

"Well," replied Mike, "the service, food and ambiance is delightful. Thank you, Jill. I feel awkward letting you pay."

"No, Sir—my treat." Jill used a credit card and waited for the waiter to return. "If you want to know the truth, Mike, I haven't bothered with anything but salads and yogurt, and, God forbid, Taco Bell since John's been gone. This was truly my treat!" She laughed.

"Ready? We have a forty-minute ride."

"I'm ready Mike, and thanks for letting me do this."

"You tell your husband he's a lucky guy," he said, pulling her chair out for her. "I hope we all can get together some day."

"I tell him every day!" replied Jill. They left the restaurant and headed north—out of the city.

On the way back, Jill talked about her lost friend. "I really miss Joanne. It's going to be so hard going through her things tomorrow. Through the years, we've given each other so much stuff. I hate to run across that. I still hope that her death was an accident. I really do."

"For a lot of reasons," responded Mike, "I do too."

Jill checked into The Victorian Lady and had a long hot bath in eucalyptus oil, courtesy of the hosts. When she returned to her room, there was a hot pot of steeping Sleepytime tea and a jigger of brandy on her night stand. *Just what I need, after a flight, an Italian meal and a half carafe of Chianti,* she thought. By the time she finished the pot of tea, her eyes nearly closed without her noticing, and she slept without incident for nine long, peaceful hours.

Mike Staples returned home to Kimberly. His welcome was warm and inviting, and he knew this was for real.

Chapter Twenty-five

Wednesday, July 15, 1998

Roger Maxco had finished reading the reports from his staff at various warehouses around the country. Production had increased dramatically the past week and it looked as though he could satisfy the gluttonous appetite of Alexis Kardonoff and his Russian friends. Even the production of the questionable cancer vaccine had accelerated.

He had resigned Tom Elliot to the fact that although they had made substantial progress in purifying the vaccine, at least by FDA standards, it was still unacceptable. Elliot had agreed, however, to meet the production level. The shipments would be ready by July 20. In seven days, the illegal, unapproved, life-threatening merchandise would be shipped all over the world without the slightest chance of tracing it back to him, and Roger would be rich beyond his wildest dreams. He would also be safely out of the country.

"Carol, see if you can reach Lowe. I need to talk to him."

"Yes, Sir, right away." It took Carol several minutes. She finally located him on his car phone.

"Mr. Maxco, Mr. Lowe is on his mobile phone."

Roger picked up the phone. "Michael, get to another phone and call me back. There's no privacy on these."

"I'm heading for your office," came the curt reply. Be there in fifteen minutes."

"See you then, Michael." Roger hung up the phone and began to make notes for the meeting with Michael He began a checklist.

- ✓ Remind Michael of July 20 date.
- ✓ Make sure the sell-off of the stock he owned and controlled was set with automatic transfers of funds.
- ✓ Arrange payoffs for Tom Elliot and all other key players involved

✓ Write statement absolving Elizabeth Martin of any connection with the illegal shipments and any other activities that may be construed as questionable manage-ment practices.
✓ Assure simultaneous transfer of $900 million by Russians. Coordinate wire transfers and confirmation of purchase order codes
✓ Confirm readiness of aircraft for departure—Moscow, Paris, Krakow, Berlin and Amsterdam

For now, time was on Roger's side. He knew this was incredibly difficult to hold together under the pressures of the past few weeks. It was important that no one, other than the Russians, know how close he was to completing his grandiose scheme. Roger reflected on the changes that had occurred and what he perceived to be his brilliant response to each situation.

Staring out the window, he thought proudly to himself, *I've come a long way—from Marshall Hall and Julian Weitzel to an entirely new plan—the Russians. Damn, I would have liked to outsmart the SEC and the FDA. In a way,* he reminded himself, *I have. The drugs and the vaccine will make me a billion dollars. Screw the stock manipulations—too complicated. This is much cleaner.*

Michael Lowe had arrived, breaking his reverie. Roger ceremoniously handed Michael the checklist.

"The news is good today, Michael. We are right on schedule—Tom Elliot has come through and all production quotas are being met. There is a lot of work to do but I see no problems. What do you think?"

"It's going to happen, Roger. Hopefully, no one will panic. The Russians have not been helpful. Elizabeth is on guard and the FBI is taking a hard look. Frankly, I'm glad Kardonoff moved up the schedule. I'm not sure we could hold all of this together for another week."

"Very perceptive," Roger said, "I was thinking the same thing. Do you see any problem with the logistics?"

The lawyer shook his head. "The paper work is in place along with the aircraft. It's a go, so far."

"It's Monday afternoon. The flights are set for a week from

today," Roger said. "Do you recall your history—when the Germans were confused about allied invasion plans? One of the things Eisenhower did was to build fake supply bases. While the Germans were preoccupied with the bogus bases, the invasion of Normandy was launched."

"I do remember. You're absolutely right. It would be wise to set something in motion to throw off our detractors."

"Michael, we know how close Elizabeth is to Rushly. If we can convince her that whatever it is we're planning won't happen until the last week in July, that might take the heat off and assure our success." Roger began to think about a plan to fool those who were determined to curtail his nefarious scheme.

"Roger, I have an idea," Michael reached down to lift a cigar from the humidor. Lighting it slowly, he said, "Suppose we begin to cut production and to disperse some token inventories. This would give the impression that you have begun to correct the computer problems you alluded to earlier—the reason for the unusual amounts of certain drugs held in the distribution centers. Along with this diversion, you could call a Directors meeting to discuss streamlining the accounting and distribution system of Maxco-Litton worldwide." In the back of his mind, and as a last resort, the lawyer contemplated the possibility of meeting with John Rushly.

"That's very good, Michael. With the Russians looking over our shoulders, it might be wise to apprise them of our plan—keep them calm. They understand the concept of insurance."

"Don't forget Charles Nitti, Michael replied, " I am sure he is waiting with bated breath for this to end."

"An excellent point, Michael, but I don't think I'll bother with them. After all, they have already received two hundred million. They'll get the rest. It's a good plan. I think I'll have a chat with Elizabeth to start the rumor mill rolling. Tomorrow, I'll call for an emergency board meeting. Why don't you alert Alexis to our plan?"

"I'll do that, Roger. Try to think of a few more ploys to throw off Elizabeth and Rushly—little things that support what you've already initiated."

"What would I do without you?" Roger smiled at his comrade in arms. I have a few goodies up my sleeve that will disarm our

adversaries. Let me get busy on this. We'll talk again tomorrow."
"When will you see Elizabeth?" Michael asked.
"Tonight," Roger replied. "I'll see her tonight." Michael gave Roger a pensive look, then decided to leave before he said anything further.
"Good day, Roger."

Three thousand miles to the west, the torrential rains of weeks past had left their mark. Three houses on the north end of the Bay had been caught in mudslides, but were still perched precariously at the top of the cliff. Construction workers were beginning the monumental task of rebuilding the Coast Highway. The area above Bodega Bay was a mess.

Jill and Renee, oblivious to the destruction of weeks past, were enjoying a late brunch at The Sea Gull, a little restaurant on the coast, a few miles north of Bodega Bay. Jill had not spoken of the circumstances surrounding her friend's death to Joanne's daughter. It was time to clear the air.

"Renee, has anyone discussed with you the investigation into your mother's death?" she asked gingerly. If Marshall were suspect, she had to remember that he was Renee's stepfather, even though they were not best friends. "Does anyone really know what happened that dreadful Sunday afternoon? Was it an accident?"

"Jill, they've dropped it. And I don't blame them. There wasn't anything sinister. Everyone in town knows that Marshall was having an affair with Dr. Weitzel's daughter, but there wasn't anything else to it. I guess Marshall had taken my mom for a walk to ask her for a divorce. But the investigators thoroughly looked over the footprints on the cliff. There was a lot of erosion under the area where Mom was standing and it was weakened by the rain. That's all. Even the cigarette butt was explained. Earlier, Kimberly had given Marshall a half-empty pack of Kools. It was during the heated argument that he flicked the butt over the cliff. Case closed. I'm glad. I wasn't close to Marshall, but you know what? He couldn't have done anything bad to Mom or anyone else. His only concern was test tubes and getting published in JAMA, and, I guess, Kimberly Weitzel. But it's over, Jill, and you've got to let it go, too."

Where did she get all this wisdom, Jill thought, reaching out to take the hand of the little girl who had grown up before her eyes. "You're right, Renee, I guess losing her was just so hard and the circumstances so tragic, I thought by finding a reason for it all, I could cope with the loss. Maybe helping you with her things and the house, I can find closure."

"Both of us can, Jill," Renee said softly, her eyes filling with tears. "I feel bad that I never thanked Marshall for being so good to me. He didn't deserve the way I treated him. I was just so jealous when he married Mom. Oh well, tomorrow's another day to use the lessons we've learned, right?"

"Right, so let me pay the bill and let's get back to the house. Although, it's so pleasant here, I hate to leave," said Jill, transfixed by the pounding surf and clear blue ocean, clean and sparkling after all the rains.

"Do you mean the restaurant or Bodega Bay?"

"I guess both—it's 110 degrees in Scottsdale." It was the 15th of July.

"But it's a dry heat, right?" Renee said, trying to be helpful.

"Yeah," Jill grimaced, laughing, "—but so's an oven!"

Arm in arm, Joanne Hall's daughter and best friend walked to the car. Closure had begun.

Driving back to town was a delight. Jill was struck by the lack of commercial development in the area. *What a great place to hang it up,* she thought.

That afternoon, Renee presented Jill with several artifacts that the executor of Joanne's estate had earmarked for delivery to Jill. There were a few pieces of rare, fragile china and two oil seascapes by a local artist.

"This is something special, Jill." Renee handed Jill a gold and emerald pendant, delicately pieced together by a Bodega Bay jeweler.

"It's lovely," Jill whispered.

"Mom had bought it for you, Jill, a month before the accident." A rush of emotion overwhelmed them both.

"I don't know what to say," Jill replied, her voice catching. They spent the next six hours going through the dressing rooms and closets in the master bedroom. By the end of the day, they had packed twenty-one large bags, all the way to the brim, for the

Junior League truck to pick up for sale in San Francisco. Jill didn't think Bodega Bay folks needed to see Joanne's clothing all around town.

"Over a light dinner that night, at the house, Renee pulled out a nice Merlot and poured them both a glass. "Thank you for taking care of all this with me, Jill. I didn't think I could do it alone."

"That's what friends are for." A feeling of peace had settled in around the house and the kitchen even seemed cozier and more familiar. *Somehow, I don't mind being here at all, now,* Jill thought. At seven-thirty, she drove back to The Victorian Lady, ready for a good night's sleep. They would start in again tomorrow, but it was getting easier. Most of the personal effects had been taken care of, and tomorrow the antique dealers were coming to pick up the furniture for the auction.

Back at the Bed and Breakfast, Jill quickly got ready for bed and cuddled up in her Egyptian sheets in the big feather bed, her cell phone at the ready. It was after eleven in New York. She hoped her husband was still up.

He answered quickly, as if he had been waiting for her call. "Hi, honey!" he said eagerly.

She laughed happily, "Isn't Caller ID wonderful?"

"Boy, do I miss you. Did you make a lot of progress at Joanne's house?" he asked warmly.

"Tons, so much done. I could use a back rub, though. John, Bodega Bay is so beautiful, so cool and nice."

He laughed. "You're so transparent! We're not moving, Jill—although there are times when I could seriously consider the idea. What's new in California?"

"I had a nice dinner with Mike last night, worked on the house all day, the auctioneers are coming tomorrow to inventory and ship everything. Renee's given me tons of stuff, dishes, jewelry, things she doesn't want, for our house. Some rattan furniture that will be really nice on our patio, I'm having it shipped. And I'm finally dealing with Joanne's death, John. Marshall's death may have been the catalyst that started all this stuff in your case, but everyone seems pretty firmly convinced that Joanne's accident was just that, an accident."

"Good, honey, I think sometimes because we're in law enforcement, we tend to suspect everyone we meet. Oh, have you seen Kimberly?" he asked as an afterthought.

"No, not yet, but I think we're going to get together soon. Mike said he thinks because I'm—I was Joanne's friend, Kimberly feels a little guilty and intimidated. I don't blame her."

"And that's why I love you. So, when are you coming?"

"I don't know, John, there's so much to do here. I don't want Renee trying to do this alone. The job's horrendous. They had so much stuff!" She snuggled deeper into the down pillows and asked, sleepily, "What about your end?" She tried unsuccessfully to stifle a yawn.

"I guess I'm getting tired, too," he answered wearily. "Now it appears as though Maxco has found redemption." John had talked to Elizabeth and she had told him about Roger's plan to 'set things right.'

"What do you mean, John?"

"Maxco is putting on a show, I'm sure of it. He's taking care of loose ends that have been bothering Elizabeth and the authorities. He's called an emergency meeting of the board of Directors for tomorrow, trying to sooth a lot of ruffled feathers. It's too much of a turn around, too disconcerting to be genuine."

"Why would he do this so suddenly, John? It doesn't make sense."

"It could be a diversion, Jill. Maybe he's stalling for time. There is another possibility. He may be ready to initiate something close to his original plan. I know the FDA is set to stop distribution of the vaccine. The Russians have a lot to do with all of this. Roger is a real juggler. I know he is up to something big—it has to do with the Russians and drugs. I just can't seem to find the last piece of the puzzle. I'm so frustrated!"

"John, when this is over, promise me, let's get away from all this mystery and intrigue. I need a break and so do you."

"That's a promise, honey. You take care of yourself over there. We're still hearing about mudslides and houses falling into the ocean, on the news. Don't fall into any sinkholes," he teased.

"I'll be here a few more days, John. Next week, we will be together—somewhere, even if it's just for a couple days. Okay?"

"Sounds good, Jill. Take care. I love you."

"I love you, sweetheart. Call me tomorrow night."

Before leaving his office for his temporary home at the Chelsea

Inn near Sixth Avenue, John made another phone call to Elizabeth's home. He knew she always stayed up late. She picked it up immediately.

"Up late, Elizabeth?"

"What else, John? There's just too much going on to try to sleep."

"Any more surprises from Roger?"

"As a matter of fact, I was given the agenda for tomorrow's Directors meeting. It is almost apologetic declaration of all his past sins. According to this, he'll be apprising us of steps taken to eliminate future inventory problems. Dr. Elliot will be giving the board a special report on the progress of the new cancer vaccine. Maybe he got religion, John," she said wryly.

"Don't take any large bets on that, Elizabeth. I'm thinking this may all be a ruse."

"What are you thinking, John?"

"I'm becoming convinced all of this is a diversion—it has to do with timing. Tomorrow is the sixteenth. Do me a favor."

"Sure, what do you need?" She grabbed her pad and pen.

"At the meeting tomorrow, try to determine, if possible, Roger's time frame to, as he put it, '… get back to normal with inventories.' That may give us a clue with respect to the timing of his plans. I am more concerned about this vaccine getting out. The FDA has been alerted and will be taking a hard look before they consider an application for approval. Find out if Roger knows this fact. He may try giving the board a snow job to keep everyone in line. I don't trust that man at all."

"Why don't you tell me how you really feel, John." Elizabeth laughed. "I'll find out as much as I can. Arthur Litton will be there. He rarely comes anymore. But he's not a happy guy, these days. He seems unusually distressed. No doubt he'll have some hard questions for Roger."

"It should be an interesting meeting, Elizabeth. When it's over, call the office or my cellular. Incidentally, have you noticed our surveillance?"

"Yes, I have. Thanks John—I feel a lot safer."

"Call me tomorrow. Night."

"Good night, John." Elizabeth had almost asked John to come over for a nightcap. Not a good idea, she reasoned.

Thursday, July 16—8:00 a.m. Chicago

It was a blustery day—a storm was brewing over Lake Michigan with strong winds bringing hot, moist air to the citizens of Chicago. Charles Nitti had arrived at his offices just off the Loop. Christopher Santini and Tony Vittorio were enjoying their morning coffee and preparing to give their boss an update on Maxco-Litton.

"Good morning, guys," Charles gestured to Tony. " Windy out there. Let me get some coffee. What's new with our friend, Maxco?" Tony gave Charles the latest news.

"It seems Roger is backing off. He's letting down—not acting as frantic as he was last week. I don't know exactly what that means. Perhaps nothing to worry about. "

"I'm worried," Nitti said, "this guy has a lot to do to make sure we are out of his business, sale of stock, etc. Look harder. I don't want any surprises. You may have to remind him of our deadline."

"Our deadline is the same as the Russian's. He knows he has only five more days." Tony was trying to calm down his boss.

"Then why in the hell is he winding down?" Nitti was getting nervous. "I don't get it and I don't like it. We're missing something!" Reports had been surfacing that the FBI, the DEA and the IRS were all looking into the activities of Maxco-Litton and its divisions. This did not sit well with the crime boss.

"Charles," replied Chris, "it may be necessary from Roger's perspective. Being so close and under so much scrutiny, this whole thing of winding down may be a clever ploy, a plot to catch the authorities off guard. I don't know for sure, but it's possible."

"I hope you're right, Chris," Nitti said, "but if he fucks us, — I'll kill him."

"Charles, with your permission, I'll talk to him. Chris may be right—I'll find out tonight." Tony knew that his boss would leave nothing to chance. He decided to act. "It's best I talk to him," Tony said.

"Okay, but no slack. You make sure he knows that by four o'clock Monday afternoon, our group is completely paid off as planned and all ties are severed. Make that clear! Call me tonight, after you get hold of Maxco."

"I have his home phone, Roger," Tony said, relieved. "I'll

make the call and give you the news." Tony Vittorio was a peacemaker and would do anything he could to keep his boss from expressing volatile behavior. He would do his best to smooth the waters.

"Do we have anyone we can talk to on the Russian side?" Nitti wanted to cover all the bases.

"Alexis Kardonoff," replied Tony. "This guy has diplomatic status. It may take a few hours to locate him."

"Get to work on it," Nitti replied gruffly. "There's no room for error. Call me when you learn something." The mobster hoped that Maxco-Litton, insofar as the Chicago group was concerned, would be history in four more days.

John Rushly was interrupted during a briefing at his temporary office at the Federal Plaza at 8:00 a.m. on Thursday.

"Mr. Rushly, I have the Director on the line." The receptionist sounded excited.

"Director of what," asked John, distracted.

"Agent Rushly, it's the Director of the FBI, Lou Hawthorne." John felt like a fool. He practically jumped to attention before grabbing the phone.

"Special Agent John Rushly."

"John, this is Lou Hawthorne. Good morning."

"Good morning to you, Sir. This is indeed a pleasure."

"Thank you, John. I wanted to congratulate you on the work you have been doing on the Maxco-Litton case. Your superiors are impressed."

"Thank you again, Sir; I appreciate your call." John held his breath. He wasn't sure, but he didn't think the Director of the FBI called around giving pep talks to his agents.

"As you know, John, the Maxco-Litton case has taken on international overtones. We know the Russians are involved. In fact, I just got off the phone with Major Yermachenko and Captain Vasin of the Federal Security Service (FSB). They have been in touch with the CIA who called me. Mr. Tenson, the Director, would like to meet with you at the DC headquarters tomorrow."

"Yes, Sir, I'll leave this evening and check in first thing in the morning."

"Thank you, John. You know this is your case—but because of the Russians, we may have to keep the CIA advised."

"I understand, Sir. That is no problem. I look forward to meeting you in Washington."

"John, I believe Captain Vasin is on his way to Washington. He can be trusted. The FBI has worked with the FSB on many cases. You know that's an offshoot of the old KGB. As a matter of background, the work in Russia is rather nasty. Several FSB agents were killed in 1997—that gives you some idea of the violent nature of their enforcement activities."

"I never realized that, Sir. Thank you for the background. I look forward to our meeting."

"Excellent, John. See you in the morning. Goodnight."

"Goodnight, Sir."

I have arrived, he thought, replacing the phone in its cradle. *The Directors of the FBI and CIA—and Washington D.C. I can't wait to tell Jill. The CIA is a part of my investigation.* He remembered the Director's instructions, "Gather your facts, John, and be ready for an interesting meeting." I need to call Elizabeth—cancel lunch. She'll understand. Knowing he was too distracted to continue, he dismissed the staff and postponed the briefing.

John did have one concern. Suppose the CIA wants total control of the situation and lets Roger Maxco off the hook for the time being? That's not acceptable. *I'll deal with that if the time comes,* he thought.

The Director placed a call to the CIA in Langley—direct to the office of George J. Tenson. He picked up the phone.

"George here."

"George, this is Lou. Our meeting is on—11:00 a.m. tomorrow. Agent Rushly is excited about CIA participation. Will you be there?"

"The Deputy Director will be there, Lou. Thanks for your cooperation. We'll talk after the get together."

"I look forward to that—good day, George."

In the New York Russian Embassy, Alexis Kardonoff had a checklist of his own. Although Michael Lowe had alerted him with regard to what appeared to be a withdrawal from Roger's

commitment, the Russians were skeptical and distrustful of Roger. Alexis made notes of "things to do."
- ✓ Monitor warehouses
- ✓ Surveillance of Elizabeth Martin
- ✓ On the 19th, confirm presence of necessary aircraft at disposition centers
- ✓ Obtain report from our man at the Lake Placid laboratory—vaccine status
- ✓ Priority—Tight surveillance of Roger Maxco

The Russians had problems of their own. FSB officers in Moscow were holding several of Kardonoff's close associates. They were sworn to silence but one never knows. *A few more days*, Alexis thought, *and it will be all over and too late for the authorities.* Alexis's thoughts were interrupted by an important call from Newark—a major warehouse and distribution center for Maxco-Litton. It came in on a private embassy-secure line.

"This is Alexis."

"Sir, this is Robert from JFK—there is a problem here. Your man, Greenwald, is in touch with competitors. I have no knowledge of what their position is with respect to our project. I only know the calls were not authorized. They were made to Charles Nitti in Chicago."

"You have done well. How does everything else look?"

"It appears that the drug shipments are in place—no vaccines as yet."

"Keep me informed. Thank you, Robert."

Alexis believed that Greenwald could do him no harm. It was expected the Chicago group would keep tabs on Roger. They had an investment, too. However, an act of betrayal could not be tolerated. Greenwald had made a fatal mistake.

Greenwald was a plant of Charles Nitti. His decision to play both ends had paid off handsomely—expensive cars, women and an apartment in Upper Manhattan. He believed he was the only paid "observer" at the JFK facility. Actually, he had three employers—Nitti, Kardonoff and Maxco-Litton.

Wednesday evening, he left the Maxco-Litton facility and

boarded the Port Authority shuttle bus to Howard Beach. He would end up on the Eight Avenue Express to Manhattan. At 6:45 p.m. Greenwald arrived at his trendy apartment near the Metropolitan Museum of Art.

At 7:30, Greenwald walked out of his building, nodded to the doorman, and took his usual walk toward Central Park. He had no reason to be apprehensive. In a timely fashion, he had reported to his two employers—nothing unusual to relay. He had smiled as both the Chicago representative and the Russian contact reacted pleasantly—confirming their respective payment arrangements.

Traitors to the Russian cause were treated harshly. The assassin knew the rules. The victim must know he is going to die. It made the job somewhat more difficult. It meant confronting the victim—making sure he or she knew exactly what was coming—and why.

Greenwald noticed the stranger approaching from the corner across the street, about two hundred feet ahead. He froze, upon hearing his name.

"Greenwald, we need to talk." Walking briskly toward his victim, the stranger reached smoothly into his jacket.

"Who are you? What do you want?" First, fear, then panic—Greenwald listened.

"You can't have it both ways, Greenwald—it's been decided." The 9mm Glock was in full view. The silencer added to the drama. Greenwald's heart sank.

"Wait, wait. I can—"

The Glock spit out the first round, a gut shot. Greenwald reeled in pain and panic.

"No. Please, God, no—" Mercilessly, the next shot pierced his heart.

"Nothing personal, Greenwald. Strictly business." As the assassin finished his sentence, Greenwald slipped to the ground in the throes of death. In four seconds, he was dead. The stranger slipped into the night as a dark Mercedes pulled up from a block away. It was one more statistic, just another unsolved murder.

Chapter Twenty-six

Thursday, July 16, 1998

Early morning in Washington D.C. was muggy but that did not distract from the excitement felt by Special Agent John Rushly. An agent arrived at Dulles and drove him to the J. Edgar Hoover FBI Building on Pennsylvania Avenue. The meeting was set for eleven o'clock. He had a half-hour to spare. John was met by the Director and introduced to the deputy Director of the CIA and Captain Vasin of the Russian FSB. Others in attendance included Field Office heads from New York, Washington D.C. and Chicago. Maggie O'Brien, from the Miami office, stood by the coffeepot, a big smile on her face and a hot cup of coffee ready for John, in her hand.

Lou Hawthorne opened the meeting. "Staff, many of you already know John Rushly from Phoenix. He's on special assignment and has been spending a lot of time in New York." Everyone acknowledged John with a greeting or a nod.

Hawthorne continued. "In particular, I would like to welcome Captain Vasin of the Russian FSB—he has a vital interest in this case. In fact, the Captain has informed us of an incident yesterday which he believes is connected to this case. An employee of Maxco-Litton was found shot to death near his apartment in Upper Manhattan. Captain Vasin believes the man, a fellow by the name of Greenwald, was working for Alexis Kardonoff." John was surprised at the depth of knowledge displayed by the FSB. *This murder just happened and they have the crime solved,* he thought.

Hawthorne continued. "John, your work has moved steadily ahead—you're doing a great job. The fact you have a key player in the Maxco-Litton hierarchy, Elizabeth Martin, has given a real boost to your efforts. The case, as you know, is international and involves, among others, the FSB, CIA and the Bahamian police. The FBI has kept these agencies informed of our progress and we're now gleaning perspective and important evidence as a result of their efforts. Kelly Bernham, deputy Director of the CIA has some interesting information to share. Kelly—"

"Thanks Lou. I want to thank everyone here for your efforts. I'm here to assist and not to preempt your work. The concerns of the CIA are these. Number one, we're worried about the infiltration of Russian criminal elements into American businesses, elements that affect national security. Two, we're concerned about Russian diplomats utilizing their unique status to impede criminal investigations and to promote chaos in the market places of the world.

"Insofar as this case is concerned, we are also working with the DEA since we believe a Russian criminal element is seeking control of Maxco-Litton, or at least control of massive amounts of drugs. Our efforts have been coordinated with the FSB and other law enforcement agencies throughout the world to prevent this from happening."

Captain Vasin interjected a comment. "Ladies, gentlemen, earlier the Director mentioned a murder that occurred yesterday in Upper Manhattan. We have been tracking all known accomplices of Alexis Kardonoff for months. Until now, we have had no direct evidence to have him removed from the diplomatic service and returned to Russia under arrest. He has many friends in high places. We know that the man killed yesterday was providing Kardonoff valuable information about Maxco-Litton. Further, we know he double-crossed his friends in Chicago, a criminal element headed by Charles Nitti. He betrayed, of course, the American people and Maxco-Litton, his employer.

"I mention all of this because I must impress upon all of you that these men are extremely vicious. They will stop at nothing. Hundreds of our agents are killed each year in Russia. Now it is spreading to your country. Alert your men and women. Use extreme caution when attempting to question or apprehend these people." John was particularly interested in these comments. He pressed the captain.

"Captain Vasin," asked John, "from my view, we are closing in on this element and those affiliated with them. How dangerous are they when they know they are beaten?"

"Agent Rushly, I know about the 'conversation' that took place between Elizabeth Martin and these people. Do not assume anything. They may kill for a variety of reasons, some illogical. In making the arrests, no one is safe until they are totally disarmed and incarcerated."

Hawthorne wanted everyone in the room to feel comfortable talking with each other, intra-agency. The meeting would break up with various agencies agreeing to keep each party informed and to coordinate all relevant information. John had a few more comments, before he was ready to let these people go. Many of them had assisted him long distance with this case. He stood, asking for a moment of their time before breaking for lunch.

"I want to thank my colleague in Miami, Maggie O'Brien, for her help in apprehending Sweeper. That was a real break for us, Maggie. With respect to the overall investigation, I believe Maxco has made his deal with the Russians. It is going to culminate with a massive distribution of stockpiled drugs. Further, I believe one of the Maxco-Litton projects has been revived and will be a part of that deal. I have alerted the FDA to that particular problem. Since this case has taken on international proportions, the vaccine part of this alleged transaction must be of interest to agencies worldwide." The Director asked John to elaborate.

"In the early stages of this case, with the deaths of Marshall Hall and Julian Weitzel, it was apparent there had been an elaborate scheme to deceive the FDA into approving a specific cancer vaccine. The data was bad. For that reason and others, the project was initially dropped by Maxco-Litton. Roger Maxco revived it, but had already put in motion his alternative plan, the one I suspect is coming down soon. If I am right, or even close, the vaccine will be shipped out to illegal distribution centers around the world, it's a vaccine not approved by the FDA and probably dangerous to a great many people. Along with the vaccine, large stockpiles of various types of prescription drugs are earmarked for shipment. I think Maxco's is trying to meet a deadline and we have to be on our toes."

"We have our jobs to do, people," the Director added, ready to adjourn the meeting. "The stakes are enormous. Working together, this case can be put to rest. This afternoon, agency heads will be meeting with John to coordinate where we go from here. He is the point man. As a result of all of our efforts, we are getting very close. John will be available in this office the rest of the day. Once again, thanks for coming and for your cooperation."

It would be a busy afternoon. John was invited to dine with the Director—it was a proud moment to share a lunch of pastrami with kraut on rye and a root beer with the Director of the Federal Bureau of Investigation.

It was eleven o'clock in the morning, and Maxco's board of Directors meeting was in full swing. Elizabeth could hardly contain herself. She had received news that Greenwald had been shot to death.

No one had mentioned it, while settling in for the meeting. She waited for just the right time. Interrupting Roger's opening statements, she stood up. She wanted everyone's full attention and she would not be put down. "Excuse me, Roger, do you have the latest news? A man by the name of Greenwald was found murdered near his New York apartment. He worked in our JFK distribution center, another murdered employee of Maxco-Litton."

Roger was furious and immediately fired back. "Elizabeth, we have thousands of employees. This was undoubtedly a mugging, having nothing to do with his employer. I think you are being paranoid. Please allow me to continue."

She refused to sit down. Elizabeth knew better. She had already talked to one of the detectives on the scene. It was a classic Russian hit.

"Of course, Roger," she replied amiably, "continue. You certainly don't need my permission. However, I find it more than coincidental that the detectives at the scene already have decided that the Russian Mafia is responsible."

"Elizabeth, I suggest we leave these matters to the police. I am attempting to inform the board of significant changes taking place at Maxco-Litton, changes that will improve production and the control of inventory. At this time," he said, turning purposefully away from her, "may I introduce Dr. Tom Elliot. He has a few comments relating to our new product research." The board members acknowledged Elliot and he stood.

"Thank you, Roger. I just want to let everyone know we are working hard on our new cancer vaccine. It isn't ready, but substantial progress has been made. In a few months, we expect

FDA approval." Roger looked smug and satisfied.
Elizabeth raised her hand for a question, but didn't bother to wait to be recognized. "Mr. Elliot, some of the information I have received this past week suggests this vaccine is in production. Could you explain how this could be happening in light of approval of the FDA being months away?"
Elliot looked at Roger and attempted to explain, faltering slightly. "The production you refer to is really a test, not only to determine possible problems with respect to production but also to determine flaws in the vaccine resulting from the process." Elliot assumed his answer would satisfy Elizabeth and the others.
"Then I can assume," Elizabeth responded, "that you have not packed any vaccines for distribution. Is that true?" Elizabeth had acquired information that tens of thousands of vials had not only been produced, but were awaiting shipment.
"Mr. Elliot," she continued without waiting for a response, "perhaps you should check on what is going on, specifically in the San Diego facility. I suspect the same things are happening elsewhere. I do have detailed knowledge that does not support your statements."
"I'll make a note of that, Ms. Martin. I'm sure there is a logical explanation." Roger shook his head patronizingly, trying to discredit her with the board. "You all realize, of course," he smiled smoothly at the members seated around the conference table, "that Dr. Elliot is not privy to all that is happening throughout the Maxco-Litton firm with regard to production and distribution systems. Many changes are taking place—for the good. In another week we should be able to report significant streamlining in all facets of the system. That's my job. In the last few days, a lot of work has been done." Roger paused and looked around before continuing. "The meeting today was called to inform all of you that we are indeed making progress. Other matters at issue, some negative, are being handled. Thank you for coming. Let's go to work—we have a lot to do." Having summarily dismissed them all, he walked out. The meeting was over.
Elizabeth was not satisfied and wanted to alert John that Roger's new demeanor was a façade, an attempt to allay their fears and delay their actions, to put everyone at ease. Her information had contradicted Elliot's carefully crafted statements and Roger

had offered no explanation, further evidence of a colossal hoax. In addition, she knew the murder of Greenwald was no mugging. She left a message at the FBI office in D.C. John was out to lunch. Elizabeth left a message—more distressing news.

Chapter Twenty-seven

Friday, July 17, 1998—Chicago

The mood was somber. Charles Nitti had just received word that Greenwald, the man he had planted at JFK, had met an untimely death. Tony Vittorio had talked with Maxco and had also been able to reach Alexis Kardonoff. As Charles became less and less cooperative in controlling his mood, the conversation became more spirited.

"So—the goddamned Russians had to make waves. Those guys are barbarians! What the hell did that bastard Kardonoff have to say?" Nitti directed his question to Tony as he had made the calls.

"They kill for little reason, Charles. It appears your guy Greenwald was working for them, too. According to Kardonoff, it was simply necessary to set an example."

"Couldn't the dumb bastards have waited a week?" Charles knew this murder would intensify the investigation. It was the worst possible time.

"They look at it differently, Charles. In my opinion, the example was for everyone involved—Roger Maxco, and our group. Once again, they wanted to let all parties know that if things don't go well for them, no one will come out alive." Incensed, Charles blurted out his own threat.

"Maybe the goddamned Russians need their own lesson, sooner than later!"

"It's just their way," Tony said, trying to keep an even keel. "Greenwald wasn't important to anyone. We'll be out of this Monday."

"I suppose this is what we get when dealing with the likes of Roger Maxco. For his sake, we'd better be out on time."

"He has the message, Charles. My last comment to Roger was emphatic. I told him we were looking to Monday as the 'drop-dead date.' Believe me, he got the message." He smiled.

"The stock that he controls is being sold off," Charles said,

"Roger is liquidating. It's slow, but you can tell it's happening. His priority is the deal with Kardonoff. Let's hope the Russians have the cash ready."

"I understand Roger has a fail-safe system in place—unless he gets the cash, the flights never leave the ground." Tony had taken a careful look at Roger's distribution plans.

"I don't trust the Russians or Roger," said Charles.

"Something could go wrong, Charles—the FBI could figure it out and make a dramatic move. The Russians could screw up again. Roger may not be able to perform for other reasons. It's so close, all we can do is wait."

"You're right, Tony. Let's get out of this in one piece. We've been lucky Roger's actions haven't sent the FBI looking in our direction."

"We don't know that for sure." Seeing his boss's angry scowl, he quickly corrected himself, "—but I believe we're okay."

"Let's have a drink," suggested Charles, "only three more days." He reached for the Mylanta, then the bourbon.

"I'll drink to day four, Charles," Tony replied cheerfully. "We can all rest easier."

It was late afternoon on Friday in New York. John had returned from Washington and was steeped in paperwork at the Federal Plaza Building. The FBI was close to obtaining a search warrant of Maxco's executive offices. They were looking for any and all files relating to warehousing and distribution of drug inventories. The warrant would be issued at any moment.

Too impatient to wait, John called the District Attorney's office. His team of investigators was ready to act and he didn't want to lose momentum. Before the caller answered, he was interrupted by another phone call. It was the prosecutor from the DAs office, on the other line. The warrant had been signed.

"John, it's a go! We'll meet you at the Trade Center. The warrant covers all records at the Maxco-Litton offices—including Roger's personal files. I expect our team will be on site no later than 4:40 p.m."

"See you there," replied John. "Jesus, let's go! We only have forty minutes. I'm glad we could do this before the weekend." He was filled with adrenaline, and he was at once relieved and nervous.

Minutes later, the scene on the top floors of the World Trade Center could only be described as organized chaos. FBI agents swooped into every office, some carrying weapons, some carrying large, empty bank boxes to put files in. Within minutes, they had picked up all the paper shredders, preventing some loyal employee from disrupting their mission, and had begun to haul away cartons upon cartons of documents. Roger Maxco stood in the doorway to his executive office, mouth open. He was aghast.

"What the hell are you doing, Rushly?"

"Mr. Maxco, I have a search warrant and an order to retrieve all documentation and files in these offices. You, Sir, may step aside and let my agents do their job."

"This is an outrage!" Roger screamed, "you can't do this to me!" His red face made him look like he was about to have a stroke.

"We can do this and we are, Maxco," Rushly responded. "If you persist in impeding this search, I'll have you arrested. You will be held in contempt of this order." Roger backed down, glaring at Elizabeth who had come out of her office and was approaching John.

"John, my god!" Her face was white. In all her thoughts, she hadn't expected such a dramatic conclusion. "What's happening?"

"I'm sorry for the disruption—it would have been inappropriate to warn any executive officers of our court order. We should be out of here in a couple of hours." Elizabeth turned to Roger.

"This is your doing, Roger," Elizabeth retorted, realizing it was all lost. "I hope you're satisfied. You've destroyed this company. I'll never forgive you!"

Roger Maxco grabbed the wall, trying to steady himself. Holding on to the chair rail, he retreated to his office and looked inside, disbelieving. In minutes, agents had stripped it of anything recognizable. All that sat on his desk was a leather blotter, a paperweight and his coffee cup. Elizabeth immediately began calling the other Directors. She motioned to John to see her privately when he could.

"Give me a few minutes, Elizabeth," he responded. "I'll meet you in your office."

Office personnel were in a state of shock. They had heard rumors and innuendo concerning the FBI and their boss, but never expected it to come to an all-out invasion.

John Rushly, all business, directed his team to finish as soon as possible, then walked briskly to Elizabeth's office to find her sitting at her desk, a look of bewilderment on her face.

"I'm sorry, Elizabeth, but you knew this was inevitable."

He wasn't prepared for the look of pure anger he received. "You could have told me."

"Elizabeth, I couldn't let you in on it."

"I see." Elizabeth said coldly. "So, what happens next?"

"We sort it out. Our staff will work all weekend. I must tell you that we're at a critical stage in our investigation."

"Do you mean Roger may be arrested?"

"It depends on what we find. I can't comment further, Elizabeth. Just be alert and watch your back. There are a lot of dangerous people involved in all of this."

"John, Monday we will need to recover our files. Business must go on. That damn vaccine isn't the only thing we're researching and producing. We have stockholders, we have responsibilities—" Her voice began to break, as if she were just beginning to realize the enormity of all of it. "Is that possible? —to retrieve our working documents?" Elizabeth was trying desperately to mitigate the damage.

"Any files that are not relevant to our investigation will be returned, Elizabeth. I'll try to speed up the process. We should be able to bring a lot of this back on Monday."

"Thanks, John—I'm overwhelmed. Who would have known it would come to this—Maxco-Litton will be severely damaged. Oh!" she put her hand to her head as if she just remembered something vital. "I've got to call Arthur Litton. Call me tomorrow, John—I must know what you find out."

"I'll do my best, Elizabeth. It's going to be a long weekend. I have to get back to my team. I'll be in touch."

Roger was on the phone screaming to Michael, who in his most judicious manner was cautioning Roger against interfering with the search and advising him to keep quiet.

"Don't go back out into the search area, Roger. Stay put. If anyone tries to question you, tell him you have no comment. The timing is bad, very bad. We need damage control. I'm calling Kardonoff. We may be okay,— we are so close."

"Son of a bitch, Michael, we need to hold this together. I suppose these bastards are going to work all weekend?" Roger continued. "Shit, they have my personal files, goddamn it!"

"Tell me there isn't a smoking gun, Roger." Michael Lowe was getting an awful feeling in his gut.

"There's nothing there, Michael—believe me." The words rang hollow. Michael Lowe knew this search could seal his doom. He pretended to sound optimistic.

"Okay, Roger. Take my advice. We'll talk tomorrow."

Chapter Twenty-eight

Saturday, July 18, 1998

The word from Krasnogorsk, the nerve center for the Russian Mafia, located northeast of Moscow, was cautiously optimistic. Although Roger's plan of slowing down the FBI investigation apparently failed, he was able to complete the required stockpiling including the agreed-upon stocks of the new vaccine.

However, concern was mounting with news of the FBI invasion of the corporate offices of Maxco-Litton. From the Russian Embassy in New York, Alexis Kardonoff was alerting his people in Krasnogorsk. It was a one way conversation.

"Gentlemen, there is close cooperation between the FBI and our nemesis, Captain Vasin of the FSB. I can't tell you what records were seized at the Maxco-Litton offices or the nature of their content—so be alert. Shipments will leave simultaneously on Monday, July 20, 4:00 p.m. EST.

I fear my position at the Embassy may be compromised. Therefore, I am making necessary arrangements to leave, as a precaution. We have two men at each distribution center to assure compliance with the orders given by Maxco. We know that the designated planes are in place with crews standing by. Have our people alerted—Moscow, Paris, Krakow, Berlin and Amsterdam. Are there any questions?"

"No, we are ready."

Kardonoff, although in charge of the execution of Roger Maxco's grandiose plan, did not have the final word. A colleague of Captain Vasin, Major Yermachenko of the FSB, had warned the FBI of the existence of someone prominent in the hierarchy of Soviet power controlling the likes of Kardonoff and others. That explained how Kardonoff had become entrenched in the Russian Embassy. He was not above making mistakes that were noticed by his superior. In fact, the decision to kill Greenwald was looked upon as being ill timed and ill advised

The red light on his secure line signaled a call from Alexis Kardonoff's superior in Moscow. He picked up the phone.

"Yes, Sir, this is Alexis."

"Listen carefully. I have received word from the FSB that Roger Maxco maintained volumes of incriminating documents, documents now in the possession of the FBI. We cannot allow even the remotest possibility of any of this material being corroborated. After 4:00 p.m. EST, Maxco is to be eliminated at the first opportunity. Is that clear?"

"Clear, Sir." The brief conversation was over. Kardonoff breathed a sigh of relief. He had not anticipated the call and worried that the Maxco-Litton deal might be called off. The death order for Roger Maxco was satisfying.

"Roger Maxco—you deserve to die. We will transfer funds—a deal is a deal—as you Americans say. You know too much and can no longer be trusted. Kerensky is right. We will live up to our bargain—but then..."

Saturday, July 18—2:00 p.m. EST

The methodical sorting of documents was in full swing, at the makeshift temporary FBI headquarters just floors below the company they were investigating. A large conference room at the Marriott provided the setting. The FBI had rented it for the weekend in the interest of time and efficiency. There were twenty federal accountants and lawyers sifting through the information. John had summoned Elizabeth to assist in deciphering three faxes recovered from Roger's files marked Personal. They were cryptic in nature and John thought Elizabeth might be familiar with the terminology. Elizabeth arrived at 3:00 p.m.

"Good afternoon," John said, "I know this isn't what you had in mind for Saturday afternoon, but I need your help."

"Anything to move this investigation along, John," she sighed, looking defeated. "I'll be relieved when this is over. What do you have?"

"Elizabeth, we have some faxes from overseas. They seem to deal with production and distribution issues, but not in plain English." John handed her the documents.

It only took a second for her to recognize the papers. "These are faxes that came in through Roger's personal fax machine—notice the distinctive underlining of the message box. The text is unusually cryptic, John. It doesn't mean it is anything sinister. We often disguise messages because of corporate espionage."

"At least we know the message was directed to Roger. Its origination is a city northwest of Moscow—Krasnogorsk."

"To my knowledge, John, Maxco-Litton has no business connections with that city."

"It's from Roger's Russian friends, Elizabeth. We are finding several direct links to the Russian Mafia. Incidentally, is Roger staying close to home?"

"You'll have to ask him, John—you must have people watching him."

"Just thought I would ask," John said, "I suspect he confides in you from time to time." John was fishing but Elizabeth, mentally out front of most men who tried to glean information, was not biting.

"John, I prefer you ask me directly if you think I am hiding something—okay?" Once again, this clever executive outflanked John. His admiration and respect grew with each mental encounter. It was obvious she was disenchanted with this whole prospect. She had just assisted the government in bringing down the company she had helped to build.

Roger was indeed under close surveillance by the FBI. In particular, he had been visited twice by an international travel executive. The agency was located in the World Trade Center—a quick check revealed that no tickets had been purchased. The meetings were casual and there was no reason to suspect Roger was making travel arrangements. He had purchased tickets for San Francisco, a trip originally planned eight months before with Elizabeth and one other executive for Chinese trade shows. The Trade Show was scheduled for August 3-6.

"You're right, Elizabeth," John backed off, "you've always been up front with me. You deserve no less."

"Thanks, John—let's face it, this past week has been upsetting to say the least. What's going to happen, John?"

"Elizabeth, this is between you and me, okay? Probably by mid-week, you should have Maxco-Litton back under control. Monday or Tuesday you will not only be able to petition the court, but obtain a court order relieving Roger of all authority with respect to Maxco-Litton. The criminal investigation may take longer. We're not there, yet. We want him sewed up tight."

"We've drafted the necessary documents, John. Our lawyers want him out Monday. The search warrant along with previous indiscretions will assure his retirement. I don't know about the criminal end of this. It's confusing to me."

"Elizabeth, Roger did a lot of good for Maxco-Litton when he took over—that's not easy to forget. You have been working with him all this time. Distance yourself, Elizabeth. There are matters I can't discuss with you, but as a friend, I'm encouraging you to keep your distance."

"I appreciate your concern, John. I'll be okay. Well, I still have time to enjoy the weekend, such as it is, so if there is nothing pressing, I'll talk to you Monday."

"Thanks for coming down, Elizabeth. I'll be in touch." John couldn't help worrying about this classic beauty. He knew as long as Roger was around, there was danger. Some of the people he had chosen to become close to were known killers, as confirmed by the FSB.

Chapter Twenty-nine

Monday, July 20—8:00 a.m. EST

Roger Maxco had created an elaborate escape plan. Having worked on it for months, he had documents giving him several new identities—passports, driver's licenses and social security cards - all coordinated to assure that plenty of cash would be available. Transportation had been meticulously thought out—a private jet to Miami, then a commercial flight to London, Paris and Rome, each under a different alias. Nothing was left to chance. He was scheduled to leave the World Trade Center at 5:00 p.m.

Michael had opted to take his chances. He believed time was on their side. *It will be over in hours*, he thought. The two began to reminisce and discuss their success. Roger would accept no calls and instructed Carol to screen all visitors.

"They worked all weekend, Roger," Michael said, referring to the FBI. "Let's hope nothing happens today." Cautious to the end, Michael wanted to hear good news.

"Michael, I have six of the highest paid lawyers in New York working on this. They have explicit instructions, to keep the FBI at bay until mid-week. Of course, a huge bonus will give them the motivation to do their legal duty. I must admit, the search and seizure caught me by surprise—bad timing."

"What about the planes, Roger? When do they start loading? The logistics of the undertaking had always been a mystery to Michael.

"Precisely at noon, Michael—the operation begins. The planes will be fully loaded by 3:30. Everything is in place."

"What about the vaccine?" Michael replied, "how in the hell did you manage production?"

"My testing scheme worked. I thought Elizabeth was going to undo me at the last meeting. Tom Elliot did a good job. By having the materials in place and the production people standing by, it has been an all-out effort, day and night. The Russians have confirmed the amounts—100,000 vials in each flight. Their people are right on top of it. You know Greenwald worked for them. That was a message to us, '—stay on track or else.'"

"It's too rough for me, Roger. You must have guts of steel."

"It's a matter what you want, Michael, and what you are willing to do to get it. We all like to win. I happen to enjoy the race. Look, Michael, I came to Maxco-Litton and turned it around—for what? What is happening today is monumental. Sure, you lose a few friends along the way. Remember Earnest Lasko?"

"Yes, Roger, and the explanation that he had a breakdown and his family took him home to Kansas. I never bought the story."

Michael wasn't sure he wanted to know the story.

"Earnest did all the accounting. Never one to take chances, he went around me to Elizabeth Martin. He did something else. One of the Chicago boys learned he was having preliminary chats with the Internal Revenue Service. The money I obtained from Charles Nitti, let us say was tainted. They asked my permission to deal with him. He is now at the bottom of the East River, tucked away permanently in a barrel of cement. They made a special trip from Chicago to New York to do the job. Why am I telling you this? You might as well know it all."

What a goddamned monster, thought Michael, gritting his teeth. *And the man shows absolutely no remorse.* "I don't care to know it all," Michael said.

"There is no retreat, Michael. This is our last grab at the brass ring. Don't stop reaching for it now."

"Don't worry, Roger, I have my own travel plans. As soon as the money is transferred, I'm out of here."

"Stay close," Roger replied, "it's only a few more hours."

"What about Tom Elliot?" Michael asked.

"He'll get away. He's a strange guy," he shook his head. "He was never concerned about the money. Just wanted to get back at the medical establishment." Roger thought more about some of their conversations. "He never felt good about the vaccine, it never tested right. There will be some casualties. I told him that was part of the deal. Sometimes people end up with the short end of the stick. It's just business."

Monday, July 20—10:00 a.m. EST

On the 23rd floor of the Federal Plaza, John Rushly was faxing the most incriminating documents to the Attorney General. It could still be hours before an arrest warrant was issued for Roger Maxco and his conspirators. Elizabeth Martin was scheduled to be in his office at noon. She was in the process of obtaining a Writ to have Roger relieved of all authority with respect to the firm's administrative operations. The court order was expected by midafternoon.

The Director of the FBI was informed that John was on the phone—he was setting up a conference call.

"This is John Rushly."

"Stand by, John—I'm on the phone with Major Yermachenko. We're having a conference call.

"This is Major Yermachenko—is this Director Hawthorne?"

"Yes, Major, and I have Special Agent John Rushly—we are all plugged in." The Director continued:

"John, the Major believes that Kardonoff and his people are geared up for something big with Maxco-Litton. He feels it is imminent. Major, what do you think is going on?"

"Agent Rushly, Director, there is an unusual amount of communication taking place between Krasnogorsk and the principle cities of Moscow, Paris, Krakow, Berlin and Amsterdam. We have been unable to decipher exactly what is being set up, but there is no doubt it has something to do with anticipated shipments from Maxco-Litton. I am suggesting a close monitoring of all distribution centers belonging to this company."

"Major," John replied, "Immediately following the seizure of files from Maxco-Litton, I ordered our agents to increase surveillance of the distribution centers. This morning, I alerted tactical squads to be ready in the event it would be necessary to shut down the Maxco-Litton warehouses. Your information is valuable, Major. It suggests we may need FAA intervention should transport flights need to be grounded.

"John," the Director added, "the FAA has been notified and you should be getting a call from the top before long. Incidentally, I am in constant touch with the Justice Department and we should have several arrest warrants in hand by early afternoon. As we speak, indictments are being handed down which involve several key players at Maxco-Litton including, of course, the principle, Roger Maxco. Stand by, John, this could happen momentarily. Is there anything else, Major?" the Director asked.

"I suggest you take great care," came the concerned reply. "Once again, these are violent people. They will not give up easily, if challenged." The Major was right. The FSB was losing agents at an alarming rate—all killed in the line of duty.

"Your words are taken to heart, Major. Thank you for joining us and for your valuable input."

"Until later, Director Hawthorne and Agent Rushly." The Major had great concerns and wished he could be part of the American operation. His men were busy at Krasnogorsk and the principle airports of Moscow, Paris, Krakow and Berlin.

"What do you think, John, is it this close?" The Director was worried. The DEA had not taken heed of his warnings. They had refused to assign special teams to the Maxco-Litton case, arguing something about prescription drugs vs street drugs and priorities. Regardless, John was ready—it would be an FBI show.

"Sir, as soon as Maxco is put away, I'll breath easier. Whatever his plans, they may be on automatic. To answer your question: I believe everything has been prearranged between the Russians and Maxco. Yes, it could all come down at anytime."

"Be ready, John—whatever you need."

"Thank you, Sir. I'll keep you informed." John had all the equipment and men he could utilize. Now it was just a waiting game.

Monday, July 20—11:00 a.m. EST

Anticipation was building in the offices of Charles Nitti. Vittorio and Santini were present and all were discussing the Maxco-Litton problem.

"Gentlemen," Charles announced, "I believe it is going to happen. I have been assured by Roger that everything is in place. I admit, Saturday, it looked bad. Believe it or not, Roger Maxco is still in charge at Maxco-Litton."

"I'm worried about all the documentation the FBI seized. What does Roger have to say about that?" Tony was not so confident.

"You worry too much Tony. Look, it's coming up on noon. In a few hours, the Russians will be happy and we will be extricated from Maxco-Litton. Maxco will drift away, I think." Charles had misgivings. "You know, if I were Roger, I would look out for the Russians—they have a lot at stake."

"What are you saying?" Chris said. "If the Russians are happy and it all goes as planned, what's their problem?"

"Roger's been too cozy with the Russians," Charles replied. "He knows too much. We're talking the Diplomatic Corps real connections with the Soviets. Anyway, he's no longer our concern. Roger can take care of himself."

"He knows a lot about us, Charles," Tony said.

"I know. Don't worry. He's being watched. If he makes any conciliatory moves toward the authorities, he will be dealt with."

"You know, it was that bungled attempt on Marshall Hall's life that brought us into this mess. Shit, I'll tell you who is going to figure this whole thing out—the FBI. All this crap is making me nervous," Charles said, "Roger does know too much—he could bury us."

Monday, July 20—12:00 p.m. EST

"Elizabeth Martin is here, Mr. Rushly." The receptionist had been alerted that she was to arrive at noon.

"I'll be right out. We're leaving the building for lunch. Correction, we'll be in the restaurant downstairs in case of emergency."

"Yes, Sir, I'll make a note of it."

John gathered some papers, folded them into his jacket pocket and walked out to the reception area. "Elizabeth," he said, "it's good to see you."

"I'm worn out, John, but it is good to be around you." She was obviously back to her old self again, and the tension, whatever it was between them, was still there, still unspoken.

"We'll stay in the building, if you don't mind. There's a decent restaurant on the first floor."

"That's fine, John. I'm so weak from all this stress and intrigue. Maybe some food will get me going again."

"You have been through a lot, Elizabeth. It's almost over. The

Director is worried about the Russians. They are extremely dangerous. It might be wise for you to take a few days off. What do you think?" They talked quietly on the elevator on the way down, then found a table in the restaurant. They both ordered coffee.

"John, this would be the worst time for me to be away from Maxco-Litton. The dedicated people, the good people - need me. They believe in what they are doing, in spite of Roger. Are you anticipating something I should know about?" John's loyalties belonged to the FBI. He couldn't divulge critical information to someone so close to the Bureau's prime suspect, even if he did trust her implicitly.

"I'm only saying, Elizabeth, that events are moving rapidly. Roger's business friends worry me. They have no conscience. I'm concerned about your safety."

"I don't believe I am in danger, John. The episode the other day was scary, but not something I expect to happen again."

"You're not doing what they demanded, Elizabeth. You're trying to take Roger's position from him. That's what the kidnapping was all about." John was determined to convince Elizabeth to extricate herself from the offices, if only for a few days.

"John, I am sure they are aware of your raid—excuse me," she said with pretended rancor, "—your search of our offices. Now more than ever the Russians know the risks. They can't threaten the FBI and they know I have little impact on what Roger is doing now. It's gone too far. I'm not important to them."

"I hope you're right," John said, "if these people operated from some logical basis, I would feel better. We know the Russians killed Greenwald. They may have killed Earnest Lasko. He is still nowhere to be found."

"If this were going on much longer, John, I would take your advice. I —," she was interrupted by her cellular phone. "I'd better get this, John."

It was one of the Maxco-Litton lawyers. "Elizabeth," he said, "you and Arthur Litton are in absolute and total control of Maxco-Litton. The Writ was handed down ten minutes ago. I'm on my way back to the office. Just in case, I'm having a federal Marshall hand it to Roger. We can stop any activity he has in progress."

"Thank God. I'll be right there." Elizabeth looked at John and said, "I'm in control, John—Roger is out."

"I'm going with you, Elizabeth." He stood up.

"John, I'll handle this. The lawyers are meeting me and bringing a federal Marshall. You do what you need to do. I'll be at my office." John picked up the tab for the half-eaten lunch. Elizabeth was out the door and well on her way to her office.

Pulling out his phone, John called the New York Field Office. The Field Officer in charge was notified as to the events unfolding. The Bureau was put on a heightened state of alert. *If this bastard is going to do something drastic,* John thought, *he will be forced to act now.* John had one more order.

"Willis, call the Justice Department—we need those warrants, now!"

"Yes, Sir, I'm on it."

"I'm heading back," John replied, "keep the lines open!" He broke into a run.

Monday, July 20—1:15 p.m. EST

Elizabeth, the lawyers, and the federal Marshall met in the lobby and took the elevator to the Maxco-Litton reception area. Elizabeth led the way directly to Roger's office.

"Carol, is Roger in?"

"Ms. Martin, I expect him back from lunch momentarily."

"Carol."

"Yes, Ms. Martin?" She looked up at Elizabeth smugly, as usual. She knew who the head honcho was and it was her boss, not Elizabeth Martin.

"This man is a federal Marshall with a court order relieving Mr. Maxco of all duties at Maxco-Litton. You no longer work for Roger. You work directly for me."

"But, I—"

"You're fired, Carol. You have five minutes to collect your personal things and leave the building." Elizabeth had tolerated the woman's sarcastic humor and aloofness for too long. *This was her chance,* she thought, *Carol blew it.*

"You can't do this. Roger will—."

"There is no Roger, Carol. You don't get it—he's out. And so are you." Elizabeth gestured to one of the lawyers. "Escort Carol from the building—she's trespassing." Carol just had time to reach into her bottom desk drawer and grab her purse before she found herself being led to the elevator. Just then, the CEO in question arrived. Just hours away from a billion dollars and freedom, Roger sensed his potential executive demise and became suddenly irate.

"What the goddamned hell is going on here? Carol, where are you going?" In tears, the distraught Carol muttered her last words to Roger.

"I'm being discarded, like useless furniture. That bitch,—" She couldn't go on and was summarily escorted to the elevator.

"Roger Maxco?" the uniformed man held a paper in front of Roger's face.

"Who the hell do you think I am? Who the hell are you?"

"Federal Marshall, Sir—this belongs to you." Roger was handed the court order.

"For god's sake, Elizabeth," he shrieked at his former colleague, standing before him, polished and elegant as usual— "Do you know what you have done?" His mind a blur, Roger's brain was trying desperately to sort out information and options.

"My god, Elizabeth—not today. Please, not today—" his face grew ashen and he stumbled, disbelieving he had come so far, to be stopped by a lousy piece of paper. Roger had known this was the worst scenario he might have to face, but he hadn't prepared for the reality of it. After all, his plan was still running full steam ahead, on automatic pilot. *It has to happen,* he thought, looking around at the sea of faces that watched him. *My life depends on it. Shape up, Roger, stay cool,* he thought, struggling for composure. "Okay," he said finally, "it's all yours, Elizabeth. I need a vacation anyway. May I stay and gather a few personal effects?"

"Of course, Roger. You know I had no choice. This firm is bigger than you and me. I don't know how you kept everything together this long. I wouldn't worry about your job. You should be more concerned about the FBI and their investigation."

"I'll prove you all wrong, even you, Elizabeth."

"You need to vacate the office by 4:30, Roger. Please don't make another scene."

"I will gladly leave, and on time, Elizabeth. I have two hours, if you don't mind—" He pulled himself together with all the courage he could muster before turning and walking, for the last time, into his executive office.

Elizabeth thanked the Marshall and retired to the boardroom with her battery of corporate lawyers. Arthur Litton had called in ill and was not in attendance. There were certain things that Elizabeth wanted to address immediately. Roger, now alone in his misery, was unaware of her imminent plans to take over complete control of the firm.

"Gentlemen, what I am about to order may be disruptive in the short run, but we must act. I have been advised by my contact at the FBI that Roger may be planning a major movement of stockpiled pharmaceuticals. In addition, rumors persist that Dr. Tom Elliot, in concert with Roger, has produced the cancer vaccine in large quantities and may be attempting to distribute this vaccine without FDA approval. Further, I believe the arrest of Roger is imminent." The lawyers were stunned. They had been out of the loop and were aghast at what Elizabeth was suggesting.

"Pardon me, Elizabeth," said Robert Rush, lead counsel. "if what you say is only partly true, it could ruin Maxco-Litton. The legal implications are enormous—law suits from customers, investors, massive fines from various government agencies—"

"Robert," she said with her usual poise, "we are fighting for the very existence of Maxco-Litton. You are absolutely correct. Therefore, you should prepare documents notifying the heads of all warehouse departments that all scheduled or unscheduled shipments are to be stopped immediately. All aircraft owned or leased by Maxco-Litton are hereby grounded. With the faxes, include the Writ obtained this afternoon. Sign my name—By order of Elizabeth Martin. The Writ gives me absolute and uncontested authority—make that clear." The conference room phone rang. It was John Rushly.

"John, this is Elizabeth."

"Elizabeth, fill me in. I have to know what is going on over there."

"John, Roger is here but is leaving at 4:30. My lawyers are busy—I'm sending you copies of my orders to all warehouse department heads. Temporarily at least, everything is to be shut down."

"Good. When will I receive those faxes?"

"In thirty minutes, John. I guarantee it."

"Elizabeth, I'll need to see you at your office at four o'clock."

"Not very good timing, John. Is it that important?"

"Absolutely. Keep Roger there, if possible." The Attorney General of the United States had informed John that arrest warrants were being issued momentarily. He would be able to act no later than 3:45 EST.

"I'll do what I can, John. See you then." Elizabeth hung up with a sense of foreboding.

Monday, July 20—2:30 EST

Michael was in a quandary. The frantic call from Roger struck his heart like a dagger. *If the court order had come through to take Roger completely out of control,* he thought, *an arrest warrant wouldn't be far behind. If it happened today, all would be lost.* Well aware that he could be arrested at any moment, Michael listened to Roger intently.

"Michael, I need your advice," Roger was whining pathetically. "Should I leave now and hide out for the rest of the day?" Roger wasn't thinking straight. The orders from the Russians had been clear. Michael took a long, hard look at a copy of their original fax:

TO: RMML:
Expect shipments. Transfer of funds ($900 million) to be confirmed upon receipt of goods including new vaccine. Must have shipping documentation in hand to take simultaneous possession Moscow, Paris, Krakow, Berlin, and Amsterdam. Confirmation of destination codes by utilizing invoice numbers 2136789—5697654—3769245—4793654—4509123 in precise order. All verified 7/27/98. Initial transfer of funds ($200 million) 7/1/98 contingent upon acknowledgement via prior encrypted codes to this number.
LK

The plan was computerized with encrypted codes. Roger had to give the final destination codes at the time the flights left.

Instantly, the funds would be transferred. He needed to be in his office—the Russians would call and Roger would initiate the sequence by computer. It was failsafe, but no one else could do it.

"Stay where you are, Roger," Michael advised, his heart in his throat. "Roger, you have to be available. No one else can make the final entries—4:00 p.m., Roger."

"I feel dizzy, I'm not thinking straight," came the weak reply. "Of course, it's only another hour or so. God, I need a drink." Roger was coming unglued—Michael had never seen the sleazy mastermind like this.

"Roger, settle down. I'm sure the FBI isn't ready to act. Thank God the Russians moved the schedule. No way could we keep this together another week."

"Are you kidding?" Roger asked, trying to laugh. "I couldn't hold this together for another day!"

Michael was under no such constraints to stay put. He would be the one to leave.

But Roger had other ideas. He kept talking. "Michael, I want you here with me, now. We can leave together at 4:15. Elizabeth expects me out of here at 4:30. Leave for my office, now. Okay?" he added plaintively.

"Roger, I can't leave this minute. Don't worry. I'll be there within the hour."

"I'll be waiting," Roger replied, "make sure you're here."

Monday, July 20—3:30 p.m. EST

Alexis Kardonoff left the Russian Embassy heading for JFK International Airport to oversee the flight from the Maxco-Litton facility. He would make the flight to London—leaving precisely at 4:15 p.m. His ride to the airport was interrupted by a call on his mobile phone. It was one of the men at the Newark Airport. The news was disheartening.

"Sir, I recovered a fax sent out by the lawyers at Maxco-Litton. It is signed by Elizabeth Martin. Roger Maxco has been relieved of all duties as CEO. Attached to the fax is a copy of the court order obtained by the lawyers. It's effective immediately. They are shutting down everything—loading, flights—everything!" Alexis

Kardonoff had anticipated this problem. He remembered the days when Elizabeth had attempted to obtain the same order. Kardonoff initiated option two—force the issue.

"Do nothing. At four o'clock precisely, have our men commandeer the jet. Anyone who gets in our way is to be eliminated. Are the planes loaded?"

"Yes, Sir, ready to go. The pilots showed, but they may be leaving."

"Take care of that problem now. I want all the other distribution centers given the same orders. Everything happens on schedule. You know what to do."

"Yes, Sir. I am initiating option two."

Chapter Thirty

Monday, July 20—3:35 p.m. EST

"Gentlemen, start your engines." It was vintage John Rushly. The respect he commanded assured him of a motivated staff willing to serve with him at the drop of a hat. They had been waiting for this one. It would be big. Arrest warrants in hand, Rushly's handpicked agents piled rapidly into the black GMC Suburban and headed for the World Trade Center. At the same time, their colleagues, a second team, descended upon the Maxco-Litton Institute at Lake Placid. Dr. Tom Elliot and others were to be arrested.

John had earlier gathered his team and briefed them on the job at hand. "It's come down to this, gentlemen—because of the massive amount of time and effort all of you have contributed to this case, we now have our authority. Our target today is Roger Maxco. His lawyer, Michael Lowe, will also be apprehended. Both are charged with conspiracy to commit murder, conspiracy to distribute and sell illegal drugs, obstruction of justice and racketeering. As you know, the last charge comes under the broad powers of RICO. Let's go."

It was a fifteen-minute drive to the World Trade Center. John rode with the officer in charge, from the New York Field Office. Rushly's team followed in the Suburban.

Michael Lowe's timing couldn't have been worse. After parking in an outside space, he walked to the main entrance of One World Trade Center. He was oblivious to the dark sedan and black Suburban heading his way. The vehicles screeched to a stop in front of him. He looked up, confused. John Rushly stepped out confronting him.

"Michael Lowe? John Rushly, FBI."

"What is this, Agent Rushly?" Michael panicked, trying to show irritation. "I'm on my way to my client's office."

"You are under arrest. Conspiracy to commit murder,

conspiracy to distribute and sell illegal drugs, obstruction of justice and racketeering." John slapped the warrant against the lawyer's chest and his assistant read Lowe his rights, simultaneously placing the shaken man in handcuffs and escorting him to the sedan.

"Stay with him, Sam," John ordered. "We're going up." Desperate, Michael raised his voice, calling after John and the agents. "Wait, wait! Mr. Rushly, I want to make a deal. I can help you! Wait!"

"Too late, Lowe, you happen to be on the wrong side of the law." John and three other agents headed on up to Maxco's office.

Monday, July 20—3:45 EST

Roger and Elizabeth were deeply engrossed in conversation. The agents could hear their voices. John tried the doorknob, gently, quietly, then realized it was locked.

"Elizabeth, I wanted to tell you before—it's all set. I leave the country this evening. You were right all along. I'm sorry about all the trouble—but a billion dollars, Elizabeth! You can join me, anywhere. We can be together."

"For God's sake, Roger! Have you gone mad? You've totally destroyed the company and now you want to destroy both our lives?"

"Elizabeth, when I first came here, I know you had feelings for me. Aren't you willing to try? I can offer you the world, now! Join me. If not now, later."

"How I have tried to save you, Roger. When you leave, you'll be a fugitive, on the run forever. What good is all that money? Where are you going to spend it, in hiding? And what about your wife, Roger? What about her? Maybe there could have been something between us at one time, but not now. What the hell is this about, just money? I've built my own fortune, Roger, honestly. That's enough for me. If I were ever important to you, Roger, why the deceit, why the murders? It's too much to comprehend."

"It's almost time Elizabeth," Roger said, oblivious to her logic. "A few key strokes to riches and freedom."

"You're insane, Roger. God help me—I probably could have

loved you at one time. I was so impressed with your talent, your business skill. I saw you take this company and turn it into the finest pharmaceutical research and manufacturing firm in the world, all because you had an incredible insight on exactly when and how to take risks. Or so I thought. But you turned evil, Roger. Maybe you always were, I don't know. But I won't be a part of this." Roger responded.

"I have a few keys to hit, Elizabeth," he responded as if he had hardly heard her. "I'll be just a moment." In seconds, the appropriate codes were inserted and the conclusion to Roger's grandiose scheme was set in motion.

Monday, July 20—3:55 p.m. EST

The reception area was unusually quiet. There was no one outside Roger's office. Agents had scurried the clerical staff off the floor, in case of resistance. They didn't want civilians harmed. John, still standing by Roger's door, listened to the conversation inside. He wanted to be sure to locate Elizabeth, mentally, inside the executive office in case they had to break in. He didn't want her taken hostage by the CEO. There was an agent stationed near the elevators. Two agents stood on either side of the door, looking at John, waiting for the move. Nodding to them as a silent signal, he suddenly banged on the door several times. He wanted to startle Roger.

"FBI, open up! This is Agent Rushly, FBI. Open the door." He yelled twice, then heard a muffled angry voice inside, followed by movement. The agents waited with guns drawn.

Roger reluctantly opened the door and stepped back. John Rushly looked him straight in the eyes, in a stern and steady voice, he said, "Roger Maxco, you are under arrest. The charges against you include conspiracy to commit murder, conspiracy to distribute and sell illegal drugs, obstruction of justice and racketeering."

"This is outrageous!" Roger's face turned red and he sputtered, trying to catch his breath.

"Yes, it is outrageous," John replied, taking control. "You have the right to remain silent—" John continued to inform the beaten man of his rights. One of the agents handcuffed him. The other stood outside the office door. Elizabeth was standing to one side.

"Oh, God, not now!" Roger screamed. "You fools! They will kill us all! Elizabeth, do something..." He began to moan, leaning his head against the doorjamb, totally disbelieving he had come this far only to be beaten.

Elizabeth, acting as if she were in a trance, suddenly realized that her whole career, everything she had worked and struggled for, was going down the drain. All those years of seventy-hour work weeks, a total sacrifice of family and social life, no pleasure for pleasure's sake, only work, building, reaching to become the most respected female executive in the firm, perhaps the industry, it was all for nothing. She would be nothing but a joke, now, from this moment on. She knew she had to do something. As if she were a cornered animal, she reached into the right drawer of Roger's desk. Slowly, smoothly, her focused eyes glistening with tears of fear, she pulled out Roger's .38 caliber revolver. Turning toward John and the other agent, she stood with the gun in her hand. At first thought, John assumed she was going to kill Roger. As he was about to yell, Elizabeth turned toward him, the gun grasped firmly in her hand.

"I can't let you do this, John," she said weakly, in a monotone. "You don't understand. If you don't arrest Roger, then we can fix it. We'll fix it. It's not for Roger, it's for the firm." Her voice broke as she tried to continue, her normally strong, articulate speech growing weaker, harder to understand. "Please, it's my whole life, John. I didn't think it would come to this. What else will I have?"

It was clear she wasn't in control of her faculties. John knew he had to act quickly. There was no telling what she might do. He hadn't realized the toll all these weeks of intrigue had taken on her. He knew he would have only one chance to bring this to a satisfactory conclusion. Looking into her eyes, a gentle smile on his face, John reached slowly for the gun. "Elizabeth, you don't want to do this, I'll help you," he almost whispered.

His words had the opposite effect than he had intended. Before he could say anything further, Elizabeth stood up straight and ordered the other agent to remove Roger's handcuffs.

Looking squarely in John's face, she said clearly, as if someone else were controlling her mind, "I'm sorry, John, he doesn't deserve to be set free, but I can't even think of him in prison. If he's in prison, Maxco-Litton is dead. It's all gone. I can't let you do that. I have to give him a chance to leave. I can't let the Chief Executive Officer of Maxco-Litton be arrested. I'm the CFO; they'll blame me, too. Oh, God, what can I do?" She looked down at the gun in her hand, in a state of total bewilderment, as if she had never seen it before, as if she didn't know where it had come from.

John took that precise moment to act. Moving toward her slowly, he began to speak. "You don't want to do this, Elizabeth. You're a brilliant woman. None of this was your fault. You won't be held accountable. Remember, Elizabeth, you assisted the FBI all along in order to protect the firm and your stockholders. You're the hero, here." He continued to move closer, a step at a time, smiling warming. "You're just upset, Elizabeth," he said, "and rightly so. But if anyone's saved the firm, it's you. And without Roger, you can rebuild. This one vaccine isn't the only thing going for you. The board trusts you. I'll tell you what," he said, in his most confiding manner, "Agent Shelby and I will strike this from our minds. At this moment, you have the opportunity to do the right thing. The other consequences are horrific, Elizabeth. You certainly don't belong in prison, and whatever you do, Roger's going to prison regardless. For your sake and mine, Elizabeth, hand me the gun." If ever John Rushly commanded respect and attention, this was it. His voice, his manner, his body language all pleaded with her to be sensible. His eyes looked into hers and finally, finally she came out of it and returned to reality. Roger had stood transfixed at the events unfolding. He had never seen her out of control and he was stunned. Elizabeth looked at John then Roger and began to weep. She placed the gun on the desk.

"Dear God, what was I doing? Forgive me, John, I have no idea what the hell I was doing." The agent took a step forward and caught her just as her knees buckled. Leaning against him, she said, "How stupid, how stupid of me!"

"Sit down, Elizabeth," John said quietly, seating her in Roger's leather chair. "Shelby, why don't you take Maxco down and put him in the car? I'll pour her some water."

The agent looked at him questioningly, and John responded quickly. "She's done nothing but assist us for weeks. The strain was just too much. Nothing has happened in this room except the arrest of Roger Maxco. Is that clear Shelby?" Elizabeth was sobbing quietly, into her hands. Her executive secretary had just been allowed into the room and began to comfort her.

"Yes, Sir," replied Shelby, finally understanding the situation. John looked at Roger, still leaning against the wall as if he didn't have the strength to walk.

"By the way, Roger, you'll need a new lawyer. Michael Lowe is in custody." Just then, the agent who had been posted at the elevator rushed in. "Rushly, you have an urgent call. It's our team at JFK." He handed John a cell phone.

"Sir, we have a situation," the frantic voice could be heard loud and clear. "Two guys, look like Russians with AK 47s, have us pinned down. We think a 707 is being skyjacked. We've called for backup! The FAA has already shut down the entire airport." In the background, John could hear the rapid fire of automatic weapons. John shouted at Agent Shelby.

"Get on the horn! Notify Central. There may be similar problems at all Maxco-Litton distribution centers. Alert the Field Officer in charge at each location. Tell the full team to disperse. Tell them the rest of us are on our way!" Agent Shelby was left with the responsibility for transporting Roger Maxco to the federal jail. Before leaving with Roger, he called the FBI headquarters and had them alert Los Angeles, San Francisco, Newark, Minneapolis and Miami—with JFK, these were the main distribution centers utilizing aircraft by Maxco-Litton. SWAT Teams at each location were on alert—and moving into action.

Monday, July 20—4:10 p.m. EST

Airport security, local police and the FBI had sealed JFK International Airport. A command post had been set up and John was getting an overview. A New York police captain greeted Rushly.

"Agent Rushly—" he shouted, trying to be heard above the activity, "all hell has broken loose here. I understand you have arrested the principal players."

"Most of them, Captain. Thanks for your help. My men were pinned down. Is that under control? What's the status of the Russians?

"Your men are okay. Regarding the Russians, we know their boss is on the plane. He's holding the pilot and co-pilot hostage. One gunman has been killed—the other is holed up in the warehouse. Your men have a SWAT Team in place. Any suggestions?"

"Captain, tell your men I want trucks across the runway, above and behind that jet. It's not going anywhere. I know who is on that plane. Is he talking?"

The captain gave the order to block the aircraft before responding, "He has a cellular. It was off when our negotiator tried calling."

"Bring a bullhorn," John ordered. "And come with me! We're going over to the plane." The captain, FBI agents and local police had positioned themselves around the massive aircraft.

John took the bullhorn and began to address the man he knew to be on the plane. "Alexis Kardonoff, this is Special Agent John Rushly, FBI. Your plane cannot leave. You are surrounded. Our agents are at every Maxco-Litton facility. It's over; it's all over! Come out and release your hostages!" John knew that Kardonoff had little to lose. At the least, he would be deported and handed over to the FSB.

On board the aircraft, Pilot Joe Hanson and Co-Pilot Jake Baker sat silently. They knew how close to death they were. Kardonoff's henchmen with their AK 47s had made that quite clear.

"Pilot," Kardonoff said brusquely, "radio the tower and have them contact that Rushly. He will call me!" There was static on the radio, but it was clear enough to get the message through.

"Right away," replied the pilot. Radio communication was open between the aircraft and the tower. John was given the message. He took a deep breath, then quickly punched in the number.

"Agent Rushly," Kardonoff answered the ring. "It seems we have what you Americans call a Mexican standoff. I suggest you allow me to leave." He almost sounded courteous.

"Kardonoff," John replied testily, "you know the drill. It can't happen. I don't think this is a particularly good day for dying, do you? Your two gunmen are already dead. Give it up."

Kardonoff knew there was no way out. He opted to be handed

over to his own kind, reasoning that with his connections in the Kremlin, he might survive.

"Rushly, I will be handed over to the Russian Embassy. Technically, I do have diplomatic immunity."

"Stay on the line," Rushly said, "this may take a little time." *You sleazy son of a bitch,* he thought. That was the most frustrating ploy these foreign nationals used and the agency hated it.

Embassy officials were already on the scene. Representatives from the State Department had been alerted. The FSB assured the FBI that Kardonoff would be prosecuted, that his diplomatic status would be terminated. *More bloodshed has been averted,* thought John. Kardonoff had a deal. Before he left the plane, however, the Russian had one more call to make. It had been prearranged. He smiled as he gave the order. "Do it now," he commanded. "The bitch, too."

"Done."

Monday, July 20—4:30 p.m. EST

Agent Shelby and the staff had made the necessary calls to all Maxco-Litton airport distribution centers. Roger was an unhappy witness, watching his world crumble with each call made. He would now be escorted to the federal facility on Long Island.

Unknown to Roger or the FBI, his every move had been monitored for the past week. Before leaving his office, Roger turned to Elizabeth, sitting quietly in his executive chair, staring out at the New York skyline. Her face was pale and drawn. He motioned to the agent for a moment to say goodbye.

"I am so sorry, Elizabeth. I was so close. There were so many complications. I never meant to hurt you."

Elizabeth gathered every bit of poise she had ever possessed, stood up straight and tall, her elegant French twist still intact, her suit surprisingly unrumpled. Stepping out from behind the desk, she walked across the office and stood in front of him.

Neither Roger Maxco nor the agent was prepared for what would happen next. Looking her former boss in the eyes, just two feet from his face, she said between clenched teeth, "You fucking bastard, I hope you die!" And hauling back, she took aim in an instant and her open hand met with his surprised face in a resounding *smack*. She turned on her heels and walked out the door. For some inexplicable reason, she knew that was the last time she would see Roger Maxco.

Monday, July 20—4:40 p.m. EST

The dispatcher from the Communications Center intercepted the cellular transmission and called John Rushly immediately.
"Sir, listen to this. I'm replaying a call Kardonoff made just before he got off the plane." John listened intently.
"Do it now, the bitch too." John's reaction was immediate.
"Hold Kardonoff," shouted at the New York field officer. "I need to talk to him." He would have to pull out all the stops. It was imperative that he reason with Kardonoff and cancel the contract on Elizabeth. Arrangements had already been made to deliver Kardonoff to the Russian Embassy.
"Sorry, John," came the chilling response. "The Russians sent a car. He's in their custody and will not communicate with American authorities."
John had no time to waste. "Contact Agent Shelby," he replied, trying to maintain his composure. "Have him lock down *where ever he is—absolutely no movement until backup arrives*—send a team!" Seeing the inquisitive look on the agent's face, he screamed, "Do it now!" Grabbing a breath, he continued, "Contact Elizabeth Martin at Maxco-Litton, at this number, 555-1262. Tell her the orders from me are that she's not to move. Send a team there. She's a target, along with Maxco. This is top priority! Find those people and secure the scene!" He had run out of breath, and his energy was spent. After all this, from Marshall to Julian—now, Elizabeth. *After all this, I will not be responsible for her death,* he thought frantically.
"Yes, Sir," came the committed response, "We're on it!"
John breathed a sigh of relief and hoped it wasn't too late.

Monday, July 20—4:55 p.m. EST

Agent Shelby had left the building with one other agent and Roger Maxco, still in handcuffs. At West Street, the West Side

Highway, and the intersection of New Murray Street, a black, 600 Mercedes whipped around in front of the four-door Chevy Caprice. At the same time, an urgent call was coming in over the car communication system.

"Shelby, give us your position," the voice sounded urgent, unlike most trained dispatchers. "Do not proceed, I repeat, do not proceed! Stay put until backup is in place. 10-4."

The responding click told the dispatcher that Shelby had heard. But no voice responded. Hearing sounds of tires screeching followed by automatic gunfire, the dispatcher became more frantic, "Shelby, what the fuck? Shelby! What's going on?" The radio was wide open.

"Agent Shelby, respond."

Shelby was hit at the first barrage of bullets, as his partner returned fire. He was shouting. "We're under fire, I'm—agent down," he could be heard struggling, "West Street and Murray." Once again, the dispatcher heard gunfire. He couldn't see what was happening. Two men approached the car where the wounded agent sat slumped over in the front seat. Guns began blazing. Shelby tried to raise his weapon. Blood ran over the other strong hand holding the radio mike.

"Shit," came the angry whisper, "they've got us, can't hold—"

Shelby was dead. His prisoner, master white-collar criminal Roger Maxco had luckily ducked down in the back seat. In a frantic and defensive move, Agent Jim West got off eight full rounds toward the black Mercedes. The two Russians had an AK 47 and a 12 gauge Winchester Defender-00 Shot. Although one Russian was hit, it was no contest. Jim West managed to fire another four rounds and wounded the other assailant, but was cut down by the AK 47—the metal doors and shatterproof glass were no match for the barrage of armor-piercing bullets. Roger Maxco was fatally wounded, but not yet dead. He received the final blasts from the 12 gauge—in the face. Sirens wailed in the distance as the Mercedes sped away. Maxco and two federal officers were dead. Rushly was on the scene in minutes.

In a futile attempt to save a life, a paramedic labored over one of the slain officers. He thought there might have been a flicker of life, but the man was gone. The paramedic stood as John and other FBI team members approached.

"Are they alive! Is anyone alive?" John shouted, running to the scene.

"I'm sorry, sir," the paramedic responded in shock, "they are all dead." He wasn't used to seeing scenes like this. It was a blood bath. All the agents knew each other and their families, some were quite close. As one after the other appeared on the scene, there were outbursts from tears to swearing, as each tried to get a handle on exactly what had happened. John turned to the ambulance crews and firemen on the scene. He placed his hand on the shoulder of one of his dead FBI agents and spoke to the rescue units.

"These men are heroes. Treat them accordingly." Turning to one of his men, John said quietly, "See that their families receive the news from one of us. Take care of them. Now, we have to stop these bastards!" *It's probably a blessing for Roger Maxco,* he thought, trying to identify the man with no face. His cell phone rang. It was one of the agents attempting to locate Elizabeth Martin.

"John, we can't locate Elizabeth Martin. She left the building, but she's not at home."

"Keep searching," he replied, thankful she hadn't been assassinated on the scene. "Call me with anything you get."

"Yes, Sir. What's going on there, John?"

"Tragedy," John responded, "pure tragedy. We've lost two of our own." *Where in the hell did she go?* he asked himself.

Monday, July 20—5:30 p.m. EST

Elizabeth Martin was on the road in her BMW, heading for the Long Island estate of her mentor, her father figure Arthur Litton. *He was the only one who could make sense of all this*, she reasoned. She had to tell him what had happened to Roger. Her thoughts now turned to saving the firm and keeping her commitment to her thousands of employees and hundreds of stockholders.

Tears and despair enveloped her being as she reflected on her years in second position to Roger. Elizabeth had thought herself a bit infatuated with Roger shortly after he had taken over Maxco-Litton. No one had any idea she felt so strongly, not even Roger.

She had never considered an affair, although Roger had given her indicated he would have gone along even though he was married. No one had ever seen Roger's wife and he never mentioned her. No one asked. It hadn't taken long for Elizabeth to become disenchanted with him, watching his unscrupulous behavior with the board members and stockholders. And yet a part of her still admired his talent for business. She had learned a lot from him.

Driving seemed to clear her head. *You were a demon possessed, Roger. You had it all, but it wasn't enough. I can't help you now, Roger.*

She pulled into the circular drive and walked along the cobblestones past the manicured lawn and colorful gardens. She loved this peaceful estate. She could see by the cars in the driveway that Arthur Litton was at home. His wife was gone, at least her car was no where to be seen.

He greeted her at the front entry, clasping her hands tightly. His demeanor was as controlled and fatherly as always. "I've been getting reports, Elizabeth," he said gently, ushering her into the house. "Are you all right?"

She looked at him carefully. "You're not ill? I thought you were ill," she said, remembering his reason for not wanting to attend the last board meeting. His lack of response let her vent, and she had a lot to say. "No, Arthur, my friend, I am not all right. Roger has been arrested by the FBI, there have been shootings, and the press is literally going to have Maxco-Litton for lunch." Suddenly, her grief turned to anger. *What the hell is he doing here so calm and collected?* she thought. *Why wasn't he at the office helping me avert a disaster?*

He could see emotion in his protegee's normally calm demeanor. "Elizabeth," he said comfortingly, leading her to a chair in the den. "Relax. Let me fix you a drink. What would you like?"

"Something strong, something very, very strong," she replied, feeling wonderfully safe and secure. As he poured her a drink, Elizabeth peered out the window and noticed a black Mercedes pulling in behind her car.

"You have company, Arthur," she said tiredly. "I hope you can get rid of them, we need to talk." Looking more carefully at the parked car, its doors not opening to let anyone out, she thought foggily, *I wonder who that is. I think I've seen that car before."*

Arthur distracted her by handing her a chilled glass. It held a double gin and tonic. He had even added a sliver of lime, perfect host that he was.

"They're picking something up, Elizabeth," he smiled warmly. "I'll just be a moment." As Arthur left the room, the phone on the desk rang. She wouldn't have picked it up but the ringing was obsessive and there seemed to be no voice mail service to answer.

Finally, Elizabeth answered. "The Litton residence."

"Elizabeth, is that you?" the voice on the other end sounded at once shocked and relieved.

"John, I was going to call you." She started to explain, "About my behavior in the office—"

"No time, no time," he cut her off abruptly. "Elizabeth, you're in danger. There's a contract—it's the Russians! Stay where you are! I'm on my way!"

"John?" she asked quietly, fear striking inside the core of her being, "Arthur is outside, outside with—there's a black Mercedes—"

"Jesus Christ, Elizabeth—hide!" There was no mistaking the urgency in his voice. "The men who killed my agents may be there. Hide in the house! Hurry! You've got to buy time! I'm leaving now!"

John signaled his fully armed team to follow. It would take at least fifteen minutes, full out with sirens. Flashing lights, wailing sirens, four FBI cars were instantly en route to save the life of one Elizabeth Martin. And her killers were there. It would be up to her. *Stall them, Elizabeth, stall them*! John thought frantically, holding onto the dashboard for support as the sedan careened around a corner.

Arthur Litton walked slowly back into the den, alone.

"Elizabeth!" He called out to her, thinking she may have gone into the kitchen. He seemed surprised to see her standing on the landing, at the top of the staircase just above the front room.

"Arthur, I need to go to the ladies' room! I'll be right down, you don't mind? It's been a nerve-wracking day." She smiled sweetly at him, trying to figure out how to keep the men outside at bay. *Let Arthur do this as gracefully as he can,* she thought.

She remembered John's urgent message, "Buy time!" All she needed was a few minutes and he would be here. Trying not to let her fear show through her façade, she remarked. "Arthur, I know it's an imposition, but could you fix me another drink, please?"

"Of course, my dear," he responded kindly. "You take your time." He turned toward the den, giving her leave to go upstairs. *It's better this way*, he thought. *I don't want her to know I'm in on it. They'll get nervous and just come in, in a few minutes. She may not have to know.* He couldn't stand to let her know he was Roger's minion, too, and had been sucked into the whole scheme. It had been easier for Arthur to get the job done, mostly by computer, at his home, away from prying eyes at the company.

It took her several minutes to reappear. He was becoming nervous. He didn't want to cross the Russians. He waited impatiently for her to reappear.

"Why hasn't the car left?" Elizabeth said smiling.

"What on earth have you been doing up there, Elizabeth?" Arthur asked, ignoring her question. He wondered if she suspected anything.

"Why?" she asked calmly. "Am I in danger, Arthur?"

"Of course not. Now, sit down. I fixed you a fresh drink. We'll talk."

Ignoring him, Elizabeth walked to the window. The car was still there. All of a sudden it hit her. *My God*, she thought, *not Arthur! Stall for time, Elizabeth*, she kept saying to herself. *Keep watching the car.*

"Arthur," she started slowly, "I have been thinking of calling a news conference, at noon on Tuesday. We have to begin damage control. What do you think?" She knew she sounded weak and hoped he wouldn't notice the fear that was creeping back into her voice.

He had picked up on her fear. Suddenly his voice turned to stone. "There will be no news conference, Elizabeth. I'm sorry, it's over. You'll have to go with these men."

"My God, Arthur," she shrugged off all pretense. She had to know the truth, the whole truth. "How could you be involved in this? Of all people, Arthur, why you? You were like a father to me." Elizabeth began to think survival. She needed three more minutes, just three more minutes.

Arthur responded, his ego taking over. He knew she loved a quick mind, and she had been like a daughter to him. He wanted her to know why he did it, why he had to do it.

The men in the car would wait for his signal. "I didn't want to get involved, Elizabeth. It just happened. I went to Roger for money a year ago. Other than a few bad investments, I'm afraid my years of gambling had finally caught up with me, at the worst possible time. Elizabeth, you know I have three kids at Harvard. I was losing this home. My wife knows nothing about this. I needed millions. I had no choice. I'm sorry. And I'm sorry you were so naïve to think it can all be done by long hours and hard work."

"Damn you, Arthur," she turned on him with all the pent-up fear and anger she had been holding in for weeks. "Everybody's sorry! You could have come to me! All you men are fucking sorry. Bullshit!"

Wincing at the comments coming from the woman he had truly adored for the last decade and a half, he turned his steely blue eyes at her. "Those men will come in soon enough, Elizabeth. I can't help you. I just can't help you." Shame and sorrow permeated the normally distinguished, handsome face of the elderly Arthur Litton.

"Fuck you, too, Arthur. If these freaking bastards are going to kill me, you are going to watch. I want you to see what you've done, you sniveling, whining coward! You're no better than Roger, just more self-serving about your deception. There was a time, Arthur, when you and I together made a commitment to excellence. Something to be proud of, we said, in one corporate meeting after another, to our thousands of employees and our customers. You're a son of a bitch, Arthur! You're the worst kind of cheat." Although Elizabeth had turned on him with a vengeance, there was an obvious tone of fear in her voice. She knew her time was short.

5:45 p.m. EST

The solid double thud of the slamming Mercedes doors sounded like a death knell in her ears. Suddenly, another sound, a more welcome one—screeching tires. John Rushly was in the lead car. It careened into the driveway. She turned to look out the window. The Russians turned toward the caravan with guns raised. This time, the FBI didn't hesitate.

In a hail of focused automatic gunfire, the two Russians were slammed back against their car. Bullets ripped flesh, bone, glass and steel. The driver stepped out with an AK 47. Another barrage of automatic 9mm blasts cut him down.

This time, remembering their colleagues slain just hours before, the FBI was not advising anyone of their rights.

John shouted orders to his agents, "Make sure the Russians are secure." Rushing into the house, he yelled for Elizabeth.

Having stayed by the window, she stood frozen, waiting for him. "John," she shouted into the hallway, "it's Arthur! He's in on it with Roger. He ran upstairs! Try the library!"

"Arthur Litton!" John shouted. "It's the FBI! Come down the stairs." John was making his way up the stairs when he heard a loud, familiar pop come from the room at the top of the stairs, then another. Mortally wounded, Arthur Litton lay gasping for breath. He had fired two shots, grazing his temple with one, and striking his forehead with the other. Rushing to his aid, John knew the massive head wound was fatal—a few seconds later, Arthur Litton was dead.

FBI agents swarmed the house and grounds. Suddenly, the stillness throughout the house was nearly overcoming.

In a state of shock, Elizabeth stood at the bottom by the banister, facing the stairwell. "John, what—?"

"He's dead, Elizabeth—I didn't get to him in time. He took his own life."

Near collapse, Elizabeth Martin clung to the railing. She kept repeating, over and over, "John, why—my God, why?"

John Rushly tried to answer. "The age-old struggle," he said quietly, "good and evil. Mortal men making bad choices." As he made his way back down the thick, carpeted stairs, John Rushly could think of nothing he wanted more than to wrap up his reports, extensive as they would be, and fly home to Phoenix—and to his wife.